Last Stand at Boulder Ridge

*Part Two
of the Centennial
Campfire Trilogy*

By Robert V. Sobczak

and Rudi Heinrich

Last Stand at Boulder Ridge:
Part Two of the Centennial Campfire Trilogy
Copyright © 2018 by Robert V. Sobczak and Rudi Heinrich

1st Edition, April 2018

ISBN: 978-0-9982598-7-1

Praise for *Last Stand at Boulder Ridge*

"A delicious double-decker sandwich of a book so stacked high with the works that you'll vow to save the second half for later only to end up eating it all in one sitting and still have room for dessert plus a really good cup of coffee followed by an absinthe and probably the best night of sleep you've had in years."
Jacoby Smith, *Arnold's Tavern*

"The *Bridge over River Kwai* meets *The Searchers* of our generation."
Editorial, *Mechanix Illustrated*

"If you've ever eaten chicken and thought it tasted like frog legs, this is your book."
Sam Hunter, *Oklahoma Advocate*

"Saddle up and hold on tight! This book bucks, and may even throw you off, but by trails end will have you riding off into prettiest Remington sunset you've ever seen."
Bartender, *Hopscotch Inn*

"Es hat mir Spaß gemacht, nach Dinosaurierknochen zu graben."
Wilhem Horger, *Palentologia*

"Probably the greatest sequel to a debut work we've seen since Bobby Angel followed up his debut *Christmas Classics Double-Live* album with his *End of the Apocalypse* LP."
Rupert Robbins, *Guitar by the Numbers*

Back of Book

At the end of the first book, *The Legend of Campfire Charlie*, our fearless protagonist, Ranger Rusty, was wrapping up a long and rather convoluted day at the Sweetwater Visitor Center with just one final task at hand: a five minute drive down the road to a nearby campground to do his evening campfire talk. The second book, *Last Stand at Boulder Ridge*, picks up where the action to the previous novel left off: the ranger entering the fiery glow of the campfire to address the crowd ...

Robert V. Sobczak
and Rudi Heinrich are co-authors
of the Centennial Campfire Trilogy

Books include:

The Legend of Campfire Charlie

Last Stand at Boulder Ridge

Final book (yet to be named)

all gave some

The Centennial Campfire

Table of Contents

Jebediah Nightlinger: Ohhh, children ... My father was a brawny Moor, six feet six inches tall. He bound his head in a red velvet cloth. He wore a curved sword, forged from the finest Toledo steel. He captured a lady, bright and dark. He took her in his arms and wrapped her in a warm quilt and carried her off. They came to a castle and he battered down the doors with the trunk of an oak tree and KILLED EVERYBODY IN IT, just so they could rest the night. Later, while she slept, he walked the parapets ... and became a king.

Roscoe Lee Browne in *The Cowboys*
Screenplay: Irving Ravetch and Harriet Frank
Book: William Dale Jennings

There were plenty of days coming when he could fish the swamp

Ernest Hemingway
Big Two Hearted River

The Centennial Campfire
Trilogy, Volume II

Prologue

PROLOGUE

Dear Reader,

This is a continuation of a previous book.

At the end of the first book, *The Legend of Campfire Charlie*, our fearless protagonist, Ranger Rusty, was wrapping up a long and rather convoluted day at the Sweetwater Visitor Center with just one final task at hand (and seemingly well within grasp): a five minute drive down the road to a nearby campground to do his evening campfire talk.

The second book picks up where the action to the previous novel left off: the ranger entering the fiery glow of the campfire ready to address the crowd.

And so the sequel begins.

But first let's talk a little about *sequels*, or more simply *seconds* at large. While not exactly a failure of a word — as in, *"Hey, I came in second in the race!"* *"—Oh yeah? Well that stinks!"* — inspirationally it does have a semi-unshakable reputation for, no matter how close, always falling a smidge short of the preferred uppermost spot. The famous Avis slogan — "We're only number two, so *We Try Harder*" — probably puts the word in its best possible light while also serving as the exception that proves the rule: seconds are only acceptable if you're on your way up. Nobody likes slipping to second, or prefers silver to gold, or being lost in the shadows of a winner take all world.

Even for something as simple as donuts the stereotype holds true. Isn't it always the first one that tastes best? The second, well, not so much. The third? Thoroughly regrettable. More on that later. And yes, inevitably, there is a fourth, fifth, sixth until there's nothing left except an empty box and a firsthand reckoning with the law of diminishing returns (better understood as the belly-bloated regret of not having stopped at just one.)

Hollywood probably played the biggest role in simultaneously perfecting and perverting sequels to their present state, serving them up as the main course of its summer blockbuster crop and counting on them as a big, if not the biggest, slice of their bottom line. But show me a great movie and I'll name you an ill-advised *Part Two* that doesn't measure up in any number of damnable ways — whether it be trying too hard, or not trying enough, pandering to clichés or sadly slipping into a pathetic caricature of its formerly respectable self. Even in the instances where a sequel is a huge box office hit — greeted with a ceremonial sipping of the soda pop and overflow-filling of the celebratory popcorn tub (and topped off with a box of jujubes for dessert) — isn't the next morning all too often met with groggy remorse that abstinence (or the Indie film) might have been the better recourse?

Sylvester Stallone's Rocky franchise may be Tinseltown's best example of the sequel's plight. Rocky (the original) won the Oscar but lost the fight, at the end of which Apollo Creed winced — "There ain't gonna be no rematch" — at a glimpse of what lay ahead and to which, we all now know in hindsight, a swollen-eyed Rocky Balboa too rashly agreed — "Don't want one;" had only the story ended there!

Fast forward three years hence to me walking out of the theater as a ten year old kid with a feeling of *exuberant satisfaction* swirling through the cerebrum of my head: the sequel picked up just where the first left off, featuring the same characters and a similar plot and of course the build up to the climactic rematch that — *spoiler alert* — Rocky wins! For me it was a moment that everything was right with the world, not that it would last (hint: see Rocky III). But now as an adult, looking back, even the sequel (Rocky II) comes off as a cheap knockoff of the first, as inferior as it was forgettable, if also better than what came next: Rocky III, IV, V and VI. (Remember the law of diminishing returns?) Maybe the better course would have been just to kill the main character off (with an Apollo one-two punch). In retrospect, of course, it was the inverse that occurred: as, incrementally, one movie after the next, the supporting characters got the ax, thus leaving Rocky as the last man standing — the sole survivor — by the time the franchise rebooted with a completely new supporting cast.

The dirty secret of sequels (and serial novels) is the post-mortem influence they cast back in time over the original work, thus upping the ante in a way: popular and critical judgement isn't reserved on just the sequel but reopens the book on the story's entire arc. The new installment has the power to either burnish or dilute the brand, if not even bring the entire house down (and yes, we can all think of a couple of those).

•••

Second books usually come in two types, sequels if they pick up where a previous novel left off or prequels if they delve back in time before the start of the original work. Alternatively they can be a hybrid or have other slight variations such as taking the view of a different character, sometimes called a *spin off*, or retaining the same characters in a different setting or plot. In terms of the latter, that's a recipe most conducive to multiple serial works as, say, the many adventures of Sherlock Holmes which — at the risk of having a crime spree break out across Greater London as the hapless Dr. Watson bungled his way through misinterpreting obtuse clues alone all by himself (trust me, every case would have remained unsolved!) — Sir Author Conan Doyle (the author) had the literary chutzpah to kill his main character off in his prime (... with the caveat that he let Holmes' nemesis Moriarty do the dirty work of course). Sounds crazy, right? Doyle, it turns out, was no one-trick pony when it came to his craft. He enjoyed writing in a wide range of literary forms — including poetry, plays, histories and other fictional tales — all of which a full-time focus on his part-time detective threatened to seriously curtail. Are you beginning to see the author's motive? (And yes, Holmes would have, too.) As an adult I have deep respect for the author going with his heart, but I must admit as a teenage disciple of the Houndstooth-jacketed sleuth I was baffled by Doyle's preoccupation with anything else. 21B Baker Street was quite obviously his God-given purpose in life. My only wish was that he'd written more. Much to his adoring fans' delight Doyle did eventually succumb to popular demand to resurrect the snooping savant for a romp in the moors surrounding Baskerville Estate and after that one more book. As for Doyle's other works? His output was prolific and in some cases praised, if also all but forgotten in our modern age (if not well before); meanwhile Holmes continues to cheat death and live on as arguably as the world's most famous crime solver of all time, even today.

...

So, to summarize thus far: here's a user's guide to whether or not to write a sequel. Are you bereft of new ideas? If yes, write a sequel. Do you easily compromise your values (i.e. ready to be *sold out*)? If yes, write a sequel. Are you a glutton for punishment? If yes, write the sequel. Do you have absolutely nothing else better to do? Again, please write a sequel if the answer is yes. After a great original work, there is no better way to signal your willingness to tarnish your artistic worth than by indulging in a vainglorious victory lap around yesterday's accomplishments, and for what: not being content with leaving well enough alone, or more probably just to make an extra buck? Well if that's the case, why not just cut to the chase and go straight on to writing a third? More on that later.

As most succinctly invoked by Kevin Costner in *A Field of Dreams* — "Build it and they will come," original works organically *attract* an audience whereas sequels pander to stadiums that are *already filled* (with an obsequious eye for giving the fans exactly what they want). Yet so often the same people cheering for more — *"Sequel! Sequel! Sequel!"* — are the first in line to voice their feelings of disappointment at the result, it sometimes even lingering as a sour point for the rest of their lives. Or more probably, they'll get over it and delude themselves (as all fans with their heroes tend to do), coming around full circle to embrace the flawed follow-up warts and all. Trust me, there are boat loads of fans who can't get enough of Rocky IV. Or at least I know one.

But before we completely disparage the genre of the sequel as a form, it's worth contemplating Ernest Hemingway's rather renowned quote that "all modern American literature" – *ahem, listen closely* – "comes from one book by Mark Twain" – *drum roll please* – "called *The Adventures of Huckleberry Finn*" – *Now hit the cymbal! Hit it again!* That's right: A Sequel! If that bombshell isn't enough, consider this kicker: the primary character of the original (and lesser) work, the pesky Tom Sawyer, has a cameo appearance that almost, but not quite, succeeds in derailing the entire masterpiece three quarters of the way in, the meaning and damage of which scholars have grappled with ever since. Imagine that: the original tainting the sequel. *My my my look how the tables have turned!* Both figuratively and literally perhaps sequels deserve a second look (pun intended). But why are we unfairly profiling sequels? That bugs me. It really does. Isn't it about time we once and for all scrutinize sequel-less originals *(oh the shame!)* for the pitiful lack of progeny they produce.

Yes, *Hamlet* was great. But where are the sequels *Hamlet II* and *Hamlet III*? Because for my money the original leaves a load of unanswered questions on the table that Shakespeare could've done a lot worse than to give a second look (and a third, more on that later) instead of wasting time on *Henry VIII* which, according to my sources, is regarded as the Bard's least inspired work. Sure, it was an original ... but was it really necessary? On the other hand, *Henry VIII: Part 2* sounds intriguing, don't you think? But only if it was part of a full Henry Series that consisted of multiple prequels reaching back to *Henry I: In the Beginning* and running sequentially forward in time from *Henry II* to *Henry VII* culminating with a jump ahead to *Henry IX* and possibly a reboot called *Little Henry Unleashed*. (In a head nod to history, I would be remiss not to state that Shakespeare actually did write several Henry VI plays.)

We need no more evidence of the shaky ground on which sequel-less originals sit than deconstructing the *one-hit wonder* for what it really is. Sure they get lots of radio play – Gerry Rafferty's *Baker Street* and Looking Glass's *Brandy (You're a Fine Girl)* coming to mind – but let's face the facts, these *one-and-done* classics are the equivalent of celebrating a sports team with a 1-15 record, say the Baltimore Colts, for winning ... that's right ... *one lousy game.* Not an isolated event at all, one-hit wonders are usually a product of beginner's luck on first try or a tortuous tale of a downtrodden veteran finally scoring a break-through hit, the key point being this: both are bookended on either end by forgettable and fruitless attempts that never hold a candle to that one-time sublime event until – finally, as the decades pass – the erosion of time crumbles away everything else except for the granite outcrop of the one singular work. Do you follow what I'm saying? It's not like a one-hit wonder was the artist's goal. It's the one-hit wonderees that failed at the sequel not the sequel that tainted the original work. In a weird way we can again paradoxically use *Rocky* to prove the point. And by *Rocky,* I mean just *Rocky,* not *Rocky I* or *The Original Rocky* ... just *Rocky* (i.e. the stand-alone original movie as it appeared in 1976) which, through it all, somehow remains intact and unsullied by the sequels that came next, it perpetually ending on the coda of Adrienne rushing towards the ring and then through the ropes to find a fighter whose eyes had been blinded, literally swollen shut, only to have his vision immediately restored by the *miracle* of her presence (as confirmed by his simple testimony – *"Where's your hat?"*) followed by their embrace, a gush of *I Love Yous*, and a triumphant surge of adrenaline (and goosebumps) from the accompanying soundtrack. Wow, what a flick!

...

More and more it's becoming clear that the problem doesn't lie with the sequels but rather in the hidden and inherent dangers of the original work. I mean, really, let's face it – is there no bigger kiss of death than initial success? You see that with athletic talent all the time. Too much of it too early can inflict a growth-stunting reliance on physical gifts instead of learning the subtleties and craftsmanship of refining and mastering detail-oriented techniques which, combined with the Avis-inspired slogan of the upstart competition ("We Try Harder") sets the stage for the improbable but perfectly predictable outcome of even the Mighty Hare being surpassed ...

and by the Slow-going Tortoise no less. Yes, obvious in retrospect, but at the time, who would have guessed? Or take handshakes as another example of the same point. Don't take me wrong, I believe in the gripping of the flesh as much as anyone and sure, I know the routine: a firm grasp, a smile, and meaningful contact eye to eye. They say a handshake can seal the deal — okay, fine — but let's not be taken for fools. The act can be more surficial showmanship than what lies at a person's core underneath. Show me a hiring manager who trusted a first impression and I'll show you a lunchroom full of co-workers whose best explanation is puzzled looks and a postulation (accompanied by no small amount of head scratching) that the new recruit "must have interviewed well." *Pssst, by the way, that's code for saying they picked the wrong guy.* What good is a strong first impression if it's followed up by underperformance from the second act on?

It is in this same spirit that you can never truly see the original work in its proper light until the second ... and third (more on that later) ... play out. The greatest gift an artist can give is not perfection but a body of work. It's only in the liberal spilling of the ink that the full grandeur of an artistic vision can finally spread its wings and, however unlikely, at least try to take flight.

...

Last Stand at Boulder Ridge is a second book not once but twice: (1) it's the follow up to *The Legend of Campfire Charlie*, thus implying a sequel and (2) it's the second time that Rudi and I have teamed up to co-author a book which, before we go any further, is a topic in and of itself that warrants — yes, here comes that word again — a *second* look; and more specifically to the point: exactly *how do you* co-author a book?

Necessary ingredients would seem to include, in no particular order — creative chemistry for collaborating on ideas, a clear division of labor to play to one another's strengths, and — quite inescapably — a lot of writing, editing and reviewing on *both* co-author's part. What else could explain penning two books in two years? The fact that a second book *even exists* would seem to suggest that we perfected our process with the first, thus paving the way for even more rapid (and seamless) assimilation of the next.

Assuming the above is all true – *which it is not* – it still doesn't explain the inner machinations of how the co-authorship worked. Let's start with the farcical just to rule it out: did Rudi and I write alternating pages, he the left and I the right? Obviously not. The more common assumption would be we split it up by task, me one chapter and Rudi the next, or me the writer and he the reviewer or, perhaps, something as simple as sharing drafts back and forth which, in terms of equitable distribution of labor would sort of make sense ... if only any of it was true. By process of elimination that leaves pretty much only one answer left: if it's not A and it's not B, then it must be C — the two of us must have hunkered down in a cabin somewhere and just cranked the whole thing out, right? As to be expected, this is a trick question. The correct answer is actually *D: None of the Above.*

•••

In the creative business there are two types of people: process people and product people, even if in the end we are a little bit of both. While products are ultimately the goal (let's face it, no author aspires to let an idea flounder in a larval state of halfhearted attempts that never coalesce into a binded book), if you don't have "a process," there is little hope of the product ever being *made once,* let alone twice. Or a third. More on that later. Writing has a false reputation for being a glamorous trade, full of epiphanies, serotonin-soaked sentences and clinking glasses of slightly-chilled champagne (or perhaps a well-hopped IPA) when major writing milestones are met; but at its core book writing is a brutal – emphasis on *brutal* – grind (emphasis on *grind,* too): much more pick-axing in the salt mines than a leisurely swing in the garden at Shangri-La. On the other hand, if you are a "process person" writing is a grind you will enjoy, a salt lick in the wilderness of the day, the week – of life – that you will not leave to happenstance or otherwise allow to be frittered away. Benjamin Franklin's observation that "(happiness) is produced not as much by great pieces of good fortune that seldom happen as by little advantages that occur every day" was directed at life in general but equally speaks to the writing process as well. Publishing a book is a once a year or two (if not a lifetime) event whereas the *act of writing,* on the other hand, occurs *every day.* It is the writing process, not the product, that structures and gives harmony to a writer's life.

Prologue

···

Not that writing, let alone a process, was on either Rudi's or my mind when our partnership project began. Our goal was much (much) more modest — just a *half-hour* campfire talk — for the purpose of paying homage to the rapidly approaching centennial of America's National Parks, at that point just a year away. Neither of us wanted the 100th year to slip by without doing something a little bit extra that, in looking back, would give us a meaningful memory of the major milestone event and a personal feeling of satisfaction that we did our part. Our conceit was simple enough: we would ditch the Power Point projector that rangers typically rely on in modern-day campfire talks in favor of an old-fashioned two-person play that harkened back to the National Park Service's (even Shakespearean) roots. Okay, maybe not Shakespearean — as in *"Hark thou ranger, who pass hither whence the nightingale flaps. The fiery-footed steeds gallop towards the shadows of the eternal eclipse;"* but we did take our theatrical responsibilities seriously. We even wrote a script.

But by no means should a few pages of notes to help us remember our lines be confused with even an inkling of a sliver of a thought of writing a book. It was always the *"spoken word,"* our steady dialog back and forth — not anything in writing — that sparked our simple fireside play to life. About those campfire talks. The first was admittedly raw, debuting just three weeks after we'd hatched the idea, the two of us waiting in the singular flame's tungsten glow for the crowd to convene, completely *unaware* what, if anything, we had (in terms of quality content or artistic chemistry) at the same time being *fully aware* that it would only be in DOING — *not in talking about it* — that the campfire skit would, could — and eventually did — take form. From that point on no two performances were the same. Each one built on the next. Often times we'd add things in at the last second during our pre-warmup check while other times we'd extemporaneously ad lib on the spot — with every new success being counterbalanced by something else we'd mess up — all of which were capped off on our long drives back into town, fresh after each event, with a critique of what worked, what didn't quite pan out and what we needed to do to improve our fireside tale the next time around. What drove us to our version of perfection? It's hard to say. Park pride and

Centennial spirit definitely factored in, as did our own self-imposed high standards, but mostly it came down to delivering a performance the one to three dozen spectators (rarely more sometimes less) could enjoy, give them a few laughs and maybe make them think.

In total we did five shows before the onslaught of mosquitoes and spring warmth forced the winter tourists to start trickling back up north, thus bringing the swamp preserve's campfire season to a close. It was March 2015.

Rather than packing it in and winding down, however, Rudi and I were just beginning to ramp up — and not because we were using the summer sojourn to refine our play for the Park Service's momentous hundredth year coming up (although we did do a bit of that): we had begun the dubious task of trying to write a book, with *trying*, or do I mean *dubious* (probably both) being the operative words? With neither of us having previously published so much as a short story let alone a haiku, our mission amounted to more a wing and a prayer than a pre-ordained fact, and even more of a fantasy when you consider the short deadline we were putting ourselves up against. Any hope for catching the Zeitgeist of the Centennial year, so our thinking went, required us completing said book at least a few months before the official birthday on August 25th, 2016. Or in other words, we had about thirteen months.

For me the imperative was clear: there was no time to waste. Anyone familiar with the scene of Richard Dreyfus making a mountain out of mashed potatoes in *Close Encounters of the Third Kind*, my writing process began something like that (although messier and more intense). My number one rule was working on the book every day, and here's the catch: even when I didn't have my A-game. B-, C-, D-game I found a way to write. In fact, I think my fortitude to work on down days was actually the hidden secret to my success, having the effect of lowering my expectations of what could be accomplished on any given day at the same time keeping my mind sifting through the gravel and priming my pump for the slurry flumes of productivity and Eureka Moments that would eventually come when my A-game was on. Even on my good days I was quick to make peace with the sobering reality that nailing any one sentence or paragraph (let alone a chapter) on a first take was pure hubris, it only being through constant and painstaking (if also paradoxically pleasurable) repetition that suddenly the story, the character, the sequencing started to click and larger passages, chapters and eventually the book would gradually coalesce. In terms of common wisdom, I shunned certain rules, too. "Write what you know" in my view became the ultimate piece of bad advice. It is only in exploring the unknown – not the familiar – that a writer's pen comes to life. "Going with whatever works" much better described my writing approach although, if I am to be honest, I'm not even sure *writing* is the right term. My pen felt as much an artisan's tool as it did a journalistic device. Sculpturing was probably a better word for my approach, at least at first, as more times than not I found myself chipping away at an unwieldy chunk of rock on a dim dream it might take form; with carpentry also coming to mind given the way I relied on trial and error techniques to hammer in and pull out nails to try to frame up an ever evolving and shapeshifting house; and with painting being the most apropos way to describe my penchant for constantly layering over and brushing up my previous day's work. I learned that writing is as much about telling a story as it is listening to the story *tell me* what to write, it being during those quiet times that Eureka Moments would most often strike. Good stopping points were also crucial, too. There exists no bigger momentum killer to writing progress than permitting edits to pile up or allowing a vine of ripe ideas to go unplucked (and as a result irreversibly shriveling up). Writing, reviewing, editing – *and repeat* – were one and the same, a constant loop and the engine that kept my mental machinery moving steadily ahead, the story and all its component pieces fresh in my head. If that sounds arduous it was; and it wasn't. I am reminded of the movie *Space Balls* in which John Candy plays a character called a *mog*: a hybrid mix between a dog and a man. "*I'm my own best friend,*" he delightfully explains. Writing the book I discovered a similar duality within myself, as every time I returned home, there it was, the book – *that droopy-eyed dog* – begging me to go for a walk. Surely you might ask, by *walk,* I must mean that in the figurative sense, as writing quite obviously requires the exact opposite and sedentary act of sitting in one single spot – as in "*Stay mog!*" – not literally moving about. I am here to tell you that my sidewalk strolls, often at sunset and always alone, were a major part of my writing loop, on which I was happy as a mog reading and reviewing my book (all the while others would periodically pass by with their dogs on a leash). Who would have thought writing was an excuse to get exercise and fresh air!

As for my co-author's writing process: plain and simple, he didn't have one; it didn't exist. Not that he couldn't write, he could, or that he didn't have good ideas, he did (great ones in fact), but absent a process he was continually stuck in the purgatory state of sporadically penning truncated page-long vignettes, often handwritten, and − this was the real doozy − in all cases always (and I mean *always*) first drafts. Getting Rudi to expand upon his initial offerings or, God forbid, review and refine what he wrote, was the equivalent of trying to lead a mule to a water hole we would both come to learn he either couldn't or wouldn't drink. Even for sections right up his wheel house, or chapters I'd already prepped (and re-prepped) to give him a head start, the result was always the same: while Rudi could reliably count on me to steadily push any of the book's many aspects ahead, he was a Study − not in Scarlet − but of Getting Nothing Done. It hit me in waves early and then like a ton of bricks: I had agreed to a partnership that stuck me with both halves of the work.

Although the following didn't happen, my moment of reckoning with Rudi went something like this: exasperated to the hilt with the partnership's imbalanced state, I invited him to the campfire to call the whole book thing off when − just as I was getting ready to break the news − Rudi and I found ourselves immersed in a four hour dialog going back and forth with me typing as fast as we talked and me once and for all finally realizing that, as is so common in life, my co-author's most frustrating of faults was also simultaneously his most magical and preternatural of gifts, not a first-draft flunky at all: he was the Master of the First Take! Time and time again it was a skill Rudi and I would convene to exploit. Simon and Garfunkel emerged early on as the patron saints of how our partnership worked. The former is lionized today as the *artist in full* while the latter is line-itemed as the "other half" (*if that*) who was basically there to harmonize but otherwise didn't carry his own weight. I'm not here to argue that Paul Simon isn't the much more accomplished musician of the two, but really (and without a doubt) it was as Simon and Garfunkel that he, *they*, did their most memorable work. Similarly, it wasn't about the equitability of the process but the end point and creative chemistry that forged our collaborative bond. Whatever it took,

Rudi and I knew we needed each other to get this story right. Two minds, and specifically *our* minds, were better than one. It was also about being faithful to our campfire pact.

...

By January 2016, we had outdone even our own lofty expectations. We'd produced a manuscript that exceeded the length of *The Adventures of Huckleberry Finn* and *Tom Sawyer* combined in just eight months. Not only was the official birthday of the Park Service still a half a year away (meaning we had made our deadline by a wide margin, or so it seemed), volume wise we had more than one book. Surely if we had succeeded in spinning a half-hour campfire skit into a two-hundred thousand word epic tale we could find the wherewithal to subdivide the sprawling work into multiple tomes. By our initial calculations that seemed as simple as putting it on the chopping block and giving it a good couple thwacks followed by a little stitching, some rewriting and a fine chamois cloth to give it a good buff; and to be sure we weren't too far off. Just three months later the first book *The Legend of Campfire Charlie* was born. It was May 2016. We'd made our deadline and we had our book. It was one month short of the midpoint of the National Park Service's Centennial year.

All expectations were that the second book (i.e. this one) would be a similar breeze. Not only was its narrative in much better shape, in theory we'd cleared away the roadblocks and ironed out our collaborative kinks. Wow, were we wrong! Perhaps it had something to do with a sophomore slump, and to be sure spending time marketing and making paperback copies of the first played a part; as did the loss of the deadline that drove us so feverishly to finish the first; also factoring in to our delay was a minor and seemingly obscure character that Rudi had earlier introduced which, upon further review, turned out to be a much more substantial part of the story than we initially thought. But the primary reason was our desire to get the story right, and inevitably — Rudi would agree — the lion's share of that workload again falling on me.

Despite vowing early on that he was ready to "up his game" for the second book, no such renaissance took place. Not that my expectations were high. While I continued to hammer away on the story most every day, Rudi would go weeks, even months, without doing all that much — a reality I came to grips with (and learned to cope) early on by adopting an *"I didn't need him but I could use him"* approach. Not that I went completely rogue. At critical junctures I made sure to loop him in, get him caught up and bounce any number of ideas around, as it was during such banter we'd almost always connect (although Rudi sometimes needed to "drink a coke" to channel his thoughts) and even if, as time passed — *and this is key* — such rap sessions seemed to happen less and less. What had been so vital to our collaborative bond in the past were now in short supply, a rare if not endangered event. But why?

Our wayward continental drift on the second book was as obvious to see as it was impossible to stop, if also its cause was equally hard for me to diagnose. As usual, it was a confluence of many events. To be sure, the sheer length of the effort dragging on for so long played a role. Neither of us expected anything as expansive as the epic that eventually evolved. Inevitably, the frontier territory of broad-stroke storyboarding and drafting new "first takes" — Rudi's forte — took a back seat to the precision and quite quotidian task of re-writing and reviewing, a skill that Rudi (at least for a book-length work) simply did not possess, despite my repeated attempts to steer him in the right direction in honing such a craft; and one in which if I did not excel, I at least applied the necessary resolve to see through. While Rudi fancied our increasingly infrequent sessions as "when the magic of the story came to life," I had long ago forged a code that writing, like character, was best measured by not what one says in the company of others, but by what one does when nobody else is around to watch. Rudi was too often content with just "showing up" for our sittings that less and less frequently occurred and being a "no show" for the time away, out of sight, when the real writing work got done every day.

Not that the above omissions were ever done in malice or sloth, as in hindsight I have come to better understand our growing abyss as less an overt choice than an inadvertent, and perhaps inevitable, outcome of the initial conditions that had so effortlessly fueled our collaborative success from the start coming to an unceremonious stop, a trifecta of terminations that included: (1) the final curtain-call on our two-year run of "evening campfire" shows, (2) us no longer living in the same town and, biggest of all, (3) the cessation of us sharing the same commute ride in and out of work. The truth was, for much of the second book, Rudi and I really didn't see or talk to each other all that much.

And so it was, as happenchance as it had been turned on, the "spigot" of our reliable and regular hang-out time had been "turned off." Not that it mattered in my mind. Yes, those daily dialogs had been the steady flow from which our campfire talk (and then the first book) had taken root, and discussion we both looked forward to as much as we probably failed to appreciate them until they stopped; but let it be said that I also had no doubt we were bigger than that. We had since matured into good friends and bon vivants of a story that no disruption (let alone a trifling scheduling change) could block; and not that it changed my routine all that much, if at all, as most every evening I continued to work on the book.

But for Rudi, the commute represented the core of his commitment, if not its bulk — a fact which became staggeringly apparent by its loss. Instead of rising to the occasion or making adjustments to stay involved, Rudi's default strategy seemed to be the "no action" alternative; or in other words, he was on a "vacation from the book" until I returned to the commute. Weeks turned into months turned into a year: it was an event that would never occur. By that time the larger reality had set in. Rudi was increasingly unavailable in any form. Always a reliable sounding board before, the new norm was prolonged stretches without hearing back a peep, to the point that when I did reach him I would have to politely admonish him for not being in better touch, but even those occasions were the exception: more and more I felt like I was partnering with an echoless void. And mind you there were a lot of things that needed to be done, both great and small and on many fronts — characters to be developed and plot lines to be shored up not to mention the seemingly intractable problem of melding together the book's many sprawling parts. Not only saddled with doing all the work, I was also the one doing all the reaching out.

Bitterness and spite, I successfully fought those feelings off, but I would be lying if I didn't admit that doubt and disappointment crept in regarding Rudi's commitment to our partnership, the project and even me as a friend. Was our grand bargain (and the companionship that formed) really no bigger than an artifact of being "commuting chums" — us just two wayward souls killing time on a long drive — a modern day variant of "drinking buddies" who, yeah, we had fun hanging out but dispersed as soon as the booze ran dry, a collaboration built more on the flimsy foundation of "easy convenience" than on the bedrock of a deeper bond or more noble cause? The situation also churned up memories of the unfulfilled freshets I had expected from Rudi all along from Day One. At command, even a whim, he could fill up and often overflow his streambanks and breach levees with his ideas, overflowing water into a vast and vivid landscape in his mind, yet too often these were flashflood events, frustratingly infrequent, prone to go unrecorded and doomed never to last. Now, absent the spigot of easy contact time afforded by our commute, Rudi's trickle-flow of effort had all but dried up into a dry arroyo of dust.

Let it be said that if the above thoughts entered my mind — and most assuredly they did — we also had too much water under the bridge and too many horses halfway across the stream (and every other cliché in the book) to reverse course or think of giving up. Whatever the partnership was or had become (and to use another tired cliché) — *It Was What It Was*: part hastily-arranged campfire deal, part unfinished wall mural that still needed paint, and part comedy of the absurd.

I am reminded of the time rather late in the game I detected a gap in the story that wasn't essential to fill, but I thought that it would be fun to include, and seeing it to be right up Rudi's wheel house — i.e. a historical bit and another chance at one of his coveted "first takes" — I elicited his help. And to his credit he dove right in, reporting significant progress in just a few short weeks, with one minor catch: He'd written it in longhand, thus — it would take "quite some time" to type up. It was probably a month later said steno pad finally fell into my lap. I'll admit what he gave me wasn't bad. Where it lacked in plot it was rich in characters. In the parlance of the creative business it was what I'd call a "good start" (even if many weeks of brainstorming, writing and refinement still lay ahead). But the absurdity was how long it took what Rudi gave me to type up. Twenty minutes tops, no joke!

Then there were Rudi's in-depth monologues to me about a new character he'd ginned up, replete with nuanced interplay of plot lines and a ton of psychological heft, and one whom I was immediately sold on and couldn't wait to read more about. The only problem, of course, was that Rudi had only imagined the character out in his mind. The sum total of his effort on pen and paper was a single sentence ... and a short one at that!

Even now, I am unsure which was the bigger accomplishment of the two: the book's literary arc or the improbable odyssey of how our partnership worked? To be honest I am mystified by both. Indeed, creative chemistry is an alchemy that doesn't always make sense. Despite our partnership's glaring imperfections, Rudi and I never lost our easy rapport, an uncanny ability to connect on ideas, a willingness to be honest with each other (to a fault) and, perhaps most of all, a relaxation reflex when it came to working on our shared literary pursuit: it was both a diversion from real life at the same time it created a new world all its own, one that was invariably fun, rejuvenating, and over which we had some semblance of control. That being said, I would be remiss if I didn't admit to wishing I could have relied on him to do a bit more, both in terms of picking up the slack and enriching the work. Co-authoring too often for Rudi was part-time consultation work.

Yet to the end, Rudi saw himself in the mirror a vast reservoir of writing talent untapped. What I saw was somebody who didn't write, not because he was "too busy" (or whatever excuse was "handy" at the time), but because he never came to realize that writing is no more a God-given bounty than it is a singular skill "lying in-wait" (or adequately beckoned with a flip of the switch), but rather, no two ways around it, writing is above all else sacrifice and hard work: an all-consuming craft that, much like an artisan in any field knows, requires some combination of vision, tools, practice, drive and most of all *time* – precious seconds that morph into hours and months of toil that coalesce in a miraculous moment; a willingness to ride the wave of creative inspiration when it swells and a faith that "appetite will come while eating" when the desire ebbs, a cold calculus that failure and "trial and error" are the only path to success, and acquiescence that the final product is as much a reflection of what you set out to accomplish in the beginning as it is an accumulation of things you learned, discovered, ad hoc and built upon along the way. It is *doing*, not in talking, that a writer both performs *and hones* his craft.

Of course, much like taking a photograph or throwing a football, really *anybody* can write. So maybe in that regard Rudi was right. But consider there are only 32 quarterbacks who make it to the professional ranks as starters in the NFL, and only half that number who, on any given Sunday, actually win their games. It is in that spirit, I humbly submit, that perhaps the best parable for portraying Rudi's role in our partnership is as a seasoned if also underachieving second-string quarterback who, although he didn't make it on the field all that much (and, yes, had he applied himself he could have been well entrenched in the starting spot on another book), it would be incorrect to correlate his (lack of) box-score stats as having no bearing on the final scoreboard result; for, just as they are equally hard to pinpoint, he brought intangibles to the sideline that were impossible to ignore; part student part mentor — he was a "fan of the game" above all else, and one with a deft grasp of its lingo and an eye for drawing up plays from the deep historical vault and a pretty good throwing rhythm for tossing the "old pigskin" back and forth on the sideline between series to help me stay loose, and an ego that understood it wasn't about his own playing time but chalking up the victory for the team that counted most. I can honestly say my confidence soared knowing Rudi was in the wings at the same time I knew we were doomed if it came down to Rudi being on the field alone. My co-author oft prided himself on making the book *better,* to which I'd invariably respond, "— Of course, but without me there simply wouldn't exist a book *to improve upon."* If all this sounds condescending or cliché, that is not my intent. I am just trying to find words to describe (and understand myself) how our co-authorship worked.

For all the above reasons and more, the preparation of the second book, at the penning of this prologue, took over a year and a half by itself. Not that I didn't enjoy it. As you may remember I self-identify as a mog.

···

On that note I would like to draw this preamble to a close, but not without one last thought. While *Last Stand at Boulder Ridge* is indeed our second book, I am of the firm opinion that it *is not* a sequel in the true sense of the word for the simple reason that its broad strokes were written at the same exact time, *not after*, the original work; and in case you need a secondary disqualifier: unlike a true sequel, this book journeys both forward and backward (and I mean *way backward*) in time. Thus, if I can recall your attention to all that stuff I said about "seconds" and "follow up" works at the start of this prologue: Please ignore, none of it applies.

And yes, about the third. This is a trilogy so there will be one more ... we think. In the meanwhile, both Rudi and I hope you enjoy this book.

Sincerely,

Bob

Prologue

Rusty's Email

Rusty's Email

Email Inbox (127 unread messages)

Today, after 8 am

Jeff (13), unread, *Extreme Weather ALERT!*
Peleg (9), unread, *fwd: Gulf Coast Outlook*
Shawna, unread, *Python Press Release*
KOA, unread, *Survey: How was your recent stay?*
Cap'n Shane, unread, *Deluxe Tour Coupons*
Cliff (12), unread, *Safety Heads Up*
Jeff (3), unread, *Extreme Weather ALERT!*
Victoria, unread, *Albuquerque Home Sales*
Russ, unread, *Python sighting at VC*
Minnows, unread, *Skunk ape sighting*
Stanley, unread, *Nightingale seminar*
Mandy, unread, *Satchel found in map room*
Dr. Jim, unread, *Anhinga Society*
Ives, unread, *Prophets Landing*
Buckingham (1,923), unread, *Next steps*
Jeff (2), unread, *Extreme Weather ALERT!*
Hayes, unread, *Spiral notebooks*
Buck, unread, *It's been a great ride!*
Congo(2) , unread, *Your book has been shipped!*
Congo, unread, *Boulder Ridge: Heroism or Hoax*
Knoop, unread, *German translation*

Today, before 8 am

Maple, read, *Scam alert: Harpooning*
All, unread, *Get Outside Survey reminder*
Cliff (8), unread, *Safety Heads Up*
Shawna, read, *Emergency Water News*
Boots LLP, unread, *Your Recent Order*
Pip, unread, *Mason and Guy on way*
Shawna, read, *Weekly meeting notes*
Jeff, unread, *Extreme Weather ALERT!*
Mary, unread, *Buck's farewell Party*
Uncle, unread, *OR-435 EMO*
Cliff (4), unread, *Dress Code Draft Plan*
Wilcox, unread, *Out in Field Reply*

Peleg, read, *fwd: Gulf Coast Outlook*
Mandy, unread, *Stray cats at VC*
Kleal, unread, *Rusty Nails!!!!!!!*
All, unread, *Park Birthday Update*
Richard (4), unread, *Be on the lookout*
Sam, unread, *Fleet System Update*
Barry, unread, *fwd: Get Outside Survey*
Shawna, read, *Tour Bus season schedule*
HTC, read, *New Hank Trouper Release*
staff, read, *fwd: 6th Annual Expo Results*
Charity, unread, *PX000556R3432*
Clayton, unread, *Job Vacancy BORI*
Liz, unread, *Mailroom Reorg Underway*
Russ, unread, *Oil Change due GT 143M*

Yesterday

Shawna, read, *Thank you everybody!!!!!*
Cliff (4), unread, *New Committee forms*
Flask, unread, *VC gate out of order*
Clayton, read, *BORI phone lines down*
All, unread, *Mandatory online training*
Eli, unread, *Flu strain h4n1 symptoms*
Rachel, read, *Wellhead repair at 50MB*
Col. Hodges, read, *Veterans Newsletter*
Cap'n Shane, read, *Deluxe Tour News*

...

Cliff, read, *Can you help me out? Thx!*
Bob, unread, *Prep for campfire talk*
Ewel, unread, *Exotic Plant of the Day*

Two Days Ago

Shawna, read, *Effie's art show at noon*
Jeff, unread, *Extreme Weather ALERT!*

...

Rusty Misses an Email

& & & & & & & & & & & & & & &
From: Jeff
To: All Staff
When: Today
Subject: ***Extreme Weather Alert***
& & & & & & & & & & & & & & &

FYI:

Jeff − − − − − −
− − − − − − − − − − −
− − − − −, FL − − −

"If you can't learn to do something well, learn to enjoy doing it poorly."
Sean O. Shay

Sent from my mobile phone

& & & & & & & & & & & & & & &
Yesterday at 9:23 am Uldi Curios wrote:
& & & & & & & & & & & & & & &

Dear Team,

In light of the weather outlook (see Polish model) our Friday meeting has been canceled.

Sincerely,

Uldi Curios, Ph.D., P.E.,
Hydro Harmonics Int'l
Experts in Environmental
Dispute Resolution "Forging
Solutions between Nature
and Man since 19−"
Savannah Georgia Office

Disclaimer:
...

Sent by satellite

& & & & & & & & & & & & & & &
Today at 8:01 am Sonny Day
& & & & & & & & & & & & & & &

Daily Weather Report: Take heart south Florida, after weeks of unseasonably hot and humid winter weather, a much deserved cold front is finally heading our way. Expect some light drizzle sometime late Thursday afternoon as the front pushes through, followed by pleasantly crisp and cool air ushering in behind it. Weekend weather should be terrific!

Sonny − − − − − −
− − − − − − − − − − −
− − − − −, FL − − −

Sent by my newsroom iPad

& & & & & & & & & & & & & & &
Today at 4:50 am Strom D. Hunter
& & & & & & & & & & & & & & &

Issued at 0450 Fri

Surface gradients preclude early regression of fen-enhanced fog as strong 110kt jet streak (Max gust = 220 at 100 m) unseats polar restriction boundary. Expect the low-level boundary to move sub peninsula latitude between 1345-1910 SGT with 99.98 convergence within standard deviation of all most models. Outlier Polish model shows a 0.02 percent chance of dynamic truculence on multiple asymmetrical fronts along the horizontal and vertically atmospheric plains with possible retraction and reemergence of the tropical subduction zone thereby creating the theoretically possible, but never before observed, Big Omni-frontal Meteorological Breach (BOMB).

Signed,

Strom D. Hunter, Ph.D.
International One-Weather Service
— — — — — — — — — — — —
Tallahassee, FL — — —

Disclaimer: Although these data have been processed successfully on a computer system, International One-Weather Service (IOWS) can neither confirm nor deny what may or may happen as the weather quite frankly has a mind of its own. The IOWS shall not be held liable for improper or incorrect use of the data described and/or contained herein as pertaining to family reunions being held in vulnerable flood plain or coastal surge areas, deployment of umbrellas, selection of appropriate rain attire, including galoshes, or evacuations plans.

Sent from my super computer

Rusty's Email

THE RANGER

The Ranger

The ranger approached the campfire and sat down at the flame.

Of everywhere in the world he'd ever been, it felt like the place he was supposed to be.

People in the audience were sitting comfortably close with just enough room that they weren't touching, but really not much more space than that, to the point that if everyone squeezed in just a little bit more there would be room for one more spot, but probably not, or maybe perhaps.

The amphitheater was filled.

They were shoulder-to-shoulder tight.

Or about as jam packed as it got.

He was ready to commence with his campfire talk.

A few smart souls had thought out far enough ahead in advance to bring lawn chairs along, and were sitting to the side, thus giving them the equivalent of first-class seats — with ample room to kick out their legs, lean back and relax just like they did in the good old days back home; they were the seasoned and the true campfire vets and people for whom the ranger had a great deal of respect.

Simultaneously — and all in a FLASH — a splash of light lit up the night and then shined straight into the ranger's eyes thus making him momentarily go blind and also lose track of where everyone was at (not to mention seeing spots) before, like a beacon in the night, the stream of electron-excited air tilted up at a ninety degree arc penetrating deeply into the dark where it illuminated the flap-happy wings of a quivering moth and, above that, an owl gliding free in stealthy flight, before the beam dropped back down low to earth — and a smudge to the left — where it stopped, mid-row, on what must have been the amphitheater's VERY LAST spot ... and on which the man with the flashlight then wiggled the light. Predictably, that gap — three empty wooden slats of bare bench — was dead center in the middle row, at about as hard a place as possible to get for the slightly-intrusive guest with the wandering light.

"Is *THAT THERE* an empty space?" he asked. "*—Cause if so I'd like to claim it as my own.*"

His tone was polite but also "to the point," more a perfunctory afterthought than a formal request, and so it went: the man with the electric torch was *moving on in* even before he got a response.

"*Sorry ma'am ... Pardon me ... AHEM ... I'm sorry about that sir ... oh, that's wonderful ... plenty of room ... okay, almost there ...*" he said as he squeezed his way in, past the already seated patrons who scooted in their shoes and pivoted their knees and couthily cleared their belongings out of the way just in time and just enough to let the late-arriving guest get by.

He was apparently all alone.

Just himself.

Or was he only a silhouette?

And his battery-powered torch of course.

"*Almost there ... just a little further ... oh, thank'ee for moving that ... Yep ... yep ... thank'ee ... thank'ee ... there we go,*" he gestured and jived until at last he had finally arrived at his spot after which, with a polite tip of his cap, he turned back and profusely thanked everyone he had passed for whatever inconvenience had just elapsed. "*Thank y'all, most sincerely!*" he stammered, just short of a gasp, and then let out a great sigh of relief — "Ahhhhhhh" — and plopped down in the seat. Without any further ado, the man with the light sat down on the pew.

If it hadn't been before, it was now official: The amphitheater was a hundred percent full. Everyone and everything was all set. The night had begun and, with the grace of God's mercy, the day was finally done (*and oh what a marathon of a workday for the ranger it had been.*)

The late arriving guest fiddled with his thumb at the shaft and turn off the torch. Once again it was completely dark, except for the orange glow from the campfire of course.

The ranger studied the friendly faces of his fireside guests. Some had blankets wrapped around their shoulders, others jackets draped over their knees and still others wore knit caps — it was *that crisp* — making it quite a bit different from a day ago (and the many weeks before that) when an immovable mass of tropical air had stubbornly sat overtop the Florida peninsula's southern half causing not just unseasonably warmer winter weather but making it, well, *hotter than crap*. That air had been a tepid and stagnant stew of supersaturated sponge-soaked air which hemmed and hawed and finally hung up — STUCK — into a standstill of unrelenting warmth which, each morning at dawn, took the form of a stillborn and protracted foggy haze (which left behind a moist film on the ground as if it had rained) thus blurring the line between heaven and earth and turning the whole world into a uniform and amorphous gooey gray; under whose cloak the ranger had driven into work — or scratch that, rather "*crawled,* if not "*crept*" (as, half a world away, where he served as a soldier everyone still slept, the ranger fighting the urge not to let his mind slip back into that past and instead staying focused on his immediate task) — moving forward in space and farther away in time from all that, even if at only the slowest of super slow-motion rates, him having to continuously *tip-tap-tap* at the pedal between his accelerator and clutch — THE BRAKE — all the while he craned his neck to keep his face up close to the translucent dash, looking out and fully ready at any moment to press that middle pedal all the way down on the floor deck with a SMASH when — *lo' and behold* — he broke out of his slow-motion rolling reverie to find himself doing *exactly that,* as indicated by a gyration of noise that sounded something like this, "— *ScrreeEEEETTTCHHH-AAAAHHHHH-ERRRNTT!!!*"

And so it was the ranger and his truck came to an abrupt and complete stop — just inches short of a doe in the middle of the asphalt on the road in front. The deer had soft brown fur and an innocent gaze with a belly that had fallen; quite obviously she was carrying a fawn: a mother with her unborn baby two hearts pounding as one; followed by a huff and a puff and a hoof push into flight, as suddenly as she appeared the apparition of the deer was gone out of sight.

The startled ranger sat speechless at his wheel scanning from side to side as he struggled to catch his breath. Once again he had avoided the most grisly of fates: eye witness to a bloody death and one that could have quite possibly included himself, and the fawn of course who would be born in days.

Suddenly alert, the ranger reengaged his clutch and shifted back up into gear to resume his way into work which, it should be pointed out, was in complete contradiction to that stagnant slug of tropical-warmed air that, well, just wouldn't shift, not a single inch. It just sat and it sat and ... *IT* ... *SAT* ... and just when common meteorological wisdom said it should have long

passed ... *IT ... SAT ... AND ... IT ... SAT ... AND ... IT ... SAT*
some more, a fat cat on its haunches with no willingness to
budge.

Days turned into weeks turned into a *month*. It was a New
World Order of the atmosphere: a perpetual fog that lurked in
the purgatory space of being neither day nor night, and for
evermore, or maybe not quite; for, just when the weather
seemed like it would never change there came a wisp of a hint
that it just might, at the benevolent hands − or rather, "fist" −
of a mighty arctic blast barreling southbound on a runaway train
called a Polar Express.

Not that the stationary mass of sedentary air wasted a single
thought on stepping aside, it instead (as do fat cats) quite
happily lounged on its pillow with not an inkling of alarm, just a
prolonged and gaping yawn, as it pushed and pawed and then all
but collapsed as it relapsed into its never ending nap, completely
unaware and without a care of the train wreck of an atmospheric
collision heading its way.

When the brawl finally came it didn't disappoint − *and Oh,
What a Sight!* − full of *THRASHES* and *CRASHES* and torrents
of light as the dueling masses of air, one warm the other cold,
went full bore into their tropospheric fight; buckets of rain and
gusts that ripped, lightning followed by thunder, the sky a cat's
ARCHING back. A hiss and a scream and a rapid-fire attacking
paw, followed by series of *KA-BOOMS* and *BA-BANGS* and other
such noise. As to who would win it was hard to say until, in a
blink of an eye, it was as clear as day. Cold air from the
Continent was plowing ahead as warm air from the Equator got
smushed back in retreat. At long last − *and Halleluiah!* − the
tropical intruder had met its defeat. It was a glorious event. A
hero's homecoming surprise. Cool air and clear skies had
triumphantly arrived!

The ranger was quite pleased (and too a bit relieved) with
the result. The change in weather could be described no other
way than *Heaven Sent:* Crisp air, treetops bending in the breeze
and the Milky Way above in clear view, its infinite celestial sea.
Or in the simplest terms, it felt good on his cheeks. It filled his
heart to the brim with a sense he had a new lease on life.

And so it was, the ranger was ready to proceed ... except for
one minor problem: the image on his tiny PC wasn't transferring
up on the big outdoor screen. Whether one or the other or both
were at fault, the two companion pieces were unable or

unwilling to talk, not unlike a hopelessly mismatched couple on a dreadful blind date. Nothing the ranger did seemed to work: a reboot, trying again, pressing every button, reconnecting, jiggling the wires and even a control-alt-delete. If that wasn't bad enough it was only about to get worse.

First a puff.

Next came an acrid whiff of smoke.

And just like that, in a blink, the entire outdoor screen went blank.

Except for the campfire, the entire amphitheater was black.

The show was obviously over.

Or, maybe not.

In an instant, out of nowhere, the giant screen magically *LIT UP!* The ranger slowly followed the beam to its source, tracking it overtop the campfire and into the crowd until it finally stopped dead center in the middle row at what appeared to be the very last spot that had been filled. But of course! It was the flashlight of the late-arriving guest.

The Ranger

BOOK 3
SANDBOX

Sandbox

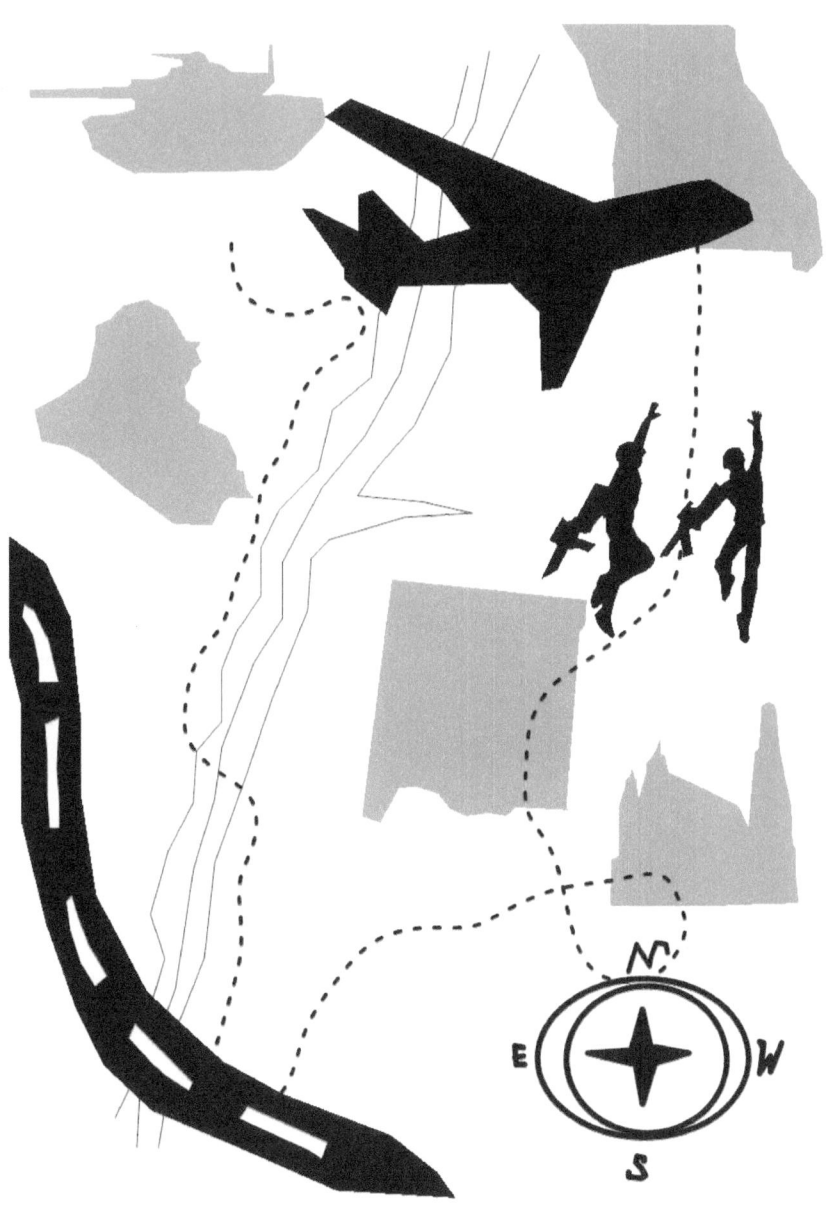

Sandbox

Chapter 1
Lonesome Campfire Blues

Rusty never gave serious thought to becoming a ranger when he returned home. He wasn't sure why. He just didn't. Instead he tried his hand at what he knew. At what he knew he was good at. He knew how to build things. He enjoyed working outside with his hands. He had done that before he left and figured he would do it again when he returned home, if *home* was the place he was at.

Rusty wrote a letter to Marshall Creutz while he was still overseas.

He trusted Marshall.

He knew he could help out.

Marshall had a job waiting for Rusty when he returned. He was happy about that. This time it wasn't on the line working on a crew but directly for the general to make sure all the subcontractors did their jobs right. Mostly they did. Rusty was a natural fit for that work. It suited him well enough.

"Glad to have you back," Marshall said with a slap on Rusty's back a few weeks in. "Glad to have you back in one piece."

Rusty nodded in acknowledgement as a cement mixer rumbled through. He had just tested the load to make sure it made spec. A half a year ago they had to tear down two walls because they didn't cure right. At least that was Marshall's view of events.

"A bad batch?" Rusty asked.

Marshall shook his head. "Yeah, but we let them pour so it was my fault. Buck stops here." He bounced his thumb off his chest as he said it. "Would've caught 'em with one simple test."

That's all Rusty needed to know. All the trucks that came through from that point on he personally inspected. It was as much about doing it right as not letting his boss down.

"Really good to have you back in one piece," Marshall repeated. It was mid afternoon on a Friday. "Why don't you take the rest of the day off ... on me." Rusty said no but Marshall insisted. Rusty respected him too much to turn him down. He accepted his offer.

"And you're in for golf tomorrow, right?"

Rusty nodded. "Tee off 7 am sharp I'm there."

That night on his couch Rusty sat there and starred.

He drove to the pub down the road to drink a beer. It felt good to be alone among people, just listening to the sounds. The bartender asked him if he wanted another beer and he said yes. Rusty looked at himself in multiple mirrors behind the bar and overhead. He thought back to what Marshall said about it being good that he was in "one piece." Looking at those mirrors his torso in one and his legs in another and hands in the reflection of the brass banister by his beer he no longer felt that way one bit.

Or maybe the problem was just the opposite.

Maybe it was being in one piece that bothered him most.

Rusty thought about the guys. How some of them made it back like him but then about the others, too. Some of them he saw go down. Others he just never saw again. Some of them he saw lose parts of their bodies. Some had dazed others panicked looks on their faces. Others he just looked into their eyes and knew they were no longer there. Each one had been so alive and then like that they were gone. Never to come back. Rusty wasn't sure where they went. There was a side of him that wanted to go there. Just to see where they were at. Just to see they were alright.

He tried to forget then an hour later he'd realize he hadn't thought about anything else.

It didn't seem like a war even if that's what they called it. It never occurred to him that they were hard times when they were happening. It seemed frustrating more than anything else. But more and more looking back he found it hard to swallow. Hard to choke back. In his throat he had a perpetual lump. What they called the war was actually the easy part. As far as he could tell they had won it without as little as a fight. At the time that was a relief but now looking back he could see that was eerie, too. That something wasn't right.

The desert was dry and lifeless. Riding in the armored truck on the dry desert floor, an infinity of nothingness ahead and behind, he wondered why in God's name anyone would choose to live in such inhospitable terrain. It was scorching hot and blighted. Bone crushingly sad. Of course he knew they didn't choose at all.

They were just born there.

You can't do anything about that.

That's probably what made him miss back home the most.

During nights at camp they made campfires with wood from the gulches where the water once or sometimes ran. Private Rusty sat at the fire studying the flame. Nights were cool in the desert. Sometimes windy. They set up special breaks to cut the wind. The other soldiers that sat around the fire spoke about where they had come from. Rusty liked to hear their stories. He had never been to the places they described. Kenny was bragging about New Mexico. Rusty was surprised to hear it was so cold.

"Snow in a desert?" Rusty said in disbelief. "I could use some of that tomorrow at noon."

"How 'bout you Herms? What state did you ride in from?" Kenny blurted out.

Herman looked at him with a cold reptilian stare. "Suburban Virginia. Hated it."

What Herman hated even more Rusty could tell was Kenny's newly-dubbed nickname for him.

Kenny prodded the fire with a stick like he was adjusting something glowing in the embers that needed fixed.

"Never did understand that about that state."

An uncomfortable pause filled the air. Rusty felt compelled to jump in.

"What ... didn't you ... understand ...?" Rusty haltingly asked keeping a careful eye towards Herman to gauge his response.

"Doesn't make sense to have a West ... *and not an 'East'"* Kenny authoritatively stated as if speaking for the group. "Silly to have just a plain old Virginie by itself. Actually Old Virginie and New Virginie would make more sense. Just like they did with Jersey."

Herman inhaled.

It looked like he was going to say something.

But then he didn't.

Rusty felt uncomfortable. Why was Kenny always dragging him into these sorts of things? Or was it Rusty always jumping in the middle thinking he could smooth things out? Rusty just didn't want a senseless altercation to occur.

Rusty stabbed at an educated guess, "— Isn't it historical? I think it has something to do with ..." he began to surmise when Kenny predictably broke in.

"Yeah, I know that, but so what. Same thing with Carolina and Dakota? They both got split north and south. You don't have South Dakota and just Dakota. See what I mean?"

Rusty tried again to interject, to clear things up. "What happened was ..."

But Kenny kept on talking.

"It's like having a *hot faucet* and then just *a faucet*," Kenny continued. "It's just common sense the other one has to be *cold.*"

Rusty looked at Herman. He had impeccable posture and was staring straight ahead. He looked unusually relaxed. Was he even hearing anything Kenny was saying? Maybe he heard it all and just didn't care.

Kenny suddenly stopped himself in mid-thought as if a light went off in his head and shifted gears. "But then again water out of the cold spigot is never *really cold*, is it?" he deduced as he thrust his finger into the air like a detective following a fresh lead. "Not ice cold anyhow. Don't you think?"

"More *Luke warm,*" Rusty eagerly affirmed.

"That's right!" Kenny nodded his head with a satisfied look. "It just doesn't sound right to say Hot and Lukewarm."

Rusty looked relieved. "Well ... there you have it."

Herman stood up and walked away without saying a word.

Rusty raised his eyebrow. "You think he's mad?"

Kenny looked at him quizzically. *"Mad about what?"*

"I don't know. Life." Rusty looked into the fire. "Being stuck with us."

"Well better us than out there ... with the jackals." Kenny motioned into the darkness, "— Or whatever the hell that thing is that howls every night."

The two of them listen to the fire crackle and hiss.

"How 'bout you?" Kenny said looking at Rusty. "What's it like where you come from?"

"Born or raised?"

"Hell, I don't care. You can pick either one."

Rusty looked into the campfire.

"Long story or short?"

"Would you get on with it for Pete's sake! How 'bout a story about a state you've *ain't never* been to. That'll work, too."

Rusty poked a stick into the fire and started to exhale.

Rusty couldn't tell if the campaign was dragging on or just getting started. There was a pit in his stomach that was starting to grow. For the first time ever he had an insatiable urge to be nowhere else in the entire world except home.

But where was home?

Rusty considered himself an American first. He knew that more than ever now that he was on the outside looking in, overseas. He was the same as the other guys. It didn't matter which state. Wherever they were from they were mostly all the same. Or familiar at least. He could see it in their mannerisms. He could hear it in the way they spoke. More similar than different but also no two of them were alike. Rusty just had to meet an American *once* and it was like he knew the person for life. The natives he met he struggled to keep straight in his head. Not that the places he saw weren't interesting or the people he met often generous and polite. It was just a sense that over time his gravity of being, who he was and why he was living, was starting to dissolve even if — and thankfully — or so he thought at the time, he was still in one piece.

As for a state, Rusty considered himself a Missourian first. No state was more American than another but you'd have trouble convincing Rusty that good ol' Missoura wasn't at the top of the list. He thought about his trips as a kid to the Gateway Arch. How that silver rainbow was the doorway that connected the American East to the American West. How it was the inverted cradle where two mighty rivers met. The spot on the map where men and women of that bygone era, the pioneers, hopped from boats into wagons and wagons into boats and some probably on horseback and also on foot, too, all setting out to wherever they were going and continued going until they got there and finally stopped and put down roots.

Rusty thought about when he went to the top of the arch to the narrow window and looked out to the West, how he couldn't see a single thing except city sprawl. But then again maybe now, in retrospect, when he squinted his eyes, he could actually see it all: the Great Rocky Mountains pushing up out of the horizon marking the end of the Great Plains. Or how in the other direction when he looked East he could almost make out that thin sliver of Atlantic Ocean blue and even hear it, too, its waves curling and clapping down on the sandy shores, its salty mist drifting in the air. Or directly down below how the muddy waters of the Mighty Mississippi and Missouri Rivers merged, how they twisted and turned but pretty much went straight south right past New Orleans and from there spilled out into the Gulf of Mexico, those same rolling waters also carrying the multi-ton cargo ships on a reverse trip into the heart of the nation on the strength of her serpentine liquid back.

Missouri could seem like a sleepy backwaters but the view from that arch confirmed that it was the center of it all, too.

Why was it then at that campfire with Kenny that the thing that filled his mind was not America or Missouri but the southern end of Florida instead, the place that he went with his father, the soggy patch of untamed wilderness they called the Big Cypress Swamp?

Maybe the barren flat desert had finally worn him thin. Flat dry dirt as far as the eye could see.

Rusty swept his hand across the fire and tried to explain the majesty and magnitude of the marshy Florida expanse.

"Like a fertile crescent ... an infinite oasis ... as far as the eye can see," Rusty whispered in a hushed but captivating tone.

Kenny looked at him enthusiastically as if he had suddenly developed an unquenchable thirst.

He licked his lips.

"Hell, open up the gates, I'm ready to drink the whole thing dry right now!"

Rusty looked at Kenny bemused.

That was exactly the problem. How did he know? What used to be free and flowing and uncontained, man had turned into an intricate series of gates and pumps and water control rules which in theory maximized the water's use but in reality created one crisis after another always blamed on nature when invariably it was man messing with Mother Nature that was the root of the despair.

Rusty recounted to Kenny the story of being on the airboat with his father, how they arrived at a place called Prophets Landing in the angled light of the late afternoon sun; how Rusty wondered why they were leaving then and not in the morning when there was more daylight to spare; how his father backed the trailer into the water until the airboat started to float — Rusty on the bow with a rope that he threw to his father to drag the metal vessel back to the bank so he could hop aboard without getting his feet wet; how Rusty sat on the front seat that had metal legs that were bolted to the deck and his father sat in the elevated captain's chair behind him; how what he saw in the slanted but still strong Florida sunshine as they left the landing, through a narrow gauntlet to the main glade, a shallow sea of water as far as the eye could see, was as shocking as it soothed his eyes, it all flying past them at airplane fast speed – a labyrinth of tall grasses and an infinite expanse of Lilliputian trees; how where his father sat was at or above the canopy top of that ancient forest of tiny trees; how he could see overtop of it all – *King of the Glades* – flying faster than a herd of antelope on the open Serengeti Plain.

Kenny gawked at Rusty with a combined sense of intrigue and disbelief.

Rusty struggled to attach words to the long-dormant memories that the campfire was stirring up: How his father's airboat had no brakes and no steering wheel just a shaft to shift the air foils behind the blur of the airplane propeller caged in back and how it wasn't just any airplane, how it was salvaged from a WWII era P-51 Mustang and how his father who understood doing things with his hands built it from scratch and constantly tinkered with it on the spot, how he had his tools with him, or at least some of them, at all times wherever he went.

It wasn't so much a ride as it was a sensation. Not flying, not floating, not four wheeling but somehow all three.

At some point Rusty's father hollered ahead for him to hold on tight as he thrust the steering shaft forward forcing the boat to do a one hundred and eighty degree spin, the boat then decelerating backwards and ever so briefly but not quite coming to a stop before at that same moment accelerating forward again, them in perpetual motion — not one time on that trip did they actually stop — his father not steering into the trail but straight through the tall grass making a new trail (or were they widening out the one that was there?) mashing it down, then going another couple hundred feet forward before hollering out again and doing the same and then the third time he did it a bird that looked like a chicken with a blaze of purple feathers on its chest flapped up onto Rusty's lap, squawked, and immediately flew away.

It wasn't until the airboat finally slowed and came off plane, quickly followed by the cessation of the gale force wind blowing on his face and the quieting of the thunder-rumbling whirl of the caged propeller behind, them then just puttering to tie up at Gumbo's dock, Rusty's father instructing him to lasso the rope to a piling — that the trancelike suspension of disbelief came to an end.

Stepping out on the dock was like waking up from a dream.

Rusty looked at the camp then back at the airboat. The silver ship sat there silent in the still water like H.G. Well's Time Traveling Machine. Their destination (if *that* was it?) looked like nothing more than a dilapidated shack that human kind had left behind and long since forgot.

Rusty didn't know where and he didn't know why. All he knew was that with no small effort they were there.

They had finally arrived.

Chapter 2
Finger Lickin' Frog Legs

The fire danced in Rusty's eyes as he reminisced.

"That's about as far away from civilization as I'd ever been ... until I landed here."

"Yeah, ain't that something," Kenny agreed. "Supposed to be where it all got started, too."

"The birthplace of civilization," Rusty confirmed.

Kenny flicked a twig in the flame. "Hell, you'd think they'd have it perfected by now. You know, figured it out. Instead, man, this place ... it's a barren mess."

"Wore out is more like it," Rusty mumbled, not sure if he was talking about the land or himself.

For the first time in a long while, talking about Florida by the campfire made Rusty feel at home. Maybe where you're born *does matter*. Even if you only stay there just an instant. Wherever you're born is always in your blood.

"Hell, Missouri has swamps, too, don't it?" Kenny asked.

"Used to but they drained 'em all. Farm land now, or what hasn't turned into suburbs at least. The levee's the only thing holding the water back."

"That and an act of God."

"*Nawww,*" Rusty countered, as if correcting the facts. "An Act of God might someday be the one thing that returns it back."

"Ha! Back to wetlands ... birds would like it anyhow."

"Not that we'll ever be around to see it."

"Fun to *think about* anyhow, don't ya think," Kenny said introspectively. "—You know, rewinding back the clock. Wish I could do that sometimes with a couple of things I guess."

Rusty looked at him intrigued. "*Oh yeah, like what?*"

Kenny shrugged. "I don't know. Some little things. Others big." He picked up some tiny pebbles around his feet and threw them one by one into the flame.

"Like back in Albuquerque ... foothills used to be right out my back door. Now you gotta drive near an hour to get past all the houses. Damn near need a pair of military goggles to even see an undeveloped foothill these days."

"You get up in them mountains much?" Rusty inquired.

"No, unfortunately not," Kenny lamented. "Mostly the desert floor. You know, four wheelin'. But always wanted to. Not sure why I didn't. Climbing the Sandias. It's really supposed to be beautiful up there."

Kenny prodded at the fire with a stick like he was dry mixing concrete under the flame. He had a faraway look in his eye.

"Saddest thing at this point," Kenny shook his head in disbelief. "— I think I know more about this God Foresaken Desert than I do any of it back home."

Kenny and Rusty listened to and watched the fire crackle and spit embers into the sky. It was pitch dark on the ground, black. Overhead was a roofless clear shot into the universe, the beginning of time, that infinite void.

Ten thousand miles West and what seemed even further back in time it was under that same sky of stars that Rusty and his father, just an hour or two after they arrived at that shack, got back on the airboat and headed out into the opal dark night, this time the two of them donning miner lamps strapped to the front of their heads in addition to a giant floodlight his father rigged to his seat, the two of them skidding overtop the half-submerged saw grass like an out-of-control comet running raucous through the dark void and newly formed constellations on the water, all unnamed: alligator eyes popping up and shining and then submerging down into the liquid ink again, frog eyes blinking and blazing in midair on the grass blade ends, and raccoon eyes cautiously watching from the safety of willow branches and live oaks reaching out from the high-ground tree islands that, like lonely and barely inhabitable planets, sporadically spotted the glades as they sped past.

Higher still and as far away then as Rusty and Kenny were sitting under them now, the cosmic pinpricks of the almighty universe quivered above.

Rusty had no idea where they were going until he saw it and then he knew they were *there:* back at the spot his father had matted down the grass with the multiple turns.

Rusty's father slowed the airboat to an idle and handed him a barbed trident that he called a gig. It was taller than Rusty about five feet long.

"Watch how I do it," his father explained as he shined the beam of his headlamp into the mesmerized eyes of an alien-like amphibian staring back. With a quick thrust his father jabbed the talon-sharp tips of the trident through the soft underbelly of the hapless frog. It barely gave a croak as into the bucket it went.

Rusty didn't like it but he did as he was told.

Easier than catching fish out of a bucket, there was a frog at the end of every isolated blade, the few that still stood upright that is, or that had righted themselves after being matted down earlier in the day.

In no time at all they filled two buckets after which his father gave the sign. Their job was done. They'd collected enough. It was time to go back.

Rusty's father spun the airboat into a circle before righting it in the direction of the trail. As they headed south back on plane, Rusty spotted the Southern Cross hovering just above the horizon line as the night air blew across his face.

Rusty looked up and watched it all whiz by, the celestial bodies above a blur and his mind feeling the same.

He was tired.

It had been a long day.

Rusty's father was elated when they tied back up at the dock. "A feast of legs for breakfast," he said as if it was going to be the most extravagant affair.

Rusty couldn't imagine eating a single frog let alone two whole bucket's full. All he could figure was that his father was going to have to eat both.

Ramshackled as it was, Rusty was relieved to be there ... inside ... home ... or wherever it was they were. It was Spartan but dry and, after his father and he hunted down and slapped dead the few they'd brought in on the walk from the dock to the front door, free of mosquitoes, too. (As for the spiders unfortunately he couldn't say the same.)

All Rusty wanted to do was sleep.

His father had meticulously shown him everything about the camp before they went frogging: how the generator worked, what each building was for, where the spot lights and other necessities were. It was thus to Rusty's surprise his father was reviewing it again as soon as they returned.

"Now the building is secure. Just stay in here and you'll be safe until I return."

"You're leaving?" Rusty said in disbelief while at the same time trying to hold back his frightful concern and, as does a son in the presence of his father, also act composed.

"Listen, ain't nobody out here within ... a hundred square miles. Only thing to be afraid of is the dark ... and that don't bite."

...

"Sounds like a real heart-warming father son experience," Kenny chuckled as he reached for an MRE. "If you were a dog that's what they'd call: *Sending You Away To The Farm.*"

Kenny carefully read the side of the pouch and gave a disappointed look. "Tell ya what, all this froggin' business is making me hungry," he said as he ripped it open anyway. "Whadaya say butt munch... wanna trade your chili for this Mac & Cheese?"

Rusty didn't bother looking up.

"Oh yeah, it's all miserable. Whatever. Fine."

"Bet you and your old man harpooned some *coons* and *squirrels* out there, too, while you were at it?"

Rusty threw his half empty water bottle at Kenny. It would have hit him square in the head if he hadn't covered up. It deflected off his hands and bounced into the dirt.

"Hey, how 'bout a little conservation! This is the desert, you know!" Kenny shot back. "— Waste not want not. We gotta save every drop."

"Consider yourself lucky," Rusty rebuked. "—If we were back in the States it would have been a bottle of booze.

"Probably real high end stuff, too."

"You got that right, I was thinking Scotch."

Kenny's eye's bugged out. "Yuck, you don't mean Cutty Shark?"

"Not Cutty Shark! I'm talking a *high-end* single malt."

"Ha! How about some *Manachevits!?*" Kenny whimsically jeered. "That'd be more your old man's style from the sounds of it. And who needs a carpet when you got water up to your ankles. Come to think of it, I bet he was making *moonshine*. I bet *that's where* your old man went." Kenny broke out into delightful song to cap it all off. *"Your hooooouse ... is made of tiirrrrrrres ... and you get your cloooo-oooooothes ... from traaaaaaash fiiiiires."*

Rusty cut him off abruptly mid verse. "That's a bunch of bull crap, Kenny!" he said in an irritated tone. "— Not in a million years would my father do that *sort of stuff!*"

"Listen, I didn't mean to ..."

Rusty waved him off.

"No worries. I'm not mad. I'm just ... I don't what I am, *not anymore.*"

Rusty balanced the last of the large pieces of wood tee pee style against the flame.

"What did the frog legs, when you ate them — *you did eat them, right?* — taste like?" Kenny inquired with a pseudo-serious look on his face, or was he on the verge of cracking up?

Rusty gave Kenny a thoughtful look. "Well, that's a good question. I guess I'd have to say ..."

Kenny didn't let him finish: "Lem'me guess — Finger licking good! I bet just like chicken! Oh, that is rich! Ha-ha-ha! That is rich, Rusty! Ha-ha-ha! You're killin' me! Ha-ha-ha!" Kenny howled in delight as he leaned backwards and let himself go, thumping into the dust.

Rusty didn't find it funny at all, not one bit.

Kenny was a jackass, simple as that.

But for some reason he couldn't help himself. Just like Kenny he, too, started to laugh. First a chuckle and then another despite continuing to try to engage Kenny in a serious tone.

"You're a real ... Kenny ... you know that ... you're just a ..." Rusty gamely attempted to admonish his friend before succumbing to the situation and giving up. "You're just lucky it's me. Because somebody else. Herman. Anybody. They'd just kill you on the spot."

"Yes! Please! Yes Kill Me!" Kenny riotously roared, all the while wiggling his fingers in front of his face deliriously repeating *"finger ... lickin' ... good!"* to the stars. The delirium of the day and the absurdity of the sight had finally taken their toll. It was impossible to be mad at Kenny. Rusty slowly but surely gave in and broke out into an uncontrollable belly laugh himself.

"They ... were ... really good!"

"Finger lickin' good!"

"I'm serious ... I swear it ..." Rusty tried to say but could not get out on account of the belly laugh exasperating all the air from his lungs. Drool, not words, was the result, thus causing the hilarity engulfing Kenny to amp up another notch.

"You're SERIOUS!? Frog legs! The Colonel's Frog Legs ... *Colonel ... Freakin' ... Rothstein's Frog Legs!* .... Oh My God! ... Finger licking ... Colonel Rothstein's Frog Legs ... Fa-fa-fa ... *Florida Fried Frog!* ... Quit it would ya Rusty ... Damn, I'm crying it's so damn funny. I can't ... get ... a hold of myself!"

Finally Kenny rolled to his side and stood up.

He brushed the powder off his uniform as best he could.

Why or if any of it was funny at all wasn't clear other than it sure felt good to laugh.

"So seriously," Kenny said, still trying to catch his breath. "He left you there ... all alone ... in the middle of the night with ... I don't know ... alligators ... snakes ... the boogeyman ... and all the other creepy creatures that live out there in the swamp?"

"Worst part about it," Rusty had to nostalgically admit, "— The front door didn't even lock. Just a screen door with a metal hook and eye latch. I didn't find humor in that one bit."

Kenny shook his head. "Seems like an awful lot of effort ... *and risky*," Kenny marveled "— All that work to make a meal out of frog legs you could have got just as easy in town at KFC."

"Funny, I know," Rusty concurred as the fire reflected in his eyes. "But I can't tell you how much I'd pay to have a bucket of skinned frog legs in front of us now. Beat the hell out of this Mac & Cheese anyhow."

Rusty was surprised by how much he remembered. The details. Little things that happened he assumed were long forgot. It was something about the campfire, a relaxation reflex around it, that helped loosen up his mind so the memories could well up.

The more Rusty talked about it the more he was convinced that the trip held clues to the answer he sought: about his father, who Campfire Charlie was and the fate of the swamp. Talking about it helped bring things to the surface at the same time it alerted him how much he still didn't know ... and probably never would.

Chapter 3
Horton's Airboat Rides Again

Rusty listened to the airboat fade into the distance but never quite disappear. That's when he realized the sound he was still hearing was a mosquito hovering midair by his ear. He clapped at it once, twice and then again. On the third try he successfully smacked and smushed the tiny intruder between his hands. He opened and looked at it in his palm, a brown speck and a tiny blot of blood. The airboat sound was gone. It was official: it was just him alone in the shack. He flexed his index finger on his thumb ready to flick it off when for the first time he noticed the peculiar beam of wood running along the ceiling.

Or was it a log?

Rusty approached it for a better look.

What at first glance appeared to be senseless graffiti he could see closer up was a kind of "sign in" book of the many people who had visited the camp. It dated back years if not decades. Rusty inspected the signature beam closely. It ran fifteen twenty feet across the center of the room. It was low enough for him to read but too high for him to touch. Not only just names, there were personalized notes, too. Rusty read them one by one to see how many names he could recognize and to decipher to what degree any of the longer free-handed messages made sense.

It didn't take long for Rusty to see it was a virtual *Who's Who List* of the swamp. Many of the men his father spoke about (and some of them he had met) had their full signatures or short hands scrawled in ink and knife cuts across the beam where once had been bark. It reminded Rusty of the many signatures that jam packed the hardened white plaster of Elliot's cast, the time he broke his arm, names written this way and that, at angles and different colored pens until about every last space was filled up. It almost seemed worthwhile to break his arm judging from all the attention he got. As he looked up at the beam Rusty wondered if his grade-school chum ever saved the plaster cast, or did it just all go into the trash when they cut it off. He probably had a photo or two of it at least. Elliot had bragged to all the girls how the doctor was going to use a little round saw to cut if off and how if he wasn't careful the blade could easy slice into his skin but that he wasn't afraid at all.

Rusty refocused his attention on the beam. Albert Lee Hodge stuck out as the John Hancock of them all. His name was among the largest and most distinctive – bold stokes of perfectly looped cursive ink deeply impregnated into the wood. Next Rusty spotted H U D D Y modestly written in capital script, not too far from *Eddie* and *Derby-Hat Dave*. Between every name he knew were a dozen or two he had no clue. There was Greg Kleal and Dan Vukovich, too. When he saw Sick Sidney, written in his telltale shaky script, it brought a smile to Rusty's face and there it was, not too far down the length of wood, proof that Randle Devine sometimes – maybe more years past – broke free from the short leash of managing his store.

Next to Reverend Devine's signature was a smiley face which after the fact, possibly a good decade later, somebody had scribbled in a thick shaggy beard with a permanent Sharpie pen. Maybe it was Randle himself?

Rusty also took time to read the other graffiti and notes between scanning for names. One read – "*Open 24/7.*" Another read, – "*Should've brought more gas. Leaving by foot now.*" Between Dan Vuchovich and Greg Kleal was written "*Tweetly Dee*" and "*Tweetly Dumb.*" Another set of initials, in this case two – *CML* and *SB* – was contained in the shape of a heart with a "*plus sign*" between them, or was it a sign of the cross? Rusty assumed it to be of a young couple who were once, maybe still, madly in love.

Rusty found Sandy Parrish's name next. At least that's who Rusty assumed it was. All it said was *Sandy* with no last name after that. Under his name was an unmistakable sketch of an orchid with an arrow at the end of a sign post, the kind you see at remote crossroads, pointing to a "*W*" (Rusty assumed to mean West) and, in microscopic Latin lettering, *Charlemagnus echolokwequus* overtop the common name *Charlie in the Box*: the rarest (some said no longer existent) orchid of the swamp. Typical for Sandy, Rusty thought, to scribble a botanical name. In boredom Rusty followed the direction the arrow pointed across the rounded underside of the log and then up the other side to find, surely by chance, that it pointed more or less precisely to a rather sprawling exposition of script that, at first glance, was simply too small to make out. Rusty stood on his tippy toes and even then had to squint.

"There's no limit ..." is all he could make out. The script was too faint after that to read on account of the dim lighting of the two incandescent lightbulbs and the shadows they cast along the beam.

Rusty pulled a chair over from the wall and hopped up. A spider scurried into the corner towards a shadow just beyond the light. Satisfied it was a safe distance away, Rusty turned his attention back to the log, and specifically to the words, which were clearer and readable if also incomplete:

> *"There's no limit to what a man can do or*
> *the places he can go if he doesn't mind ..."*

It was disappointing to see the original ending had been crossed out. Why or who did it Rusty had no idea. In its place was a dark and expansive blot of black and blue ink and divots in the wood. A couple alternative endings were written off to the side, with *"suffering the consequences"* and *"keeping one step ahead of the law"* popping out the most.

The multitude of endings made Rusty laugh as much as leave him wondering what the original ending was. He shook his head in vague recollection. He'd heard of the saying before, somewhere, but on the spot he couldn't quite recall what it was or who said it, or if he'd read it in a book or a magazine perhaps. Not that he gave it much more than a passing thought. There was still a lot more of the log to see.

He hopped down to the floor and slid the chair back against the wall.

In doing so, Rusty noticed both vertical support posts (the two pieces of milled lumber that held up the log at either end) were similarly scrawled with names, too. Those signatures seemed newer and were separated by more space. One of them he even recognized, or so he could only assume, the letters — *S h a n e* — written at the bottom of the post, about four feet high, in the deliberately drawn handwriting of a preschooler's pen. Just above it was the name *Allen* and in parenthesis by it, just to be sure — *Shane's big brother* — preceded by a dash. There was also somebody named RIP etched more recently just above and to the right.

Rusty walked across the room to inspect the other post but didn't see any names he recognized other than *S h u l a   i s   G o d* stenciled in at chest height.

Rusty thought about the story Randle "The Reverend" Divine told him about Coach Shula stopping for gas at Monroe Station and immediately Campfire Charlie came to mind. If such a man existed — given *that story,* and so many of the others his father had told him over the years — it would only make sense that his name would be prominently displayed on the beam, too. It wasn't. Then again neither was his father's. Rusty found the absence of both men's name disappointing to say the least, as if after so many years the sign-in log still lay incomplete.

Rusty went over the beam again to give it a more meticulous look. He noticed many names and messages he'd missed, with two proximate yet paradoxical pieces of advice catching his eye:

All Ye Who Enter Beware

and

Warning: Stay Inside.

Rusty tried to contemplate how exactly the two conflicting recommendations might apply to him. One interpretation would be that he'd just made a *one-way* airboat ride. If "staying inside" meant staying safe then there might be a chance he would never get back home, at least not without his father's help. Or was the beware warning not about the wilderness but what might lie inside the shack? What if his father died? Nobody, not a soul, even knew where he was, or him how to get back ... at least without getting eaten alive by alligators or, and this would be the biggest irony, trying to slog back through the watery wilderness and dying of thirst. Instinctively Rusty jumped around backwards to make sure he wasn't about to be attacked only a moment later trying to calm himself down and gather his thoughts. He was going to make himself woozy with worry if he didn't get a grip. True, any and all of his interpretations of the warnings were not good but, like a proverb in a fortune cookie, they were probably no more his destiny than they were words of strangers written on a giant piece of wood. Never once could he remember reading a fortune in a cookie that ever came true. The same applied to horoscopes, too. The trick with them was that they were written so vaguely that they could be interpreted in any number of ways. Horoscopes were less about the truth than they were a way to exonerate one's responsibility, a handy excuse, for whatever did or didn't happen; a way of laying the culpability at the feet of some other larger force. It was on that last thought that Rusty made peace with the cryptic words of warning on the log, and which also coincided with him spotting a third quote in the same area that he'd previously missed:

Not a fit night for beast nor man.

Rusty's thoughts again returned to his father. What sort of business was he doing in the middle of nowhere on an airboat alone in the night. And what if he never came back?

Rusty caught himself.

There he was overthinking everything again.

If there was one person he never had to worry about, it was his father. He could take care of anything or any situation. He was sure of that. In some strange way the quote gave him new hope that his father's name was up on the beam or the posts, and thus Rusty resumed his search, going back over the names he'd already seen mixed in with new little details that emerged: But as for his original quest he still came up one name short.

As far as he could tell his father's name wasn't there.

Rusty tried to imagine how his father would have signed his name if he did. Probably somewhere high up on the log and prominently displayed like Albert Lee Hodge.

•••

Rusty laid down on the cot.

A half hour later he was sitting on the edge of the bed staring across the dark room. He reached down to the floor and grabbed the flashlight by the shaft then pushed the button forward until the spotlight appeared. He shined the light at the wall until he found the door and then followed the beam into the main room, an area that combined a kitchen and a living room all in one. The same counter that held the sink also horseshoed around into the middle of the room to form a rectangular table that had barstools on the far side and custom-built shelving built within. Several of the cubbies were filled with stacks of magazines. Judging from the first few, the magazines weren't exactly up on current events, let along even in circulation. Among them were a *Mechanix Illustrated, a Real Men Digest,* a *Sports Trails Quarterly,* and a *True War* — all publications he had no idea even existed, let alone who read them or what they were about. A quarter way down the pile, he finally found a magazine he recognized: it was a *Life Magazine,* just like the ones that covered the coffee table in the waiting room of his dentist's office in Missouri up North, although quite a bit older as judged by the date on the front cover he was looking at. The magazine was older than him. It featured fighter jets rocketing over South Vietnam. The deeper he went in the pile the older the magazines got to the point he surmised they were older than his father, not that he knew exactly when his father was born. Rusty decided that was something he should know and was going to ask him as soon as he returned. Rusty thought for a moment about that. He'd never seen a childhood photo of his father or had any idea what he looked like when he was a boy. Rusty had no reason – or evidence anyhow – to suggest otherwise that he wasn't a full grown man his whole life.

The *Mechanix Illustrated* featured a photo of a teenage boy gripping a metal wheel of a complicated machine much in the manner that a captain does for steering a ship, although in this case with no nautical intent. The boy appeared to be inside a windowless room of a factory where they fabricated intricate metal parts. On the inside he found an article that at the top in bold red typeface read — *"HERE'S A CAR"* — and then in smaller black letters under it — *"You'd Like To Own"* — only it wasn't a car at all: it had giant wheels on it and an open top that gave the appearance of a doctored-up military truck.

A few pages in was a man with horned-rimmed glasses and a pipe under the title: *"The Man Who Brings Engines to Life."* Rusty initially thought the man to be a mechanic judging by the intricate (almost lifelike) cartoon sketches drawn on each corner of the two-page spread. One was a helicopter, another of a powerful engine and the third a battleship. It wasn't the accuracy but the anthropomorphic features on each one that made them unique. The helicopter was adorned with the stodgy face of an British aviator. The gas-powered engine sported the muscular arms of a body builder which, somewhat comically, it was using to pull its own crank! The boat paradoxically boasted legs, four of them, that it was using to doggy paddle to shore where it opened a large metal door on its chest through which a squadron of soldiers burst out onto the beach. The man wasn't an engineer at all, but a Disney-style cartoonist, or maybe a little of both.

The cover of the *Real Men* magazine painted a hair-raising scene of two boys dueling with what looked like harpoons in a turbulent whitewater stream chock full of tree trunks that had recently been cut down. The teenager in the blue shirt had his harpoon raised high and ready to strike a slightly older (and notably uglier) man cowering down in a red and black checked shirt. Rusty saw no way the ugly man in the red flannel could survive ... or not be very badly injured at least, leaving him to wonder what bad deed he could have committed to deserve such a fate. Under the image it read *"Moscow's Top Military Secrets Exposed: THE RED PLAN TO CONQUER AMERICA."*

Also featured on the front cover were *"I Was Kidnapped by a Wolfpack of Castro's Terror Maidens"* and *"Wild Vacationing Wives Are Destroying Palm Beach."* Rusty thumbed through the magazines and saw more of the same. Predictably they were way out of date, too. That's when he leaned back from the counter and noticed a stack of newspapers on the shelf underneath.

The one on top was the Gold Coast Gazeteer for Monday, Tuesday and Wednesday September 15, 16 and 17. Rusty looked for the year but it was too faded to see. The front headline was *"Hundreds Escape Flood."* Rusty looked at the photo that accompanied it. A man and his dog were paddling in a row boat down the middle of a road. The dog looked happy enough. The subtitle in smaller print read *"Bigger Canals and Levees Planned in Storm's Wake."* Rusty read through the article from front to back. The flooding was especially bad in the one particular spot because of its location downstream of newly installed agricultural pumps. "Don't make sense they flood us out but keep the tomatoes dry?" a local homeowner decried. A representative from the Farm Bureau encouraged all local homeowners to do their part by "proactively planting hedgerows of water-slurping maleleuca trees, recently shipped in from Australia" – and *"available for free!"* – to help *"stomp out natural floods when they occur."* On the bottom corner there was an advertisement for a Heliomaxer Radio for $19.99, it claiming its product to be capable of *"Tuning in Foreign Stations as Far Away as Mars*."* There was more fine print at the bottom that Rusty didn't read.

Rusty paged through the rest of the paper and then picked up the one underneath. The world seemed simpler back then from what he could judge. And a little more black and white. The articles were obviously slanted more than they were factual but in a way that was colorful and entertaining, too, as if good story telling was more important than telling the absolute truth even if, the truth as they knew it at the time was what they reported, too. To Rusty that was a startling contrast to the stale and stoic reporting of the Evening Nightly News he sometimes watched around the television set up north with Dwight.

Or maybe him liking these newspapers was just a sign he was getting older, growing up. Rusty decided on the spot he'd give reading the Post-Dispatch another chance when he got back to Missouri, assuming he wasn't stuck at the ramshackled camp for life.

It was quiet in the room except for the crinkling and flapping sound of him handling the pages and dark except for the spot where he shined the flashlight's beam.

A bit unexpectedly Rusty found himself engrossed in a story continued from an earlier page without even the benefit of the opening paragraphs or even what its title was − rather, it was the odd photograph featured near the middle crease of the back pages that caught his eye. And it was only because he was reading the "Salty Says" fishing report on the Delray Fishing Tournament, the lucky winner − *a Mr. Charles Monteray of Ernst, Michigan, hauling in the biggest prize: A 75 pound sailfish six miles offshore* − that he even noticed the photograph at all.

The scene was nondescript enough, probably common in the swamp. It featured a man yanking on a taut rope with all his might (while simultaneously trying to smile). The rope was angled upward and over the top of a horizontal log and then dropped vertically down. A gigantic alligator lay prostrate, supported by a hook and a cradle, at the rope's end. The scaly beast was presumably dead but looked peaceful enough − even smiling perhaps. Its beefy tail spilled beyond the confines of the crib onto the ground.

Above the photo at the top of the article the headline read *"GATORS"* in large print followed by *"Continued from Page 2"* after that. Rusty turned back to the start of the story. *"Illegal Poaching Has Gators On Brink"* the title read. Then he read the line underneath and that's when his eyes really lit up.

It was his father's name!

His father was the author. Rusty couldn't believe it. With great interest and just as much pride, he eagerly read the article from front to back. The subject would have surprised Rusty had he not heard it firsthand before. Crooked game wardens, not the poachers, were the primary gator problem in the swamp. A since vanished game warden, a man by the name of Jimmy Thistle, was cited as lying at the epicenter of the spilt blood and bad feelings that had emerged and who in the article was described as *"the original hatchet man whose name, even now, is spoken in whispers for fear of retribution from the law."* The story went on to explain how a well-funded coastal merchant class was brought in to strictly enforce new quotas *"far below a living wage that any honest working gator hunter could earn"* all the while *"turning a blind eye"* to the syndicate who were hauling in truckloads of gators by the week to private dealers along the coast and further upstate. The current game warden, a man by the name of Chester (Chaz) McElliot, admitted that *"mistakes had been made,"* but really, by the time the article was written, the poaching had played out because the gator population was so low. The only option was to shut the hunt down. The last line was a quote from Chaz. *"— The alligator is not a cuddly creature but it's one that we aim to protect."*

Rusty looked at the photograph of the man with the gator. Either the man was very short or the gator was abnormally large — thirteen feet at a minimum even if the man was just five and a half feet tall. That meant the man had to be incredibly, almost supernaturally, strong to hoist a gator so high. Or maybe it was an optical illusion? The more Rusty looked at it the more he couldn't tell if the man was standing directly under the horizontal beam from which the gator hung or well behind in the distance a good five or ten feet.

Rusty looked back and forth at the gator and the man in attempt to better judge.

Also confounding matters was the man's face. It was blurred as if he had turned his head just as the photo was snapped, as if somebody or something got his attention or called his name — or he was shaking his head to keep a giant deerfly at bay? The latter hypothesis was possibly corroborated by a suspicious speck not too far from the gentleman's face. Rusty was well aware of how annoying the bugs could be from an unpleasant kamikaze attack (and large welt) from one of the unrelenting creatures earlier in the trip. That's when it occurred to Rusty that it was neither the man nor the gator that caught his eye at all, but rather the cradle of a contraption – *the log* – from which the gator hung.

Something about it tickled at the back of his mind. Where was it that he saw that log before? Rusty paused to think. It was in looking up to ponder that a jolt of electricity shot through his spine.

All in a flash the Eureka Moment hit!

Aha! Of course!

The log in the paper was the very same one he was sitting under in the dimly-illuminated shack. Or at least that was his hunch. Was it possible they were the same? Probably not. In any event, Rusty shined the flashlight back and forth between the newspaper and the log overhead to double check. The irony was that the log in the photo looked new at the same time the photo in the newspaper had bleached with time and grown faint; meanwhile the log above his head was in real space — right in front of him clear as his flashlight could shine — but also dulled from the elements and grooved by the passage of time. But just like the features in an old portrait of a child shine through in the face of an adult (no matter how old), Rusty reasoned there very may well be a clearly identifiable trait that connected the "black and white" image on the paper to the real-life log above his head.

Rusty went back and forth between the two of them several times in attempt to confirm. The more he did it, the more he wasn't sure. It looked the same, but he couldn't find a slam dunk clue either. The photograph was simply too small to scrutinize with any level of detail and the log overhead too cluttered with signatures to see any of its "original markings" underneath. Rusty reached the tentative conclusion that such gator frames and cradles were probably commonplace back in those days.

The chore of looking back at the beam reminded Rusty how earlier he was equally frustrated not to find his father's name. If he couldn't prove the signature beam was the same in the photo he was newly resolved to at least confirm the presence of his father's name on the log. After all, he was a journalist. That probably made him locally famous, or at least semi well known, in the swamp, and would have also instilled him with the importance of leaving behind his mark.

Rusty shined the flashlight at "*S h a n e*" near the bottom of the back post.

Slowly.

Meticulously.

With full attention.

He worked his way up.

In a strange way, by using the flashlight, he felt like he could canvas the wooden relic, inch by inch – one spot then the next and then the next – much more thoroughly than earlier in the evening in the imperfectly projected illumination of the room's uncovered incandescent lights.

Bottom to top, he worked his way across, first the front-door side of the beam, then the side that faced the kitchen and finally the bottom that faced the back wall before ending up at the top of the other vertical beam where he worked his way down to the inscription that read: *S h u l a   i s   G o d*. Now Rusty was positive. There was no Henry and no Hank. There wasn't a single indication that his father was ever there. Maybe he went by a different name, or his initials perhaps.

Rusty stepped away from the beam in failure and a bit frustrated, too. Hadn't his father only been to the cabin about a hundred times? He didn't know the exact number but could only assume.

Quickly and without thinking Rusty ran the flashlight beam from *Shane* to *Shula* across the entire signatory frame when without even looking for it — from the corner of his eye — something popped out. He reverse traced the beam from his flashlight back up to the center of the log, just above where the pulley long ago in that photo once hung, and there it was: plain as day, not written but rather whittled away with a knife, seven letters carved in a row, each one three to four times bigger than any of the other signatures that had been written at every angle overtop:

C h a r l i e.

Rusty couldn't believe it at the same time he shivered with delight. It was dim. It was faint. But it was there for sure. After so many stories of the mystery man, had he finally found proof? All Rusty could definitively say with any authority was that he was suddenly very, very tired. His eyes were drooping. The rush of adrenaline that gushed through his body after his improbable discovery had pretty much washed away any and all the energy he had left. Fatigue had fallen over him like a ton of bricks.

Rusty shined the flashlight back on the newspaper and folded it up then put it on top of the others and returned them just as he found them to the shelf underneath. He did the same with the magazines on the countertop, too, chronological order from oldest to youngest, neatly stacked. In doing so, as he pushed the magazines against the wall, he noticed an empty can with its label still intact. It read *"Libby's Corned Beef Hash."* Its original contents long ago eaten as an entrée at the camp, the rippled shell of tin had been salvaged to serve as a makeshift container for a few pencils and pens.

One of the writing utensils in particular caught Rusty's attention for the reason that, and perhaps only because, his mother and Dwight had bought him a similar-styled pen as a momento from Six Flags a few years back, only it had "The Comet" roller coaster inside.

Rusty picked the pen out of the can.

The front shaft where you gripped it to write was solid blue with silver script that read, *"Horton's Airboat Rides, Frog Town, Florida, USA."* The back half was a transparent glass tube filled with clear fluid that contained a miniature airboat on the inside. Rusty tilted the pen at an angle and watched the airboat slowly slide to the other end. He remembered endlessly doing the same thing with his roller coaster pen over and over again on the ride back from Six Flags and later on in his room at his desk.

That's when it occurred to Rusty exactly what he needed to do.

With his flashlight in one hand and the pen in the other, he slid the barstool to the middle of the room and then climbed up the rungs until he was standing upright on top and in reach of the log. In a blank spot he pressed the ballpoint pen from Frog Town against the wood.

Back on the floor he shined the light back up to inspect what he'd done. His father's name wasn't there, but his now was, all contained within the dot in the *"i"* so long ago whittled to spell Charlie's name.

Chapter 4
Glen Canyon Dam of the Swamp

When Rusty opened his eyes it was already early dawn but it wasn't the light, rather the sound, that woke him up. His first inclination was to wave his hand around his head to bat away another mosquito when he realized there was no bug there. It gradually grew louder and louder until finally it was a deafening roar as if the bug had become imbedded inside his inner ear when suddenly he sat up to the sound of a propeller jauntily coming to a stop. It was an airboat. Rusty was getting ready to head to the door when he heard voices of one man and then another but it wasn't until he got to the screen door that it was confirmed. Neither man was his father. Nor was it his father's boat. The one man, the driver, had a pot belly and slicked back black hair. The other was lanky with a hillbilly beard and wore what appeared to be a railroad engineer's cap. At the time he wasn't sure whether to produce himself at the door or run and hide in back. He was thinking that the space in the corner of the top bunk would be the perfect spot when the man with the slicked back hair (who as soon as he opened his mouth Rusty renamed him in his mind to The-Man-with-Rusty-Nails-in-his-Throat) called out in a scratchy baritone voice.

"Rusty, you in there?"

The man with the hillbilly beard gave a friendly wave confirming he saw the boy at the door.

Not knowing what else to do Rusty flicked open the latch with his index finger and approached the two men. The man with the rusty nails in his throat introduced himself as Johnny Gumm. The other man just Ed.

"Your father's still out I see," Johnny observed.

"Out skinning frogs," Rusty confirmed. With the arrival of the two visitors he perhaps finally understood why his father had made mention of "*a feast.*"

The two men looked at each other but didn't say anything. "Frog legs, well — of course," Johnny Gumm repeated in a semi-incredulous voice.

"Didn't want to attract the alligators to the camp," Rusty explained in case they didn't already know.

Johnny shook his head. "Not gonna argue with Henry on that."

"How long has he been gone?"

Rusty tried to think. "He left when it was still dark. A couple hours ago, at least. Probably more."

...

Johnny was tending to a smoldering pile of blackened chunks of wood on an outdoor grill when another airboat became audible in the distant slough.

Rusty pointed toward the sound. "Can you year that? It's probably my father."

"I hear him, Lima Charlie," Johnny bellowed like a bullfrog. "— A load of frog legs. Just in time. The grill's all set."

Rusty went out to the edge of the dock to see if he could spot him while Ed, lanky as he was, climbed to the top of the roof and waved his arms like a makeshift lighthouse to guide him in.

Ed must have been hungry, too.

"Lima Charlie?" Rusty murmured to himself and then walked up to Johnny Gumm to repeat. *"Lima Charlie?"*

Johnny smiled wryly as he stoked at the wood. "Just some old military slang. Us war dogs. It's just how we speak."

Rusty looked at him blankly. He didn't get it.

"Lima Charlie ... as in Loud and Clear."

...

The airboat came to an abrupt stop about a hundred feet from the dock and then from there it puttered in. Rusty looked at the airboat. It was his father alright. But something looked different. That's when he realized the vessel was loaded with black plastic bags – all of them full – covered with a brown tarp.

"What's in all the sacks?" Rusty asked as he met his father at the dock. The first thing that occurred to him was that he was confiscating, or rather – *rescuing* – more plants just like he'd seen him do before on the buggy ride when Sid Gruman's boys got stuck in the mud.

"Just a bunch of trash," his father said nonchalantly, walking Rusty away.

"Trash? Way out here?" Rusty was confused. "— How did you see it in the dark?"

Before Rusty's father could respond the man with the Hillbilly Beard came up and extended his hand to shake.

"Your reputation precedes you," the one man said to the other with a respectful look.

"Always wondered when we might meet," the other responded in kind.

The men embraced like they were old friends, or was it the first time they met?

Rusty's father waved to Johnny. "— Hope you brought some corned hash!"

"You know I did Henry. Now bring over them frog legs would ya, you son of a gun?" Johnny crudely croaked, although not using those exact words, after which Johnny turned to Rusty with an apologetic grin. "You'll have to excuse my French. Grew up my whole life talkin' to swamp rats. Only language they understand."

Henry greeted Johnny with a hearty slap on the back followed up in short order by Ed joining them in a conversation on topics and people and places that Rusty didn't know. Rusty had always admired his father's easy rapport with other men and these two he could see were no different; it was like they all knew each other from a long time ago even if it had been a long time since they last met, or in the case of his father and Ed, if in fact it was the first time they'd ever met at all. For Rusty it was impossible to fully understand the context of the event. It was a man's world and he was a boy. There were so many things he didn't know. Johnny brought a large tin platter of steaming frog legs over to the picnic table that was shaded by a huge Gumbo branch. The branch's orange bark was peeling off in spots like sunburnt skin, although not a sign of weakness — it rather revealed the strength of the muscular woody tissue underneath. The frog legs smelled terrific and had a taste that did not disappoint, and far better than a bucket of boring chicken: they were a perfect culinary re-creation of the swamp. Or was he just hungry? Chicken too would have probably also hit the spot. All the while they ate the three men reminisced about their comings and goings and the good times they'd spent. Johnny left and returned several times to the grill to replenish the tray. By his final trip back the bones were stacked high.

"Sick Sid. So, how is that old codger? Heard he took a turn for the worse."

"Oh, you know," Rusty's father nodded slightly with a smile. "— *Same old Sid.* As long as he's complainin' you know he's doin' good. Or good enough. The day he quits crying, actually, is when I'm gonna worry. That's when we'll know it's *really bad.*"

"Me, I'm just the opposite." Johnny croaked. "The only cure I know is to ignore every ache and pain I got."

Ed sort of hunched over with his hand stroking his beard in deep thought. "Not a bad place to die if you ask me – out in the middle of nowhere in the swamp."

"Beats being knifed in the back behind the Hialeah Track, anyhow" Rusty's father exhaled.

The three men laughed.

"Yeah. God rest his soul. But it's all the same really, ain't it. All you can hope for is to push it off as long as possible," Johnny soberly observed. "— As long as the Good Lord will allow."

"But not long enough that they hook you up to a bunch of tubes," Ed resolutely shot back. "My last breath, when I breath it, is gonna be on *my terms*, nobody else's. Not on a hospital bed and not on life support. I guarantee you that!"

The melancholic turn in topic caused the conversation to stall. Rusty looked at his father, then to Ed and then at Johnny Gumm. Henry raised his eyebrows. "Well I guess I'd have to think that one over when the time comes." He looked at Johnny like there was something else to discuss. "—Shall we?" Johnny dutifully obliged by standing and walking over to retrieve a leather briefcase he had leaning against the Gumbo trunk, although before commencing he had one final thought on the previous topic. "You know I've had a couple stints in the hospital myself. *Sometimes YOU DO get better.*"

He flopped the case with a thud on the table and was about to open it (and had already popped free one latch) when he looked at the table and realized their wasn't enough space.

"First thing first," Johnny said as he picked up the towering platter of bones and carefully walked them to the water's edge.

"Gator bait!" he bellowed as he carelessly hurled the carcass remains into the flooded grass.

Rusty was speechless. Wasn't the whole point of his father going to skin the frogs last night to do just the opposite — to keep the blood and guts as far away from camp as possible? The same rule applied to never dumping bacon grease near camp for fear of attracting bears. Rusty looked searchingly at Ed's face and his father's for any sense of alarm only to find none.

"Now show us what we're up against," Ed ordered as Johnny removed the map from his briefcase and spread it out. Ed grabbed one corner and Rusty's father the other as Johnny picked up a rock and then one more. Rusty found two more rocks by the trunk of the Gumbo tree which Henry and Ed put at the other corners to keep the creased paper lying flat. The four of them huddled around the map as Johnny explained the lay of the land: where the water came in and where it went out, where the existing water infrastructure was and where the new airport was going to be built. Finally he speculated where the new canals and levees were gonna go in after that.

"You see on this side," he pointed to the East, "is all about storing and conveying water. That's where they're focusing all their attention. "But on this side," he said pointing to the West, "— It's not about the water, no sir. It's about *conveying land*."

"Oh, I see. It's a water shift," Ed said as he stroked his hillbilly beard and pointed to a specific spot on the map. "This side's gonna get too much, over here not enough."

"Well it's a *shifty* shift," Henry spoke up. "They're doing it on the sly. It was never written up in any of the reports. This side was supposed to be untouched. It took us up to now to figure out what's going on and hell, now it's probably too late. Had I not been flying we would have missed the whole thing."

"Let me tell ya, Henry. If we don't stop this one it's all over." Johnny swept his hand over the entire picnic table and, in the same motion, up towards the airboats and out across the distant swamp beyond. Rusty turned to where he was pointing. As far as his eye could see it was nothing but water-flooded glades.

When he turned back to the table Johnny was looking straight at Ed, "Gonna be the ..." Rusty paused a moment to think of the exact name, as he'd said it, and then like that it popped into his head, "— The *Glen Canyon* Dam of the Swamp."

"When's the last time anybody around here was able to stop a Drainage District canal?" Ed inquired.

Johnny Gumm gave a blank stare. Rusty could see a sickness bordering on rage in his father's and Johnny Gumm's eyes. This time the Drainage District and developers had gone too far. But there didn't seem to be any stopping them either.

"Ever since the *Drowning Horse Report*, and even before that, it's been petal on the metal ... those developers and canal builders getting whatever they want." Johnny sighed. "We thought we were protected, but now ... it's only a matter of time."

The man with the hillbilly beard didn't seem fazed. "The secret to stopping a runaway train," he roguishly smiled as he adjusted his cap, "— is finding a way to slow it down."

"Dammit, I was hoping we could just derail the hole darn thing and be done with it," Johnny howled.

"Well my view on this, Gentlemen," Henry exhaled, "— and I know the four of us agree, is that there's no limit to what a man can accomplish if he doesn't mind who gets the credit."

"Are you talking the airport or the levee?"

"I'm thinking both."

•••

Kenny interrupted to make an important point.

"So the man with the Hillbilly Beard said that to your father, *not the other way around?*"

Rusty thought for a moment and then confirmed.

Kenny continued. "— Because if that Ed's the Ed I'm thinking it might just be ... and *are you sure* that's exactly what they said?"

"Well it's been a long time," Rusty conceded. "— But that's how I remember it."

Kenny traced a stick in the sand. "I mean I know it's a longshot. And by long shot I mean *a really long shot*. But the way you describe it: *that wasn't Edward Abbey, you don't think?* Did he ever work in the Everglades as a ranger? If so," Kenny paused. "—I think it might've been him."

Rusty was dimly familiar with the name but sort of doubtful, too. "Park Ranger! My father wouldn't have anything to do with that."

"I mean he's dead now," Kenny clarified.

"Dead?" Rusty echoed in a hollow voice, "— *What's your proof?"*

"Proof?" Kenny laughed. "Oh, I don't know. I read it in the newspaper. We're only talking *Edward Abbey*. His death made

74

the Evening Nightly News. You know Edward Abbey was, *IS*, really famous out West."

"Oh, you mean *him*," Rusty replied, quickly regathering himself.

Kenny looked at Rusty strangely, slightly squinting, not quite sure what his friend's reaction meant. "I mean, if his name was Ed. And he had a hillbilly beard. And if they really specifically mentioned Glen Canyon Dam. *You're sure about that, right?* Because that's what his book *Desert Solitaire* was all about."

"About saving the canyon?"

"Hell no!" Kenny blurted. "The canyon, they flooded that puppy out. The book was sort of a eulogy for the canyon that got destroyed by the rising pool." He broke a twig he was holding in half and tossed both ends in the flame. "— It's better known as Lake Powell today."

Rusty scoffed. "Well, a bunch of good that book did! Sounds like a big waste of time."

"Ohhh, he wrote *that* book, too," Kenny rebutted with a wag of his finger. "It's called the *Monkey Wrench Gang*. In that book they blow the whole damn dam up. Fictional of course, but semi-autobiographical, too."

"Probably what he'd *wished* he'd done in real life," Rusty guessed.

"You got that right!" Kenny enthusiastically agreed. "Now that'd be a good one to turn the clock back on. Lake Powell. Let me tell ya, it's really bizarre. It's a blaze of blue water in the middle of the desert. Drier than this place even, or about just the same. Hell, ol' Ed Abbey is probably rolling in his grave — *wherever that's at* — thinking about all them fat ass idiots in houseboats chugging beer and tossing their empty cans out on the lake." Kenny paused as he chuckled to himself. "Thing about Edward Abbey, you know, as passionate as he was about nature, he was actually a litter bug. He had a really bad habit of tossing beer cans along the side of the road everywhere he drove."

"An environmental litter bug? Now there's a contradiction."

"Conventional wisdom would say you're right. But Edward Abbey wasn't exactly, what's the term: *Politically Correct*. Still, I bet it must burn him up. That's assuming you can still think when you die," Kenny added as he scratched his scalp. "— *You can* still think when your dead, *right?*"

"What'ya mean *wherever* he's at," Rusty interrupted, going back to a previous point.

"Well ... he died. That much they know. Or think they know. After that nobody, except his closest apostles at the time, are really sure. There's theories about it. But you know, his inner circle made a promise. They're all tight lipped."

"So he could still be alive?"

"As alive as Elvis I guess," Kenny joked only to have his answer elevate him up onto a more philosophical plane. "The thing about The King and Ed Abby is all you really have to do is listen to *Are You Lonesome Tonight* or read *Hayduke Lives* and you'd swear they were right next to you talking in your ear like they were still alive.

"And who's Hayduke?" Rusty asked, trying to follow along.

"That was Edward Abbey's alter ego in the *Monkey Wrench Gang*," Kenny explained. "Do you see what I'm saying? I think if you leave something behind, like Elvis did with his hit songs or Ed Abbey did with his books, there's a part of you that never dies. *Does that make sense?*"

Kenny thought about it some more. "When you read any of Edward Abbey's books it makes you feel like you're riding shotgun in the passenger seat with him in his truck. More than feel: *you're actually there!*"

"And chucking the beer cans out the window, littering too, I guess?" Rusty sarcastically asked. "The guy sounds like quite a saint."

"You know, not that I'd do it myself, but I sort of like the unrepentant litter bug in him."

"Yeah, none of your best heroes are perfect, that's for sure." Rusty admitted in a halfhearted attempt to rationalize the act. "— Everybody has a fatal flaw."

"Well, hopefully not *fatal*," Kenny cracked. "Anyhow, something like that. Sad really when you think about it. Lake Powell flooded out what was the most inaccessible canyon country in the whole United States. Used to be a multi-day trip to this place called Rainbow Arch. Hell, my brothers and I jet-skied there in under an hour from the house boat we rented at the marina. That always burned Edward Abbey up."

Rusty tried to imagine the geological feature in his mind but kept defaulting to an image of the silver-plated Gateway Arch in St. Louis he'd seen so many times in his youth.

Kenny continued: "Lake Powell's water line goes right up to its edge. The engineers wanted to go another twenty feet higher. Would've flooded the whole damn thing out if they had. But as a nod to some Enviros they stopped it short."

"Small victories."

"Actually, you're not too far off. Some say that's where the modern-day environmental movement got its start."

"Because it was part of Arches?" Rusty asked.

Kenny shook his head to the contrary. "That's a completely different park, in the corner of Utah, further to the southeast. But Arches National Park *is* where Ed Abbey wrote his book."

"Which one?"

"Desert Solitaire."

...

Rusty liked listening to Kenny's stories out West. It sounded like interesting country and country to which he'd never been. That made Rusty think: maybe it would be good country for the two of them — both Kenny and him together — to someday explore, when they got back — *if they got back* he corrected himself as he knocked his knuckles three times against the side of his head. Could it have really been Edward Abbey at the picnic table at Gumbo's Camp so long ago that day as Kenny seemed to suggest? Rusty tried to think back. If he hated dams he sure as hell would've hated levees. If it was him, Rusty wondered which persona was at the picnic table that day? Was it the resigned man who wrote *Desert Solitaire* to document the wilderness canyon in its unadulterated state one last time before the earthmoving machines came crashing in to cut off the water spigot once and for good? Or was it the resolute man who was all ready to hatch a plan to monkey wrench the whole works like in his other book, *Hayduke Lives*? Was that what Ed meant when he mentioned "slowing down a runaway train?" The more Rusty thought about it the more of a likelihood it seemed to be. The best Rusty could say was that he couldn't rule anything out. "I'd just have to look at a photo of Edward Abbey to know for sure," he finally offered as the next logical step.

All of a sudden Kenny seemed skeptical.

"You know, the more I think about it, the more I think it probably *wasn't* him."

Somewhat crestfallen Rusty was taken aback. "— No? Why not?"

"Well for one, there's only a couple hundred thousand Eds in the world. And two, what in the name of Heaven would Edward Abbey be doing in the middle of some God Forsaken swamp."

"You said so yourself he was a park ranger. Don't they get moved all over the country to all the parks?"

"All I'm just saying is that there's hillbilly bearded guys named Ed littered all over that backwoods swamp. And from the sounds of it I bet your father probably knew every one of 'em."

Kenny and Rusty looked at the dying flame. The wood was mostly consumed but the slag pile of embers was still emitting heat. "How about stateside," Rusty floated as an idea, "— when we get back why don't the two of us go out West. To Arches. And maybe try and figure this Edward Abbey mystery out." Rusty thought about it some more. "Plus it would be fun just to drive around. We'll reminisce about all the good ol' days in the war overseas."

"Ha!" Kenny concurred. "Sounds like a good plan. And a hell of a lot better than sitting around at the lodge with a bunch of World War II vets telling us everything we did wrong."

"Arches?" Kenny closed his eyes and repeated, "— Sure, why the hell not."

Chapter 5
Go West Young Man

The war progressed wonderfully. Better than they ever expected. Day after day there was never a fight. When they finally arrived at their destination it was abandoned, too. Days later the war was declared won to great fanfare at home. Of course on the line he and everyone else knew nothing was won. You don't win anything that easy, especially a war.

"You want another beer, bud?" The bartender asked.

Rusty looked down into his mug.

"Maybe one more."

···

Rusty made tee time the next morning. His first hit off the tee went straight and long.

"That's a good strike, Rusty. A damn good strike. Who'd think you go off to war and come back with such a fine stroke?"

Rusty laughed, "Those care packages of golf balls you sent didn't hurt."

"Yeah, driving golf balls ... it's the best way I know anyway for clearing the mind."

Rusty laughed but this time not so much. What type of soldier returns from war a better golfer? Not a good one anyway. And a lower handicap at that. Rusty had never golfed a better round or been so disappointed in himself.

That following Monday Rusty gave his two weeks notice.

Marshall looked at him surprised.

"I just need time."

Marshall shook his head. He understood but didn't understand. "Take as much time as you need."

···

Rusty was in his truck driving south.

He didn't want any payments, no paperwork, so he paid cash.

The money he didn't spend on his truck he had in his pocket.

That was all the money he had to his name.

It wasn't much.

It was enough.

His only plan was to keep driving.

He'd drive until he had nothing in his pocket and no debt to his name.

That was the extent of his plan.

It was a good plan.

The Mississippi River was beside him to the left.

Just past the exit to Jackson Island he turned on his headlights.

It was getting dark.

A pair of silver eyes popped out on the side of the road, and then another.

It was a mother deer and her fawn.

The fawn's eyes followed Rusty as he slowed down.

The mother looked around.

Rusty imagined himself in a single engine plane like his father flying as far as he wanted. He looked at the gas tank. The needle pointed to just above a half tank. It felt more like half empty. He'd drive it until it got close to E and then fill it up and keep driving. Or maybe he'd let it drop below E and just ditch his truck and take off by foot from there. He was in that sort of mood.

He felt dead on the inside.

Like he didn't care.

The road was empty.

Single lane.

He hadn't hit the interstate yet.

Maybe he wouldn't make it that far.

At least not tonight.

When he saw it was a National Forest he decided to stop.

His mind wasn't right and he knew it.

It would do for the night.

He cleared out a spot to pitch his tent and took from his truck his Coleman stove and lantern that one and then the other he lit. He wasn't a fancy cook but he knew how to make good camping food. He fried an egg with a slab of spam and some cheddar cheese melted over top all squished between the bottom and top halves of a dinner roll. For dessert he had raisins mixed in with some sunflower and pumpkin seeds. He cleaned the flatware while it was still warm. It felt good to be in nature, to simplify. It made him feel in control. He grabbed a Hank Trouper comic book he had with him in the metal milk crate in the back of his truck. Sometimes at night he looked at those for no other reason than to fall asleep.

Rusty briefly studied the cover and then opened it up, somewhere in the middle so he could read forward and back. He liked doing that. It made the past seem as much of a mystery as the future was on the pages ahead. Everything was dark except for the lantern glow around him and his book.

Hank Trouper was floating down a river with Huckleberry his dog on a little wooden raft. It reminded Rusty of the Rubico, its banks wooded and its current running smooth. Hank Trouper had his pants rolled up and his feet in the water as Huckleberry ran around the edge of the raft sticking his snoot towards the surface and barking at the fish. Hank and Huckleberry made life look so easy. Floating downstream. Not a worry in the world. Life was as simple as that.

A sunset spread across the last panel on the lower right. It looked warm and inviting, a rich magenta glow.

Rusty turned the page.

On the first panel, top left, it was completely dark. Night. The stars up above reflected in the water below. Huckleberry bit at them thinking they were fish. All he came up with was a wet snout. On the next panel those sparkly treats disappeared. The water was dead. Just inky black. A blanket of fog had moved in. Huckleberry went to the center of the raft and sat close up against Hank. The two could see each other but just barely and that was about it.

The next panel was surprising because it showed the river again but from the distance as if it was drawn overhead by the vantage of a small engine plane like the kind his father flew. To Rusty's surprise, the blanket of fog didn't cover the whole country at all, it was rather just a thin ribbon of meandering murkiness that slithered through the valley like a snake. Away from the river up on the hills the stars were still shining bright in the night sky. On the right side of the panel Rusty could see what looked like bubbles or mist disrupting the fog. The next panel zoomed in to a giant sign stuck in the mud on the river bank that Hank couldn't see. The fog was thick as pea soup. By mistake they had taken the wrong fork. Instead of entering into the bypass canal they were still heading down the main branch where the channel widened and the current slowed to a crawl. At first Hank didn't know why. And not that he cared. It was late and he needed some sleep. They would figure it out in the morning after the fog lifted and they got some rest. Huckleberry didn't like him doing that. He started biting at Hank's pant leg trying to tell him something. He didn't want Hank going to sleep.

"Cut that out!" Hank ordered to no avail.

That's when Hank started to hear what Huckleberry already knew and Rusty saw from the safety of his warm lantern glow: the muffled roar of a waterfall rapidly approaching downstream! Hank was frantic. Terrified. He did his best to paddle in reverse. Upstream. But his effort was all for naught. The current was pulling him down toward the lip of the spill-over dam. After that it was into the torrent below.

•••

Rusty woke up in a start by the campfire. The flame was gone. The embers cold. He pushed his palm against his chest and then his fingers on his brow. He was still there. Not dead. He listened to the sounds. An owl. The wind in the trees. Then it was quiet again.

That's when he heard it.

A crunch in the brush, then another. Then one more. Like steps of an animal or human. Then it stopped. Rusty kept listening. Something, or someone, was still there.

Rusty straightened up. He put one knee on the ground and hunched his shoulders down in a military pose and then relaxed his eyes to expand his peripheral view. He quieted his breath. When, if, the sound came again he would be able to pinpoint its exact spot. He wasn't out of the woods but he was in a more advantageous spot. When the sound came again he wouldn't pause he would strike he had his hand on his knife and the only thing he could feel was the rhythmic thumping of his heart like a drum. He counted the beats to stay awake but before he could help it he was counting sheep. A moment later he was again fast asleep.

•••

Rusty woke up at some point later crouching in the same spot. His head was slumped forward. There was a puddle of drool below him in the dirt.

It took a moment for him to come to.

To shake off the sleep.

To remember who he was.

He felt his face again.

Still there.

His name was Rusty.

That much he knew.

He didn't know much else.

There was a muted light to the East. It was dim, not dark. The sun hadn't risen but it was getting close. There were more sounds. The lonesome call of a dove. A vehicle in the distance on some faraway road, unseen. There was also a small flame, barely the size of a candle, visible in the center of the campfire ring. That confused Rusty. The fire had been cold when he had woken before.

At least that's how he remembered it.

Now he wasn't sure.

The images of what he had been dreaming started to race, and simultaneously erase, through his head. He tried to grab onto them to give them sense but like a wad of old photographs being flipped fifty-two card style in front of his face — each card individually and all together flying out of the deck into oblivion, over the abyss — the images, what they meant and how they were connected eviscerated as soon as they appeared. The moment it made sense was the same moment it also all immediately vanished, not only from his mind but leaving the earth, too.

By the time Rusty stood upright his mind was blank and he had a mild migraine like he'd been hit in the head.

Then in a flash it all came racing back like a flood.

For a final fleeting second his dream returned.

They were moving fast but also standing still, too. It didn't make sense at all until he looked down and saw they were on a river filled with floating logs. When he studied the logs more closely he realized they were actually people being swept away. Rusty wanted to help them but the harder he tried the quicker everything else sped up to the point all and everyone would have been lost downstream if it wasn't for the man standing next to him wearing a Stetson hat who effortlessly pulled people to safety from all sides, left and right. Rusty tried to look at the man but couldn't see his face. Every time he thought he was going to get a good look the man turned. Eventually by luck Rusty did finally catch a glimpse of the man's face followed by a fleeting moment of deep understanding of his place in the universe, it enriching his head and filling his heart, only in the same instant to see the man had disappeared, leaving Rusty with no recollection of who or where he was, or if he was ever there at all. Rusty looked down into the turbulent waters and pulled a postcard from the stream. He recognized it immediately by the photograph, an alligator in the Everglades. He turned it over. It was blank on the other side. Rusty looked up. Several people were waving goodbye. Now he was the one speeding past everyone in the current, everything around him turning into a blur, him bracing for impact, ready for a crash when in a moment of total awareness he reached out his hand to another hand and triumphantly clasped.

•••

"Kenny!" Rusty gasped, startling himself back awake.

He was looking at the ground.

Sprigs of grass, dirt, leaves. Not much.

He was in the middle of the woods alone looking at a campfire its flame out but its embers still warm him crouched down when he finally remembered where he was and why he was on one knee.

To hell with his dream.

He just wanted to get in his truck and be gone.

Rusty cleaned his campsite in five minutes and was ready to go. The moment he was about to turn the key in the ignition something told him to stop.

"What the hell," he said to himself as he threw up his hands and pushed open the door. He walked through the underbrush in the general direction where he thought he heard the footsteps hours before.

Predictably there was nothing there.

Just trash.

Stupid trash.

Even in a National Forest.

Trash.

He went back to his truck to get a plastic bag and his Cruetz Construction work gloves to pick it up.

Old beer cans. Bohemian Bush Beer was the brand. An oily rag. Empty shot gun shell casings. A ripped open bag of fast food from which dropped out a few fries. An empty box of Duralogs. It was weathered but still readable. A family of four looked out at Rusty from the side of the cardboard box. A husband and wife at either end with two beautiful children, both under ten, in between. Each of them held a stick speared at the tip with a perfectly white marshmallow roasting above the Duralog flame. *"Ideal for Campfire Cookouts"* it read in an oval-shaped red polygon to the right.

Rusty stuffed what he'd already bagged into the Duraflame box when he heard a familiar sound: an approaching truck.

Rusty emerged from the brush holding the box as the four-wheel drive vehicle pulled in.

It was a wildlife ranger.

"Litter patrol," Rusty flatly explained before he'd even been asked. He tilted the box of loose items for the ranger to see.

"Everything else okay?"

Rusty sighed, "— Just had to rest my eyes is all."

"Military?" The ranger asked.

"Army. Sixth Infrantry Regiment. Last six overseas," Rusty instinctively replied.

"Navy. SEA BEE. Served seven years. Last two in the Sandbox," the ranger offered about himself. "— Just got back a year ago last June."

The ranger took a quick look at Rusty's truck.

"Going any place ... specific?"

Rusty didn't respond.

The ranger understood.

"I was there, too," he said. "You'll figure it out."

Chapter 6
Five Year Flight

Rusty was happy to be back on the road.

He picked up the Interstate, Westbound.

At first it was rolling and wooded.

Next thing he knew — it could have been two hours or it could have been ten days — everything was flat.

Rusty pulled off at a rest area.

His tank was on empty. He needed gas.

He watched the digits advance on the LCD screen. He noticed how the gallons moved slow and the dollars moved fast. He thought back to the old pumps, how they were mechanically controlled. The days when the gallons moved faster than dollars. He doubted those days would ever return.

Rusty's thoughts drifted back in time to when the gas station attendants met you outside at the pump, how Dwight didn't get out of his truck, how he just rolled down his window and told the attendant to fill it up which he did holding the nozzle handle down with a clip in the back so he could squeegee off the windshield with blue fluid, first one side and then the other. Rusty thought back to how when the tank was filled the lever automatically shut off with a snap of metal on metal which was the cue for the attendant to hand pump the rest, to get to an even dollar so the change would be exact, just cash. Dwight would then hand a ten or twenty dollar bill through the window which the attendant meticulously placed in the back of his greasy wad of bills – twenties, tens, fives and ones – handing back whatever was required to make change and then they would be on their way.

There were always three vending machines against the wall. One was for soft drinks, another for junk food and the other for cigarettes.

Sometimes Dwight would give Rusty money to buy a pack. It was something about the thud of the Camels on the tray after he pulled the metal knob that Rusty always liked. "You get to be my age, you'll see, pretty much coffee and cigarettes are the only thing you can't go without."

Rusty scanned across the length of the mega convenience store while he held his hand on the pump. It was a grocery store compared to the fill up stations he remembered as a kid. He couldn't leave the pump because it didn't have a hook in back to hold the latch. In the old days that was the standard, just like you always paid after, not before, you got the gas.

When the handle shut off he looked up at the LCD screen. He pumped the handle until it rounded up to an even number. Before he went in to pick up his change he grasped the handle of the squeegee from the holster and ran it across his windshield both sides. The bugs smeared at first before the blue fluid soaked in and he could wipe the glass clean. He had to press hard.

Inside the attendant asked him what pump.

"I'm at fourteen," Rusty replied. He looked at the cigarettes. "And I'll also take a pack of Camels Turkish Gold." He didn't smoke them but they brought back memories; he liked the smell of unburnt tobacco in his truck. On the other hand, maybe he would smoke one. For Dwight. For old time's sake.

He took three ones and a quarter out of his pocket to even up.

She gave him back change.

He dropped the coins in a cup.

He didn't bother to look if it was for charity or a tip.

He didn't care.

He had a full tank.

That was good enough.

...

Rusty never thought he was making a difference when he was over there but now that he was back he wondered if it wouldn't be best for him to return.

Better yet, if he could go back in time.

That would be best of all, and maybe his only hope.

Boot camp was where it all started. The overwhelming thought in his mind when he signed up was that he wouldn't make it. Sometimes you need a mindset like that to make it through. There was a side of him now that wished that was true. He'd heard stories about how tough it was and how there were other people he knew who were way tougher than him and more dedicated to the cause but who didn't make the cut. Rusty thought back to the first time he proved himself under fire when it counted most. That's when the men saw they could rely on him and didn't have to hold his hand or think of him as a liability. There was an ease and the relaxation around men who respected who he was and what he could do. It was a long initiation into it and one that quite frankly he couldn't see coming to an end. It wasn't until Corporal Rothstein, who had done nothing but give him a hard time for months on end, unexpectedly addressed him by his first name and asked him to throw him a soda out of the fridge.

"So what did you think about Bilbo down at the mess hall?"

Rusty turned around to see if Corporal Rothstein was talking to someone else.

No one else was behind him.

"Oh that, yeah," Rusty laughed. "Bilbo's nuts. You won't see me doing that."

"That's why we like having you around here, Rusty. Good to have *adult supervision.*"

Rusty didn't quite know what to make of that other than everyone else in the room seemed to take cue. From that point forward as far as the unit was concerned Rusty was a "made man."

"That was huge," Kenny told him afterwards, the two of them walking away from the mess hall under the harsh glow of the night security lights. "That's as sure a sign there is they're eyeing to move you up the ranks."

Rusty was doubtful. "More than likely he was just in a good mood. I just happened to be there."

Kenny shook his head. "I was standing right next to you. Slim, too. But it was *you* he said it to. Hell, he even knew your name."

"Move up the ranks?" Rusty scoffed. "If that means staying here a single day longer than I have to, then you can count me out."

Kenny pointed up at the moon. Its face was cool, serene, familiar – about as close to home as they got. "I always wondered what it would be like to walk on the surface of the moon. Now, between all the rocks and dust, and having to trudge around in all our body armor — I think I finally know. The thing about this place, though, it's a lot closer to Mars."

"Well, the good news on that," Rusty said pointing up. "Just another hundred and — *what is it,* thirty three days, right? — and they'll be sending us back to earth."

"But who's counting, right?" Kenny concurred with a laugh as he reached up and knocked on Rusty's noggin three times. "What's your take on the man on the moon — *friend or foe?"*

"Definitely friend."

"That's what I think, too," Kenny agreed. "Funny how he never looks straight at you. It's like he's looking over you, at a slant. In *that direction,"* Kenny pointed.

Rusty looked at where Kenny was pointing. A man was approaching them. A corporal. He was running neither fast nor slow. At first he thought it was just coincidence but as the man got closer Rusty could see he was heading straight for them.

The corporal stopped in front of Rusty. "Everyone's looking for you," he said slightly out of breath.

When Rusty didn't respond immediately, Kenny inquired for him. *"Why?* What's going on?" He tried to say it in a way not to sound concerned. "— *This isn't about ..."*

"No, none of that," the officer answered in a monotone voice. He turned to Rusty. "Your presence is requested at the HQ Tent. It's something ... it's ... news from home."

Private Rusty closed his eyes to give himself some room to think.

"Is it serious?"

The corporal either couldn't or wouldn't elaborate. "My orders were to find you and bring you back. Your presence is required at the Commanding Officer's tent."

"Now?"

"They said right away."

The three of them cut diagonal across the gravely earth. Rusty looked up at the moon. The moon stared straight back.

"I'll be right here, okay," Kenny said when they finally arrived. They were at the entryway to the tent. "I'm not going anywhere, man. I'll be right here."

Rusty was led inside where he was greeted by the CO himself. Next to him sat a chaplain. He had a grim look in his eyes.

Rusty's mind went numb.

He felt like he was standing on the surface of the moon.

West Texas amazed Rusty as much as it frightened him, sixty miles an hour moving west, rubber gripping asphalt, axles turning, tires rolling ahead, the thin ribbon of road narrowing to a point on the distant horizon, a barren expanse of uninhabitable land on either side both left and right as far as he could see. No water. No vegetation. Just rock and sand. But something about it comforted him, too. He rolled down the window and rested his elbow on the sill. He put his hand into the wind. He wasn't playing the radio. He just wanted to listen to the quiet even if it wasn't quiet one bit.

Just him and the rustling of the air blowing past.

It put him in a trance.

The blades of the giant turbines spun up ahead in the distance. They looked slow but maybe that was just because the blades were so big and so high off the ground. Wind power in oil country? There was something paradoxical about that.

When Rusty saw his first derrick he understood why it looked familiar. Deserts and oil went together he figured. He didn't know why that was the case or if it was the rule. Eighty five million barrels pumped from the ground every day, three hundred and sixty five days per year. It was a finite supply. Once burned it would be gone for good. Not that anybody cared. Rusty didn't know if that bothered him or made him feel better. What he did know was that for extended moments, some lasting only a few seconds and other times running on for miles, he felt like he was heading back in time to the place he had left behind. It scared him at first before filling him with a deep calm.

Up ahead a billboard approached.

Welcome to New Mexico
The Land of Enchantment

On it were two hot peppers, one green and the other red.

At first it didn't look any different than Texas. Then it did. Derricks gave way to a kaleidoscope of colors. Still desert. But richer. The landscape seemed more alive. He had a vague sense that he was rising up in elevation, too. Just like on the runway in the airplane on his way out.

He was heading to BWI.

From there overseas.

A man in a sports coat and blue oxford greeted him as he walked by.

"Thank you for your service," the man said.

Private Rusty thought how he hadn't done anything yet. He nodded anyway.

When it came time to board the plane they invited service men and women and anyone who needed assistance to board first. There was a mother with a boy in a wheelchair who couldn't walk unassisted. Private Rusty waited for them and then afterwards joined the group.

The plane was small and crickety, not as big as he thought and it used propellers instead of jets. The flight attendant gave instructions from the front. She was good looking. Her skirt hugged tight against her hips and her blouse was open the first two buttons down from the top. She wore a stylish yellow scarf around her neck. Private Rusty moved to the center seat in the back when he saw it was only half full. It felt good to stretch out his legs.

On the plane he stared out the window. There were some thin clouds but not enough that he couldn't still see the land below. He tried to guess the states as he flew over them. The rivers and coastal inlets gave him the best clues.

Rusty looked out towards the eastern horizon. That's where he was going. Frankfurt first, then there. It was illuminated and bright. Too bright. Appearances can be deceiving is all he could think.

When the plane started to descend he knew the water body was the Chesapeake Bay.

Private Rusty closed his eyes. He hadn't slept well the night before because he had to wake up early. The terminal was busy. He got on a bigger plane to head East overseas.

At some point on the flight, not too far long after takeoff and soon after the meal, the monotonous white noise in the cabin put him to sleep.

Five years later it was the same sound that woke him up.

There was a tray of food in front of him.

He hadn't eaten a thing.

Rusty looked out the window.

For the longest time it was nothing but deep blue.

Then there it was.

The beach.

Green.

The coast.
Dover.
That's where Kenny came in.
The wheels touched down.
His plane decelerated to a stop.
Like it or not, Rusty was home.
He had arrived at BWI.

Chapter 7
House Hunting at the Hopscotch

Rusty took the envelope out from the glovebox and pulled the map off the dash. As far as he could tell he was at the right spot.

823 Luzon Avenue

Rusty had imagined Albuquerque would be like driving through a parking lot. He was surprised to find the subdivision looked just like what he knew back in Missouri growing up.

Rusty put the truck back in gear and drove forward. When he got close he parked cattycorner, across the avenue on the other side. He folded up the map and placed it next to him on the empty passenger's side seat.

Rusty looked out through the windshield at the house.

A man was washing a car on the driveway in front.

Rusty hesitated.

He'd thought quite a bit about what he would say. He'd even written a letter and was going to just send it by mail. Then he got the idea he should hand deliver it. He'd always wondered what they'd be like and now there he was. Or was it even them? Maybe it was someone else. Maybe he had the wrong address or they had moved. Or maybe they'd *moved on*. Maybe the last thing they needed was him showing up to stir up the pot. Back home growing up, Rusty thought back to how there were three Creekside Courts at various points along Rubico Creek which wasn't a big deal until there was a fire and the Creekside the firefighters got to last was where the house had already burned down. Maybe there were three Luzerns and two of them got switched.

As usual he was reading too much into things. Or was he just looking for an excuse? Dwight had always said "not to force things. When the timing doesn't feel right, that's when you back away." More and more Rusty could see the things Dwight said made sense. He was practical. He had black and white rules. The house wasn't going anywhere. He could always go back.

Rusty was ready to do just that when the man washing the car turned to him to offer help. The hose was still running.

"Is everything okay? You look lost."

Rusty fumbled for the right words — anything actually — to say when the front door opened. A teenager walked out.

"Is everything okay, Dad?" he asked. He glanced cautiously towards Rusty.

"Oh no, everything's fine."

The father looked at Rusty intently.

"You're not here for the open house?"

"Open ... house?"

He turned back to his son and said something Rusty couldn't quite follow at the same time Rusty noticed the For Sale sign in the yard across the street. Underneath was a smaller sign. It read Open House.

"Oh yeah, I'm sorry," Rusty said unconvincingly as he assessed the situation. "I'm here for the Open House. There it is. From ten to three. I just didn't see the sign."

"Well you better hurry up because," he looked at his watch. "It's just five minutes 'til ..."

"Right! Right!" Rusty sputtered. He was about to step over the curb to offer his hand to shake when a disturbance of some sort on the inside of the house caused the man to abruptly drop the hose and rush inside.

Rusty watched the running water. It appeared to be soaking in at first but then all of a sudden he noticed a dark stain on the sidewalk where the water ran out on the cement.

•••

"*Welcome, come on in,*" a voice sang from behind him on the porch. "*— The door's open.*"

Rusty entered.

"I'll be right with you in one minute," she motioned as he stepped inside. Her hands were neatly manicured and she smelled strongly of a flowery perfume. "— I'm just finishing up.

Spec sheets are around the corner on the new granite countertops."

Rusty was glad to be told what to do. The soldier in him liked that. The realtor turned her attention back to the couple.

"Based on what I'm hearing, this house pretty much has everything you're looking for," Rusty listened from the front room. "The right school district. You're really close to downtown. And I'm sure you noticed the great views of the mountains."

Rusty peeked out the window to see for himself. Mountains? All he could see was other homes. Maybe she was talking about the windows in back.

"I know it looks dated and I can show you a lot bigger houses in the foothills for the same price, but the trend is really starting to reverse. More and more everyone wants to be closer to downtown." The realtor's heals clicked across the clay tiles. "And like I said, they are pretty firm with their price. Homes in this area often go higher than listed. But they'll entertain offers, too, if it's a cash deal."

Rusty laughed to himself as he scanned for and then found the asking price on the right-hand side of the sheet. Cash deal? It seemed like a ridiculous amount. The realtor left with the couple through the front door. A minute later she walked through the same door inside.

"Okay, now it's your turn," she said as she returned from the front porch. "My name is Victoria and you are ..."

She didn't give him a chance to answer. "Oh great, *Rusty*, there you are," she said looking at the paper. "I see you signed in. Okay ... yes ... yes. Oh, and right here, if you can add your email address, and your phone number, too."

Rusty hesitated. "Well, I'm sort of between phone numbers ... for the time being."

"Of course, not a problem," she said with a super understanding smile. Her teeth were incredibly white. "— Just fill out whatever you can. Tell you what, let me just show you the place."

"Is my mother's number okay?"

"As long as it's a number I can reach you at, that'll work."

Rusty put the pen back on the counter when he was through.

"So are you new to the area? Relocating for work?"

"Well I'm kind of between work right now."

They walked into the front room.

"And do you have a family, because this is a perfect split floor design, three beds and two baths."

"Well, not a wife ... and no kids ... not yet ... but I'm hoping ... eventually."

"Are you relocating from somewhere else in town, because if so I can help you sell that place, too. It's a great time to upgrade with the interest rates being so low. And if you look at the kitchen back here by the ..."

Suddenly she cut off.

"Sir, the kitchen is back here. Is there something in the front yard you would like to see?"

Rusty was peering out across the avenue through the newly installed plantation blinds. "How about the neighborhood?" he asked as he looked out.

"It's an established neighborhood. Working class mostly. But it's starting to convert. A lot of young professionals are moving in."

"And how about the *neighbors*," Rusty more specifically asked, pointing to the man and his teenage son. They were back outside rubbing down the car with terry cloth rags.

The realtor joined him at the window. "It's definitely a good neighborhood. They'd probably be happy to talk to you on your way out. They are a very nice family. They've been here a long time."

"That's a great idea!" Rusty energetically agreed.

"So, like I was saying about the kitchen ..." the realtor continued as Rusty followed her towards the back.

Rusty graciously thanked her for her time at the front door. He was carrying a glossy purple folder with her business card paper-clipped to the front. It was the best that he'd felt in days, almost normal, although the feeling didn't last long.

His heart sank the moment he turned around.

The car was gone.

In its place was just a wet spot on the driveway.

•••

Rusty found a KOA on the outskirts of town up in the foothills and rented a site for the night. He was at a loss.

After setting up his tent and cooking a meal he decided to take a walk. It looked a lot different than the desert overseas; refreshed and more natural, not as worn out. The air was breezy and a little cold. Rusty walked on the loose rocks of the road shoulder towards a neon sign just down a path by the side of the road which he couldn't read until he got up close.

The Hopscotch Inn

Good enough.

Not that there was anything else.

A few locals sat scattershot around the tables. An attractive blond tended the bar. Otherwise it was empty. It looked like a slow night.

"What can I get for ya?" she asked.

"Whatever," Rusty nodded at the tap. "—Or, actually, cancel that. I'll have a scotch."

"A scotch it is. How's Cutty Shark?"

"Great."

"On the rocks?"

Rusty nodded. "That's fine."

Rusty felt the lump in his throat welling up and the room pulling his mood down. He looked at the fluorescent dartboard and thought something looked sinister about the logo on the bottom. A Frederick Remington-style print hung from the wall. Two cowboys riding into the sunset. Rusty stood up to read the nameplate on the bottom. "Utah Country." He studied the canvas close up. What had looked like a three-dimensional space of open country from his seat was all an illusion, just splotches of multicolored oil splattered and stroked on a taut canvas within a frame of deeply-stained wood. He wondered who the artist was and how it ended up in the bar. After a while it started to bother Rusty to the point that he couldn't stand to look at it anymore.

Rusty moved to a new seat so he could look the other way.

"The same thing, scotch on the rocks?" the bartender asked.

Rusty looked down at his glass. It was empty.

"So what brings you to town?"

"Well I'm just, um, you know ..."

"Passing through?"

Rusty nodded. "That's right, yeah. Just passing through. To see a friend."

Two tables away Rusty overheard a couple talking about their hike from earlier in the day.

"Say, you wouldn't happen to know where to pick up Spandral Trail?"

"Yeah, I know exactly where it is," the man responded. "But it's a serious hike. It's a very steep ascent. Way more than a one day round trip. *Is it just you?*"

Rusty stared back blankly, not answering.

"Because I definitely don't recommend hiking it alone."

Chapter 8
Spandral Trail or Bust

It was still dark the next morning when Rusty woke up.

The arrow pointed one way to the interstate, to the right. Rusty turned left.

The road was straight and flat. Not paved. A plume of smoke kicked up behind him as he drove. Houses got fewer and farther apart to the point they looked more like ranches until there was nothing at all, just desert, and then there he was.

It was more or less just like the man had explained. The road would get windy at the base of the foothills, then there'd be a cattle crossing and it was the next right after that. Rusty insisted he didn't want the topo map when the man offered it to him but he was glad to have it now.

Rusty got out of his truck.

He reached for the sky and yawned.

He wasn't tired he was ready to go.

There wasn't a sign to say one way or the other if he was wrong or right. Rusty double checked the topo map in search of clues. He looked at the canyon entrance and then compared it to the tightly-spaced parallel lines.

In back he found his boots and laced them up. They had served him well before and they would serve him well here. You have to go into each mission thinking that way. Hope for the best. Plan for the worst. He didn't know about the first part but about the second he was sure.

He didn't delay. He didn't doubt.

He packed light.

He didn't need much.

A few minutes down the path he encountered the sign.

Spandral Trail

There was a rectangle of rusted metal below it that read *"No Services Beyond This Point. Hike At Your Own Risk."* There was also a water tight box. He opened it to see what was inside. A notebook. He flipped to the last entry. Two people. A Mack and Christine K. In the space after their name they wrote "To the falls and back." Rusty put the notebook back in the box, unsigned. He returned the latch back into the eyehole and continued down the trail.

It sort of surprised him to be walking downhill. According to the topo map the full ascent was over four thousand feet up. Could that be right? Why would he be walking down if he had to hike up so high. Ten minutes later he understood. It wasn't until the canyon entrance that the trail started its ascent. He checked the map just to be sure. The climb would be slow on the first half through the canyon and then steep on the switchbacks after that. He was already thirsty. That was a bad sign. Not that he cared.

Entering the canyon took longer than he thought it would. The trail hugged up against the sheer cliff wall on the left. It was well shaded in the morning sun. At first so was the whole canyon but that began to change as the sun climbed up. The opposite wall lit up first. The illumination slowly spread into the middle to the creek. Rusty looked down. He was about two hundred feet above the creek, or something like that. It was hard to tell. He could hear it more than see it. When he could see it, usually it was a short reach, a snippet at best. Not that he ever stopped to look at it for long. He had a long way yet to go.

The canyon part of the trail was not a steady *up and up* but more like a roller coaster ride with mini valleys and peaks with not much in the way of flatness in between. The parts where he climbed up, the sound of the water grew, usually from a run of rapids and sometimes a mini waterfall or two. On the down slopes the opposite occurred. The creek quieted to a trickle. Rusty knelt by its bank and touched the water with his hand as he came to a crossing. Cool. Wet. He quickly stood up. He hopped from rock to rock to rock and then to the dry and loose gravel on the other side of the crystal clear stream. The trail crisscrossed the creek a couple times like that. The higher he climbed the smaller the stream got, even if — as judged from the rounded corners of the boulders the current jockeyed around — the mountain freshet gushed at much higher levels, at times probably making it impossible to cross. He periodically passed washouts and repair work to the trail along the way. The fixes were primitive. Just some rocks lined up with cobbly dirt shoveled in behind. Rusty wondered what it looked like when the great floods washed through and thought about how nature always undoes everything man pursues.

Eventually Rusty found his way to the source, a solid red rock. Water rainbowed out of an ancient crack at its base. Rusty put his hand in the water and then raised his hand to his face. The wetness felt good. Cold. Ice cold. Much colder than you get from a kitchen sink. He opened his mouth and let the water pour inside. He could feel its coolness going all the way down.

It was his last chance for water. The man at the Hopscotch had circled that on the map. Last chance for water he wrote with an arrow pointing to the spot. It was also the takeoff point for the steep staircase of switchbacks onward and upward above.

Rusty emptied out the water he still had in his canteen and refilled it to the brim. Mountain fed and straight from the rock it didn't get any purer than that. He turned around and looked down the gauntlet of rock he'd just navigated up. As best he could he followed the creek with his eyes to where it spilled out on the desert floor. It looked hazy. Unreal. Cottonwood trees lined up like pilgrims along the riparian seam. Their green fluorescents quivered at the altar of the mountain-cooled stream. Rusty turned his head away and looked up to the ridgeline and, although he couldn't see it, in the direction of the Spandrals after that.

The trail looked rugged. Daunting. Maybe impossible was the better word.

But others had done it before so he would do the same.

He didn't have any doubts.

Or maybe he didn't care.

Rusty was happy to be done with the canyon and on to the switchback part of the trail. His progress was encouraging at first. No more wasting time weaving up the slow slant of the canyon fetch. He was marching onward and upward straight up. Well, maybe not a hundred percent straight. It would be better described as following the path of an almost fully extended wood rule, a trail that zigzagged up the cliff face to the left and the right, not unlike the measuring device that Dwight so often used at the construction site.

One foot after the other after the next and up the wood rule he stepped until at an inclined and obtuse angle of the articulated measuring stick's metal joint he turned and continued his way up the rocky path.

At some point the soles of his feet started to get warm, or as Kenny used to say, "— started to bark."

"Ya hear 'em?"

"Hear what?"

"Two dogs barking. Ya hear it?"

"I don't hear nothing."

"It's my feet, they're starting to hurt."

"We better stop."

"Not for me!"

"No, for your feet. I can hear them starting to bark."

Up ahead Rusty spotted a good rock with shade that he could lean against to take a break. When he got there he saw an even better rock with a bigger shadow which he leaned against and then sat down. Rusty laughed to himself about his dogs. His feet fit like a glove into his military boots. That was a revelation from the start and probably the thing that set him apart. He could even wear them without socks. That brought a lot of laughs from the other guys, Kenny the most. *"Forgot to do your laundry did ya?"* he would invariably joke. Of course it was the little stuff not any one thing that won him respect. Over time the little stuff added up. Kenny wore the heaviest duty socks they had and even then he'd still get blisters that would make him wince, although eventually he learned his limits and when he needed to rest his dogs during which he swore the one thing he wished was that he had better feet. Maybe on the switchbacks Rusty had finally met his match. The rocks were sharp and cooked and stabbed at his feet. It was a good pain because it made him feel like he finally understood what Kenny meant.

Rusty stood up and tried to shake it off. He didn't like where his thoughts were going. The only way to keep his head clear was to keep moving ahead. Actually, not ahead ... *up*. And up and up. An endless up.

One step after the other after the other and up.

One foot after the other after the other. Repeat

Rusty let his gaze slip into the canyon below. The seep with the ice cold water was out of sight. At the next switchback he looked up to gage the ridgeline to see if he'd made any progress.

If he had, he couldn't tell. It looked the same unreachable distance away.

Rusty plodded on. He wasn't fatalistic he was just realistic.

He found it best to just stare at the trail, at the rocks where he was putting his feet. Everything else he tried to block out. The straightest shot between Point Alpha and Point Beta was to forget every other letter Charlie to Omega.

Rusty corrected himself.

He meant Zulu.

He should've eaten a bigger breakfast.

His body was starting to move away from his mind. His thoughts were beginning to warp.

Rusty overran a switchback and then another. The first one he found his way back easy but the second time not so much. The third time the soles of his boots started to slide like he'd stepped on marbles on a granite floor sending him through the door towards and over the edge of the rock ledge. At the last second the rubber of his soles miraculously gripped on the stone. Rusty stood over the precipice panting. He was an inch maybe less away from a straight-down thousand foot vertical drop. He instinctively tried to swallow but he couldn't. His throat was too dry. His heart beat against the inside of his chest like somebody stomping on the foot pedal of a drum. One boot then the next he shimmied his feet back to safety. He backtracked from there as best he could until he found the main trail. Or was it the trail? He couldn't tell. His eyes stung from sweat making it hard to see. There was only one trail. That had to be it. He walked on it stupidly in the wrong direction before realizing it was too easy and he needed to turn around. He needed to be going *up*, not down. He looked up for the ridgeline but it was too steep to see. The wooden rule was no longer lying at an angle, it was like he was climbing a ladder straight up a wall on his hands and knees.

One foot up, then another, then again.

One foot up, again … again.

The only way forward was to block everything else out.

There was nothing else.

Just him and his boots and rocks and the trail.

One foot up … breathe … take a breath.

One foot … scramble slip … take another step.

Rusty felt numb. The numbness felt good. Feeling numb was progress. One step and then another and then another and

then again. One step then another then another then again.
One step then another then another then again.

...

Rusty saw lights.
Lots of lights.
Then darkness.
Lots of darkness.
Sounds popped in and out of his ears followed by a long
silence. Strange voices came and went. Some were no closer
than a few feet away. Others far in the distance.
It was just Kenny and him.
They were both alive.
That meant they had a chance.
There was still daylight outside. Rusty wished that there
wasn't. He looked out again. Three hundred and sixty degrees
of wasteland in every direction.
"What now?" Kenny whimpered. The joking in his voice
was gone.
Rusty shook his head.
He didn't know.
What he did know was if they'd gotten into it they could get
out.
Rusty tried to think about what his father would do, how it
was with his BB gun he first taught him how to shoot, how
before he intervened he had blamed his errant shooting on the
gun not himself and how it took him by so much surprise when
his father nonchalantly asked for a try with the same gun and
quickly proceeded to shoot every one of those cans down.
"The trick," his father told him, "is to lean your left side on a
hard edge. Then you aim it up from there. Understand?"
Rusty wasn't sure but he tried it anyhow.
The door frame kept him still. It stabilized his arm.
He raised the gun to his shoulder and positioned the scope
to his eye.
The can was in the cross hairs.
He pulled the trigger.
The can went flying into the air.
He looked at his father who nodded his head with approval.
"Keep going," he said. "Do it again."
And again and again and still another time and then again
and again until the next time he tried it and without even

thinking he just raised the gun to his shoulder and the scope to his eye and pulled the trigger. This time it was a buck in the crosshairs a hundred feet ahead. The animal lurched ahead then fell to the ground.

If Rusty knew anything he understood the angles. Rusty knew how to make the geometry in his head come true with his hands and, if need be, he could do the same with a plan.

A simple plan.

Its execution precise.

This mess would take time.

Rusty knew that most of all.

"We sit tight until dark."

Kenny seemed doubtful. "Sit tight? ... *dark?*"

Rusty pulled a deck of cards from his pocket and slid them out of the box. "How 'bout some Six Hand."

Kenny looked at him blankly.

"The usual?" Kenny asked.

Rusty nodded.

"Dime a point."

Chapter 9
Climbing the Stegosaurus' Back

Rusty woke in a trance smoking a Turkish Gold on the shaded side of a pyramidal shaped rock. He didn't remember stopping until it was time to go and then he did. Rusty looked up. The ridgeline was a thousand feet straight overhead. Line of sight he followed it to the right until – it had to be – he was looking straight at the Spandrals. Or a good chunk of it at least.

Rusty gulped greedily at his canteen.

He tried to stop but couldn't.

He gulped some more.

The canteen was less than half full. He shook it. Actually closer to an eighth.

Rusty slid off the rock and continued up the trail.

One foot over the other over the other over the next and repeat. One step repeat repeat repeat.

The higher he hiked the farther the ridgeline the Spandrals his life seemed to retreat. Or was he tantalizingly close?

An hour later he was still in the switchbacks with no end in sight.

Another hour passed and it was still the same.

The ridge taunted and leered at him from above.

Rusty tried to block it out.

One foot over the other over the other over the next and repeat.

Rusty looked down. He was delirious. The canyon — the same one that cut a gaping hole in the mountain side visible from tens of miles across the desert floor, the same one that dwarfed him as he trekked ant-like along the base of its towering walls, and the same one that like a giant venomous snakehead had hissed at him with its liquid serpentine tongue and swallowed him whole into its open jaws — was no longer visible from the expansive vantage of his lofty perch.

Not visible at all.

No longer visible one bit.

Rusty scanned down across the desert floor. Or was it a mirage? He was closer to the view that the astronauts saw from the window of Apollo 13 than he was to God's Green Earth. None of it looked real. Not anymore. It was a place unto which he was now detached. A separate space.

Or was he looking into a mirror at who he had become?

It looked thirsty.

Rusty took another drink from his canteen.

At first he was just sucking at air until he arched his back and tilted his neck as far as it went and then there it was: the last drop. There was nothing left. That was the bad news. The good news was he'd made it up to the ridge. He was done with the switchbacks he was happy about that. No longer up and up it was now just a flat walk, or so he thought. Now he saw otherwise. A giant mound of rock loomed in front of him.

It looked like .... He couldn't think of words to describe it. The word he was trying to think of was evading his grasp.

Rusty laughed morbidly at his mistake.

Unlike the switchbacks that continuously and unrelentingly went straight up and up and more up, he somehow got it in his mind that the walk along the ridge would be easy and flat. It was not. It was not and it would not be anything close. What he saw in front of him was a roller coaster ride suspended in space, reminiscent of his hike up the mouth of canyon with the exception that the ascents and descents were ten times as great and a hundred times more cruel. The ridgeline was a series of rocky outcrops and death-defying drops that – at least from the angle he was looking – took on the form of the armored plates a Stegosaurus's back.

How could he have miscalculated the topo map so poorly?

Rusty didn't dwell on the question.

He pushed ahead to the creature's tail of stone.

One step after the other after the other after the other don't stop.

One step after the other after the other.

Don't stop.

Keep going.

Going. going. Going. Step step step.

The ups were deceivingly long, or was he just getting tired? Walking down the plates of the Stegosaurus's arched back was a welcome relief but never long enough before once again he was on his way back up another spike of stone. Harder than even the ups was fighting the feelings of having to stop on the way down. Above all Rusty knew he couldn't stop. Sitting would be succumbing and once he sat he would be stuck.

...

Kenny was nervous to the point he felt sick. He kept repeating things. *"What in the hell? What the hell?"*

Rusty tried to stay relaxed. He listened to Kenny say "What the hell?" a couple more times as he continued to think. Calm as a duck his mind was paddling nonstop underneath.

"We can't just run unless you wanna get yourself killed."

Kenny looked at Rusty trying to understand.

The first step of understanding was accepting their fate.

If Rusty had a plan then he'd go with that.

"So you think we can get out of this?"

"If we got in here we can get out. It may take time. And it'll take us some luck. But there's a way if we're patient. We take it step by step."

Communication was down. That's what Kenny hated the most. Rusty didn't like it either but it didn't change their plan. They had to be a hundred percent self-sufficient. Rusty was comfortable with that.

Rusty went over it again in his head to make sure it was right.

They'd sit tight as long as it was daylight. It was suicide to venture out before night. Rusty warned Kenny that there would be a reflex to want to move as soon as it turned dark but that they would have to resist. They wouldn't make their first move until the moment the moon lifted up and was no longer touching the earth.

"You got that?"

Kenny nodded.

"We'll v-line to the ridgeline on the west slope and head south from there. For now, we hunker down. We wait."

Kenny was on one side and Rusty on the other.

They were both slouched down.

Seconds turned to minutes turned to hours but eventually their time came.

The moon was floating just above the horizon, its umbilical cord to earth about to detach.

Rusty and Kenny were running low for the dark splotch on the ground ahead.

Their boots thumped as they ran with the moon staring sideways from above.

Rusty turned back to make eye contact with Kenny. He pointed two fingers to his eyes and then up ahead. They were moving again. Boots thumping. The terrain was more rocky than sandy. It was like running on asphalt that had been washed over with dirt.

Rusty was relieved when they made it to the lunar shade on the west slope of the ridge but even then he never broke stride. Kenny followed. They were heading south. It was just like Rusty planned. Just like he hoped. Their feet thumped on the dirt but otherwise there was no other sound, no stomping just panting and thumping on the rocky ground.

Rusty waved back his hand and quieted his breath.

Kenny dropped one knee to the ground the same.

They scanned ahead and to the side to see what approached.

Both their hearts pounded as they scanned out in front.

Nothing.

They were good.

Again and just like that they were thump-running south.

An hour later their pace started to slow. They were about half the distance they needed to go.

Kenny spotted a ditch.

"I need a break."

Rusty did too.

"We sit tight ... here ... until morning 4 am," Rusty decided on the spot as he reigned in his breath. His heart was pounding on the inside like the sound of raindrops on a roof.

Kenny looked at him nervously, impatiently.

"We're making great ground. Let's keep at it. Our momentum is up."

Rusty could have kept going, too. There was a side of him that wanted to throw all caution to the wind and gun it nonstop.

But that wasn't the plan.

The plan was to hold up.

The moon had now risen over a quarter arc in the sky. They still had shade on the west side of the ridge but from this point forward (as the moon rose up) it would be getting less and less.

The plan was to wait it out until the moon worked its way across the sky and started its descent to the horizon on the west. That's when the shade would switch to the east slope of the ridge, under the cover of which they could continue south.

Rusty looked again.

Maybe Kenny was right.

But something or somebody was holding him back.

Rusty looked at the moon. He wasn't looking at a celestial body he was looking at its face and not just any old face but at a face he knew well, a face that he trusted as much if not more than his own. In a flash Rusty thought back to his mother and him, the two of them, in her car, driving north, the moon following them down every road she turned, first through the neighborhoods, the houses shuttered and dark, and then next up the main road across the causeway on which they took flight, onto the mainland, past the scattered strip malls and under the lonely lamp lights, and then finally on the interstate and only then did his mother finally breathe a sigh of relief, her gripping the wheel as Rusty began to doze off, him almost but not quite yet falling asleep as he glanced out the back window one last time – not at the road or for the man they were leaving behind, but up in the sky at the man on the moon who was following them like a balloon on a string.

The moon had moved with him north to Missouri and now here it was with him again.

The same moon.

The same face.

It didn't say a thing. It just silently stared back. As if to say everything would work out. That everything would be alright.

Kenny was having trouble catching his breath. He pulled his binoculars out of his pack. He shakily peered out over the edge.

"It's looks clear," he panted. "I say we go."

Rusty scanned across the moonscape methodically using plain sight and then reached out his arm toward Kenny and said, "Here, let me have a look." Nothing seemed out of the ordinary but still something didn't seem right. The next moment the moon rose an increment of an arc higher and Rusty saw why. One, two, three ... four ... Rusty counted over a half dozen pickups and jeeps with people, combatants, milling about, keeping guard on a saddle in the ridge up ahead. They possibly might have been able to duck down undetected in another ditch had they continued on, but chances were just as good whoever they were would have spotted them first. That would have been all she wrote. The odds weren't good.

Rusty looked up and thanked the moon.

Kenny was sitting down in the ditch with his back against the wall.

He'd fallen asleep.

Rusty closed his eyes, too.

...

Rusty rustled Kenny awake by the shoulder.

The moment they made eye contact they both knew what to do.

Lickety split, they were out of the ditch hunched over and scurrying up to a spot that slightly dipped and then up and over to the east slope they went. The ridge didn't go a hundred percent in the direction they needed it to but it was the best and only escape route they had.

Their boots thudded on the ground. They stopped. They listened. They continued thudding. They didn't think they just went they stayed low their backs bent.

Up ahead and to the left a dark spot appeared. The spot grew. They thudded some more. Next time Rusty looked the spot was a line but with depth, it was deep, not too deep, a seam. It was exactly the break Rusty was hoping for: a dry gully gulch carved out from an ephemeral desert stream. Mr. Moon in the sky had gotten them this far. Now it was up to Mr. Water to lead them the rest of the way out. It wouldn't take them all the way there but it would get them close enough, and then from there a Hail Mary pass to safety was all they would need. Still a long shot. But doable. They had a chance.

The soil was soft but not too soft so when they ran they didn't sink down. They followed a game trail through a thicket of branches that brushed up on their sides. A Persian doe and her fawn watched them in the darkness as they ran by. Two soldiers in the dry river bed they barely made a sound. Twigs branches dirt, one foot then the next then the next and the next. Periodically the sandy bottom gave way to an uneven cobbly bed where the thicket opened but mostly the trail was quite narrow and thin.

At some point the eastern sky started to pale. It was still dark just not pitch black, a gray goo-ish glow. The sun hadn't risen and the moon was still up. Rusty thanked the moon that was about to leave and the water that wasn't there and deer for clearing the path through which they sped. This was it. They were at their spot. Everything had fallen in place just as they needed, even better than they could have hoped. From here on out all they'd need was a little luck. The moon was disappearing behind the craggy ridgeline to the west.

"It's all yours Kenny. Go for it. I got your back."

Kenny was still sucking air.

"No, definitely you go, man. I'm beat. Besides, I'm a better shot."

Rusty looked at him unsure.

Kenny nodded.

The two embraced.

"Brothers for life."

"God Damned right!"

Rusty rose out of the dusty arroyo like a creature escaping from purgatory to stake its claim on a second life. Slow at first, his forward momentum gradually picked up. One stride after the other. It was barely daybreak and he could already feel the sun's heat. He turned back to look at it. Massive and fiery and incredibly bright. It nearly blinded him. He immediately turned around. He never broke stride. One eye looking forward the other down at the ground. At any moment he knew his life could be over. He listened for gun fire between the rhythmic thud of his boots on the ground, but the sound never came and with each step he was that much closer to home.

Other than that one time Rusty did not turn back.

An eternity later Rusty arrived on the other side.

The Hail Mary pass was complete.

He was sitting in the safety of the palm of Bravo Charlie's hands.

"Holy Shit, you aren't one of those two privates ..."

Rusty was about to nod his head yes when behind him the sound finally came. From the direction of the arroyo an unmistakable *tat-tat-tat tat-tat-tat* rang out.

Then silence.

A very long silence.

His ears were clogged with the drum of his heart.

Rusty closed his eyes.

A moment later he opened them up as a dust cloud stormed in.

112

"You scared the hell out of us," Rusty exhaled with relief as Kenny appeared.

A solider flipped them both a bottle of water from a cooler packed in ice.

"Walk in the cake!" Kenny laughed, almost hysterically, as he found a shady spot and collapsed in the dirt. The other soldiers gathered around.

Kenny cracked open the water.

"Ice cold ... just like I like it," he said as he poured the liquid overtop his head.

Chapter 10
Schnitzel and Noodles

Rusty's lips were dry.

Cracked.

Not that he could feel it.

He was that numb.

He had climbed to the top of the stegosaurus's back and was now on his way down, almost to its neck.

He still had to hike up a few more armored plates, but mostly he was going down more than he was climbing up. The outline of what he thought was the Spandrals was now in clear view. All he had to do was cross the parapet of the stegosaurus's neck. He wondered why they called it the Spandrals and not the Head of the Stegosaurus instead. What did the Spandrals even mean? It didn't make sense. The loose rocks that had crumbled and poked under the soles of his boots the entire way up were now gone. He was walking across a smooth marble bridge that rounded off down into nothingness on each side, all chiseled from a single stone.

The closer Rusty got the less certain he was.

Was it the Spandrals?

All he knew was that's where the path led.

There was no other path.

At least as far as he could tell.

It had to be the Spandrals. What else could it be?

...

Rusty wasn't sure what to do.

Other than making it there he didn't have a plan.

He slid his pack off his back and lifted himself up on a rock. It felt good to let his feet hang free. He swung them back and forth in the air and let his back hunch.

114

He tried to swallow but he couldn't. His throat was that dry.

He took an apple out of his pack, red skin and white pulp. There was a side of him that wanted to bite into it just to suck out the juice; but he did not. He hurled it into the void as far as he could instead. He listened for the sound of it hitting something. There was no sound. He immediately wanted it back. He looked at what else he had brought. Not much. Matches. Some photos. A bandana. He'd purposely packed light.

Usually Rusty would make a campfire but up in the Spandrals, if that was where he was at, it was nothing more than a denuded dead end of solid sterile rock which long ago even before the dinosaurs were born had been being pulverized, pressurized and pushed up to its current spot, it remaining to the present day an unfinished and long dormant masterwork. Rusty was in awe of its immensity. How in the hell did so much rock get so far up?

Rusty wondered the same thing about himself.

He hadn't passed a tree let alone a twig, not even a dead piece of grass, since midway up the switchbacks at the place he got lost.

Rusty pushed out the tray of the box and took a match.

He slid the red head across the striker until halfway across it ignited into a flame.

Light.

Rusty had never thought of himself as religious but he never thought he was not religious either, even if he never went regularly to any church or synagogue or tabernacle or mosque.

Rusty tried to pray but couldn't.

Praying was the only way you could prove God existed. The only evidence of that proof was a thing called faith. And if you didn't pray or couldn't pray then you didn't have faith and if you didn't have faith then you didn't have God.

The time Steve invited him to mass flew into his head without warning. It was at the end of a Saturday, not quite evening, at dusk. Seeing Rusty had nothing else to do Steve invited him to join along, whether out of pity or politeness or that it was just the right thing to do.

On the car ride in back Steve asked him if he'd ever been baptized.

Rusty didn't know at the time but he said "yes" just to put the matter to rest and let the conversation pass.

Steve's voice echoed in Rusty's head up on the rock. "Because people who don't get baptized don't go to Heaven. And if you commit suicide you can't go to Heaven even if you are baptized. It's in the Bible."

At the time Rusty didn't know if either were true but Steve seemed sure.

That bothered Rusty then even if "so what" was all he could think about it now.

Rusty thought back to sitting in the pews: Steve to his right and an old man and his wife to his left, people in the row in front and also behind, the inside of the church was pretty much packed.

Rusty felt penned in.

He was glad he went but even happier when it was finally done and they all stood up to leave. It wasn't that he didn't like it, as if it were repellent. Although he wondered what was accomplished when the ceremony was through. Rather he felt out of place. Like he didn't belong. The whole mass Rusty had to guess what was coming next. When to *stand up* when to *sit down*. When to *kneel down*. When to *speak* and *what* to say. When to *sing*. Rusty didn't know the words to any of the songs. The others around him seemed to know every note and gesture by heart, like it was programmed into them by the Almighty himself at birth. One of the songs even sounded like the Bobby Angel hit, *Let your Light Shine Through,* from the B-Side of *Man on the Moon LP,* a simple but catchy song that had been coopted as the anthem of choice for any number of social causes where the downtrodden needed a voice. He watched the people as they followed along in unison with the priest. Rusty wondered if when they looked at him they could sense his unease. That he was out of place. That he didn't belong. Rusty decided it was something you had to be born with, something that you had to do all the time, something that had to be passed down from your father and your mother and father's mother before that. It didn't matter how hard he tried he couldn't overcome that. Did his father even have a religion? Or was he a descendant of some pagan tribe?

He didn't know.

The door on the way out was crowded. Rusty felt cramped. Like they were livestock in a pen. To Rusty a church didn't seem like a place you'd find God. God would need someplace much bigger with more space to spread out. How was it even possible for God to be at every church all at once? Did every church have a different God? Was there only one God that was right?

Rusty wondered how many wars and how much civil unrest God had caused, one side claiming him against the next, and the other way around. Then again that Almighty Being could probably take credit for ending the same wars and bringing peace, too. Rusty thought how people claimed God to justify they were right, as a way to absolve their sins, as an excuse to do whatever they wanted, whatever they pleased. Our God is better than your God. God loves us more than he loves you. Our God versus your God but really the reason for fighting was much more primal than that.

Rusty laughed to himself about Liberty being the reason for the war. Spreading Freedom. Evoking the highest when it was really about the bottom of the barrel all along. Nobody said it but it couldn't be more obvious. Transparent. Clear as a forty two gallon barrel of crude.

But still, despite man's misuse of God, there was still a big side of Rusty that couldn't help but believe. Or want to believe at least.

God was always that thing bigger than us, and just beyond. That thing that couldn't be understood.

Natural forces.

The infinite universe.

The other side of death.

People prayed to that Unknown and All-knowing Creator who was out there, somewhere, for ... He ... She ... It (maybe God was just a force) to help them understand. Or if not understand then to at least put them at peace with the wicked world, its whimsical ways and when their time came to gracefully and serenely and with dignity lay their body down to rest.

The Deep Sleep.

A Soul.

Did it exist?

If it did, in time – everyone's time – it would eventually be the only thing that was left.

The human soul and the Face of God. These were two things Rusty had never seen.

What did God look like and if not in a church then where did God live? Maybe God had been out on the open road with him all along, in the distance peering up over the horizon, reaching out and grabbing his truck and guiding it with the palm of his hand. Or maybe when he was hiking up Spandral Trail it was God's pointer finger and thumb that gently pinched him at the collar and guided him up. Or here at the Spandrals — if the Spandrals was in fact where he was? Maybe God was sitting beside him, unseen.

Rusty's mind raced back to arriving in Vienna. On R & R. Just Kenny and him. The two of them climbing up the stairwell from the dungeon dark subway into the fresh illumination of a flickering and civilized sun.

Rusty had not set out to see the cathedral but now that they were there he convinced Kenny to at least have a look.

"And then we find a place to eat, right?" Kenny insisted. He looked at Rusty exasperated. Couldn't he see he was starving? "— I've been dreaming of chowing down a good schnitzel and noodles for *practically a year!"*

The door looked old and creaky. Medieval. Surprisingly it opened with relative ease.

On the inside it took Rusty's eyes a moment to adjust.

"You ain't religious, are ya?" Kenny asked under his breath, cupping his hand over his mouth.

Rusty bent his neck back and back and back (and still back) in attempt to find if and where the ceiling began only to discover it was not a structure at all but rather a spiritually enhanced part of the sky.

Rusty knew a little bit about what it took to build even something relatively simple as a residential house. The money, the materials, the machinery, the men. But most of all it was time and hard work. Those houses didn't build themselves. Not in a night and not in a week. It took months of hard labor and discipline. Sweat and sheer force.

This in comparison was on a scale beyond anything he could comprehend. The most baffling part was that it was built centuries ago. How could the men manage to build something so mammoth and meticulous at the same time? Every square inch was a work of art.

It wasn't so much that the ceiling was so high as it was the wall was so tall, mostly glass and with no supports. He knew from working construction how much that violated all sorts of engineering rules. Dwight would have said the same if also going on to explain how it was the flying buttresses on the outside, out of view, that kept the inside up. Otherwise the entire thing would buckle and collapse, into a pile of ruins, under its own weight.

The masonry work looked impossibly intricate. He could spend days, weeks, years in the one spot he was standing and probably never take it all in. The walls draped down from the ceiling in a cascade of kaleidoscopic colored glass letting in light from all sides while a circular dome on the ceiling simultaneously rained down illumination from above. The light felt soft and cool where he was standing on the floor, almost like moonlight.

Rusty still couldn't prove there was a God but standing there inside the cathedral he had no doubt there wasn't one either.

Religious? Kenny's question caught him off guard. Technically he was an adult but he still didn't know. He liked in America how there was a separation between church and state. He considered himself secular but didn't everyone also have a spiritual self. Even money was emblazoned with "In God We Trust" across all dollar denominations and every last cent.

"As much as anybody I guess," Rusty responded optimistically but also not without a hint of doubt.

Rusty turned to gauge Kenny's reaction but he was no longer there.

Rusty walked down the aisle.

Scattered in the pews were a few people: sitting, praying, kneeling down. They were mostly older. In contrast to how Rusty felt about himself, they looked like they belonged, praying with a precision that was even more sacred than the structure itself. Rusty tried to walk softly. The shaded illumination of the masonry and glass strangely amplified and muffled every sound.

He found an empty pew and sat down.

Rusty knew he couldn't pray but he tried to pretend. He closed his eyes. It was dark. Quiet. So quiet he could actually hear the absence of sound, as if it were a void, a gateway, for leaving the earth. He covered his palms in front of his face. He listened with his ears, his head and his heart for somebody out there, anybody, to give him a sign. He waited. He listened. He waited some more. He tried to say a prayer but it didn't come out right. His mind drifted off. He sat quietly in his thoughts. Was there a particular way he should be doing it? And even if there was and he did it, would it do any good?

What do you pray for anyhow?

World peace? The end of wars? That the bad things that are happening or are about to happen go away and go away for good? Do you pray for a lucky break or for things not to change? That seemed like a stupid thing to pray considering everything eventually does.

So many people and so many prayers. Rusty looked at an old woman in front of him who he was sure was a nun. He wondered what it would be like to serve God like that. For an entire life. With everything you were. No distractions just you and God. To live in confidence and without doubt. To know one's payers were if not always answered then at least heard. If anyone knew God Rusty reasoned on the spot that it was her.

Suddenly it hit Rusty and he knew what to pray for.

It was obvious.

He folded his hands.

He put down his head.

Another ninety nine days and a gentle breeze at their backs.

He said it again, this time moving his lips. "Another ninety days and a gentle breeze at our backs."

Rusty waved his hand to get Kenny's attention.

Kenny saw him. "Schnitzel and noodles!" he enthusiastically mouthed back.

Rusty propped open the giant medieval door with his foot, first Kenny then him sliding out. Rusty shielded his face from the brightness with his hand as he made his way down the marble steps. It took his eyes a moment to adjust.

"You really looked like a natural in there ...," Kenny said as they turned a corner and headed down the street. "— Kneeling and praying. You looked like an old pro."

Rusty didn't respond.

He didn't know what to say.

Not that Kenny was looking for an answer.

He was completely consumed by the sights and sounds on the street.

The people were what he liked to look at most of all, especially the women wearing the fashions that neither Rusty nor Kenny had ever seen in the states.

"All the styles stateside," Kenny confided as they walked. "— They show up here at least two years before."

"I bet it's probably Paris where they show up first, don't you think?" Rusty guessed.

120

They stopped at a busy intersection and waited for the pedestrian light to tell them it was okay to cross.

"You aren't afraid of dying? That wasn't what ... *that* ..." Kenny said motioning back towards St. Stephens, "— was all about?"

Rusty raised his eyebrow as the crossing sign lit up.

"Well, I dunno. About as much as the next guy, I guess."

"You don't mean me?" Kenny laughed as he poked Rusty in the ribs and pointed at their feet, "— Cause *I'm the guy* standing right next to you."

Rusty immediately corrected himself. "No I didn't mean it like that."

"It just looked like ... in the church ... you know ... that you were ... making good with God?"

Rusty didn't answer.

"No worries because I was doing the same," Kenny explained. "— Figured I'd say a prayer for you, us, since we were in there, and there really wasn't much else to do." Kenny smiled. "You know, simple things. That's the trick to praying. You can't go *too big*. A good prayer for you would be to ask God to let you win a few extra hands of Six Hand. Hell, I'm up over a hundred points on you from the train!"

"Ten dollars and sixty cents."

"That's a round of beers!"

As they turned the corner, they found themselves staring straight at two attractive young women standing under an awning of an open air corner café.

One had on a pair of tall black boots and wore a gray jacket tied tight at the waist, the bottom end of which came down just above her mid-thigh high maroon dress. The other wore pants that cut short mid-calf with flat shoes ballerina style and a tan sash across her neck that also doubled as her blouse.

Rusty looked up at the sign, "– *Plachutta*. How does that sound?"

"Looks even better!" Kenny said with an uptick in his voice as he nudged at Rusty's arm and jumped up to click his heals together in delight. "Schnitzel," he pointed. "And noodles. Here we come! You don't see schnitzel and noodles like that in the good ol' U S of A."

•••

Rusty watched the match burn down to his fingers.

He let it sting a little before he blew it out. Everything was completely dark again. He was alone except for the smell of the burnt wood.

Rusty tried to think what Kenny would say.

"I told you so! Ain't this place boss. *Ain't it!* That's my town down there. Not no fancy park, but *waaaayyyyy better* than your half a McDonald's Gateway Arch!"

Rusty blew a puff of air out of his nose as he laughed to himself. How could it be that shoe box sized window was so small yet he remembered so much? Now here he was almost two miles high up with the stars and all he saw was total dark.

Rusty closed and opened his eyes.

Both were equally black.

He hoisted himself upright on the rock and started to walk straight ahead.

He had no idea where the next step might land, or not land.

Land ... or ... not land.

Land or ... not land.

Land or not land.

Rusty stopped mid step when suddenly it appeared.

A thin line of luminescence across the craggy rock of the ridge.

Then a sliver.

Then a quarter.

Then a full half.

Finally there it was.

The full moon floating free in the night.

Rusty stared at the moon.

The moon stared back.

His old friend.

Rusty reached out to touch its ashen face. It seemed that close.

He whiffed.

At the same time he whiffed he wobbled and looked down to find himself standing at the end of the road: on the outermost tip of a stone plank with nothing above and nothing below. Just one more step and down into the dungeon of infinite doom and despair, that great void, the easy and early out, he would have dropped into, he would have for eternity sank.

Rusty looked at his old friend.

The glowing white orb.

Other than his heart beating he couldn't hear a thing.

Chapter 11
Falling Back to Earth

Rusty followed the moonlight off of the Spandrals.

First he crossed over the parapet of the dinosaur's outstretched neck to the stegosaurus's back which he climbed up to the top and then down its armored plates until finally he reached the end of its tail where the ridgeline met the deep descent into the switchbacks where he paused unsure what to do.

Everything below was pitch black. Judging from the angle of the moon it would stay that way for some time. That meant he would have to wait. Or he could go now and take his chances that he wouldn't miss any of the switchback's many sharp turns and walk off the edge into the darkness and then that would be it.

Overriding everything else was a biological urge.

He wanted to live.

He needed a drink.

Death was inevitable unless he got one soon.

There was no time to waste.

His life depended on getting down to the rock where the water rainbowed out.

The first few switchbacks were easy. It felt good to be going downhill, continuously, just letting gravity do the work. The only part that was tricky was seeing the sharp turns in the dark and planting his boots just right.

Then his feet started to hurt.

Soon after that he felt a burn in his thighs.

Each step thereafter he felt a stabbing pain until not many steps after that knives were wrenching in both his legs all the time.

His brakes were failing.

He couldn't slow down.

He tried to stop but he couldn't he was going too fast maybe it wasn't his brakes but his thirst his mouth was paradoxically dry and foaming with a salty surf that was pushing his foot on the accelerator the same time the knives in his thighs were yelling at him to stop his mind going manic to the point he couldn't think straight as he tried to find a way to extend the zigzagging wood rule of the switchbacks into the long slide in the game of *Shoots and Ladders* that would deliver him to the bottom of the board immediately all at once.

The first time he fell he bounced right back up.

The second time took longer.

When he touched his elbow with his hand he felt wetness.

Blood.

He brought his hand to his mouth.

It was warm but it was wet. It tasted good. Dracula style he tried to drink himself dry but he couldn't figure out a way to get his elbow in his mouth or his mouth to his elbow he wasn't sure which one to which.

Rusty fell again.

This time unlike the two before he kept going.

He'd finally found that shoot.

It wasn't a smooth slide but it was fast.

He hit things. Sharp things. He hit them hard. It didn't feel good and then he didn't feel anything at all. How strange, Rusty thought, when he finally stood up, how his elbow didn't hurt at all although he was overwhelmed by throbbing inside his skull. He thought he heard water only to discover the sound he was hearing was something dripping from his ear. He touched it with his hand and brought his hand to his mouth. It tasted salty. A fluid of some sort.

Which way was down?

He couldn't decide.

He looked one way then the next and then up in the air.

Rusty took two steps forward then two steps to the left before turning back the other way. He paused. He sat down. He tried to stand up but couldn't.

Rusty closed his eyes and then opened them to find himself staring into the Face of God.

Soothing and pure.

The Almighty's unadulterated white light?

Rusty closed his eyes and opened them again.

He tried to focus on what was in front of him and then he closed his eyes for good.

Some time later he woke up.

The moon was straight above him looking down.

He waited.

He looked up and listened.

He waited some more.

Rusty closed his eyes.

Rusty opened his eyes and heard a sound.

He pulled at the bottom of his ear to dislodge some dirt and listened some more.

It sounded familiar

He looked at his elbow. Was it really bleeding that bad?

It felt crusty and stiff. No longer wet.

He listened again.

He tried to stand up but he couldn't.

He tried again and couldn't again.

A second time he tried and couldn't so he decided to worm his way to the sound.

He pulled his body across the rocks, through a thicket, into the reeds.

He'd made it.

To water.

Sweet water.

He pulled his entire body in the current and fell asleep.

A deep sleep.

A sleep to end all sleeps.

•••

Rusty didn't expect to come up on a camp.

He didn't remember one on his way in.

He took cover behind a boulder beside the trail to think it through. He looked at his elbow. It didn't hurt nor was it bleeding. It seemed alright. Maybe it had all just been a bad dream. Maybe his fall wasn't that bad. Maybe it was his other arm. He looked at that one and it was the same. Maybe it was the mineral water from the spring. Maybe it washed the blood away.

Sleeping is good for the heeling process, too.

How long had he been asleep? It could have been an hour, possibly many hours, even days. Rusty didn't know.

He tried to process what he saw up ahead. Five or six pickup trucks. A horse. Several men circled around a campfire. Others were clustered in groups. Some of the men had long rifles. Another a bowie knife. All of them had menacing looks. A man in a Stetson hat was standing behind the fire prodding it with a long stick.

Were they gathering for a meeting, maybe they were on a hunting trip, or was there going to be a fight?

Rusty was about to turn around when he noticed it was too late.

The man in the Stetson hat was staring him down.

It seemed senseless trying to escape.

Rusty stepped away from the boulder to reveal himself in plain sight. He put his hands up and walked towards the campfire. He went slowly. He tried to look strong. He wanted them to know that he was not afraid.

Rusty was terrified.

The man's face was hidden under the shadow of his hat. Rusty turned around to look at the moon. There it was. It had his back.

"Henry's son, right?"

A jolt ran down Rusty's spine.

How did he know?

Rusty tried to say something but his voice vanished in the crackle of the campfire as he approached.

The man in the Stetson hat responded with a shrug.

"Say boys, you seen Henry 'round?"

The men shook their heads solemnly.

None of them seemed to know.

"Hey butt munch, maybe you took a wrong turn at Albuquerque," a voice interjected from the side. Rusty turned expecting to see Kenny in full battle fatigues and eating an MRE only to instead hear the same voice coming from a different direction, "You got anything to trade for this chili?" the voice said again. Rusty spun around and spun around again and then fell down.

The man with the Stetson gripped Rusty firmly by the elbow and pulled him up. "You can't hang around here," he said. "You have to follow me."

"Kenny, is that you? Kenny!"

There was no response.

"Where are we going?" Rusty asked.

126

The man in the Stetson hat was now ahead of him. Rusty tried to run to catch up. His side hurt. "Wait up. Wait up." Rusty called again. "I can't keep up."

What had been a rocky desert trail gave way to deep sand, almost like a beach, although the sound he was hearing was not the surf, but splashing from his feet. Looking down he was surprised to discover he was slogging through a foot-deep freshwater marsh, an oasis perhaps, when he again looked up to find himself staring at an altered, if also eerily familiar, view: a shallowly-flooded expanse of cord grasses as far as his eye could see peppered with domes of cypress trees, islands of slash pine and a red-shouldered hawk soaring through the sky. Immediately up ahead and to the side, the sound of a motor revved to a start. As soon as he saw the silhouette of the machine — its giant rubber tires and hulking frame — it all made sense. It was his father's swamp buggy. The man with the Stetson was sitting behind the wheel.

Rusty stopped to catch his breath.

After that everything went black.

The Ranger, Continued

THE RANGER
Continued

The Ranger, Continued

The spot of light danced along the length and then diagonally across the large outdoor screen as the ranger clicked away at his keyboard and mouse, *click ... tap ... click tap ... click.*

He was trying to get his Power Point to work.

Getting it started was sometimes the hardest part.

Click ... tap ... click tap ... click

As for that light, it made for a ghostly sight, swirling in a figure-eight and rapidly spasming into other geometrical shapes before lifting up and off into the inky-twinkly night above, and which — upon completing a full lunar arc — landed back down on solid turf to once again, for a second time, shine squarely into the ranger's eyes.

"Now, I cain't speak for every man, woman and child," the shadowy figure on the business end of the laser beam of light opined. "— But from where I'm at, right ch'ere, I cain't see a darn thang, NO SIR."

Indeed, there was no mincing the facts.

The outdoor screen was completely blank and, except for the campfire, the rest of the amphitheater was black. Not counting the SPLASH OF LIGHT from the flashlight of course.

The ranger was about to respond when, in a half-hearted attempt to tiptoe around the truth and his mind flashing back to a memory of a simpler time in his youth, his thoughts unconsciously drifted off, in fast retreat, back deep into the past, to the billboard-sized screen at the drive-in movie theatre — *The Big H* — on the edge of the town he used to call home when he was a pint-sized kid; all the while, of course, he continued to *click, tip ... tap ... click tap ... click*

There she was: three stories tall above and behind the trees, Princess Leia with her trademark hair and flowing white dress. Was it even *legal* for him to be looking through the glass, even if all he could do was catch a fleeting glimpse? They hadn't bought a ticket, true, but as long as his mother didn't stop the car it was probably *okay* to look is all he could guess, and so he pressed against the glass and watched – not unlike an opportunistic Peeking Tom – as the would-be queen resolutely (if also with resignation) prepared herself to enter the satellite ship that would blast her to safety off into outer space as the capsule of a car where he and his mother sat shot through the darkness under the moon and stars, the ephemeral angle that had allowed him to surreptitiously see the movie screen now gone – it vanishing without a trace – leaving him gazing at the lonely glow of the dashboard lights from behind, in the backseat, and his mother up front clenching her hands at the wheel and staring through the windshield at the dotted yellow line's relentless retreat.

Even back then, as a boy, the ranger couldn't help but think how that giant screen had been an eyesore throughout the entirety of the sun-drenched day, a useless and ugly monument in fact, and a poorly placed one at that: put not in front but *behind* the trees. And unlike the advertisement-slathered billboards that lined the shoulder of the main drag going in and out of town, it was a screen that was an ashen blank slate, one hundred percent a monochrome white – except for at night when it became undeniably ALIVE! – leaving him with no other wish, as they drove past, than to *BE THERE* first hand, sitting straight in front, at any of *The Big H's* many vacant spots instead of puttering forward on the lonely asphalt path, going back to the apartment they called home to watch a little bit of boring TV and be all cooped up before getting tucked into bed for the night; not that his idealized vision of what it should be would ever be satiated by seeing the real thing: case in point being when he eventually got to go to the drive-in to see a movie for the very first time. The giant screen didn't so much serve up the sanctuary and glitz of a motion-picture house as it resembled being squeezed into a traffic jam of an overflowing grocery store parking lot, and a staticky one at that – *Scratch crackle SCREETCH* – a garbling sound that was monotone and flat, not even counting the discomfort of having to crane his neck to view the screen's full extent; washing the bugs off the front of the windshield beforehand definitely would have helped.

Movie theaters were meant to be inside, not out, thus making *The Big H* an unwelcomed affront to the natural law of the semi-understood-but-never-to-be-fully-known universe, a violation that was confirmed and capped off (and poetically so, as if the darkened trees that encircled the amphitheater had gotten the last laugh) when that long-ago-but-now-forgotten motion picture show *JARRED* to an utter and abrupt stop at the most inopportune of spots, the soundtrack still blaring and the screen going completely black.

At first there was silence, then there was a shout, *"Hey, what the hell!?"* a bellicose voice belted out — followed in short order by a cacophonous orchestral of too-many-horns-to-count and a litany of similarly-themed complaints — *"WHAT A RIP OFF!"* and *"I Want My Money Back!"* and *"LAST TIME I COME HERE!"* — that reached a chaotic crescendo before, energy spent, they gradually trailed off as, one by one, the vehicles rolled away though the front gate and back on the road to wherever and whichever direction they called home.

By that time the industrial-strength overhead lamps had already buzzed on — *ZUMM-ZZZZ-na-ZZZZAAAA-ZUM-ZZZZZAAAA* — casting a shadowless glare and merciless light on a parking lot previously cloaked in comforting dark and sugar coated on top with sprinkles of magical movie dust that the high-wattage surge immediately snuffed out, incinerating the cinematic trance on the spot, as the voice of the manager interrupted over the AV speakers to announce.

"Blump ... ka-thump ... Errrrnt ... We are sorry to inform you ... *BLEEEEEP* ... that an equipment malfunction has occurred. *Vrrrennntt.* Please follow the attendants with the flags and you will be presented a discount coupon at the front gate ... *THUMP ... BLEEP ...* Again, we apologize for any inconvenience this may have caused. And thank you for your patronage to ... *The Big H ... You're Drive In ... ERRRRRNT ... Movie Home.* We look forward to seeing you again soon."

Fast forward a couple decades hence, to the present tense, and so sat the ranger with a not-all-that-different situation on his hands, leaving him wondering what excuse he would have to drum up for the departing guests as they left: a few kind words and maybe a handshake perhaps? Or would it be the other way around: the jilted patrons consoling him not to sweat it one bit or to get too upset, *"Our deepest condolences"* and *"You certainly TRIED your best"* followed up with a supercilious *"Maybe you should GET AWAY and take some time off."*

Of course, he wasn't quite at that point — at least not yet, in fact not even close — as any of the patrons could easily attest by the intense look on the ranger's face, one committed to blocking out all distractions both small and great, as he continued to *click* and *tap* and ... *TO* ... *PATIENTLY* ... *WAIT* ... for the hourglass icon and its incessant tumbling to hurry up. He watched it quite stupidly as it flipped and it flopped, end over end, grain by grain drizzling out, a drip-drip and a drop-drop, drop-drip, drip-drop until — *Gasp!* — the sandglass suddenly stopped (and not just your typical pause, no, this time it had a truly ominous look) to which the ranger quietly gave a hard swallow — *Ga-Gulp!* — as he pressed his palm against the side of his neck and tried his very best to keep his wits, to project an air that, well, it was all part of the act, and that the ill-timed delay didn't phase him one bit; despite the chill in the air, he could feel beads of perspiration starting to drip down the back of his neck.

"Just one more moment," he said as he tensed with a sense, nonetheless, that indeed something was slightly off kilter, not a hundred percent correct, as he floundered to get the projector to react to the keyboard commands from his usually trusty laptop, the futility of which was laid bare by the lingering smell of burnt electrical dust. It was the telltale sign that the light bulb filament in the projector had burnt out.

Nonetheless the ranger pressed on, less in hope for achieving success than in an instinctive and quite delusional quest to push off the inevitable failure he was still unprepared to admit, if also quite aware it was one he was *sooner than later* going to have to confront ... all the while the tepid glow of the tiny monitor reflected off the oily sheen of his face. In a previous era, such a sight would have been a signal that the hapless ranger needed immediate medical help, an emergency response, that he was very very (very) sick, or perhaps in need of a firm Heimlich thrust to quickly dislodge a glump of unchewed food stuck midway down his esophagus even if, on this particular eve, in the modern age, the ranger's bent back and listless hunch (including a wide-open mouth and a string of drool dribbling from his lip, his skin a clammy cerulean tint) were neither signs of sloth nor sickness but rather a testament to the ardor of his dedication and industriousness. He epitomized productivity to the max. A worker in front of his computer. Nobody was going to argue about that.

It was then, out of nowhere, that it appeared, and oh what a sight, an angelic apparition: it was a BEAM OF LIGHT! Although it was not quite like he'd imagined, as its orientation wasn't exactly right. Instead of shining from the projector up on the giant screen *in front* (as he had hoped), the illumination was streaming down on his hands *from behind* as he continued to type.

"YEP, Yep, yep. Reckoned it wouldn't hurt to give ya a lil' extra light," an approaching voice announced loud enough for everyone to hear followed up by a much more softly render message straight into the ranger's ear, "*— Psst, can you hear me? I'm purty sure that there light bulb is BURNT OUT.*"

The ranger turned around with a bit of a shock at the sight of seeing the shadowy figure so close up: a bushy growth of whiskers spiraling out from under his nose and a thick pair of glasses simultaneously magnifying and obscuring his bulging eyes beneath. It was the late-arriving guest.

To be sure, although it was not a hundred percent cure, the light in that brief moment didn't hurt, that is, at least not at first, although sadly it didn't last for long, as the self-anointed patron saint of what was most assuredly a lost cause hurriedly shined the light away, thus making it *darker* than it was before the unsolicited offering of illumination occurred, and in doing so planted the following question in the ranger's head: Might it have been *more preferable* if the strange man hadn't shined the light at all?

Once again the ranger watched the light take flight, scurrying across the amphitheater like an angel through the night before coming to rest on an attending patron's face, a man with a shaggy Zach Galifianakis beard, if also with a tad more gray which, on second thought, gave him a decidedly more Steve Wozniakian look, a correction of which was immediately validated the moment the elder statesman opened his mouth to expound with a timely and technically insightful thought.

"Well, is it a *pre or post* Y2K version? Because if its pre-1999, you can't run the DOS application without the patch."

Tap ... tap ... double click ... Tap-tip

"Did you say WHYY TWOOO KAYY?" the late-arriving man sang out perhaps a decibel too loud as he simultaneously summersault-flipped the flashlight end over end into the nocturnal air.

"Ha! Oh yeah, I remember that!" another voice called out.

"YEP ... Yep ... yep. Brings back memories, sure does. With my Why-Two-Kay stockpile of marshmallows I was good to go on food for a year. Had me quite an extensive stash of them jet-puffed fluffs in my fallout shelter."

"*Marshmallows!*" a woman burst out loud from an aisle seat. "— Ever think of going with just straight sugar cubes instead."

"Not with my teeth ma'am. The marshmallows are much preferred. Just a lot more softer on the gums."

"Ha! Isn't that funny how we all prepared for the worst," the Zack Wozniakian looking guy interjected with a nostalgic sigh. "—And then nothing happened."

"Huh!? Whadaya mean *nuthin'* happened!?"

"Yeah, that's a crock!" another dissenting spoke up. "It set the stage for a domino effect of *really bad* events starting with the Dot Com Bust ..."

The mustachioed man thrust his finger into the air as if to deliver an important point, only to fizzle into a thought he probably should have kept to himself. "Ya know, if a genie ever gave me three wishes," he whimsically mused, "— the first thing I'd ask for is a pack of them jet-puffed marshmallows to fall out of the sky on my head."

Not that any of the patrons were paying attention to the man. Instead, the conversation picked up where the previous line of thought about the world's current state of affairs had left off.

"Do you really think it started with Y2K? I kinda thought that was a false alarm."

"And then a year or two later, Nine Eleven. That was by far the worst!"

"Followed by the housing bubble bust, the financial crisis crash, climate change, the war on ... darn near everything; the bad news just keeps on rolling in."

"YEP Yep yep, it's been a real bad run. I'll give ya that," The mustachioed man conceded as he shined his light on the ground and then bent down to pick something up. It was a clear plastic bag with little globules of white inside. "Sure does seem like every step forward we take two steps back."

"Well, whatever started it, I never thought I'd see more change in my life than my grandparents. And I'm only fifty three!"

"Were the nineties really that much better?" a teenager asked in a bemused tone.

"Life moved a lot slower for one thing, that's for sure."

"Halleluiah to that!"

"Well I'll be," the mustachioed man gaffed, "—It's a bag of puffs!" Amazed at his find, he shined his flashlight up at the stars.

"Actually," a voice from a nearby lawn chair spoke up. "I think that bag's ...."

"*Pssst,*" another whispered to interrupt. "*He's already touched it.* Just let him keep it. I have two more fresh bags in the truck."

The woman in the aisle seat continued: "Even little things, like my father reading the newspaper around the kitchen table, are suddenly gone. The practice no longer exists."

"Yeah, you got that right!"

"These days everybody's hunching over a computer screen pretty much everywhere you go."

"So true. Everybody's plugged in all the time!"

"Even at a campfire! It's sad."

"Sure does seem like the Golden Age has come and gone ..."

"Not that you ever realize it's the Golden Age at the time."

"And by the time you do it's too late."

"Yeah, you got that right. Like the time I sold my entire vinyl record collection at a yard sale for a quarter a piece. I'd give anything now to get those disks back."

"YEP Yep yep, sure do wonder how we got SO FAR off track!?'" the mustachioed man pondered as he ripped open his newly-found bag of puffs and popped a couple marshmallows in his mouth. "Anybody else ... *gobble gobble* ... want one ... *gobble gobble gulp* ... sure are good ... *gobble gobble* ... just what I needed ... *gulp* ... really hits the spot."

And thus it was, whether subconsciously or not, that the wayward ranger once again drifted off on the gentle breeze of his own thoughts, into a deeply repressed if also meticulously kept amphitheater of his own mind, rewinding back in time, to that glittery era when and where Bobby Angel burst on the scene and of whom, a decade or two hence — by happenstance — the then twelve year old ranger was first introduced while browsing through the bottom shelf of the mahogany wood console in the den of his friend's quite sizeable house (not too far from the basketball courts) on top of which sat a turntable spinning at slow-motion thirty-three revolution speed and below which were dozens of vinyl records vertically squished, including a rare mint-condition first-edition of the enigmatic artist's *End of the Apocalypse* LP, one of only a few thousand made before detection of two flaws brought its production to a grinding halt, the first of which centered on a rash of reports detailing how disillusioned teens were slashing their wrists on the razor-sharp edges of the LP's quadruple disks with the second swirling around rumors that transcendental mind-altering gas was leaching out of the album's three-dimensional cover art when left out in the sun too long, thus deluding the nation's impressionable youth into believing that locking themselves in the backseat of their parent's cars — windows rolled up tight as they sipped ice cold cokes — would help open their minds to new horizons and other hallucinogenic effects, the surprising upshot of which, from a conservative middle-America point of view, was its supposed role in ending the societal scourge of juveniles sniffing model airplane glue in backyard sheds, thus making the second design flaw, well, "maybe not so bad."

Unlike as was standard issue in the day, the *The End of the Apocalypse LP* contained not one, but rather three disks (not including the fourth that was discovered years later by an Angelhead in a double layer of felt behind a hidden flap) each of which could be opened at the adjoining pleats, like an accordion folded Rand McNally gas-station map, or alternatively unzipped and reattached with a combination of buttons, magnets and Velcro clasps that worked in tandem with a brass chain, a pulley and other hydraulic parts to turn the avant-guard offering into a three-dimensional display that in theory should have made the album "the easiest thing to spot" if it weren't for the fact you could be staring straight at the LPs many shape-shifting forms and never know it was a record at all, let alone a Bobby Angel masterwork, the album alternatively resembling a naval ship cracked in half or a UFO making a lunar pass depending on how you folded it back up (and that was assuming none of the detachable pieces got lost); it laying bare a whole new world that no one before or since had ever seen let alone thought up — the type of album you could never get tired of no matter how many times you looked; in fact you could listen to the entire album front and back and front and back and front and back (and front and back) and barely put a dent in trying to digest all the album's intricate array of art — which was centered mostly around obscure collector-edition photographs of Bobby Angel displaying various states of indifference to the lens — with the icing on the cake being the warning labels that were slathered on the album's outer skin, front and back, cram packed with line after line of legalese that was as illegible as it was cryptic in disclosing the product's supposed risks — *"Do Not Handle Without Rubber Gloves, Gas Mask Highly Recommended"* and *"Keep All Windows and Doors Ajar if Opened in a Confined Space"* being among its most easy to follow pieces of advice — thus doing the C-G-D strumming chord artist a backhanded favor of sorts: the aftermarket stickers quickly became the album's primary and most recognizable mark, not to be confused with the "unofficial" street handle given to the album by the "Kingmaker of All Things Rock," Rupert Robbins, in his scathing review in the highly influential *Guitar By The Numbers* magazine, opining that *"Bobby Angel is so far ahead of his time on this one, he'll have to wait until Hell Freezes Over for this sh— to catch on,"* a prediction that was made all the more prescient by the high-flying flagship monthly publication going defunct by decade's end in a large part due to its inability to stay relevant amid new strumming trends, a development of which Bobby Angel was rumored to have responded to by saying "maybe after the apocalypse we can all eat cake" as he parted his hair during the sitting that produced the iconic poster that so many adoring Angelphiles push-pinned to the back of their bedroom doors and tried to imitate.

By that time, mint-condition copies had become so rare that a semi-lucrative counterfeit market had sprung up, making it second to only Canadian bacon on the list of North America's most smuggled consumable goods, thus motivating border patrol agents to retrain their canine units to detect the scent of polyvinyl chloride instead of cooked ham and embargo-minded politicians to upend a trade agreement in a diplomatic dust up that the liberal press dubbed "The Second Sombrero Wars."

Despite, or perhaps because, of the intense scrutiny surrounding the record's botched release, even the most basic facts of the album somehow managed to remain quagmired in misunderstanding and disbelief with closure on any one front growing increasingly remote while also being exacerbated and made more complex as time passed by a slew of new conspiracy theories spawning forth and spinning off (and subsequently metasizing into new lives all their own) which in turn became fodder for half-baked pseudo-intellectual debates that found traction on underground college radio stations where highly-caffeinated DJs talked ad infinitum into the night about the album's influence on secular and religious tastes all the while a new and contradictory school of thought emerged to suggest that, based on the math, the record was perhaps, in its simplest form, nothing more than a clever publicity stunt — the suppression of sales forming the counterintuitive linchpin of its transcendent success and utter inaccessibility fueling the fodder that grew its myth — the masterstroke of which perhaps was duping the artist into believing that was what he had envisioned all along — or was Bobby Angel "extremely distraught" over the marketing botch? As usual, nobody (not even Bobby Angel or maybe only Bobby Angel) had a clue.

Just when it looked like it couldn't get any worse, the matter took a nose dive into the abyss of a protracted proxy battle that played out in plain sight as Bobby Angel plied his craft into refining the now famous Yukon-Mexicali Sound on a side project with the *Transatlantic Harmony Experiment* quintet, better known simply by the acronym T.H.E. and best remembered for the *Clogging to the Oldies* tour, a venue that pitted the rhythm guitarist in the red scarf (whom Bobby Angel famously slighted by wearing a terry cloth hooded vest) against the rest of the more seasoned studio session band, much to ticket scalpers delight: for them acrimonious internal disputes only heightened the resale price of their obstructed-view seats; and to be sure, Bobby Angel knew how to play the part by finding a way to hide from the spotlight (and let others duke it out) by way of finding sanctuary in a primitive windowless hut nestled deep in a valley retreat [a locale that was later rumored to be his inspiration for his smash hit *No Name Lake* and soon thereafter to become an unofficial mecca that crunchy Angelheads spent years, even decades, wandering remote backwoods trails in the Catskills and the Monongahela forests trying to locate] in part to free himself from the turmoil but mostly to *pour* himself into his art, and in this instance, quite literally so, by teaming up with Little Dutchboy's upstart competitor to launch a cutting edge new line of paints — featuring a novel spectrum of colors that nobody had ever seen — and which a group of upstart Polygonists used as inspiration to push the envelope with a genre of underexplored shapes [called Nautical Horns, including the sub-families Maxiflucitoids and Inverse Points] that would have caused an even bigger splash if it wasn't for the surprise seventh-hour ruling that overturned the lower court's decision to "grant a stay" on Bobby Angel's estranged record company's request to release a second-edition of the *End of the Apocalypse* LP that, in the judge's own words [the Honorable Melvin Etus's] "was a fraudulent perversion of the artist's original work," to the near universal applause among the people and lauded in the press;" for not only did the charlatan second edition contain just one disk (i.e. a truncation that was achieved by arbitrarily axing each track by a third, resulting in the abrupt cut off of most songs mid riff) its packaging had been reduced to a single sleeve, just a front and a back, thus stripping the masterwork of its many iconic detachable parts, with the big implication being that it was no longer capable of unfolding and opening up; or in other words, it was an "all too easy to recognize" shadow of its former self, not even mentioning the price-killing Saskatchewan knockoff which you could buy at a tenth of the price overseas (and featured a 45, not a 33, speed disk) that were being shipped in mass in unmarked container ships at major launching points across the outskirts of Old Quebec which Alcohol, Tobacco and Firearms agents proved either unable or not willing to intercept thus causing long-haul trucking companies to be stuck with the bill and bulk rail car shipments stranded at inland hubs where, when discovered, they were burned in bulk on the spot, generating a plume of putrid purple smoke to which a new generation of aspiring Angelheads erroneously flocked, clogging up tollways and pushing traffic out on rusty barbed wire lined cow paths, all in hope of getting a chance to whiff the magical gas on their way to buy scalped tickets for the on-again-off-again *Bobby Angel and T.H.E. Clogging to the Oldies* tour; and possibly recording a bootleg tape, making some of them hundreds of thousands of dollars richer overnight and, unexpectedly, also turning them into paranoid freaks: recordings from Waukesha and Duluth, depending on their quality, were worth anywhere from the price of a lava lamp to more than some fan's entire estates, leading to a rash of home invasions in which fourteen carrot gems and priceless bone china sets were left lying in place untouched amid a mess of vinyl disks littered about scattershot on oriental rug-adorned hard wood floors consequently causing fans that hadn't been robbed to hide their proud possession as best they could [often in the unlikeliest of places such as underneath hollowed-out table pads on top of which sat knickknacks of various sorts, such as Hummel ceramic figurines, say, one of a boy sitting in a meadow playing a flute to a yellow bird, singing along, on the tippy toe end of his outstretched bare feet and another of a little girl with a red bow feeding a spotted fawn with her hand, and similar keepsakes all so sweet]; or even going so far as disavowing Bobby Angel in public as a way to foil any would-be burglars who might be in earshot, slurring him as a washed up yodeling bum; the backdrop of which proved to be the perfect stage for the enigmatic artist to return from his exile retreat, his fan's all clamoring to hear a sequel track, only to greet a new generation of devotees with another lines of paints (this time a beguiling spectrum of "new grays") and a string of Greatest Hits albums instead, that all went platinum three in a row back to back, the third of which was all new material, or as was typical with the artist, par for the course — Nothing Bobby Angel did made any sense.

As the decades played out, revisionist history started to see the situation in a whole new light, to which the prize-winning economist Clarence Q. Lubin's career took flight — him donning a maroon turtle neck, a Hounds Tooth jacket and goatee beard (to perfectly play the part) — by coaxing his pal in the Chemistry Department, Christoff Vonn Sieht, whom he played pickle ball with at lunch, to use his mass spectrometer and other sophisticated and non-invasive techniques to scientifically prove (with reproducible test results) that the fabled album in actuality contained not a single molecule of any poisonous gas (not even lead paint) or, in sum: the urban legend surrounding the album's toxic fumes was *"a bunch of crap,"* a point that he emphasized to much acclaim by sitting in his Peugeot 504 parked in the summer sun for four hours straight — windows rolled up and chain smoking Camel cigarettes — and somehow managing to emerge, unscathed and alive, amid the flashes of newspaper reporters covering the stunt, all topped off with the perfect pre-meditated quote rolling off his tongue, "other than being a little parched, I'm kinda feelin' sort of fine," which not coincidently was an oft recited lyric from the titular song on the debut Christmas album disk that had so long ago catapulted Bobby Angel's name to dinner table recognition across the continental

US, and thus clearing the path for a wide range of orchestral-minded traveling troubadours to follow suit.

Incredibly, after so many years of focusing on the lead up and outfall of its release, critics were finally getting around to delving into the one thing they more or less ignored and which turned out to be the most dangerous aspect of the master work — *it's words.* Not that doing so was a simple listening act: by this point the most prominent sound emitted from the dwindling stock of heirloom disks was a warped and wobbly hiss overtop infinitesimally faint ramblings that were hard to distinguish (if also unmistakably recognizable as Bobby Angel's warbling voice) although admittedly to his legion of fervent fans, the *True Believers,* that was just part of the fun — playing them over and over (and over) again helped them perfect their trademark Bobby Angel dance (a fusion of square dancing, the rumba and contemporary tap) at the same time it opened their minds to delving into the state of the universe and the depths of where Bobby Angel's mind was at — which had led to the unexpected discovery that, to a point, the more the record wore out, the louder and louder it got (notching a full thirteen on the Polk Brother's one to twelve scale), but — with an unexpected twist — it was not the sound of the A-side track *playing forward* but rather the B-side playing *in reverse* that was the louder of the two sounds if also an unintelligible one at that, and one that most people believed would "never be cracked" until a group of out-of-work stenographers (having lost their jobs to Bosley's tape machine) started to pick out words and phrases, thus unleashing a footrace among the assorted *Friends of the Angelheads* groups to see who could unravel the deeply coded message first, a quest that was repeatedly stymied by the over-worn albums having a tendency to overheat if played for too long without a break, and thereby spontaneously combusting into a heap of dust (leading to a flurry of lawsuits that were settled in highrise offices out of court) or was it, as the Nobel Prize winning and Honorary Chair of the Von Leigwig Society Dr. Clarence Q. Lubin claimed — "all just part of Bobby Angel's grand design?"

Clues could be gleaned in copious amounts to prove either point.

A revisionist frenzy among the elites was mirrored by waning interest among the working class, it more and more being seen as a relic of the past, a quaint reminder of an era gone by; that was, until a tell-all Bobby Angel memoir was leaked featuring an endless stream of subconscious thoughts which, for the most part, were as obtuse as they were hard to pronounce (including two chapters written entirely in Linear B) but which was nonetheless received with critical praise for shedding light on his "Windowless Hut" renaissance period during which Bobby Angel and T.H.E. perfected the Yankee Doodle sound that simultaneously fueled a national craze and reaffirmed the artist's deep historical roots – with the quartet of bag piper Dan "Company Man" Richt, "Big Mack" Jack on the keys, Manny Hudson on the horns, and Brooks River on the bass doing all the heavy lifting on the melody and harmony work while the lightweight rhythm guitarist Timmy "Two" Timer (as always, donning his red scarf) cashed in as the lyricist with the copyright checks, plowing all his ethically-impaired proceeds into underwater real estate deals off the Jamaican coast, thereby leaving the rest of the band practically penniless except for a lifetime supply of free paints which, in a horrid twist, a despondent "Company Man" Dan – fresh off the wagon – relapsed and drank himself to death, thus eliminating any hope for a *Happily Ever After Bobby Angel and T.H.E.* reunion tour.

By that time, the imbroglio over the album being safe or unsafe or generating one or multiple bootlegs had become overblown and beside the point for the reason that the original intent of the safety warnings so direly stamped on the first edition had become turned inside out: connoisseurs of the album were wearing silk gloves and surgical masks to protect the fragile album from harmful biological and atmospheric contaminants. Or in other words, the new imperative was protecting the album from the people, not the people from the art.

It was then like that, as quick as a snap, as inexplicably as it had started, the ranger's mental missive on Bobby Angel trailed off at just about the same time the affable banter previously being enjoyed among the patrons of the amphitheater came to an awkward pause. The void was palpable. Whereas before everyone was talking, the mood had turned. Nobody was saying a word. It was as quiet as could be. Just the sound of crickets chirping. Singing frogs. The crackling flame.

And then it came. A singular clap. One palm to the other. It was a resonate smack. Then another and another at an accelerating pace. It was the mustachioed man, of course, clapping his hands as fast as he could.

"WHADAYA SAY EVERBODY!" the slightly off-centered man cheered. *"Wow, wasn't that great everybody. What a terrific Campfire Talk! How 'bout it! Let's all give the ranger a real big round of applause!"*

The ranger was more than a little embarrassed, and especially so for the guest. What in the world he could have ever done to become the man's Number One Fan was beyond his comprehension, or anybody's guess. But astonishingly, there he was − fully invested as if it was his mission in life − giving it *his all* trying to rally the crowd into an encore salute for a show that not only hadn't started but was now safe to say, never would. The ranger's efforts, the show, the evening were pretty much caput (i.e. making the event not unlike a defective fire cracker that simply wasn't going to go off). The man was obviously and quite obliviously out of touch, if also harmless in his support as well. Sometimes people need a mission for the sake of doing something even if, as in this case, it was senseless and without a point.

"JUST A MINOR TECHNICAL DELAY, FOLKS!" he proclaimed to the packed house as he continued to clap while also, at the same time, he coyly cupped his hands to mutter some more helpful tidbits of information under his breath. *"Say, you DO KNOW the bulb is dead?"*

The ranger rolled his eyes at the news. "Yeah," he mumbled. "−This has really turned into a real fubar alright."

"Ha! A FUBAR? Not even close," the man with the light whispered under his breath. "− Ain't no Sunday school picnic, I'll give ya that. Maybe a SNAFU at the worst. But definitely not a FUBAR, *not yet."*

"Yeah ... well ... whatever ... pretty much the same result."

"HOW 'BOUT IT FOLKS, LET'S HEAR IT FOR THE RANGER!" the whiskered man again belted out, this time less to elicit a response than to drown out the ranger's predictably feeble attempt at an excuse and again using the diversionary drumming of his palms to continue his covert pep-talk. "Listen here, ranger," he said, leaning in with a lecturing tone, "− Better broken equipment and a functioning ranger than functioning equipment and a ranger that don't work." The man patted his chest. "Trust me, Donnie here, I've seen a lot worse. In fact, as

145

far as I'm concerned, and when you look back you'll see: this is all a blessin' in disguise."

"HA! A blessing in disguise? Oh yeah, right!" the ranger sarcastically spat back, although it should be noted he was more than a bit caught off guard by the unexpected revelation of the stranger's name. If the man had introduced himself before, the ranger couldn't recall ... other than *there was something* about the name Donnie that vaguely rang a bell.

"Could be wrong," the bespectacled man who called himself Donnie casually quipped, "but I don't think that I am."

"In fact, I have a hunch all this equipment is what's stifflin' your thoughts." He emphasized the point by touching the end of his flashlight to the PC lid and pushing it shut with a gentle thrust. "And say, why don't you unplug both of them cords while you're at it. See 'em there? Right down at your feet. Okay, good, now grab that end and let's move this puppy out of the way. You ready? One ... two ... three ... LIFT!"

The ranger lunged forward to prevent the table from tilting and spilling everything off, and then — finding himself stuck — helped the late-arriving guest carry the gurney of wounded equipment away. "*Pardon me, ma'am ... no sir you're fine ... Okay, keep 'er steady ... just a little further ... oh, thank'ee, sir for moving your chair ... Much obliged! Ya still got it?... good. How 'bout over here?*"

The ranger looked up. They were under the floodlight in back. It was turned off. Dark. "Yeah okay, this works."

"Exactly what I was thinkin', too! Funny don't ya think how great minds think alike?"

The ranger and the stranger lowered the table down until all four feet were back on the ground. The ranger looked at the darkened floodlight overhead. Instinctively, without thought, the ranger reached for the switch to turn it on. After all, the show was over. Timing was right to call it a night, to flood the amphitheater with electric lamp light. The ranger was surprised to find his effort stymied by the firm grip of Donnie's hand around his wrist.

"You flip on the light and you'll gonna KILL the entire vibe."

"But the ..."

"Hey!!! You listen to me, Ranger. It's still not a FUBAR. UNDERSTOOD!"

"Um, pardon me," a patron interrupted, obviously speaking on behalf of the crowd. "— Did I hear you say the show's over? Does that mean we should all leave?"

"Well I hope not!" a woman on the other corner rose to his defense. "—I've been looking forward to this campfire talk *all day!*"

"Yeah," the bearded man next to her decreed. "How about just telling us some ranger stories? You must have a lot of those ..."

"Well ... um ... yeah ... I mean ... um"

Somewhat predictably it was the late-arriving guest who stepped in to answer on the faltering ranger's behalf. "Ha, KHEN-HE? You bet he can. Look at him. The man IS A LIVE and God for honest park ranger. The computer might've crashed but as far as I KHEN tell, HE ISN'T DEAD. TRUST ME."

The mustachioed man sauntered up the center aisle like he owned the place. The fire light cast his shadow on the giant outdoor screen twenty feet tall. He formed his hands in the shape of an old-fashioned megaphone and hollered toward the ranger in back. "THE THING ABOUT A RANGER IS THEY ALWAYS HAVE A BACKUP PLAN, A SECOND LIFE-LINE, FOR *JUST IN CASE. AIN'T THAT RIGHT?"*

The entire crowd turned back in unison to hear the ranger's response.

Not that the dumfounded ranger had one. The best he could muster was a nervous cough and a few mumbled words.

"Well, ahem, the, um, well, ahem ..."

"Ya hear that folks? Don't anybody go anywhere!" the strange guest [Donnie was his name] enthusiastically endorsed. "KHEN-HE? Ha! You heard it yourselves, just like he SAYS. When life knocks you down you GET up off YOUR BUTT. You get UP. Everybody's HERE. Everything we need. NOW get up here ranger. Come on. Let's get this show going in full gear."

"Full gear?" the ranger laughed to himself in self defeat. No, this show was definitely over. Simple as that. How could it not be? There was no mincing the facts. Without pause the ranger again reached with his finger to flick on the switch and turn on the light — and had actually proceeded as far as pushing it half way up — when *something* the strange guest had just said (either explicitly or between the lines) struck him deep down in his heart to the point that the ranger's own inner voice firmly and quite resolutely sang out for him to STOP and reverse course.

147

And so he did, and so it was: the switch of the floodlight got pushed back down to off.

The amphitheater remained dark.

Except for the campfire.

And the flashlight of course.

Sure, the mustachioed man was a "bit eccentric," the ranger thought, but he was also right. It was an age-old mistake to confuse the messenger with the message. The computer and projector were extras, *not essentials*. Everything he needed was already at hand: a campfire, a ranger and a very nice crowd. The equipment was superfluous. It simply didn't have to be so complex.

The mustachioed man beamed with pride as he watched the ranger amble up the center aisle to join him up front, whereupon he greeted the rejuvenated ranger with a giant and heartfelt pat on the back. "The stage is all yours, fella. I'll be on the other side of the campfire roastin' marshmallows on a stick, just in case you need me. But I don't think you will."

The ranger patiently (and thankfully) watched as the stranger exited stage left when, in an instant, it clicked: the identity of his "campfire coach" popped in his head. But of course, he was the same vagabond of a visitor who'd helped him raise Old Glory in front of the Visitor Center earlier in the day. And he was the same famished freeloader who insisted on paying for his junk food with a handful of eclectic coins. And he was the same worn-out wanderer who'd fallen asleep in the auditorium as the park movie played. And he was the same slumbering snorer whom he had discretely closed the door for so he could rest in peace. And he was the same enigmatic guest he'd gone back to check on an hour or so later only to discover him missing without a trace. The ranger had always wondered where or in which direction the homeless guy had gone and now he knew: just a few miles down the road to his campfire talk; and that his name was "Donnie" – perhaps that was another clue. In a weird way everything was starting to make sense. As bad as things had gone – starting with an odyssey of a long day at the Sweetwater Visitor Center and now capped off by an equally frustrating start to his campfire talk – there was a good side to it all, too: he could at least be thankful that the many campfire guests had not left, at least not yet. Still that didn't solve what he could or should or would be talking about next. The ranger was reminded of a recurring nightmare he'd had since his youth of showing up late to class having completely forgotten to study for the big test, always waking up just in time and just before the teacher stamped his paper with a Big Fat F. The ranger felt similar relieved, if also having no idea how to start or what to say. Fortunately an empathetic soul threw him a lifeline from not too far away.

"Tell us where you're from, start with that?"

"Well, I grew up in Missouri."

"Born *and* raised?" another voice shouted out.

"Actually, I was born ... *down here.*"

"In South Florida? Whoa, that makes you a native. I bet you've really seen this place change. I'm in the middle of reading *Land Remembered*. The governor, I can't remember which one, just a few terms back, he wanted to make it required reading for every new Floridian. Make it a law that everyone got a copy of their own."

The ranger sort of liked the idea. "Well, it's definitely a terrific read."

"But not as good as *Wildman of the Glades*?" another voice from the side abruptly sang out.

The ranger couldn't help but roll his eyes. "Well some books, *ahem*, you gotta take with a big grain of salt," he gestured with reassurance to the onlooking crowd.

"Oh that guy's the REAL DEAL. His story is as incredible as it is legit. I have an autographed copy and I already read it twice. Cap'n Shane is a legend in these parts. Between his statue in front of his airboat operation, all the billboards and of course his book, he's pretty much ubiquitous wherever you look. Problem is, most of the people who could corroborate his escapades are in jail, missing ... or dead. Yeah, hasn't always been 'live and let live' in the swamp, if you know what I mean."

The ranger was about to interrupt when he thought to just let the man speak his peace.

"Shane says the old code he grew up by 'went extinct' when the park moved in. Honoring handshakes and settling disputes with barroom brawls got replaced with paperwork and unreadable laws. Shane even played a big role in establishing the park, before they turned against him. You know, speculation runs rampant that he still uses his business to launder his square grouper loot. That ol' Shane, he's a wily operator, especially how he fans the flames in his book. The guy even survived a wicked airboat crash. That's what gave him his limp. He's everything and all that. The whole bit."

The ranger nodded his head as he circled counterclockwise around the flame. He reached his hand toward the heat. It felt good. Warm. His story-telling juices were starting to flow. He was getting an idea of the direction he wanted to go.

"Well, there's a lot of stories out there," the ranger agreed. "But let me tell ya something. Even if they're *all true* and you read *every book*, the one thing I can tell you for certain is that you're not gonna find everything you need to know in the *written word*."

"That's why you gotta get out on The Deluxe Tour with Cap'n Shane! It's worth every penny."

This time someone else did the ranger's bidding for him. "SHHHH!" a woman nudged on the man's shoulder from behind. "I can't hear the ranger with you speaking so much!"

The ranger politely tipped the brim of his hat towards the woman to show his thanks as an air pocket in a log popped a thousand ashen sparkles upward and outward into the dark.

"I've actually heard it said that most of history, about ninety percent, probably more than that, never makes it into books. Never even gets written down. Imagine that. Ninety percent of history. Ninety percent. Lost to time."

The ranger gestured to the crackling flame.

"That's where the campfire comes in."

BOOK 4
THE ROUND UP

The Round Up

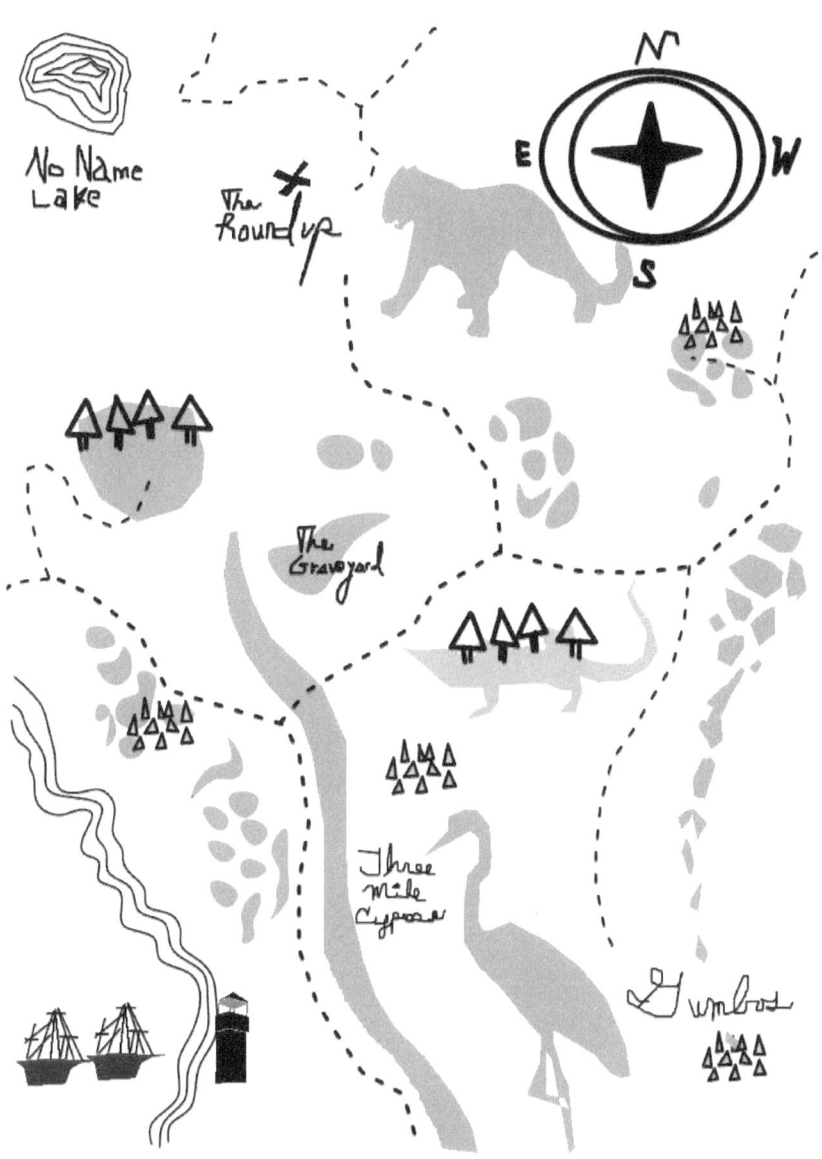

No Name Lake

The Round Up

The Graveyard

Three Mile Cypress

Gunbos

The Round Up

Chapter 1:
Outmanned, Outgunned and Alone

Nov 5, 1856

My thoughts are drawn to the grandeur of the land. While the majority of those posted in this desolate corner of the world lack an appreciation for its beauty and rusticity, I have taken to it with all the alacrity of a fish long out of water. The endless sunshine and sandy soil of the hammocks, the baked scent of wet pine needles after a torrent and the crispness of the mild winter breezes suit me. I have not a thought for Ohio. I am awestruck by the enormity and grandeur of the trees and their reflection on the waters. Following the arboreal behemoths to their apogee in the heavens, I am seized with euphoria unlike any I have ever experienced, myself flying in the treetops. My epiphanies are only broken by the tapping of – behold! – two great woodpeckers. My soul has landed and a peace has settled upon me as if I have found something in this wild and verdant firmament that I can keep. The moment still lingers, entrenched in my soul somehow. Should I perish here, I am not disturbed by my crude flesh dissolving into the subterranean waters below, long after my soul has quietly slipped into the humid ether.

Nov 9

A preposterously thick fog rolls in from the coast.

The men gather at the shoreline to watch it approach. Two of the new privates, Doane and Foster, are overtaken by the dense mist on their way back to the fort, although the sour juice may have been a factor, too.

Nov 10

I am startled awake by distant screaming and the smell of smoke.

I go to the East Tower to steady my nerves. There is a dim glow in the distance across the river. Likely an Indian blaze.

Nov 11

The platoon is ambushed and harried by hostile Indians at Bishop's Hope.

We suffer a casualty. One Andrew Stafford, our chief surveyor and mapper, is shot in the shoulder by an arrow as we ford a muddy plain. The attack comes from the direction of a long strand astride the lagoon. We return fire only to be greeted by the surprise of a second and more substantive volley from a nearby bluff. On a good note it looks like Stafford will pull through. His wound is tended to quickly. There seems slim chance of putrification.

Nov 13

The Indians are outgunning us at every turn.

The days of easily repelling the primitive raids have given way to protracted battles of increasing complexity and daring. Firearms, not the bow and arrow, have become their weapon of choice. Shadows Inside's warriors anticipate our every move.

Nov 15

Danforth returns to the fort with a refugee of war, a teenage boy named Simon.

The young lad is badly rattled and barely able to speak. Danforth had encountered him by chance on the coastal trail during one of his scouting missions and immediately recognized him as the eldest son of a homesteader from the North Bluff named Thompson.

Nov 16

After a day of rest and a good meal, Simon is finally able to speak.

He describes a wonderful life on their homestead: plentiful game, year-round crops, and a ready market with passing ships. Then came the evening of the dense fog. I nod to the lad that I remember the night well. Silence gives way to a frightening sound, the plunging of a heavy chain to a bottomless depth and the splashing of paddles and men's voices approaching the shore. His father hollers several times for the mysterious guests to leave, but to no avail: the door is battered open with a series of violent strikes at the hands of hulking silhouette that emerges from an eerie green glow. "It was a PI-PI-PIRATE in a BA-BA-BLACK HAT," Simon swears. "Nothing but BA-BA-BONES and a PA-PA-PEG for a foot!" The poor boy breaks down in tears as he recounts the rest: a giant silver sword sinking straight through his father's chest and out the other side of his back, a gaggle of similarly skeletal sailors bursting in from behind, one smashing everything to smithereens with a club and another an axe, culminating in flames consuming the house. Danforth confirms that the homestead is indeed obliterated beyond a trace. All that remains is a mound of shell it was built on and several piles of freshly dug up limey rock at various spots.

Nov 17
Danforth and I both confer in private and agree.

The boy has been through a tragedy of immense proportions and is obviously delusional. Shadows Inside's warriors — *not pirates* — are the perpetrators of this heinous crime. The savages are well known to adorn themselves in clothing and other goods that they pilfer during their raids. One story comes to mind from many years back, during the Creek War, when a group of Cherokees waylaid a traveling troop of Shakespearean actors and stripped them naked of all their clothing. One can imagine something similar here. In accordance with the severity of the situation, I have advised Kerr to plan a counter attack and instructed Danforth to scout down where Shadows Inside is stowing his fleet of canoes.

Nov 19
Simon has been stung by a scorpion in the latrine.

His foot is engorged the size of a cannonball and hot as the Devil. Danforth has sedated him with a tincture of elder willow and anise until the swelling subsides.

Nov 21
Our retaliatory strike fails miserably.

Kerr's vessel is pushed with the current and strands on a shoal. Half the men wade through the shallows to take positions on the bank while another contingent, led by Jeffers, fires a small cannon. The blast flushes a cataclysm of squawking waterfowl into the sky. Quite a few collide and plunge into the shallows. Simon clubs several of the thrashing birds for us to enjoy at the campfire later tonight. One of the feisty animals still has enough life in it to jab Simon in the ear, giving us all a well-deserved laugh. It is a fine county indeed where the game kill each other without need for wasting gunpowder or shot. As for the savages, they manage to escape unharmed in the commotion.

Nov 27
Danforth taps Stafford's map with confidence.

He believes he's finally found where the rendezvous between the Cuban smugglers and the savages is taking place: a cluster of islands near the river's mouth which the naval squadron dare not patrol for fear of running aground because of treacherous currents and coral reefs. He hopes to find out more in the days ahead.

Nov 29
Stafford's condition worsens.

Danforth provides assurance that his intervention with his sour milk of opiate and medicinal herbs will have him on his feet soon enough.

Dec 1
The consequences of our failure to secure the interior continue to mount.

Refugees are flocking to the fort. A shanty town has formed. Around a dozen families in all. Should these family's linger, I feel they may become dependent on government largesse, a situation I do not wish to manage.

Dec 4
The men's spirits are sorely lagging.

The imperative seems clear: we must halt the flow of smuggled arms and increase the firepower of the fort. We are in desperate need of a decisive victory that will break the will of Shadows Inside and his clan.

Dec 6
I am astounded by Stafford's rapid deterioration of body and mind. The few words I can make out when he tries to speak make little sense. Something about "folding the map at Waxy Hadjo's Inlet, holding it towards the sun in reverse, and looking

for what's buried between a 'Double Ewe' and a 'Why.'" He stares through me as if looking toward the horizon at a faraway ship.

Dec 8
Danforth greets me this morning with unfortunate news: Stafford is dead.

Chapter 2:
Swamp Buggy Ride to The Lodge

The swamp buggy rolled through a marl prairie towards a tall stand of trees.

The thigh-high grass gave the illusion of an even surface, but underneath the ground was pockmarked with grooves and crannies that the makeshift machine chugged up and down and around. Rusty's father was behind the wheel driving. Tate sat shotgun beside him on a cracked-vinyl bucket seat that was dry rot underneath. Huddy stood like a ship captain at the helm immediately behind them, in the middle of the buggy, gripping his hands around the roll bar, as he stared ahead at the approaching trees. Sandy Parrish slouched back in leisurely repose on one of the two twin cushioned bench seats that ran lengthwise down the back. He had one leg propped up on the bench and was munching on an apple as he watched the scenery slowly go by in reverse. Rusty sat upright and wide eyed in the middle of the opposite bench, just doing his best not to fall off.

"You sure you don't want an apple?" Sandy asked as he tossed the core over the rail.

Rusty was hungry but he shook his head no.

"Sure are tasty."

"No," Rusty refused more resolutely, this time out loud.

Huddy's gaze lifted as the backwoods buggy approached a grove. He wasn't a big man, but he was naturally strong, solid as a rock and wiry as ironwood, with a voice that was deep and steady and easy to trust; and ebony skin that had barely wrinkled despite many decades under the sun.

It didn't take Rusty long to sense this part of the swamp was different. He had heard that the really big cypress trees had been cut down during World War II, but if they had he couldn't tell ... at least not up to this point. To him all the trees looked big. Other than the trail — which was rutted in spots and sometimes widened, too, as a vestige of other outdoorsmen using the same route — everything else looked pristine, untouched, about as far away from civilization as you could possibly get, not a place that had been crisscrossed with rails and invaded with heavy machinery to cut down and haul the giant trees out. But this grove was different. That much he could see. The girth of the trunks were much wider and the trees were more generously spaced out underneath. The undergrowth was spare. The tops of the trees far away.

Giant palmetto fronds brushed up against the elevated sides of the buggy as they bumped up and down on the trail, crinkling and crunching and making other such scratching sounds. Rusty was thankful the seats were padded, and also so high up. He listened to the assortment of dry sedges getting flattened under the weight of the buggy's jumbo-jet tires as they rolled across the spongy earth.

At the same time Huddy's gaze seemed lost in the canopy, Rusty's father was looking down into the thickness of the brush. "See that," he pointed towards the thicket.

"I'M LOOKING AT THEM," Huddy confirmed in his booming baritone voice as he leaned back as far as he could go, one hand on the roll bar his other on the crown of his head so as to prevent his hat from falling off; "— AND THEY'RE MAGNIFICENT."

Rusty kept looking up and down to see what the two men were looking at. How could it be that they were facing in two completely different directions? One man was *looking up* and the other man *looking down* — yet, quixotically, they seemed to be talking about the same thing. Rusty's father shifted the drive shaft and lurched the buggy in reverse. The engine squealed in protest at the sudden change in course, but quickly fell in line with a guttural hum. As for the passengers, not all were as quick to adjust.

"Whoa! Henry!" Sandy howled as he jostled back and forth in his seat. "— A *little warning* would be nice!" While Sandy Parrish wasn't a man you would describe as completely untroubled by surrounding events, his scientific inquisitiveness served as his natural antidote to the many distractions and petty grudges that so often afflicted quotidian thought. Part of his being caught off guard might very well have been attributed to his preoccupation in trying to identify rare plants hidden amidst the foliage they passed — a bounty of grasses, trees and air plants of every type.

The buggy momentarily stopped as Henry once again looked intently across the forest floor, *but at what?* Rusty tried to decipher what it could possibly be. His father's brow wrinkled a certain way when he was trying to figure something out, whether it be an engine problem or an intricacy on a map. All Rusty saw was a green thicket, a hodgepodge of temperate and tropical plants. Out of the corner of his eye he suddenly caught a glance of something, through a break in the greenery. Or was his mind just playing tricks? Then in a blink it was gone. It didn't help that his father had shifted the swamp buggy out of reverse and they were bouncing and bumping ahead back up the trail. Tate sloppily swiped out some chaw from underneath his lower lip and pinched more tobacco out of his pouch. He packed it against his gum as Huddy started mumbling a prayer towards the tops of the ancient trees.

> "I AM UNWORTHY.
> UNWORTHY TO CAST
> A SHADOW IN THIS
> HOLY PLACE"

The buggy chugged along for a good while with nobody saying a word. The only sound came from the machine. The grumble of the engine. The slow churn of the wheels. Eventually Sandy spoke up. "Some pretty good shade here, Huddy. I guess I'd be remiss if I didn't thank you for leaving us *at least some* of the Virgins," Sandy smirked. He turned to Rusty with a coy wink as the baffled boy struggled to follow along. *"Old Growth shade,"* the plant aficionado effused, *"—It just don't get no better than that. Last of the Giants, Rusty."*

Huddy inhaled deeply, almost repentantly. He chose his words carefully. "LIKE YOU Doctor Sandy, I TOO AM THANKFUL for what is STILL LEFT."

The men's heads bobbed and weaved as the buggy bounced ahead. Everyone except for Huddy had to speak louder than normal to overcome the noisy racket of squeaking metal and rubber contorting against uneven earth. Tate turned around in obvious irritation at the tone of Sandy's remark as he pointed a threatening finger towards the unsuspecting botanist, *"— Now listen here you hypocritical son of a ..."*

Huddy silently and politely held up his hand to cut Tate off, not that he disagreed with the big man, but out of principle:

Huddy was a man that could fight his own fights, even if he was a peacemaker at heart. "YES, Doctor Sandy," Huddy confessed. "— IT IS TRUE. I did. CUT THEM DOWN." The low-decibel pitch of his voice vibrated off the trunks of the many giant trees. "—I cut them with THESE HANDS. THESE BONES. THIS FLESH." It wasn't apparent if Huddy was directing his comment at Sandy or pleading his case straight to the trees. "— Look upon us, OH LORD. And FORGIVE US for what WE DID."

The buggy abruptly dropped down at a gravity-defying angle. Rusty was convinced without a doubt that the buggy would tilt over, first on two wheels and quickly thereafter plop over on its side like a turtle stranded upside down on its shell. How could it not? The machine was tilted forty five degrees into a dinosaur-sized rut. The welded metal and oversized bolts croaked and moaned a cacophony of "*Errrrrrnt-crunk-ga-TONKs*" and other sounds like that. But if Henry was even the tiniest bit concerned, he didn't show it. Completely unfazed he continued to steer the buggy forward at the awkward slant.

Tate and Rusty grabbed tight onto the metal perimeter railing just in time as Sandy flung forward out of his seat toward a protruding metal joint. For a scary second it looked like it was going to end with a gruesome collision of hard steal puncturing soft flesh. Rusty took a moment to think about what they would do if Sandy, or any of them, actually did get seriously hurt. They were in the middle of nowhere. It was over a day's trip back to pavement alone, and a couple hours ride into town from there to the closest hospital. Injuries take on a whole new dimension in a wilderness so remote.

"Jesus Henry! Can you give us some warning on those ... *damned deep holes!?*" Sandy protested. "—And since when did this trail get so bad. I thought you were a better driver than that."

In complete contrast to Sandy, Huddy stood like a pillar, his boot soles welded to the metal deck. Rusty was shocked to see that he wasn't even holding onto the roll bar with his hands. Instead he had both arms raised high over his head, reaching upward, with his palms turned skyward to catch the light. As Rusty and Sandy braced with both feet and both hands with everything they had, Huddy stood immobile and immune to the commotion created by the high-seas jostling up and down and back and forth, anchored by a ballast somewhere deep in his soul; or was his sturdiness a secondary offshoot of his communion with the towering trees? What was clear was that Sandy's comment was still weighing on Huddy's mind. "—You should KNOW. When I CUT THOSE TREES. I did it with SOUND HEART. Papa, Uncle Lincoln and me, a MERE BOY. They were HARD days. The BEST PAY we could find. A DEAL with the Devil? Maybe. But it was MY LIFE. THAT KNIFE. EIGHT FEET LONG. RAZOR-SHARP TEETH. Other men GREW RICH on those trees. For us it was just an HONEST DAY'S PAY."

The buggy eased down into a flooded stretch of trail. Rusty turned back to watch the churned liquid rush to the side like the parting Red Sea; it was similar to the wake left behind by a motor boat revving full throttle up on plane across a saltwater bay although in this case it was much muddier and ten times more slow. Rusty continued watching until the turbid and tannic water retreated back into the center of the trail.

"At least he didn't steal no orchids!" Tate sounded back as he spat in his can, "— Don't take but elementary schoolin' to know orchids ain't replaceable, either." Loren "Gator" Tate was a big and burly man who had spent "the better part of half a century" trying to hack a living out of the swamp. The sum total of his efforts he had to show for it was his jerry-rigged backcountry camp, on land he didn't own, and a perpetual sense of optimism that things would always work out. Among Tate's favorite hobbies were chewing tobacco, whittling sticks and doing whatever it took to get under Sandy Parrish's skin.

"Tate, how many times do I have to tell you that *collecting specimens* isn't stealing!" Sandy professorially snapped back.

"A plant's a plant, ain't that right Henry," Tate said as he nudged at the ever diligent driver's side to confirm. "— Taking a thing like an orchid ain't moral. Them ain't ord'nary plants. If your gonna look at 'em close, seems kinda mean to pluck 'em and put 'em in some hothouse. Lazy as well."

Rusty spotted a red-shouldered hawk perched on sentry duty overhead at the same moment the buggy bulldozed through a tangle of branches that was blocking the path. The front grill and large tires of the machine easily obliterated the rotten wood with a cacophonous crunch followed by a series of snaps and pops, spooking the watchful raptor up and away out of sight.

"Jesus, Tate!" Sandy howled as shards of broken wood and leaves fell across the deck. "I can take your toothless accusations about my orchid research, but how about a little notice on the wood chunks catapulting us in back. The guy riding shotgun has responsibilities. If you're not up to them, get your fat ass back here so I can do the job!"

Tate's eyes bulged with fury. "Don't *yooouuu* tell me about pulling my fair share, Parrish! *I'll take it from a lot of people but not from no glorified orchid poacher!*"

Henry slowed the buggy down to honor Sandy's request, or was he stopping for something else? Rusty was puzzled to see his father once again studying the undergrowth in the adjacent woods. His brow raised and furrowed as he scanned for some mysterious quality in the bush. Rusty stood up on the bench in back to try to catch a glimpse for himself without any luck. As far as he could tell there wasn't anything unusual there — just the giant tree trunks, interwoven spirals of palmetto fronds, a cornucopia of bromeliads and an assortment of other flora. More and more, thanks to his father, he was able to identify many of the plants by their common, and sometimes their scientific, names: muhlenbergia, cardinal plant, hymenocallis, Caroline's Wish and resurrection fern just to name a few in view.

Then he saw it!

It was blurry and fleeting but sure enough there it was, and then in an instant it was gone; or was it ever there even at all?

...

Tate was happy as a clam at his success in getting under Sandy's skin. He spat victoriously off the side of the buggy. "A little hard to cast that first stone when ya live in a glass house, *ain't it Parrish?*" Tate admonished. "— With all your egg-headed book learning I'd of thought you, of all people, would be the first to understand there ain't no difference between orchid thieving and cutting old-growth out of these woods. Lord knows the Parrish clan made a lot more cash off of harvestin' orchids in Homestead than fishin' Mullet down in Snake Bight."

Rusty attention was momentarily distracted by two deer grazing in the distant prairie when, in his peripheral vision, he spotted an approaching curtain of vegetation barreling towards them from overhead. "Take cover!" Rusty warned as he ducked down.

"Oh, that t'aint nothing," Tate laughed with reassurance as the dangling curtain of greenery gently fanned across everyone's heads. "—Just a bunch of Spanish Moss. Soft as a baby's behind."

Sandy grabbed a piece to show Rusty the subtle intricacy of the plant.

"Well there you go at it again," Tate mocked. "More *specimen collectin'* I suppose."

"At least I didn't hunt gators to extirpation." Sandy acerbically bit back. He turned to Rusty with an *"oops look"* on his face as if he had just let a poorly kept secret out of the bag. *"— You know that's how he got his name."*

"Not true!" Tate countered with grave offense. *"—* You know that's a lie Parrish! I hunted gator, but we was doin' like we always done. We never shot out all the gators in a hole. I t'werent no glorified Wild West buffalo hunter shooting crocs from the back of the caboose for kicks." Tate turned attentively to Rusty to set the record straight, talking to him in a hushed voice. *"Shush, everybody knows the name Gator don't mean nothin' in these parts.* If I had a nickel for every feller in Florida named 'Gator', I'd be a millionaire by now."

"Millionaire?" Sandy snidely remarked. "—Sounds like another one of your failed *'get-rich'* schemes to me. And that your side-stepping the issue, too."

"Maybe my momma gave me that name, Parrish," Tate speculated in his own defense. "—Maybe it happened so long ago I *plumb forgot*, ever think about that?"

"More like *repressed*," Sandy corrected as he eased back horizontally on his cushion to watch the passing treetops with a satisfied expression of a man that had won. "I don't blame ya, Tate," he added. *"—* I would've learned to block it out, too, if my conscience was saddled with the long list of crocodilian atrocities you've committed."

Sandy seized the moment of silence that followed to set the story straight on the sanctity of his own ecological ethics. "And for the record, every orchid I sell *in town* is an orchid that doesn't get *pilfered* out of the swamp. Sure I make a profit, but I fixed the problem. And I also give back fifteen percent. Market solutions save ecosystems, not good intents. The road to perdition is paved with 'em ya know."

Out of nowhere Huddy spoke up in Tate's defense. "WELL, if that's the case, the way I REMEMBER IT, if there is ANY ONE person to THANK for SAVING the VIRGINS that are LEFT: That person would have to be Loren GATOR Tate."

"What!!!!" Sandy clamored as he clutched at his hat, "— Thank Tate, um, *forrrrr what!?* Showing up *too late* maybe.

Huddy, you know better than anybody that most of the virgin groves were clear cut by the time Tate reported for work."

The big man was delighted by Huddy's unexpected gesture of gratitude. Rarely one to smile, Tate's face lit up to reveal a malformed set of discolored and missing teeth. *"Now you listen to Huddy,"* Tate joyfully jowled as he spat tobacco juice on a frond as it passed by. "Ya see, the name 'Gator' is an honorarium, my red badge o' courage, and I wear it with pride." Tate looked up and squinted at a sunbeam shining through the foliage above. "Ain't sayin' I'm not guilty of some things, but it's easy to point the finger in retrospect if that's your game. Truth is, what Huddy and the rest of the lumbermen did with the cypress was our patriotic duty. It helped us win the Second World War."

"Did you serve overseas?" Rusty asked Tate, wondering if that's how he and his father met.

"No," Tate replied, "— The day after Pearl Harbor got bombed I tried to volunteer, but I was too busted up. Bad knees. The government said my experience as a citrus farmer in on the Lake Wales Ridge would be enough. Orange juice was a prized wartime commodity for feeding the troops. Problem was — after the Saint Nicholas Freeze of '40 and Canker Blight o' 41 near wiped out every tree in the groves I worked — they had no choice but to let me go. That's how I found my way south and picked up work with the logging operations. Once J.P. Hackett saw that I knew how to run a crew, he made me a saw boss out here. Little bit o' luck didn't hurt neither after the previous saw boss, what's his name, got mauled by a bear and quit."

Sandy leaned over to Rusty to try to explain: "That guy J.P. Hacket they're talking about. He was the foreman for the logging mill, a business interest of the big guy up top, Mr. Gilchrest, himself."

"Mr. Gilchrest?"

"That's right. Claude Gilchrest, he was sort of the king around here," Sandy offered. "—He pretty much owned the *entire* swamp. He had a vision of turning this place into 'The Detroit of the South.' He wanted to build a factory town along the Trail and ship cars 'round the world out of Port Miami. It certainly didn't turn out that way, but his family owns plenty of real estate."

"Emperor CLAUDIUS, we used to CALL HIM," Huddy recalled.

Sandy nodded. "He'd strategically buy land, build roads and circumvent the competition. He started in the twenties hawking his 'Swamp Paradise' on street corners in Miami. He bought hundreds of thousands of acres after the bust. Folks laughed then."

"Anyhow," Tate continued. "J.P. was quick to hone in on my skills. Had I'd gotten in earlier and played my cards right, I would've easily worked my way up the corporate chain at the mill in Perry and that's a fact. But the logging business was long in the tooth by the time I showed up. We was at the cusp of either cuttin' 'em all down, or trying to save what was left. Somebody had to speak up. But Ol' J.P., no, he didn't like my proselytizing one bit. He tried to quiet me down by agreeing to bring it up to the board but it didn't take me long to see he was draggin' his feet. That's when I took matters in my own hands with the Audubon folks and, for that matter — purty much anybody who'd listen." Tate paused as a light went off in his head. "Oh yeah, that's right!" he said with a victorious thrust of his finger in the air as the distant memory roared back. "J.P. about flipped his lid when I brought up saving the Danforth Tract: *What's your deal, Lorenzo!? You just won't quit will ya? You're like a damned alligator that's got ahold of something and just won't let go 'til it gets beat with a shovel.'* After that nobody called me Loren anymore. Everybody just called me *'Gator Tate.'*"

Huddy's shoulders shuddered a bit as he let go a laugh. "Remember the meeting where J.P. got SO MAD at you he THREATENED to cut you IN HALF with the WHIPSAW if you talked about it ANOTHER PEEP!"

Tate chuckled. "He was a hard nut to crack, alright. But he come around. At the Langford Lumber Christmas pary in '56 J.P. pulled me into a corner and confided to me that he was gonna talk to the board before operations ceased the next year. Not that there was all that much left. Just a couple minor groves and the Danforth Tract."

Rusty definitely liked that version of how Tate got his name better, but he still wasn't sure — not that he had all that much time to think: the buggy accelerated down into a mini-canyon where it splatted as it bottomed out. The machine's frame rattled and moaned as it contorted over the rocks. They were now entering a straight stretch of trail. The rubber nobbies of the giant wheels gripped the uneven limestone and smashed down knee-high grass. The men were looking in every direction — except for Rusty's father, of course. Predictably he was once again scanning at ground level. *But for what?*

"Ya know, I guess in my own small way I did help play a role in savin' what's left," Tate mused in the softer and more conciliatory tone of a man who understood he'd been bestowed an individual accolade he didn't fully deserve. "Truth be told, it took many people — *not just me* — to save the trees." Tate reached back for the roll bar so he could better explain. "A lotta fellers died working these trees. It was dangerous work but it helped us win the war."

"Did you know anyone personally that got killed cutting the cypress, Mr. Tate?"

Huddy spoke up before Tate could process the thought. "My Uncle LINCOLN ... He DIED cutting the trees ... CRUSHED between two logs ... SQUEEZED to death while he was HOOKING the BIG LOGS on THE CRANE."

"Lincoln was one hell of a log dogger, lightning fast! But sometimes a man ain't fast enough," Tate added gravely.

"It's been FORTY YEARS," Huddy confirmed. "— I'm OLD ENOUGH to be his FATHER now."

"Yeah, time flies, sure does," Sandy whimsically sighed as he watched the scenery go by in reverse. "About feels how long we've been on this trail."

Huddy continued: "FUNNY how I can FEEL his EYES looking DOWN on me. AFTER ALL THESE YEARS not a day passes that I DON'T FEEL THEM. Up there with SWEET JESUS. Up in the CLOUDS. Like I'm still a LITTLE LAMB. Like I'm STILL a lost CHILD."

"That was a sad, sad day," said Tate. Rusty noticed the burly man's eyes moistening and a quivering in his jaw. "I had to go to the quarters and let Huddy's father know that Link was gone." Gator Tate nudged Henry on the side and made a gesture for him to stop. Henry cut the engine. "Okay, gentlemen," Tate said in as best as he could muster a magnanimous tone. "I'd like to propose that we all bow heads in a moment of silence for Lincoln ..."

He turned to Huddy for clarification. *"Was the last name Johnson?"*

Huddy nodded that it was.

"Then a moment of silence it is, for Lincoln Johnson!" Tate officially announced.

Everyone put their heads down to show their respects. Rusty listened to the wind blow through the leaves and the fronds but it was mostly silence. Nothing else. The branches creaked slightly as they gently swayed back and forth. Out of nowhere, a giant bird landed with great force on a tree above them prompting everyone to look up. It was a pileated woodpecker. The bird hammered with its beak and ripped off giants chunks of the bark. Tate ended the moment of silence as the black white and red plumed bird flew away, humbly mumbling an Amen and making a sign of the cross. One by one the other men put their hats back on. Henry turned the key and the engine rumbled back to life. Once again they were rolling forward up the trail.

•••

The perpetually-lounging secular professor sang out a light-hearted "Halleluiah" to the minor victory of finally getting back on track and moving up trail — not that he was completely off the hook. Huddy had a question specifically for him that really put him on the spot, "—So, Doctor Sandy, if you don't see the FACE OF GOD, what do you see when you LOOK UP at the trees?"

The inquiry seemed to genuinely catch Sandy off guard, a somewhat surprising reaction considering he was the person who started the conversation with his sarcastic allusion to Huddy's previous life as a sawyer decades ago. Sandy was never one to rush out an answer without letting it soak in and stew around for a while. He joined his hands behind the back of his head in a relaxed semi-inclined state of deep thought. A minute or so down the trail Sandy was ready with a response.

"I guess when I look up, the thing I see most is ... *trees.*"

"Well duh," Tate mocked.

"*Tall* trees," Sandy specified.

"There ya have it folks! Truly profound insight. And how many years of schoolin' did it take you to come up with that?" Tate scoffed as he rolled his eyes.

"And all about five hundred years old."

"*What!!!! Only five hun'ert year's old!? That's a bunch of bunk!*" Tate spewed. A steady drip of tobacco drooled out of his mouth and down his double chin. "*Five hun—? How does that explain the Tyrannosaurus Rex hip bone I have in front of my camp?*"

Sandy sighed condescendingly. "Tate! That ... chunk ... of: How Many Times Do I Have To Tell You! It's nothing more than a slab of limerock that got wedged up in the roots of a felled pine tree. Probably from the Labor Day Storm of '35."

Tate's ears flattened. *"Noooo,"* he said defensively. *"I even showed it to ..."*

"I don't care if you showed it to *Charlie* for cryin' out loud!" Sandy sang out at the top of his lungs. "It's a proven fact: all these trees started growing on the same day, week or year ... about a half a millennium ago, underneath of which, if you core down into the peat — *and I have* — there's a thick layer of ash?

"That's right," Tate defiantly shot back, detecting an opportunity to use Sandy's new information to support his own mis-interpretation of the facts. "That's the ash from the meteor God used to kill the dinosaurs off ... some forty thousand ... forty thousand ... four thousand ... years back. Just like the Bible says." He shook his head at Rusty in disbelief. "Five hun'ert years old. What a bunch of balarky! That's ridiculous!"

Ready to go to any length to prove Sandy Parrish wrong, Tate used his fingers as a primitive math device to countdown the centuries five hundred years back. "Eighteen hun'ert ... okay, um ... seventeen hun'ert ... and then ... um ... sixteen hun'ert ... *fifteen hun'ert. Ah ha!* I get it Sandy! I see what you're tryin' to say — the ol' 1492 Columbus sailed the ocean blue — *But you're wrong. Dead wrong. I'm a lot smarter than ya think."*

Rusty still didn't get it. 1492? "Huh?"

"Sandy's got Chris Columbus and Johnny Appleseed all mixed up in his head," Tate wheezed into Rusty's ear, under his breath, before turning back to Sandy to more formally refute. *"Soooo,* let me get this right. According to your theory, the first thing Ol' Columbus did when he floated over on the Mayflower was *plant* a bunch of cypress trees?" Tate chortled at the absurdity. *"—Like that makes any sense."*

Sandy shook his head with a measure of admiration. "Actually Tate," Sandy jibbed, "—that's not bad. Other than Columbus never stepping foot in, *ahem,* Florida, and oh yeah, by the way, it was the Pilgrims, *ahem,* not Columbus who sailed over on the Mayflower, and they landed in, *ahem,* Cape Cod, not Florida. But, wow, I have to hand it to you Tate, you're pretty darn close. Quite honestly, I'm Impressed."

"I don't like your haughty tone, Parrish!"

"I'm sorry, Loren. I don't mean to jerk your chain. It's just the Caloosa Indians lived here for thousands of years. And then we come over for what, the past few hundred, and mess it all up."

"What side of history are you on anyhow, Sandy?" Tate interrogated suspiciously. "— Sounds like the traitor side. We won the war fair and square and that's a fact."

"The war?"

"The Indian wars, Seminole War, Boulder Ridge ... you name it."

"But Boulder Ridge was a ..."

"Don't try to trip me up with details, Parrish. The truth is ..."

"The truth is irrefutable, and quite sad," Sandy cut in. "Most Native American civilizations were crippled by the microbial storm we brought over, not any war heroics on our part."

"*Storm?*" Tate queried. "You ain't talking the Labor Day Hurricane of '35?"

"Tate, I'm talking about smallpox, influenza, and all the other diseases we introduced to the shores of the New World."

Gator Tate shook his head with a pitiful look. "Sandy, there you go re-gurgle-atin' more of your nonsense from your high falutin' books. It's all a bunch of hooey. And you cain't prove none of what you're sayin', neither. At least I got a dinosaur bone to back me up."

Sandy threw up his hands in defeat. "Well fellas, you can lead a mule to water but you can't make him drink."

"You callin' me a jackass, Parrish!?"

"All's I'm saying is these trees are about all the proof you need," Sandy said pointing up. "Whether you accept it or not, Loren, that's your choice. The truth is the Indians extensively burned. The same way we spread fire across the hunting grounds to flush up new growth and attract the deer, the Indians did the same *just on a much larger scale.*"

Tate shook his head pridefully but didn't say no.

"Everything we're looking at used to be fire-swept prairie and open herbaceous marsh," Sandy added. "And then came the Columbian Invasion. The disease. The collapse. Without regular fire on the landscape, that opened the door for the trees to *move in.*"

"*Moving Trees!?*" Tate's eyes lit up in victorious delight, "— Ha, I got ya! Since when did trees get feet? I rest my case!"

Just in time Henry gave a shout for everyone to duck as — *Thwat thwat thwat thwat thwat thwat thwat* — the buggy barged through a tunnel of low hanging branches. From there the trail opened into an interior marsh. Rusty was more than a little baffled by the recent conversation, as was Huddy, too. "THE WAY you say it, DOCTOR SANDY," Huddy deliberated as he held one hand on the roll bar. "These GIANT TREES are nothing but a MISTAKE?"

"Kind of a letdown, don't you think?" Henry agreed. Up until that point it was unclear if he was even listening at all. Rusty's father was often like that. He'd let everybody say their peace first and then chime in with a conclusive thought at the end to tie it together. "— Gotta admit, as pretty as they look, it's a pretty sad story to know they got their start as *overgrown weeds.*"

"Overgrown WEEDS!" Huddy responded with a booming laugh, as if it finally clicked. "J.P. HACKET .... HA HA HA ... USE TO SAY the EXACT SAME THING ... HA HA HA ... That the TREES were NO BETTER than OVERGROWN WEEDS ... HA HA HA ... That the only reason GOD put them on EARTH ... HA HA HA ... was for man to CUT THEM DOWN ... HA HA HA ... just like WEEDS!"

Sandy was floored by the revelation. "*Did he really say that?* Wow! That's a significant historical point. He actually called the old growth trees ... '*Weeds?*' That's incredible, Huddy."

"I heard him call 'em that, too," Tate testified, "—But I'm purty sure he was just repeating what he heard coming down from the board in Perry. If they weren't making money off of them, they called them weeds. J.P. was a company man through and through."

"And Huddy, just to be clear on what you said earlier," Sandy tried to clarify, "— What was it, in your recollection, that Tate '*actually did*' — other than '*just talk*'— to deserve so much credit for saving the trees, *nickname not withstanding?*"

"Sandy I did plenty. As much as anyone. When my day came I took a stand."

"Gator, I don't doubt it. I just want to hear it from Huddy is all."

Rusty tucked his head down and grabbed hold as branches rubbed up against him on the inside of a tight bend. The more the men spoke, the more confusing the story got. As believable as Tate's story sounded, Sandy seemed skeptical and Tate slightly defensive as if something was being held back. Or maybe the entire story was made up. Or maybe the true answer, if an answer ever existed, was lost to time, forgot.

Huddy's face broadened into a bright smile. "WHAT DID HE DO? *Whhhhhaaaaat did heeee doooo!?* He SHOWED UP! That's WHAT! From that point FORWARD, we all knew the WHOLE operation was *CURSED!!!*"

Huddy erupted into booming laughter that filled the woods — "HA-HA-HA-HA!" — followed by the rest of the men infectiously joining in. Even Rusty found himself uncontrollably giggling, although he wasn't sure why or what about. Most perplexing of all was the unexpected sight of seeing the butt of the joke joyously chuckling along, too.

"Gotta admit myself," Tate confessed, "— Despite ample efforts to the contrary, I *never did* possess much of a financial magic touch."

"Good to see you ain't still bitter about your failed Frog LEGGZZZZZ scheme," Sandy snickered as he thought back to the low-budget TV commercial Tate had made to tout his fledging business. "That jingle at the end, *'Remember folks, that's Frog Legs with a ZEE-ee-e!'* was classic. Must have cost you a small fortune to get air time like that — during *Bowling for Dollars*. That was a prime time slot!"

"Market forces turned against me there, too. I can't deny that. And I only made matters worse when I doubled down as the market peaked." Tate snapped his fingers. "Then just like that, I lost it all when it collapsed — *purty much everything overnight.*"

The buggy chugged up the trail as they continued to talk.

"What in the hell were you thinking pumping your *whole nest egg* into Frog Legz?" Sandy pondered out loud while simultaneously stifling a laugh. "And if you didn't get it the first time," Sandy added, "— Remember folks, that's Frog Legz with a *ZEEee-e—e!!!*"

What at first had been funny seemed to stir up bad memories with Tate. He spat contemptuously into the passing brush.

"Now you shut your trap!" the big man aggressively barked. "Those TV and radio spots brought 'em in by the droves from the coast. Shoulda trademarked that jingle, too." In a huff Tate

turned back and feigned using the roll bar as a barrier to prevent him from attacking the botanical whiz. "Not everybody has life served up on a silver platter for 'em, Parrish. Some of us gotta *take risks* — and some of them sizeable — if we aim to sock away any cash. *Ain't that right, Henry?*"

It was unclear if Henry heard — let alone agreed — with Tate's question, possibly explained by his concentration on maneuvering along a complex series of turns on the trail. In the meanwhile, the initial wave of bitterness having passed, Tate had been overtaken by the spellbound look of a never-say-die entrepreneur who still had work to do: a man who judged his success more by the grandeur of his dreams than the economic outcome or any financial rewards. He was an idea guy first and a schemer to the end. Decades after its demise, in his mind his Frog Legz vision was all still within reach, his eternal muse. "— *Her* ... I mean ... them frog Legz were the most *beautiful thing*. I can still see 'em now." He stretched his arm out and groped at the air with a bedazzled look. "Had stores on *both coast* when my operation was at its peak."

"He means *stands*," Sandy interrupted to differentiate the subtle — yet important — point, for the record, just in case anybody was taking notes.

"And a *vertically-integrated* business model, too." Tate boasted. "The only thing I regret is ..."

The conversation was suddenly cut off as the buggy bumped up and down through a labyrinth of deep ruts. The wheels spun violently before gaining traction and resuming ahead. Rusty's father veered the buggy to the edge of the trail so that the wheels on the left were in the middle of the cobbly rut and the other two on the right were angled up on more stable land. Once again, he was slouching in his seat and looking just over the palmettos at something he saw, *but what?* Finally this time Rusty saw it, too! It was the faintest wisp of smoke, and then in a flash it was gone. Or maybe Rusty was imagining things, again. Henry carefully maneuvered the giant machine to traverse a fallen pine tree, first rolling over the front tires and following up with the back. It reminded Rusty of the speeds bumps in town only ten times as high.

By the time they were back on even ground the conversation had changed. This time Rusty's father took the lead. "Okay, Okay Okay. I wouldn't be deifying or demonizing anybody for anything that did or didn't get left behind," he said as if to set the record straight. "Truth is, the tracts that got saved, those trees weren't very big. And the ones they did clear cut, they're growing back."

"Man, just think about it," Sandy said in amazement of the full sum of the conversation and the grandeur of the view as it rolled past. "A man like Claudius Gilchrest. One man, he owned the entire swamp ... *all the way to the coast.*"

"*EMPORER CLAUDIUS,*" Huddy nostalgically concurred. "That's how we THOUGHT OF HIM back in the days when I still swung the ax."

"And a *benevolent ruler he was,* too," Tate added. "He let us be, let us have the run o' these woods."

"Robin Hood and his band of merry misfits and outlaws," Sandy said under his breath.

"There is no LOVE like that from a FATHER who gives you THE KEYS to HIS KINGDOM and lets you DO AS YOU PLEASE," Huddy bellowed as he stared up in the trees.

Once again the buggy hit a rocky stretch. All the men except Huddy grabbed on for dear life. Rusty was still trying to process everything the men said as he gripped on tight. All the new information was interesting but distorted his understanding of the swamp and, more than that, who his father was. He'd always thought of his father as the highest form of royalty in the swamp, maybe not its ruler but definitely an archduke or equivalent rank, and definitely not an outlaw. His father didn't wear a gold crown or parade around with a scepter staff or have papers decreeing it all his own, but nobody knew the country better, to him not a single square inch of its endless miles seemed unknown. He tried to imagine what Emperor Claudius looked like and what he saw when he first arrived, presumably by boat, to stake out his claim, and wondered in awe how any one man could ever manage to purchase so much land.

•••

As the buggy slowed to a stop Rusty's father jerked it into reverse. Rusty saw it coming this time and braced himself, but to the ever-lounging Sandy it once again came as an unwelcome surprise. *"Henry, for the love of God!"* the irritated passenger yelped. *"—Can you once and for all please tell us what in the criminy you're stopping to look at!?"*

Henry shut off the engine and turned back.

"Didn't anybody else see the extinguished campfires?"

"Campfires?"

"That's right," Henry confirmed. "—I counted no less than nine of them coming up the trail."

In a moment of clarity Rusty grabbed hold of the roll bar and hoisted himself on the bench. Just out past the bend he saw another plume of smoke. "There's another up ahead," he pointed enthusiastically if also a little perplexed. He had no idea what the presence of the campfires meant, good or bad, other than he was finally glad to learn what had been preoccupying his father's thoughts the entire ride up.

"Then there you have it," Henry declared, "— *Make it Ten.* Good to know somebody else is paying attention." Rusty couldn't help but notice a hint of admiration in his father's voice.

"Well I guess that means we have company," Sandy shrugged nonchalantly not thinking it to be a big deal. "After all it is the Round Up. Didn't really think it would be just us."

With the buggy once again moving forward Sandy picked up where the previous conversation left off. "The truth is, these trees would've come down, too. Could've cut them and milled them in the name of business to make an easy buck. But the big money wasn't in the woods anymore, it was along the coast. Cutting trees was small potatoes compared to building condos and strip malls and golf courses. The bigwigs diverted all their capital into that."

"Then, by the time they got around to returning to cut the rest of them down," Rusty's father chimed in to finish the thought, "—The Environmental Movement had taken root. In fact, it was those *same coastal condos* that brought the Tree Huggers in."

Sandy smiled at the irony. "Sort of backfired don't you think?"

Huddy shook his head at the absurdity of it all. "WELL ... Here's THANKSGIVING to ... WHO EVER ... or WHAT EVER ... saved THESE TREES. You can CALL them a WEED if you like, Doctor Sandy, or a MISTAKE ... But for the LOVE of SWEET JESUS ... and Uncle LINCOLN ... to me they are a FORETASTE OF HEAVEN."

The buggy rolled forward.

After a tense and sometimes baffling ride up, Rusty was finally starting to feel comfortable with the situation, the surroundings and his place among the men, maybe because he spotted the last — *the tenth* — campfire, maybe because he'd made his father proud. Whatever the reason, he was feeling a little more at ease to the point that without even thinking about it he spontaneously started whistling a tune with no idea what it was other than the notes seemed to naturally, musically, flow.

Rusty immediately stopped when Tate turned back with a flabbergasted look. "My God, that song! I haven't heard it in years!"

"Not since I was a boy," Huddy confirmed.

When Rusty shrugged obliviously — he hadn't the faintest idea what the song could be — his father piped in with the correct answer: "Of course it's *Rising of the Moon*;" not that he dwelled on it or wanted to discuss anything else. Something was bothering his father but as usual he didn't say what, and as usual it could be a list of any number of things: the impending arrival at their destination, the Round Up, or the unidentified guest who made the fires, or quite possibly it was something else — or maybe it was the whistling or that Rusty didn't know the name of the song? More than likely it was nothing at all. His father was a man of long silences and few words.

The good news was that they were getting close. It was easy to see they had entered a stretch of trail that was less traveled. The path looked more manicured and there were no ruts. Around the next bend there it was staring them in the face: a horizontal board nailed about fifteen feet in the air between two tall pine trees.

Across the wood plank it read "THE LODGE."

Chapter 3:
Danforth Takes Control

Jan 13, 1857

Danforth returns from the interior to a hero's welcome.

We look forward to finding out more in the days ahead. Danforth's insight into this country and its present situation, both military and economic, is deep. I cannot spare this man. His knowledge and talents are critical to the success of the mission here.

Jan 14

The men hang on Danforth's every word around the campfire.

Danforth elicits the help of a convalescing Simon to demonstrate how he thwarted an ambush from a savage dropping down from a branch overhanging the trail. Simon is unable to speak except for a pitiful croaking noise after Danforth's series of roundhouse flips and kicks to the ribs, culminating in a cartilage-cracking wrenching of his arm. Danforth opens his satchel to reveal several items the fleeing brave had left behind: a Spanish pistolera, a bag full of arrowheads, and a couple of trinkets made of obsidian and pearl.

Jan 15

I meet with Danforth to discuss business.

While the other men eat rations closer to that of the commoners, barely above the sustenance of the savages' corn or their malodorous meal of smoked mullet or snook, for me the duck is as satisfying to the stomach as it is salubrious to the mind. Tobacco and sour juice afterwards only heightens the delectable nature of the feast.

Jan 16

Ever the forward thinker, Danforth espouses the somewhat counterintuitive view that "settlements, not surveying" are most crucial to dismantling the Indian's supply line of smuggled goods. He alludes to the Armed Occupation Act as being key. They must be confident that the Army will support them at their homesteads. Arming the refugees and a sustained resettlement effort is our vital next step. Any offensive into the interior is premature until "ten times" the current settlers are in place to burn back and drain the thicket behind which the savages hide.

Jan 19
Danforth continues to promote the virtues of the Rapid-fire Rotary gun.

The weapon has received much acclaim for winning the peace on the Hobart Plain. Danforth and I raucously laugh amid a haze of swirling smoke as he describes the use of the weapon to kill seven savages in a single turn of the crank and putting the others into retreat. Just to think, the work of an entire platoon accomplished with a single twist of the wrist. Oh the marvels of this modern age!

Jan 22
Danforth again wins the shooting contest with ease.

On a challenge afterwards he splits a swamp apple from fifty paces off the top of Simon's head. Danforth credits his deft use of the weapon to the Kentucky frontier of his youth where he regularly relied on the arrow and bow's silent stealth to hunt small game as a result of most of the big game already being killed off.

Jan 23
Enjoying stewed duck and oysters with Danforth as we discuss our current situation.

Danforth gives me hope that we are "past the worst of it" and that "good days lie ahead." All indications are that Shadows Inside is ready to strike a deal. Meanwhile, Danforth's resettlement of the refugees has gone forward without a hitch thanks to a novel financial arrangement backed by the Harvie Trading Co. where he trades his pelts. While Danforth profits from the deal, he is also taking on most of the financial risk. Bottom line: the fort benefits without any direct expense to our books.

Feb 1

The Rapid-fire Rotary Cannon has arrived!

Simon demonstrates its proficiency by obliterating a nearby cypress tree, in the process killing a dozen birds, probably more. We all laugh heartily as the powerful kickback propels Simon backwards over the edge of the bluff onto a sulphurous mud flat. Upon regaining consciousness, Simon insists in his typical babbling that it was a cannon ball fired from the deck of a "Spanish Galleon" that knocked him out, and that further, he has knowledge of a plan by the pirates to overthrow the fort.

Feb 3

Shadows Inside again refuses the terms of the treaty.

The Great Chief's resolve is deep. He claims that his band of braves has not been involved in the recent skirmishes as he has relocated his people well beyond the Great Falls, a natural feature of great splenditude I have heard many stories about but never seen. In his own words, "— The white man's ink and paper might as well be words spoken into the wind that disappears as soon as it dries. All their promises are lies. It was here that we were born, that our navel was cut and with our blood dropping into the ground it made the land dear to us. We will never leave."

Feb 4

Yet another lightning strike on the East Tower.

Simon was knocked clear out of the tower and mildly singed, but it could have been much worse. Foster eventually finds him hanging upside down from the sharpened point of one of the palisades. Wiggins is soon on hand to administer salts to snap him back to life. I instruct Hardy to spread shell at the base to neutralize the polarity of the tower, a trick that I learned from Admiral Rowley's *Handbook of Physics and Control of Natural Occurrences*.

Feb 7

The column led by Kerr returns with devastating news.

The Rapid-Fire Rotary Gun fell overboard in a dangerous eddy not properly indicated on Stafford's map. This is a costly blunder which I will have to answer for. What good is such advanced weaponry without a good map!

Feb 8

Just when I begin to think conditions are improving, it turns out we are much worse off than I thought. We are spending too many resources defending the new settlers and too much of our rations feeding their mouths.

Feb 10

Simon has taken ill with two goose-egg size lumps on either side of his throat and a constant ringing in his ears. He resembles some phantasm of the deep. I have ordered the beleaguered lad quarantined in a windowless hut in the dunes by the lagoon until his symptoms subside.

Feb 13

Whooping cough runs rampant through the settlements.
The wicked cold weather is not helping in the least.

Feb 14

Simon's odd habit of lighting busk fires continues to unnerve the sickened camp.

He feeds the flame with feathers and other debris that he scavenges along the surf all hours of the day and night. Danforth's intervention with his tincture of natural remedies and mild opiates only seems to make matters worse.

Feb 15

I am awoken from a deep slumber.

Climbing the East Tower to have a better look, I am greeted by the sight of Simon dancing wildly around the pulsing flame and beating a drum. His words are incredibly clear considering the distance. "The Galleon's arrived! The Galleon's arrived!" he repeatedly moans as he paces back and forth along the water's edge. My gaze across the placid scene reveals only the glow of the moon and nothing else. "Some in chains, oh! The chains!" he continues to chant at the top of his lungs. "— Down down down, they drowned! Captor and captive, drowned by the long black chain! From the salty foam they rose! Give it 'em back that what ain't your'n! A throat they'll cut for every pound of gold you stole!"

Chapter 4:
Abandoned Ghost Town Gets New Life

Rusty couldn't believe they had finally arrived at The Lodge. Though he hadn't thought about it in a specific sense, a vague outline of the place had taken form in his head as they rode up the trail. His father told him that The Lodge was built in the days before the Tamiami Trail was even a thought. A relic of the Florida frontier. That image was pretty much obliterated the moment The Lodge came into sight. Instead of a picturesque alpine A-frame with a stone fireplace and an elk head mounted on the wall, Rusty found himself looking at a hodgepodge of materials and structures more notable for *not matching* than any one building standing out. It looked less architectural than an abstract piece of art: a quaint collage of incongruous angles beneath the patchy shade of towering trees. Building materials include two-by-fours, tin, ply board, brick, some recycled aluminum, and a spongy-looking white rock. The backwoods country club even had what appeared to be the green blaze of a golf-course fairway on the other side of a row of slash pine trees in back. After all the buildup about The Lodge and the Round Up, Rusty felt a little letdown. How many times had he heard in conversations prior to the trip how the Round Up was going to "settle things" and how it was "symbolic" they were holding it up at The Lodge? Instead it had the abandoned look of a ghost town from out West after the price of silver had collapsed; certainly not a venue for holding an important event. A bushy-tailed brown squirrel scrambled across the ground and then up a tree trunk and across a branch. It was The Lodge's only sign of life. Rusty shrugged to himself. Maybe sometimes you throw a party and nobody shows up. Not that he was complaining. He was happy with it being only them for now. They were probably just the first ones to arrive. That was probably part of the plan.

183

Tate was still laughing about the "fake panther" trick they played on him just after the entrance sign on their way in.

"We really got ya on that one! But don't ya worry. We get all the *new comers* on that. Ya t'weren't first and ya won't be the last."

"It's kind of a rite of passage," Sandy admitted. "A stupid rite of passage, but a rite of passage all the same."

"They say getting scared is as good for your health as a belly laugh," Tate continued, "— I read that in a magazine. I think it was in a *Man's Life*. Always had the best articles in there. Shame about it going out of print. Basically what it said was that getting chased by a wild animal, *and the bigger the better*, is actually good for ya. Helps free up the bad chemicals in your brain, stuff like that. So yeah, we have fun with it, but it also adds to the overall salubrious effect of being out in nature, too. And look on the bright side, now you can think of yourself as ... one of us."

Rusty was still a bit embarrassed. "So everybody gets fooled?"

"And trust me, most a lot worse," Tate chortled as he patted Rusty on the back. "— Wish I had a picture of everyone's face when we take 'em around that bend. Not everybody admits it, but they all get a pretty good jolt ... except for Old Man Hodge," Tate clarified at the end. "That mean ol' cuss ain't scared 'o nothin'."

"*Well of course not Albert Lee, you dimwit!*" Sandy howled. "Why would the man ever be afraid of something he built himself."

"Actually," Tate said a bit haughtily, "—that isn't a hun'ert percent correct. That wooden wildcat used to sit on top of Julius Silver's hardware store in Old Miami. Duffy got a hold of it after Julius passed, I think through Barb, who was pretty much liquitating everything she wasn't throwing out. Or maybe it was Jack Sprat, ya remember him? Anyhow, somehow it got saved and found its way out to The Lodge. Yes, it was Old Man Hodge who first nailed it to a tree. But it wasn't until Walter Gruman, *'Toots' as we all called him*, hung it from a cable and the modern-day incarnation started to take shape.

"TOOTS, yes indeed, he was a MIGHTY FINE harmonica player," Huddy reminisced. "NEVER heard a finer player before OR EVER SINCE."

"And then Eddie," Tate continued, "— he was the one that added the wood mask that gives it its real three-dimensional look. Um, oh yes, and then there was Melonie Robertson. What was it, five or fifteen years back, she gave it a fresh coat of paint?" Tate's eyes beamed as he expounded on the historical fine points and many ins and outs of the gag. "The trick is, just like we got you, first you gotta get 'em to bite on the whole *'rattlesnake country'* bit. Once I seen you looking down, you mightn't have noticed it, I sort of shifted to the left so I was square in front of ya. I seen some people do it without the opening part, but it never works out as good." Gator Tate paused as if he'd just struck gold with a new idea. "Ya know, now that we're on the subject, there's a side of me that thinks I should write it down in an instruction booklet, or maybe patent the design. I bet people'd pay good money for a trick panther of their own, don't ya think?"

Sandy's eyes rolled. "Given your marketing genius, Tate, I don't see what could possibly go wrong. It's a huge payday in the making. My only suggesting is that you consider calling it *'Panther Legz.'* Oh, and by the way," Sandy turned to Rusty to add, "— that would be Panther Legz *with a ZEE-ee-e.*"

Rusty half expected Tate to retaliate to Sandy's dripping sarcasm. Instead, the big man was enrapt in a gleeful trance as he juggled the scheme in his head.

Meanwhile, Rusty's father was already up on the front porch of what appeared to be the compound's main structure, or the sturdiest as least, with thick limestone walls capped off with a red tin roof. Typical of most camps his father had taken him to there was no lock or key at the front door, just a metal eyehole and a latch. With a flick of his finger and the tiniest push the screen door swung open and Henry walked inside. Tate hobbled up the stairs behind him, but quickly veered right towards an upright barrel at the end of the porch. *"Hooooo-eeee! Look-ee this!"* the big man exclaimed with delight as he lifted up the lid. "Ol' Albert Lee's got a barrel-full of possums and 'coons! Just the way we used to keep our meat pickled before refrigerators. Brings back memories, yessir!"

Tate pulled one of the alien-looking carcasses out of the salty brine by the tail just as Rusty approached, allowing the boy to get a glimpse of the gruesome scene within: a good dozen skinned mammals, possums, a squirrel, and possibly a raccoon all floating inside a salty broth. Rusty quickly backed away and went inside.

"Just US tonight, RIGHT?" Huddy tried to clarify.

Henry nodded. "And Vuke and Kleal if they show."

"*Vuke's coming?*" Sandy gaped. "— I thought he was *going away* for a while."

Henry eased over to the sink. It had an old-time spigot that you had to hand pump to get water to flow. A line of tin cups hung on little brass hooks on the wall. "Nope, that all blew over."

Sandy seemed skeptical. "A little too quick, don't you think? Considering the circumstances."

Outside Huddy and Tate could be heard debating the merits of preserving meat in brine. "YEP, Brings back LOTS OF MEMORIES ... MOST OF 'EM BAD."

"Speak for yourself, Johnson," said Tate as he reached down further in the barrel. "Something about pickled game just agrees with me, or maybe I just prefer those simpler times."

"PAPA bought us a fridge after a YEAR OR TWO in Hopeland," Huddy reminisced. "Been keeping my meat ON ICE ever since. TASTES BETTER."

Sandy reiterated his concern, "I just don't like it Henry. I'm tellin' ya, something just ain't ..." only to be drowned out by the squeaking of the metal lever. Henry continued to pump until a stream of water gushed out the iron spout. Once the water cleared, Henry filled up a cup and passed it to Rusty. "There ya go, take a drink."

"Drilled a deep well. Makes a difference."

The coolness of the water quickly gave way to bitterness as Rusty gulped it down. It didn't taste like normal water but Rusty didn't care. He was thirsty from the long buggy ride up.

Tate's eyes bulged with disapproval as he shuffled through the door. "T'aint drank water since ... *forever*, Henry. You know that."

Huddy didn't hesitate one bit. He guzzled his cup straight down and walked over for a second cup. "Been a LONG TIME since I tasted water THAT GOOD."

"Ohhh, awwwlllrright," Tate finally caved in. "— Give me a cup, for ceremonial sake." Execution of the seemingly simple act immediately stalled, not unlike a man afraid of heights trying to summon the courage to cross a suspension bridge. He pinched his nostrils as he brought the cup's brim trepidatiously to his lips like it was piping-hot soup, mostly slurping air. He struggled mightily to take even one sip.

"SO, just to be SURE," Huddy asked as he leaned against the counter and savored his cup, "—About HOLDING our LITTLE ROUND UP at THE LODGE. Old man Hodge *IS ON BOARD*, right?" Huddy turned to a conspicuously nervous Tate, "— I JUST want to BE SURE."

"Oh! Hello Mr. Hodge. Good to see you." Sandy sang out through the front door, "Not to worry, it's just me and the boys ... and *Loren Tate* inside. You do remember Loren *'Deer Guts'* Tate, right!?"

Rusty joined Sandy at the door to get a better look at the proprietor. To his surprise, nobody was there. Sandy nudged Rusty on the side to play along.

"Um actually, Albert Lee, Tate's in the back room, by the way, going through some of your things. I'm kinda surprised to see ya because, ol' Tate, the way he was talking, it sounded like you'd passed."

"That ain't true!" Tate hollered with a panic-stricken voice as he shakily spilled the inedible liquid out of his cup. "Mr. Albert, um, can you hear me out, um, about them deer guts," he stammered as he grabbed a rag to clean up around the sink. "— That was, um, a complete misunderstanding, I can assure you that I had no idea I was on your propitty."

Tate's burgeoning panic attack defused to confusion at the door. *"So, where'd he go? Where's Albert Lee?"* Tate asked as he looked around in every direction.

"Um, well, he was just there," Sandy shrugged in an effort to sustain the charade. "I guess he must've just stepped away, maybe *to get his shotgun.*" He nudged Rusty on the side. *"—Ain't that right?"*

"Shotgun!!! Man I knew coming out here was a bad idea," Tate gasped in a high pitched voice.

When the chorus of laughter broke out, Tate knew he'd been had. "Relax, Tate, would ya!? Albert Lee ain't here, at least not yet. *It's just us,"* Sandy confirmed as he followed Rusty's line of sight up towards the canopy, "—and that barred owl up in the tree."

"Hell Tate, it's been what, fifteen years, at least. Don't ya think ol' Albert Lee's done forgot about those deer guts by now? Yeah, it attracted a sow and her cubs, and he almost got attacked on his way to the outhouse, but he did survive."

"So he ain't here!?" Tate repeated, just to be sure. "—Thank goodness. But be careful, would ya. A fella my age don't need that type o' stress." The big man moved his hand to various parts of his chest in search of the beat of his heart, but unable to find it, settled on rubbing his stomach. "Say Huddy, how long ya think it'll be before we eat? The earlier the better for me."

Henry took the cue without missing a beat. The joking was done. Time was a-wasting and they had a lot to do. The men knew their roles. Huddy was in charge of chuck wagon, Sandy the lead on prepping the camp for the anticipated crowd, and Tate the point man on catching as many fish as he could from the bass pond out back, on the other side of the fairway, for Huddy to fry up. "Already got my shady spot picked out," the big man said as he excused himself with a tip of his hat, "— And in case you don't get a chance to see her yourselves, I'll be sure to tell ol' Gertie Gator you fellas said hello!"

Henry lit a cigarillo, deeply inhaled, then exhaled through his nostrils as he shook out the match. "Don't know if this is the end or the beginning," he said to Sandy. "— Might just be a little bit of both."

Chapter 5:
Lt. Thursby French Reports to Duty

Mar 1, 1857

A mirthful ray of hope penetrates the leaden skies of my war hardened heart.

Earlier today at the wharf I was overtaken by the sound of someone whistling the most mellifluous rendition of the old Irish tune *The Rising of the Moon* that I have ever heard. Perhaps the fair winds of good fortune have finally shifted our way.

Mar 3

It is with great delight that I make acquaintance of the whimsical whistler himself, a Lt. Thursby French. His papers show him to be a commissioned officer sent by the way of New Orleans with sealed orders from Washington D.C. His salary is to be paid in full straight from the War Department and at no expense to the fort — an unusual situation to be sure; but neither am I one to judge a gifted horse by its teeth. He is accompanied at all times by a shorter, dark and rather taciturn man named Guess, presumably his servant. Not unusual for a man of his rank.

I will allow him to settle in before finding out more.

Mar 5

French approaches me with an offer I cannot refuse:

As so it is, French will serve as the new cartographer and surveyor of the fort, in place of Stafford — effective immediately.

Mar 7

Am already having misgivings about my rash decision.

Staggering heat, torrential rains, and lack of normal geographic landmarks will surely foil any chance for French's success. The resurgent Indian attacks make it the worst time possible for bringing on a novice hand. French will soon discover the interior to be a desert of marshes and islands from which the Indians disappear and reappear like phantoms. The savage's have increasingly come to view surveyors, not soldiers, as the primary enemy they face by way of the invisible lines they cast over the land. The Indian name for survey literally translates to "Shaman of the White Men's World." I fear French walks in the footsteps of Stafford in this regard, especially in light of his penchant to travel into the interior alone.

Mar 15
Lt. French arrival has been accompanied by a run of good luck.

Kerr reports the discovery of a rancid pile of dead animals on his most recent raid, a surefire sign of the Indian's descent from subsistence hunting to rapacious slaughter of their hunting grounds in order to satiate the smuggler's demands for pelts. Ford meanwhile returns to the fort with thirteen bottles of rum. I am convinced that the smuggler's introduction of liquor is playing a role in the savage's decline. I've ordered all contraband secured under lock and key with the other perishable goods.

Mar 17
It hasn't taken long for French to become a favorite among the men.

A week ago coming in first over Danforth in the shooting competition and now finding a sunken ship just south of the river's mouth, and to a tee almost at the exact same spot marked for its dangerous currents on Stafford's map. The naval brigade eagerly anticipates catching a glimpse of the wreck whenever patrols pass that way. Rumor has spread that it might be a Spanish galleon.

Mar 20
The men continue to find merry fishing for treasure at the wreck.

The water is so clear it appears only an arm's reach away — as if you could touch it — but a plumb bob lowered by Guess shows it to be five fathoms deep. Under French's direction the men use long ropes attached to a pulley and anchor with some success. A few gold doubloons, Spanish in origin, are recovered from the shallows nearby.

Mar 21
Simon is stung by a giant ray fish on a free dive down to the wreck. The poison appears to have entered his head judging from the resurgence of his cockamamie about an imminent pirate attack. He blathers on endlessly about a crew of skeletal pirates fast at work aboard the sunken galleon preparing to overthrow the fort led by a "Big Man with a Black Hat."

Mar 22
French is paying the men in equal shares for the full bounty of everything they pull up, redeemable from the U.S. Treasury directly to each man or a named heir upon completion of their tour of duty.
I have never seen the men's morale so high.

Mar 25
I run into Danforth by chance at the settlements this morning.
He is leisurely enjoying a smoke with his sister Gwynne, her husband Isaac and their six children who hail from their homestead near Fort King. Isaac resembles Danforth but lacks his easy manner. He has the habit of eating palmetto berries, a rancid fruit that he cannot stomach. Soon enough the conversation turns to the wreck. Danforth calls the whole situation a "distraction to the fort's mission" and speculates it to be nothing more than an "old slaver ship that got pushed off course by a storm and stranded on a shoal." He ends on the practical point that "the resources of the fort are best used fighting the savages, not scaring up some sunken ship's curse." He also questions the legality of French's promises on the salvaged items and is deeply suspicious of Guess.

Mar 27
Why Guess doesn't bother me more I am at a loss.
Judging from the chestnut color of his skin he is obviously part Indian, and thus technically-speaking an enemy of the fort. I had initially thought him to be no older than Simon as judged by his height until hearing his deeply resonate bassoon of a voice; I am now of an opinion that he is older than me. He

appears to understand English quite well, although he and French always speak in the heathen Muskogee tongue. French's reputation and rank protects the half-breed for now.

Mar 30
More rumors about French are starting to spread throughout camp.

Kerr spotted him talking to a group of wandering Indians from the distance on the North Bluff, not a part of Shadows Inside's band of warriors but still a concern. Barton, a corporal from the mountains of North Carolina who understands some Cherokee, claims to have overheard French discussing with Guess the location of several more wrecks.

Apr 1
I arrive at the campfire to find a wooden mask being consumed in flames.

Hardy quickly fills me in on events: Simon had taken it upon himself to perform a rain dance around the campfire while adorning a mask he'd recovered from the wreck the fortnight before, partly in hopes of relieving the drought but mostly just for jest – and much to the merriment of the men – when an inebriated MacGraw, slurring his words, takes to chasing him around the campfire with a knife under the conviction Simon is one of Shadows Inside's braves. Danforth steps out of the darkness to quell the unrest, knocking MacGraw out cold with his fist and ripping the mask off Simon's face and throwing it in the flame. It is soon thereafter that I arrive and promptly start scribing Danforth's words as he addresses the men.

"I would've warned ya ... but looks like I missed me chance. Guess it never occurred to any of ya that stuff yer pullin' up from the wreck might be cursed, did ya!? HA! That ain't just any old wreck, I'll have ya know: It's the doomed slaver ship from some two centuries back. 1685 was the year to be exact. Sailing out of Curacao bound for New Orleans from the Bight of Benin. No that ain't any ol' boat! It was captained by none other than Dutchman Davey himself." A chatter breaks out among the men the moment they hear the name, followed by a whimpering voice "— Di-Di-Did you say Du-Du-Dutchman Da-Da-Davey?" "THAT'S RIGHT!" Danforth barks back. "How y'all feelin' now knowing ya messin' with the Dutchman's ship? Ya know he don't take no prisoners. *All of ya and any of ya, he'll take ya down with his ship!"* Contrary to the other men's reaction, Simon takes delight in what he hears, as it serves to vindicate his sanity and validate his claims of repeated sightings of pirate in recent months. As if often the case around campfires, Danforth's voice starts to mimic the tenor and tone of the fabled captain he is talking about as his story resumes. "The Gulf ... oh, me safe harbor ... we'd made our port ... oh, the Gulf, it looked placid enough ... TOO PLACID ... That's when the patch of blue sky above us raced north OUT OF SIGHT and an UTTER DARKNESS from the South swiftly grabbed us by the throat. Gentle swales at first. Just a gentle bump EVERY HOUR on the nose. Oh, but how they grew! Five, Ten, Twenty, FORTY, A HUNDRED FOOT SEAS. ROGUE WAVES crashing in from left and RIGHT. There was no longer UP or DOWN or NORTH or SOUTH it was just a Wall of Water and Wind, the Eye of God, a Vengeant God, maybe even the DEVIL himself!" A voice in the darkness fretfully pipes up. "But Di-Di-Di Captain Davey actually escape?" Danforth shakes his head in condemnation like he knows the answer but isn't of a mind to give it away: "I guess we'll be finding out shortly, wont we, now that ya'll gone messin' with his ship."

Chapter 6:
Reunion with Big Elmer

1 pm

As inexplicably as it had previously entered his head, just as quickly it was gone. No matter how hard he tried, Rusty was unable to replicate the mysterious song he had unwittingly whistled on the ride in.

Tate sang along gleefully to the Rusty's failed attempt: *"Camp town races here we come, doo-da doo-da.* Always loved that song. Brings back memories when I was a boy and my Uncle Arby used to whistle that tune when he took me to the track. But he'd only whistle if he'd won. I learned a lot of cuss words from him when he didn't."

"Hey, let's not forget about Rusty," Sandy interrupted. "Wouldn't be right to just leave him sitting around."

"Good point!" Tate sang out in high spirits. "How about we post Rusty up the trail so he can get Vuke and Kleal on the panther trick as they turn up into camp."

"That's the dumbest thing I've heard come out of your mouth all trip ... *so far,*" Sandy scoffed. "First off, I'll believe it when I see it if they show, and second off, they'd probably open fire with a gun."

"At the panther? Yeah, that would be a shame to mess it up."

"NO! You idiot. Not the panther. *At Rusty!*"

"Oh, I didn't mean it like that," Tate embarrassedly reassessed as another idea went off in his head. He turned to Rusty. "How 'bout ya join me at the fishing pond with a pad of paper and pen? If you know how to write, I have a hun'erts of ideas in my head."

"Maybe it's better if Rusty shadows me?" Sandy offered as a better alternative. "— I'll fill you in on the fine points of running

194

this camp. No time like the present to pass information down from one generation to the next."

"WHY NOT give him a REAL JOB," Huddy broke in. "The runway's all overgrown. It definitely needs to be MOWED?"

Runway? Did he say ... *runway?* All of a sudden it clicked. So that's what the long linear stretch of bright green lawn was. Not a golf course. In hindsight it made perfect sense. Anybody who wanted to shoot a round of golf would surely do so at any one of the dozens of new golf courses in town by the coast. But a runway seemed almost as farfetched. Who in their right mind would try to land a plane way out in a place like this, so far in the middle of nowhere? Not that Rusty had much of a chance to think it all through. He was hustling as fast as he could just to stay even with Sandy. Despite his laid-back demeanor the entire buggy ride up, Sandy Parrish ambled ahead effortlessly. If you had to pick an animal he most closely resembled it would be a great blue heron or a wood stork thanks to his disproportionally long and bony legs. It was a characteristic that probably went hand in hand with him being such a good botanist — helping him see above and walk through the tall cord grass. "First thing first, we'll need some gasoline," Sandy explained as he led the way. "Always amazed how Albert keeps this place up. He's ... getting up there in the years. He's gotta be ... in his ... eighties ... I guess ... but still going stong. Albert is not one to go Gently into that Good Night." The tenor of Sandy's voice changed as he recited something from memory, "— *Old age should burn and rave at close of day, Rage, rage against the dying of the light.*" Sandy stopped and looked at Rusty. "You ever read any Dylan Thomas?" Not that he gave him all too long to respond. "Well you should, put it on your list," he said and quickly returned to walking at his fast pace as he recited another line of the poet's work:

> *"Though wise men at their end know dark is right,*
> *because their words had forked no lightning they*
> *do not go gentle into that good night."*

At the machine shed Sandy picked up a gas can and gave it a shake. On the other side of the dilapidated outbuilding Sandy swung open a heavy door to reveal a huge contraption of green metal several feet across. "Not exactly your average everyday backcountry camp generator. It's the closest thing in these parts to Okeechobee Power and Light. Down the way, over there, it's even wired in to Tinker's Camp, too."

"Who is Albert Lee Hodge? And why is Tate so scared of him?" Rusty asked just as Sandy pulled on the cord to the generator. It took four yanks to bring the machine to life. Sandy nudged the choke back to adjust the engine to a higher pitched and less rumbly sound. "Last ... *vrumm* ... of a dying ... *brum* ... breed," Sandy shouted back above the din of the engine to explain. "The thing about Albert ... *vrumm vrum* ... long before the Trail ... *grumble brum* .... and then once they subdivided ... *rumble vrum* ... that was back in ... *wrum brum.*"

The racket from the generator dropped off as they rounded the corner towards another structure, a lean-too with three sides open and a row of covered equipment lined up in back, except for a gap. "Hmmm, the mower's missing." Sandy seemed momentarily caught off guard but just as quickly gathered his thoughts. "Bet it's down at Tinker's camp."

"Actually, I think I saw it at the end of the strip," Rusty recalled.

"Hmmm, that means somebody is here. All the same. Well, just to be sure let's fill up this can with gas."

"And how about the key?" Rusty added.

"It's in the ignition. This far out in the country you put the key any other place and it'll just get lost."

...

Rusty had never mowed a lawn before, let alone an airstrip. He was honored to have the responsibility but felt a little overwhelmed, too. "And don't forget to also sweep for rocks," Sandy instructed him as he walked away. "It's gotta be smooth as a baby's behind for ... *ahem* ... our special guest of honor ... *ahem* ... flying in."

Rusty was truly perplexed: what could be so important or urgent that somebody would be crazy (and rich) enough to fly an airplane out to such a remote camp? Trying to land a plane in the middle of the woods seemed dangerous. Even with the gators and snakes, the ground was definitely a much safer route. Maybe the guest of honor was Charlie. Or maybe Charlie was the one who'd driven the mower to the strip. Rusty recalled how Huddy had said that Charlie had already passed through when they picked him up the day before, so maybe he was the one lighting campfires along the way to The Lodge? Or was it Mr. Hodge? Not that any of it made any sense.

Halfway to the riding mover Rusty met up with Gator Tate on his way to the pond.

"Here, let me give you a hand with the can," Tate offered as they crossed paths.

"No, I got it," Rusty waved him off. "— This is my job."

"That's the spirit! Gotta take care of yourself out here," Gator said with a big pat on the back. "—We call it *rugged Individualism.* It's what spending time in the woods is all about."

Rusty nodded over to the fishing hole. "So, how many fish do you think you can catch?"

"Well, I reckon as many as we need. But you know the old Indian sayin': *Gator don't eat all the fish in the pond.* I use the same principal when I go fishin'." Tate nodded his head toward the rather large reptile floating twenty feet away, "— T'aint that right Gertie! Us gators we both think alike!"

Rusty was surprised by the size of the creature relative to the pond. Gertie looked huge. Or maybe the optical illusion was the other way around. Perhaps the pond was just that small. If he could find a loose rock he could easily throw it from bank to bank. Unfortunately there were no loose rocks to be found. The rock that he saw exposed at the small lake was a contiguous slab that he'd need a hammer to chip a piece off. It was a bit ironic to Rusty as well, thinking back: despite buggying through an endless series of giant puddles and low-lying cypress forest on their trip to the The Lodge, this dinky little pond was probably the deepest open water body he'd seen in two days. "And believe it or not," Tate marveled, "—This here fishing hole is as deep as the Big O ... in most spots."

Rusty's recollection of airboating on Lake Okeechobee — was it two trips back? — was still vivid in his mind. They went so far out they completely lost sight of the bank, the only thing they could see was water and sky. "But Lake Okeechobee, I was out there with my father. It's more like a *bay* than it is *a lake.* It must be a thousand times the size."

"But shallower than Gertie's pond," Tate marveled. "—And that's a fact. The Big Lake actually used to be the source of this here swamp, until the engineers walled the thing off. Sad really. Farmers get rich and us swamp rats get stuck with what's left." Tate continued. "Anyhow, to make a long story short. Albert

Lee and his daddy dug this fishing hole to harvest the fill for the runway, plus used some extra rock to fill in the low spots around camp. Basically, what I'm trying to say: Gertie's pond is a man-made lake. Not that she cares."

"Tell you what," Gator huffed. "When you get done mowing, why don't ya join me over here. I'll show you all my tricks for hooking bass. Might be the makings of a good instructional booklet. There's a lot of people interested in catching fish, don't ya think? And don't bother lugging the can all the way down yonder. My guess is the mower still has gas."

...

Sure enough, Tate was right. The machine revved to a start with a turn of key. No need to add gas. For the first time ever, and in the middle of nowhere, he was cutting grass.

It didn't take Rusty long into it to understand why the task was left partway done. The mower was slow and the fairway — or rather, scratch that, *"air strip"* is what he meant — was long, a quarter mile at least. But he had to concentrate, too. And it wasn't about just clocking time or making the lawn look pretty: he had to make it *safe* for landing a plane! That meant clearing any and all debris, both loose rocks and stray branches, not just cutting grass. It didn't take Rusty long to see that he was in for a long afternoon, a lot of stopping and starting and figuring things out, learning on the fly just like his father said life was all about. Speaking of such, it was only after he had ran the mower down a full half a length of the strip that he turned back to discover that he'd only *matted down* the grass. Fortunately nobody else was watching and it was an easy fix. A quick push of the lever to lower the blades and Rusty was off and rolling again down the strip, this time with the satisfaction of hearing the grass being snipped.

With each new row his confidence grew. But the more he mowed the more imperfections he saw, especially along the edges as the result of fallen branches and one or two fairly good sized trunks. Some of those were too big to lift forcing him to kick them loose with his boots or lever them up with a stick.

Sandy was waving him down in front of one such log. "Saw this was a big one. Thought you could use some help." Rolling it over revealed a coiled up rattlesnake. "—Kinda had a hunch we might find a rattler." Sandy used a long branch to prod it along.

"Actually used to catch these things when I was a boy your age for money."

"To sell as pets?" Rusty guessed.

"No, not pets. *To milk.* There were two snake catchers, Ben Reed and another out of Miami named George Smith. Both payed a half dollar a snake. The venom was used in the medical field before modern-day pharmaceutical cures."

"Sounds dangerous," Rusty added.

"Thing is we didn't even do it for the money. Mostly it was just about fun, you know, the adventure of it all. Plus it was going to a good cause."

Sandy walked with Rusty back to the mower. "Had the same kind of mower at Snake Bight. Took a half a day to mow that ... before we sold out to the government. Now it's all grown over. Last time I drove by it I couldn't bear to look. I guess on the good side at least Dad didn't have to see it go to hell." Sandy shook his head trying to free himself from his pessimistic thoughts. "—Real good job on the mowing, Rus'. Just don't forget to lift up the mower blades if you see any rocks."

With the return of the repetitive clipping and the snipping Rusty's thoughts quickly drifted off, not because he was bored but because he had slipped into a groove: redundant work had the contrary effect of consuming one's body at the same time it allowed the mind space to free itself up and wander off. In this case Rusty found himself drifting back in time on the twilight trip with his father in the airboat down to Gumbos, how when they first arrived he thought the camp looked like a shack but how by the time they departed it had magically transformed into a one-of-a-kind palace he would never forget. He could almost hear the scratchy bull-frog croak of Johnny Gumm's voice as they sat at the picnic table and discussed any number of things great and small, some that Rusty could remember and others he couldn't immediately recall. Judging from the predictions on the Round Up, Rusty figured he'd be seeing the man in the days to come. As Rusty turned the wheel of the the mower The Lodge came into full view. No, it wasn't a beach resort to be sure, but considering how far out it was in the swamp, and inaccessible by way of a normal road (not to mention it was hours away from the closest store), there was no better word for describing it than a backcountry resort. It didn't have a golf course or a color TV, but it did have a runway that looked like a fairway and a limerock lined pond that was pretty darn close to a pool. It wasn't as aquamarine clear nor with a high dive like the triangular pool at the modern-day Trail's End Lodge and Motor Inn down on the Tamiami Trail but it did have a rope swing that hung from a branch with blocks of wood hammered on a tree trunk next to it that led to a makeshift launch pad at the crook of a large branch that overhung the pond. Rusty imagined himself swooshing down and then swinging up as he held tight on the rope, and then with a flare of a trapeze artist, letting go and flying freeform through the air (perhaps even doing a flip or two) before landing with two feet planted square down on Gertie the Alligator's back and waterskiing around to the crowd's delight as they watched from bleacher seats on the sandy beach at Cypress Gardens Amusement Park. Rusty laughed to himself thinking how — whenever that commercial played, back up north in the cramped apartment in Missouri's suburban outskirts, usually during the Evening Nightly News — there was always a twinkle in his stepdad Dwight's eye, "Tell you what, if I ever make it to Florida, seeing the waterski show at Cypress Gardens, that's gonna be the first thing I do!"

···

2 pm
The sight of a new buggy in camp caught Rusty's eye.

He parked the mower and ran towards The Lodge. Boisterous voices became louder and louder as Rusty approached. He was crestfallen but nonetheless happy to see who it was: Dan "Vuke" Vukovich and Greg Kleal, two of his dad's good chums from the old days, friendships that reached back to even before their days in the swamp. Dan was a huge man, sporting the size and athletic build of a pro-football player. He was holding a beer in his left hand and had his foot planted on a cooler in front of him like it was a treasure chest he'd just dug up from a deserted beach. Rusty immediately recalled the many stories his father told about how he'd met Dan while stationed at Homestead Air Force Base and how they spent their weekends fishing in the Keys and running around the swamp. After they got out of the Air Force they both got pilot's licenses and jobs as crop-dusters in Homestead.

That's where they met Greg. Greg Kleal was born outside of Detroit and had worked in a travelling carnival owned by his grandfather. The family wintered in Key West, and Greg had spent his high school years there, mainly getting into trouble according to the wild stories he told. He did a tour in the Navy and had become an aircraft mechanic before plying his trade for a crop-dusting company in Homestead. Though Rusty liked Greg, he could always sense something dangerous beneath his jolly exterior, as if his easy smile and ready laugh was a reflex for covering up a darker and barbaric truth, and one that Rusty probably didn't want to know.

Greg Kleal's pear-shaped frame jiggled as he slapped Rusty a high five. *"Just look at this guy! Look … At … This … Guy!"*

Dan grabbed him by the shoulder and gave him a solid one-armed hug.

"Lookin' more and more like yer ol' man!" Dan marveled as he scanned around camp. "— So, where is that old swamp rat?"

"He just went out …"

Greg smiled knowingly. "Of course. Never could keep Henry in camp too long."

Dan hopped back on the buggy to toss down some gear to Greg. Out of nowhere Sandy stepped in front of the last bag and intercepted it before it could reach Greg.

"What's in here?" He said curiously. "Sort of feels like wads of cash."

"Fumble-rooskeeeee!!!" Kleal yapped as he gave the bag a pop, dislodging it from Sandy's possession and quickly picking it up. "Why don't we keep this one up there," Greg advised to Vuke as he hurled it back up. Dan silently concurred as he stashed the bag into a metal box and locked it with a key.

"Let me tell ya, Sandy. It's been a crazy couple weeks. Good to get up here to unwind a bit. Any word on who's all coming?" Vuke asked.

"The good news for you is that Pepe's gonna be a no-show," Sandy shrugged as Huddy Johnson approached. "—Otherwise you'll have to wait and ask Henry. Huds and me we're just really along for the ride. I would guess the usual suspects but really I don't have a clue."

"For the record, me and Pepe: we patched things up. Just hooked him up with a new high-powered rifle and some ammo. You heard what happened to his dogs."

"WEAPONIZING an ENEMY?" Huddy asked.

"Huddy … *Jeesssuuss* … he's a friend. Like I said we worked things out."

"YOU WORKED THINGS OUT WITH PEPE?" Huddy seemed as incredulous as he was impressed.

"Vuke and him sort of bonded over their hatred for the government thing," Kleal chortled.

"Hey, the United States is the greatest country in the history of the earth. I just hate to see what all the stupid liberals and the Commie lovin' lefties in charge are doing to mess it all up. Pepe ever tell you his run ins with the IRS? Brothers for life once he told me about that. They purposely go after conservatives, you know. There's numbers on that."

"Just another way the Government is trying to destroy our way of life," Kleal spat to the ground grimacing. "Now ya got me all worked up. Toss me a beer would ya."

"OH, I SEE. The TWO OF YOU have a COMMON ENEMY," Huddy warily responded. "—So that makes him ... *YOUR* ... *FRIEND?*"

"All I'm saying is if they want to ever come collectin', they best be ready for World War III. I've got Ground Zero for the revolution staked out at my camp."

"Camp? Don't you mean *bunker?*"

"*Laugh all you want now, Parrish. Ha. Ha.* We'll see who's prepared when the Commies strike. The Russians are training Latin America terrorist in Cuba for an invasion of Miami. You see the latest edition of SOF?"

"*S ... O ... F?*" Sandy repeated with a scrunched up face.

"Soldier of Freedom. Don't play dumb." Vuke shook his head. "Pisses me off about you liberals. Took a good thing, the Constitution, and now look what we got. Ya know, one in twenty Cuban refugees is a Castro plant. Moscow gives the word, they'll probably take out Miami first. And *I'm talkin' with nukes!*"

Sandy rolled his eyes and looked at Kleal. "W-a-s h-e l-i-k-e t-h-i-s t-h-e w-h-o-l-e w-a-y u-p?" he mouthed. "Listen Dan," I'm not gonna argue with you. But why would they bomb Miami if it's filled with Castro plants?"

Greg started jiggling with laughter. "Hey Vuke, remember that time, the three of us, you me and Henry first went to Miller's Cave?"

Vuke seemed to brighten up at the memory. "Yeah, Henry might've been the new guy back then, but he set the tone for our group. That was the dawn of a new era. A changing of the guard."

Sandy turned to Rusty. "Some of the stories with your father. Let me tell ya, they're legendary in these parts."

"Yeah, they were the Good Ol' Days alright," Kleal sighed under his breath.

"Still are! Still could be!" Vuke rebuked as a field of furrows formed over his brow. "That's the thing that pisses me off. The whole country is going into the toilet."

"Speaking of shitters," Kleal added as he poured the remainder of his beer down his throat – *BEEELLLLCCHH!* "I gotta go see a man about a horse."

"Hey Dan, you couldn't give me a hand with some of the equipment in back. Not sure who used the tractor but it's sort of a mess."

"Awww Hell, Parrish. I'm up here to relax – you know that – to blow off a little steam, especially in light of recent events. Not get bogged down with work."

"Tell you what, Dan. Gimme an hour. After that you're off the clock."

"Puuuurrrrr-fect!" Kleal laughed as he headed toward the outhouse. "– It's gonna take me a good hour *at least* to take a crap."

"Oh, alright," Vuke surrendered. "—Let's go give it a look."

Rusty used the break in conversation to politely excuse himself from the camp. Mowing the grass had given him a mission, and it was a mission he aimed on finishing up. It also gave him the satisfaction that he was earning his stay.

•••

3 pm

Tate yanked at the line but the fish got away just as Rusty walked up.

The big man pointed to the large crocodilian in the middle of the pond. "Cain't tell ya how many times I sat on this bucket and just spilled out my guts to Ol' Gertie. And God Bless Her, she's about the best listener I know. She never interrupts or gives advice. She just listens."

"That's a lot of fish!" Rusty commented on Tate's haul.

"Yep, sure is," Tate acknowledged as he gazed out at the pond. "Had Greg bring over an extra cooler. The way they're talking, we're gonna have a big crowd."

"Dan seemed really upset, not like I remember him. Is something up?"

"Oh, no, I don't think so. Sometimes he just has to get things off his chest. And then he comes around."

"So, how many do you think they'll be ... in total?" Rusty asked. There were just a couple of bunks in the cabin, definitely not enough for a large crowd. More than likely there were going to be a lot of tents and tarps.

Tate couldn't say for sure. "Sounds like a couple dozen at least. Word got out. Might need to fish us out a gator to feed the whole lot." As if on cue the giant gator submerged under the surface. Gator Tate gave a flummoxed look. *"Oh Gertie, come on! You know I wasn't talking about you!"*

"You don't think ... that Gertie ... *actually understood?*"

Tate sort of nodded. "I don't know if it's like that with anybody else, but gators seem to understand everything I say. Especially Gertie."

"That's why they gave you your name, right?" Rusty asked in an effort to finally get the record straight.

Tate thought for a moment as he cast the line. "Ya know, God's honest truth. The more I think it over the more I think I might've actually given it to myself."

The big man's reverie ended abruptly as his fishing line grew taunt.

"Oh My Lord! I think I just hooked Ol' Elmer!" he grunted. Tate jammed the end of the rod into his belly and spun at the wheel. *"— Bugger's been playing games with me all day, but this time he's all mine!"* Tate struggled mightily to keep his footing against the powerful pull of the bull fish. Or maybe Tate was just tuckered out from a long day. "I just ain't what I used to be. Especially since I haven't been properly fed. *And Elmer knows it!"*

It was Tug o' War for the ages. And it could have gone either way. Splashing and cursing, and back and forth: up until the last moment it was hard to say who had the upper hand. Even when Gator Tate triumphantly pulled the pond's biggest fish up out of the water, Elmer refused to give up.

"You aren't gonna keep him?"

"Hell no!" Tate giddily laughed. "— Jus' sometimes a fish like ol' Elmer's gotta be shown who's the boss."

Rusty watched with relief as the old codger deftly dislodged the hook from the strong-tailed fish, and then with surprise as the old bass pro unexpectedly plopped Elmer in his chest. "Hold on tight!" Tate exclaimed. "I'd put him back myself if my back weren't so messed up." Elmer flipped and flopped in attempt to force himself free from Rusty's double-armed cradle hold as Tate directed him along the bank to a sandy spot under a laurel oak. "That looks good, put him in there."

After a small splash, Elmer spun around in place, like the hands of a wrist watch being manually adjusted to the correct time, before darting away out of sight into the inky depths of the pond.

...

4 pm

Rusty was enjoying himself relaxing in The Lodge reading the book he'd found on the shelf when he heard all hell starting to break loose on the porch.

Tate and Sandy were going at it face to face, about an inch apart, and raving mad. Whatever had been said, it appeared to be the final straw on the camel's back of a long simmering feud that was well beyond repair of words. "Now you listen here you UPPITY SON OF A BITCH!" Tate threatened as he cocked back his clenched fist.

A clang of a cowbell rang on perfect cue as if to indicate the opening round of a heavy-weight fight. Rusty imagined the crush of Tate's knuckles against Sandy's spectacled face followed by the botanical professor retaliating back with a roundhouse to the big man's blubbery belly (and in all probability bouncing back, Tate was that fat.) As the bell continued to ring, Huddy's voice filled the air: *"CHOW TIME!* Come and get it! *GIT IT 'FORE IT'S GONE!"*

And just like that Gator Tate disappeared around the bend faster than a thoroughbred horse galloping around first quarter length at the track. The crusty old codger wasn't mad at all, just crabby from needing something to eat — and about as thankful as Rusty had heard him all trip. *"God bless ya, Huddy! Oh this is Heaven! Hea-ven!"* Tate sang as he barreled down the path toward the aroma. *"God bless! God bless!"*

Chapter 7:
Swords at Dawn to Settle the Score

Apr 2, 1857
Unending rain all day and rations are running low.

Three days hence the mosquitoes will make life miserable beyond compare. I have ordered the men to prepare smudge fires to ward off the pests as we await supplies.

Apr 18
French presents me with perplexing news.

He has concluded that Stafford's map is largely incorrect — even "doctored up" — as if Stafford wished to hide something. I heard him out but refrained from any judgement one way or the other until I can study the matter more closely for myself.

Apr 28
A new rumor is circulating that French is a spy.

He has yet to reveal his mission here. The men speculate that he is using his titular role as a surveyor to cover up the true nature of his work. I gather the men to allay their fears, assuring them that bringing French on as surveyor was my decision, *not his*. There is eye rolling and much scoffing. Ford theorizes he is a special envoy for President Pierce while Abrams is of a mind he may be signaling the British Navy from the East Tower at night.

May 3
I awake in a cold sweat lying face down on the table across Stafford's map.

Trying to remember last night ...

May 6

Danforth ridicules French's assertions about Stafford's work.

After a meal of duck and onions stewed in white sauce, we review every detail of the map. Danforth recalls the many times he used it "as his compass" to guide him deep into the interior and back. The conversation renews my confidence that the late Stafford's attention to detail and accuracy was beyond reproach. Danforth presents me with a vial of milk of opiates which he says will steady my nerves.

May 7

I awake to the sound of dirt falling on my body and face.

Am I dreaming? "Stafford!?" I call. "—Is that you? Stafford my friend? Why are you trying to bury me alive?" I ask. He looks at me but doesn't respond. "I am not dead," I explain as I crawl out of my earthen tomb. I even help him push in the remaining dirt. "Good riddance!" I laugh as I pat the dirt down with my boots and fashion a cross out of a length of twine and two sticks. By the time I look up from my prayer Stafford is gone. My pursuit of him is hobbled by a peg which has replaced my missing lower leg. Or am I running faster than I ever have before? Flying, like an eagle! I AM AN EAGLE! Over the tree tops and among the clouds. I can see everything. It's all so clear! So clear! The fort! The wreck! All the islands! Now I am flying farther inland. Over the Green Hell. Oh, the Beautiful Green Hell. Green Hell? No, a Green HEAVEN! I can see everything! Everything! Everything is so clear! And oh my Lord, My Lord, The Falls! Oh, the Falls! The Beautiful Blue Falls!

May 8

Unable … to … write.

Mind … is … in a … fog. A terrible bout of swamp fever. I am definitely in need of … some more … of the … confiscated … rum.

May 10

The sound of whistling rouses me from my stupor.

I stumble out into the brightness but find no one there. It has now been near three weeks since I've last seen French.

May 19

My condition deteriorates like the weather.

I am plagued by hallucinations and vertigo. It is as if my vision has been constricted to a small porthole of a ship. I am plagued by a reoccurring dream of shoveling all the dirt on top of Stafford's grave only to return to my quarters to the sight of him sitting inside.

Jun 1

French finally returns.

And under the cover of darkness. Something is up. I am beginning to think he and his Indian accomplice are conspiring against the fort.

Jun 8

I stop by French's quarters to find nobody there.

As it is my responsibility as the commander of the fort to squash any and all sedition before it takes root, I shoulder my way through the front door to the surprise of my life: the sight of an attacking owl swooping down at my face! Only after hitting the deck, causing a sheath of brushes to scatter about, do I discovered that dangling creature is stuffed, its lifeless body attached to the rafters by a length of twine and its wings spread wide as if in flight — nor is the creature alone. The room is filled with an eclectic flock of similarly stuffed specimens combined with an equal proliferation of canvases reflecting the various poses the animals are arranged — including a Snowy White perched on a branch, a giant woodpecker clasping to a trunk with chunks of wood flying in the air, and a Great Blue gliding in the mist of a water fall not unlike the one I've seen in my dreams. The room resembles a mirror house of natural splenditude multiplied many times the intensity of real life to the point I have trouble discerning if I am inside or out. A voice calls me from above, French's. After several failed attempts, I finally succeed in climbing the ladder to the East Tower to find French and Guess speaking in Muscogee and sipping hot tea in the cool breeze. French glances haughtily at my unsteady state as he dabs his brush with blue paint. Out of politeness I take him up on his offer for tea only to immediately spit the vile liquid out as I finally get a look at the depiction on his canvas: it's a re-creation of the Spanish galleon floating on the water, perhaps as it looked before it'd been sunk, and could it be — I squint my eyes to confirm: is that not my silhouette in the tiny porthole looking out at the rising clouds of an approaching storm!?

Jun 15

A personal slight from French at breakfast has me sorely rattled.

He dared to insinuate, within Lieutenant Kerr's hearing, to Captain Ford that my decisions favor profiteering above winning the peace. Although he doesn't come right out and say it, he also seems to imply that my penchant for sour juice and milk of opiate is enfeebling my ability to command this post — which it certainly is not! When I counter that it is he who is committing the treasonous acts, adding in as well that his tea is *"disgusting,"* he regards me with his predictably haughty visage. Accordingly, I have ordered twenty four hour guard of the confiscated rum under suspicion that he is spiking his tea.

Jun 18

I run out of my quarters in a fury to the sound of whistling only to discover it to be Kerr whom I command to stop.

Jun 22

Not just an annoyance, I am now of the opinion that French is a fraud and Guess is much worse and that both of their activities pose a grave risk to the fort. French's aloof behavior has slowly but surely undermined my authority. He comes and goes as he pleases with no respect to the chain of command. The men are increasingly following the lead of his carefree demeanor and unorthodox approach.

Jun 25

Again hearing that abominable whistling I fly out my door to the sight of Hardy whom I immediately order to the stockade to be flogged.

Jun 28

It is now open knowledge that French has sent for men from Ft Meade.

I also suspect that French is trying to poison me with his tea — just like he killed Stafford. I haven't felt right since our encounter on the East Tower. Neither are the other men doing well. They smile in front of French when I am not around, but otherwise their faces are ashen and morale is repressed.

Jul 14

I know what he's up to. I know his game. He and his Indian friend. I will stop French and I will be lauded a hero.

Jul 15, 10 am

French crosses the line!

When I order his arrest he responds arrogantly, "— On what grounds?" I laugh in his face at his pathetic pretention. He is no innocent knave! Of course it is Article 5: *Detrimental Actions and Behavior against the Command!* French tries to turn the tables by invoking his authority as an officer of the Inspector General and directs Ford to arrest me on the spot. During the impasse that follows, I remove my glove and slap him across the right cheek. French looks as me with profound disappointment, but is also calm. "So, now it's become personal. Very well then, choose your weapon. I will have satisfaction at dawn."

12 noon

Danforth does his best to steady my nerves.

We enjoy stewed duck and parsnips, my favorites, and afterwards smoke tobacco as we discuss strategy, rounded off with a fresh batch of Danforth's milk of opiates, a delectable treat. For the first time in a long while, I am back to feeling myself.

5 pm

French does not stand a chance!

Under Danforth's oversight, I practice my blade work against Simon and his makeshift sword crafted from cypress. My strikes are so ferocious I succeed in hacking his weapon into splinters and even gashing a slight wound across his arm. My confidence soars.

Jul 16

French and I meet in the clearing at dawn.

I am immediately taken aback by French's handling of his blade and quite lengthy arms. He moves first with a firesome lunge. I disengage my blade but he proves too quick for me to riposte. He follows with a series of advances which I parry as he drives me back. In a heartbeat, French pulls back and motions me forward. This is less a taunt than it is a gesture of a master training a novice. I charge at him in a rage. French calmly and deftly counters my desperate onslaught, sizing me up like a cat playing with a mouse. There is no escaping the obvious: I am clearly overmatched. In a final move of dominance, he swats my armament to the ground − leaving me weaponless − and advance-lunges the tip of his blade to my Adam's apple; it is a pitiful end to a pitiful fight. But instead of dispatching me on the spot, French withdraws his blade, sheaths it, and extracts a silver snuff box from his pocket from which he offers me to partake. Facing the river he requests my strict confidence before revealing the true nature of his mission.

Jul 19
I order Danforth to be locked in the stockade.
The charge: treason against the fort, including illegal sale of arms and pilfering Wiggin's medicine supplies, defrauding the settlers, and the murder of Andrew Stafford whom, upon French's recommendation, we hereby rename the fort in his honor.

Aug 3
Today we reach the source of the river.
Around the bend we are delighted by the sight of a small series of waterfalls, the like of which is not known in this part of the peninsula. Each fall of water is a foot higher than the last and cascades upon clear pools in limestone worn away by the eons. Countless fish teem in these pools, all alive with every shimmer of color. A great forked waterfall emerges around the bend, ten foot high at its crest, beyond which lies the source of the river. It is more than noteworthy as a spot of sublime beauty and natural repose. George informs me that bears and wildcats will sometimes come to feed on the fish, thus they call the place "Fisheating Heart of the River." I sit in a limestone encrusted pool among the fish and wash my grimy face in its clear water. I shall like to see this wonder of nature kept safe from human endeavors.

Aug 4
Shadows Inside joins us around the campfire.

He recounts the story of his people, how they found great strength in the land. They do not want to fight but they will not leave either. He is saddened by the sickness the White Man brings. He says he cannot see the treaty line but trusts me if I say it is there. He has heard many promises from the White Man but seen nothing for his people. He says his people have been witness to many of the White Man's boats. He would like to find a boat for his people to sail away. But where to? He says people should stay where they are born and make peace there, that their land is not our land. Nobody owns the land. I wish I could answer the chief that we would all soon leave so the paradise could be returned to its fullness. That I knew that would not be happening brought my spirits lower still. Once glimpsed by the covetous eye of men, paradise is forever doomed.

Aug 5

Gunfire erupts in the distance as we near the fort.

A thick fog obscures the trail. The smell of smoke mingles with the gloom. Shouting and cursing comes from all directions. There is an orange hue in the distance. My worst fears are confirmed: the fort is engulfed in flames! Men rush about fighting the blaze while others are firing in the direction of the refugee camp. Women and children shriek and scatter towards the pines. I pull Simon aside to hear his version of events, which he recounts to me with a wild eyed stare and that I immediately dismiss: His mumbles amount to nothing more than a repeat of his endless nonsense on marauding pirates from the sunken galleon storming on shore, this time freeing their triumphant leader, Danforth, from his cell and only sparing Simon's life, at Danforth's strict command, so that he shall be left behind to retell the tale.

Aug 6

The refugee uprising is quelled at dawn after torches and pitch are thrown on the roof of the blockhouse.

Lieutenant Kerr assures me it was nothing more than a riot by some of the refugees over the distribution of food. Of five prisoners, four were quickly recaptured. Only Danforth remains at large.

Chapter 8:
Stories Erupt Around the Campfire

The men gathered around the campfire all in a congenial mood, the best of friends, as if they didn't have a problem in the world. Most startling of all was to see Sandy choose a seat right next to Tate who didn't seem to begrudge him the spot one bit — and more than that, even graciously scooted over to give his erstwhile nemesis more space on the wood plank — all the while pausing not even a second from greedily shoveling food in his face. All hurt feelings or simmering feuds were put to rest when it came time for chowtime in the woods.

"Nobody gets seconds 'til I get mine," Tate garbled as victuals fell out of his mouth. "— First in line gets dibs. Them's just the rules."

Thirty minutes later the food was gone and the plates cleared off: the all-consuming spell of voracious eating was officially complete. Matches were struck and the smell of tobacco filled the air. The men settled into a rhythm of storytelling around the flame. What had been pure daylight before the meal, or at least bright enough for reading in The Lodge, had now turned into a darkening dusk that encroached ever inward on the flickering fire light.

Sandy took a splinter of wood out of the corner of his mouth. He was probably the lightest eater of the group and was the first to speak up. "*Frog legs suuuuurrre were good.* Compliments to the chef, Huddy. Well done."

"Don't thank ME. It's MR. KLEAL to whom you should TIP YOUR HAT."

Kleal was smiling ear to ear. "Actually, it was both Vuke and me. He did the gigging. I ran the boat."

213

"Well, there's frog legs *and then there's frog legs*," Sandy acknowledged as he tipped his hat to all three men involved. "— Whatever you had them marinatin' in that was some *special ...*"

"That's it!" Tate exclaimed with his pointer finger thrust vertically in the air. A Eureka Moment sizzled in his eyes. "— You used my *special sauce!"*

"Yoouuur special sauce?" Sandy said incredulously.

Tate's initial euphoria was dampened by a burgeoning wellspring of confusion. "Actually, it was naggin' at me the whole time I was eatin' 'em. Had I not been so darned famished I pro'bly woulda connected the dots sooner." He held up a bone to emphasize the point. "Those are a rip off if there ever was one of my secret sauce back from my froggin' days. *Brings back memories, Kleal."*

"Wonderin' if you'd notice," Greg chuckled proudly, still grinning. He was about to say something else when he deferred back to Tate who was on the verge of another thought. "—Go ahead."

"But that sauce. It was my ... *secret* ... recipe. A *proprietary* formula. I, we, didn't share it with a single soul. It's what set Frog Legz apart."

Sandy leaned forward to whisper into Rusty's ear, "— *That's Frog Legz with a Zeeee."*

Greg threw his hands up in the air in fake surrender like he'd been caught red handed by the FBI. "Well, I guess the cat's outatha bag,"

"But don't you worry, Gator," Vuke awkwardly slurred. "— You know us, we skinned that cat as soon as it got out. Scout's honor, nobody else knows."

Greg tapped at his noggin in confirmation. *"Don't even got it written down.* You got my word on that, Tate."

"Manny! It was Manny right?" Tate spat in the dirt with the pain of a honest business man who'd come to learn he'd been betrayed by his trusted partner of many years. He didn't even wait to hear the answer. *"So Manny gave it to ya!? Darnnitt!* He gave me his word he'd keep it safe and sound — locked in the vault — with all our cash and other paper work."

Greg rubbed his finger in a little circle across his temple as he jammed his other hand into his mouth to remove a piece of meat from a gap left behind by a missing tooth. He flicked the flesh into the flame. "Now I'm not in the business of throwing anybody under the bus," Kleal responded, *"—I want to be real clear about that."* In the code of the campfire it was his way of pleading the fifth.

"Maybe not under the bus," Vuke a bit overzealously added in. *"—But how about over the bridge? And with their feet stuck in a bucket o' cement!"*

Greg smiled from ear to ear. "Well, if a guy's got it comin' to him: Gentlemen, you probably know the rest."

A moment of campfire silence ensued. The men listened to the crackle of the logs and stared into the ember glow of the ash.

"Well, whatever," Tate expectorated. "Mighta bothered me year's back. And it's been a long time. But now that I'm advancing in age, I guess I'm softenin' up. Hate to see a family recipe like that *not get passed down* to the right folks. At this point, you guys are about the best family I got. Remind me Greg, what was my secret anyhow? It's been so damn long I done plumb forgot." Tate spat some tobacco on the ground as he tried to recollect. "I know I used a little chicory. Sour orange rinds and sugar cane slag if I remember right." Tate rubbed his hand in his face like he was trying to hold back tears. "Damn smoke in my eye," he feigned as a way to cover up his emotional turn in mood. The flame was quite obviously burning clean and funneling its embers straight up, not towards him one bit.

"Much obliged to know they pass your approval, Tate" Greg answered as he thudded his fist on his chest in a show of respect. "Means the world to me that they meet your standard."

"THE Gold Standard!" Vuke proclaimed.

One Bohemian Beer and then another was raised toward the light.

"To the Frog Legz days!" and "Amen To That!" and "All Hail Lorenzo Tate!" a succession of voices called out as, arms extended, the men leaned in to clink together their cans in a ceremonial toast.

"To Frog Legz with a Zeee-ee," Sandy snuck in before he swigged from his can.

Greg glared menacingly at Sandy. *"Give the man some respect would ya!* He single handedly revolutionized froggin' in these parts."

After mostly listening, Henry finally had something to say. "Soze, are you gonna tell the boys the *official history,* Loren?" May be a good time to finally put all the Frog Legz rumors to rest."

215

"That's Frog Legz with a zeeeeee!" Sandy gleefully repeated, unable to resist.

Kleal's nostrils flared in anger at Sandy's unwillingness to comply with his warning. The situation quickly simmered down as Henry made a calming gesture with his hand and Vuke tossed his corpulent cohort a can. *"—Anybody else ready for another cold one?"*

"Thing is Loren," Henry said as he lit a tiparillo, "— there's been so many stories circulated over the years *nobody's sure* what to believe. For posterity's sake it might be good to hear the official version, as it happened, straight from the source."

Tate rubbed his forearm across his face with a conflicted look. The memories seemed to be weighing down on him so heavily that the big man had lost his ability to speak. A moment later that theory was quickly dispelled when Tate opened his mouth and let out a giant *BUURRR-REEELLCH*. Gas, not bad blood, was the only thing holding him back.

"There, now I feel better," a refreshed Lorenzo Tate announced with a look of instant relief. "— Too much of my special Frog Legz sauce *always did* give me gas."

A burst of laughter broke out around the campfire, but just as quickly stopped. The prospect of hearing the story straight from the "Gator's mouth" was an opportunity none of the men wanted to miss. The versions of the story they did know were often conflicting or partial or too farfetched, all coming from unconfirmed sources — bystanders, minor players and gadflies — who regurgitated information that was so filtered through the grapevine and polluted by false threads that it was impossible to tell what proportion, or if any of it, matched up with the facts. This time they would finally get the full scoop, the unabridged version from the founder himself. For Tate it was as much about setting the record straight as it was getting it off (and out of) his chest. Assuming he'd be able to talk at all? Again he looked uneasy. Could it be that, after so many years, the aging entrepreneur was still in denial: unwilling or unable to objectively recall the full arc of events? Suddenly Tate was overtaken by another rapturous look as a series of baby dinosaur-sized burps burst forth through his lips — *BLURRP-BURRP-BLURP-BURP* — followed by one more for good measure: *BUR-RELLCH!*

The men took advantage of Tate's prolonged gaseous release to pass around a new round of drinks. Everyone quieted down as Tate cleared his throat followed by him spitting out some phlegm and then packing some fresh tobacco under his lower lip.

"Okay, so here's how it goes boys. Like most great ventures, I never set out from the start to build the behemoth it became. Just enjoyed froggin' down in the marshes past Hole in the Wall. Always gigged me a little extra for gas money, you know, that I'd sell out of the back off my truck off near the bend at Smokey's where the shoulder widened out. As always, I used my secret sauce to smoke 'em up just right. Business was slow at first but when word got out, it wasn't long before I had to bump up from one cooler to four. Then I got Gerald and Leroy in the fold to use their airboat to shore up my supply. Not too much longer after that Scrumptious Suzie's caught wind of what I was up to and wanted to buy me out. Offered me twenty five hun'ert on the spot, but Candy Martinelli she convinced me – *begged me actually* – to hold tight and not sell out so we could grow the operation 'ten times the size' by re-investing the profits and keeping our take-home pay lean. Tate leaned in to the fire and whispered. *"You do remember Candy Martinell?"* He drew an outline of what looked like a curvaceous vase in the air with his hands. *"Kinda hard to say 'no' to a woman like that!"*

Kleal spoke up. "Yeah, she had the *best damn legs* I've ever seen. Never since seen a woman move quite like the way she walked. It was a thing of beauty."

Vuke bit at his hand. "Yeah, that Candy was one of a kind. She sure was sweet. Capital H, O, T, HOT. Actually, hot *and sweet* at the same time."

"Kinda sounds like my sauce!" Tate cooed with a boyish grin: "Ain't gonna lie and say she didn't play a big part in me perfectin' the formula of my secret blend. In many ways she was the inspiration behind my success."

"Like any of us ever had a chance! She was way out of our league," Kleal mocked as he slurped the puddle of beer off the top of his newly opened can. "Especially you Vuke. It's laughable how much you fancy yourself a lady's man. Candy Martinelli didn't have a clue who you were."

"Well of course she knew me, but I was *only nineteen,"* Vuke blushed. "One time she even came up and squeezed my cheek."

"Oh, isn't that precious!"

"I actually went to school with her younger sister," Sandy added. "Not as good looking but she married well."

Henry nodded. "Son to the heir of the United Cane Corp, but his generation, I doubt he ever stepped foot in a field."

Huddy was seated furthest from the campfire, hunched over like he was asleep. "Of the MANY THINGS I did to HUSTLE A BUCK I am proud to say I NEVER LOWERED myself to cutting SUGAR CANE."

"Oh don't kid yourself, she was *even sweeter* than that," Tate decreed. "But don't be fooled by her good looks. She was one sharp mama, too. Even on the coldest days she never once missed a day not wearing them short shorts, *not once*. She knew how to bring 'em in and fill up the tables. Weekends were always packed."

All the talking of Miss Martinelli seemed to put the men in a trance. For a moment nobody said a word. The only sounds to be heard were the crackling embers at the center of the glowing orb and chirping of frogs and other critters out in the dark.

"Brought the customers in, that's for sure. She was smart as all get out."

Sandy leaned forward and poked the campfire with a stick.

"Whenever business got slow, *which wasn't much*, she'd walk out to the side of the road to wave her red bandana and in no time we'd have the parking lot all filled up."

"Parking lot?" Sandy repeated in a gasp. "I remember going there with Dad and we just pulled off on the shoulder of the road. Actually there was barely room for that."

"Her legs were that good. For a time we had a problem of guys just rolling in to gawk at her and not buying a single bite. That's when we, *well she actually*, got the idea of changing the floor plan."

"You mean nailing in those two by fours, like a cow pen?" Sandy said less as a question than a statement of fact.

"No, not cow," Tate corrected. "We called it the *Frog Pen.*"

"Would you let the man finish his story?" Kleal barked at Sandy with an annoyed look.

"So's anyhow, the way she set it up then, the guys couldn't get a good look at her legs unless they bought a bucket. A bushel would set you back twenty five. Minimum order was ten dollars for the adult men. She'd go from table to table turning up the charm. Sometimes she'd even treat the highest rolling customers to a signed copy of that promotional photo as an extra perk. You all remember the one I'm talking about? She was on tip toes in the foreground with her hands in the air and the store behind her in back."

"Ahem, stand," Sandy murmured.

Vuke laughed. "Tate, can't tell you how many frog legs bones I saw dumped by the base of your billboards. Men would empty out those buckets faster than lightning just to get a chance to turn around for more."

"More Candy Martinelli or frog legs?"

"With a good business model, it's all interlinked," Tate explained. "People came back for the experience as much as anything else. That's what made us so great."

"Hey," Henry interrupted as he exhaled some smoke. "— Anybody else notice the billboard by Turners is still up? That's a minor miracle of the universe if you ask me."

"Still in pretty good shape, too." Sandy added. "Can't see the frog anymore but the letter "Z" at the end is still there plain as day."

"And of course Candy's nice pair of legs!"

"What's the deal on why they never tore that one down?" Vuke asked.

"Ain't on the State easement. They can't touch it. I think it's on Indian land," Sandy guessed.

"Can't take credit for the signs," Tate added. "— They were *Manny's idea.*"

"Old Manny Pantera," Vuke scoffed. "Had that guy sized up as a Castro loyalist the moment we met. Never trusted how he was so *over the top* with his hatred for the Comandante en Jefe. It seemed like he was *playin' a part*, you know — like he was tryin' to cover something up."

"Political leanings notwithstanding, he was a good partner," Tate spat into the ground. "T'aint nobody gonna convince me otherwise on that. Those billboards single handedly tripled my profits overnight. Can't blame him for having trouble navigating the gov'ment's paperwork thing."

"Paper work nothing!" Sandy laughed. "He put them up for the price of lumber and nails ... and some shoddy construction work at that. If I remember correctly all it took was a tropical storm, not even a hurricane, to blow them all down."

"Except for the one at Turners," Henry mused. That has concrete pillars. The Indians built it to withstand a Category Five."

"Beautiful to *still* be able to see her legs on that billboard. Ten times the normal size and, other than being a little faded, it's almost like they didn't age. I'd be lying if I said I don't sometimes just pull over on the road shoulder and stare at that sign."

"It's a blessing ... that stretch of road. Scenery like that is a Gift from God. And not just because of the 'Candy Martinelli' thing. It's just nice, you know, to have a historic memento of that caliber from The Golden Age."

"Here here to that!" a voiced called as the men raised their beers and somebody else said "Amen."

"Shame about that storm," Tate frowned. "If I could pinpoint the one thing that started my decline I'd probably point to that."

"You mean to tell me ... a couple signs going down ... is what did your business in?" Dan retorted with a puzzled look.

"Well, the one down by the 12-C, it got wedged in the gate. When the water managers saw what happened, that brought the building permit folks in. Next thing I know the Health Department's casing out my joints ... and all *undercover* cars, too."

"Undercover *Health Department* cars?" Sandy inquired skeptically as he stifled a smile. "— Probably wearing dark sunglasses and overcoats, too, I bet. The whole bit."

"Not that it was a problem we couldn't handle, at least not at first," Tate recalled. "Candy knew how to soften them boys up. She had 'em eatin' free frog legs out of her hands. Sealed the deal with a signed photograph if I remember correct. Let me tell ya, fellas: at my peak I had twenty employees and half a dozen boats. We were operating twenty four seven. Man, I'm tellin' ya, I was *this close*," Tate held out his hand to make an infinitesimal space between his pointer finger and thumb, "— *This close I'm tellin' ya to becoming the McDonald's of the Swamp.*" The big man rubbed his chin with a nostalgic sigh. "Had my sights set on buying out Scrumptious Suzies too if she'd of just agreed to the right price. Even richer than Parrish there for a while," the big man beamed with pride. "Remember that, Sandy — the day I come in to your orchid house and flopped down twelve hun'ert dollars cash?"

Sandy tipped back his hat. "Never forget the day, Tate. Dad couldn't figure out if you were more interested in the plants or just rubbing all that cash in our face."

"To be honest, Sandy, I was probably doing a little of both," Tate laughed mischievously. "But actually that was one of the last times I actually had any cash. Manny was always one step ahead on the business plan, and he and Candy had me reinvesting every drop. On paper we had profits soaring through the roof, so I just kinda adopted an if-the-wheel-ain't-broke-ain't-no-need-to-go-fixing-it approach."

"*Twelve boats!* No wonder you went under! You must've *frogged out* the whole swamp!" Kleal croaked.

"No, Gerald and Leroy rotated their route. We had a steady supply chain feeding fresh meat to twelve stores ..."

"*More like shacks,*" Sandy whispered again under his breath.

"Like I was saying, I had thirteen stores up and down both coasts," Tate continued. "Even had me a Central Command. A corkboard and all. Set up in the back room of the Green Frog."

"You don't mean the back room with the *pinball machine?*" Kleal asked with surprise, as if something finally clicked.

"Yeah, that's right Greg," Tate responded. "I was so much on the road, between the coasts, I sort of used that back room of the tavern as my office. I had the map covered with thumbtacks to help me track my growing empire. Red for my stores, and blue ones to show my frogging routes, and greens my billboard locations and white ones to show me where all the Scrumptious Suzie's and other joints were at. Gotta keep an eye on the competition anybody'll tell ya that. The Green Frog was real good about letting me set up shop. They didn't charge me any rent or anything. Partly because I was a big tipper, even if — *you know how it is when cash is low* — I had them add most of my gratuities straight to my tab. Like I said, Manny took every cent I made and plowed it right back in." Tate's eyes glimmered as he painted the scene. "You should've seen it boys! The map and thumbtacks galore. I had the whole world in the palm of my hand. For the first time my entire life, I felt like I was building sumpin' bigger than myself."

The big man flopped his hands in the air and then let them collapse back down on his lap as simultaneously the glimmer in his eyes went flat. "Of all the things I lost, the thing I miss most is just looking at that map, dreamin' and schemin' about what and where to go next. It was like I was General MacAuthur moving around all of his troops." Tate sighed. "— And then came the Big Blow and it was all for naught."

"The signs falling down? Really? *That* did you in!?" Sandy scoffed.

Tate thought about it some more. "Well, actually, if I was to be honest it was more about *market forces* pulling the rug out from under my feet."

"Funny how quickly tastes can change," Kleal agreed. "The food industry can be fickle like that."

"Not at all, Greg, no that wasn't it," Tate shook his head vociferously. "Hell, ya'll *tasted 'em* here tonight! Ain't nothing going '*out of fashion*' with a product as delicious as that. God's honest truth, and this is a fact: Candy and the girls were actually turning them back the day we closed up."

"Yeah," Sandy cackled. "When word leaked out about it being the last day to get a look at Candy's legs, *I bet* you had a super colony of pickup trucks flocking in from both coasts."

"So, let me get this straight: You had all that business and you *still* had to shut down? I don't get it. *What's the catch?*"

"Department of Environmental Regulations came out with a report on mercury contamination in the Glades," Henry spoke up. "I was working the scoop on it at the time. The more I found out, the worse it got. The numbers were so bad. I knew it would be the end of Tate. Then that hotshot Yankee reporter caught wind of it. It wasn't a matter of 'if but when' and then boom — it made front cover of *The Gold Coast Gazette.*"

Tate quickly hashed through the altered economic landscape the article ushered in. "The Gov'ment calculated five ounces of frog meat two times per week as the safe limit. Overnight the math blew up in my face. I worked on the arithmetic over and over at my Central Command post at the Green Frog, but no matter how many times I did the number crunching I kept coming back with the same result: I'd have to raise my price to a *hun'ert dollars a bucket* just to break even, and a hun'ert and fit'y to keep my cash flow intact."

"Mercury? That's a laugh," Vuke sarcastically rebuked. "Now there's a government conspiracy if I ever heard one. I've been eating Glades fish half my life and never got sick once. If I remember correctly, wasn't it cockroaches that shut you down?"

Tate conceded the point. "Yeah, that's true. At my Miami store they were pretty bad."

"Plywood shacks collect 'em," Sandy pointed out.

"Manny kept blaming it on the exterminator."

"Yeah right!" Kleal burst out in disgust. The fire flickered off his receding hairline as a diabolical smile consumed his face, making it unclear if he was talking to the men or directing his comments straight into the throbbing embers of the flame. "— About the only cockroaches in your Miami joint were Manny and his friends."

Tate seemed unwilling to blame any one person or any force for his demise, but rather — like all burnt business men do in their final analysis — eventually came around to seeing it as an unfortunate and ill-timed convergence of events, some of which, had he been more proactive, he might have been able to delay but never fully prevent. "I shoulda diversified, there's no denying that. I had plans for a broader menu of wider swamp offerings all lined up: swamp cabbage, palmetto jelly, crawdads, gator tail, *the whole works*. I was even working on a Talapia pudding. But once the frog market collapsed — *my bread and butter* — it was too late."

"Weren't you serving alcohol without a permit, too?" Sandy tried to recall. "— I actually remember *that* being the last straw that tripped you up."

Tate shook his head. "No, that dust up with the Liquor Control Board. Manny had some inside connections that knew how to get that to blow over purty quick."

Tate caught himself mid thought.

"Yeah, Manny was *cool as a cucumber* in crisis. In that final year or so I found myself having to lean on him more and more. He was practically my psychologist during the run of back luck with the liquor board, the health department, the mercury crisis, and the drought."

"The drought! That's right," Sandy exclaimed. "How could I forget."

Tate continued. "Yeah, that Manny, I gotta hand it to him: He was confident as hell. Over and over he kept telling me to wait for the mercury thing to pass over, just like things always do, and we'd be right back in the driver seat callin' the shots." Tate took a deep breath. "But the thing is, we were so over extended — we literally had no cash reserves. By that time Gerald and Leroy were breathing down my neck, too." Tate pulled at his collar just remembering the hot water he got himself in. "I told Manny point blank. Let's just liquidate what we got. And maybe get in touch with Scrumptious Suzie's about my swamp cabbage recipe — see if she was interested and find out what she'd be willing to pay — because by that time, along the coast, Suzie's burgers were really starting to take off."

Sandy buried his head in his hands in a state of hilarious disbelief. "Yeah, burger with a side of swamp cabbage and Talapia pudding. *Sounds like a real feast!?*"

"So what did Manny do with all the money? You must've stockpiled a good amount of cash," Vuke inquired. "—Because by the the time Greg and I got to him he was *pretty much* broke."

"And, *ahem*, how would we know anything about that?" Greg rolled his eyes in a thinly vailed effort to shut his friend up. "I got four witnesses that can vouch I was *out of town* that entire week."

An oblivious Tate continued: "Manny and me, we were actually just a few steps away from the bank when he finally sold me over on his fail safe plan. Told me we mothball — *not abandon* — the main frogging side of the business, for the time being, until the whole hubbub on the mercury simmered down."

"And how about the liquor board violation?" Sandy asked.

"Yeah," Tate admitted, "— that was dogging us, too, but mostly it was the mercury thing." The big man pursed his mouth, stretched his hair back to make it look all slicked back, and began to speak. The moment he did Vuke broke to pieces in glee, repetitively slapping the palm of his hand on his knee in riotous anticipation of what was coming next. *"You know'a about them stoodies, so many stoodies,"* Tate perfectly aped the intonations of his old business partner's distinctive voice, *"— the next one will be a sayin' joost the opposite, how the mercury isn't bad at all, but is actually goot for your heart!"*

Kleal hailed Tate's imitation — "You got Manny spot on!" — as the men broke out into riotous laughter.

"Anyhow," Tate continued, "Manny said we put all our eggs into Miami and concentrate on the business's other side."

"Other side? You mean exterminating the cockroaches," Sandy sarcastically quipped, unable to hold back.

"Let the man finish, would ya Parrish!" Kleal glowered with his hard-to-read smile.

Tate meanwhile seemed to have lost his train of thought. The big man spit some tobacco on the ground and looked up at Greg still all confused, "— The other side ...*as in?*"

"The other side of your business," Kleal recalled, trying to tickle the aging entrepreneur's cavernous mind. "— Not the Frogs, but the ..."

"Ohhhhh," Tate said as if a lightbulb went on in his head. "—You're talkin' about when we changed the name to *just 'LEGZ.'*" The moment Tate said it Greg quickly turned towards Sandy with threatening look. The quick-witted botanist seemed to get the message, this time making no mention of the distinctive letter used to pluralize LEGZ.

Tate chuckled to himself before he began. "Yeah, Manny's idea was to open a club and just call it LEGZ ... in a warehouse off the Industrial Block. Just a ten minute drive over the causeway from Miami's main strip."

"As in *strip club?*" Sandy asked with a genuine look of curiosity. Of all the things he knew about Frog Legz this was an aspect of the business he hadn't yet heard. Kleal playfully pelted him with an empty can that he hurled from across the flame. "Anybody need another one?" he asked as he opened the cooler and softball tossed one Sandy's way.

"Much obliged," Sandy said as he cautiously tilted the brim of his hat in acknowledgment of Greg's ability to teeter-totter between generosity and vengeance in the same breath.

Tate continued: "Meanwhile Leroy and Gerald, they were pushing me for their payoff. I'd been paying them on promissory notes and future shares. Anyhow it all came to a boil one night. Gerald and Leroy cornered me by the pinball machine at the Green Frog. Told me they needed their cash and they needed it now. The only thing I could do to convince them from killing me — and you know how Gerald was a pro with throwing a knife — was the three of us to go see Manny *in person* and settle up."

"So at eleven o'clock we show up in Miami. My Lord, let me tell ya," Tate said as an aside. "— I was proud as all git out how nice that store looked. Candy's neon leg lit up *like a beacon* in the night. Sure did make the industrial district look nice. Even Leroy and Gerald seem to soften up once we got inside and they saw all the money flying around, and, oh boy, all those ladies — couldn't hold a candle to Candy, but still — they sure were a sight for sore eyes. Don't know how Manny did it, but he attracted a real high rollin' crowd."

"So let me guess — Manny never showed up."

"That was the bad news. And for a moment there I thought it was the end of my life. The good news was that a couple of ladies took a liking to Gerald and Leroy. All I could figure was Manny caught wind of what was going on and tipped them off. They kept squeezing their muscles telling them things like *'Oooh, you're so manly going out on a* boat' and *'you must get lonely being out there in woods.'* And how right they were. Out on the high seas, in the Everbushes, Gerald and Leroy were in full control, captains of their ship. But with them two ladies sitting on their laps it was like they were putty in their hands. Anyhow, next thing I remember is waking up in the pitch dark under a booth; and everyone was gone."

"That's weird. Where'd they all go?"

"I don't know. It was a long day, plus the whole lead up to the night. I must have dozed off."

"You mean *passed out?*" Sandy couldn't help sneaking in.

"Well I won't deny I didn't have a few cocktails." Tate shook his head in affirmation as he spit in his can. "Yeah, God bless Manny ... wherever he is."

"Or do you mean Rest in Peace?" Sandy laughed.

Tate looked at Sandy sideways. "You didn't have anything to do with ..."

"Whoa! Whoa! Whoa!" Sandy sang as he threw up his hands in defense. "I got nothin' against Manny, and never did! LEGZ, whatever you called it, I never once stepped foot in that place. It's just, I was just speculating because ..." Sandy looked around to confirm with everybody else. "I haven't heard a peep from the guy since. You don't think ..."

To a man everyone went quiet around the campfire, looking around at each other with shifty eyes. Rusty was confused, he didn't know what to think; nor did the oblivious Tate.

"Anyhow," Tate said, cautiously breaking the awkward silence. "— By the time I pulled myself up off the floor and made it through the door, it was sun-up and the place was crawling with cops. Even Gerald and Leroy were in cuffs."

Tate shook his head. "They took me down to the station to question me about everything I knew about Manny "El Rey" Pantera and his *Arco Platino Gang*, wanted for fraud in four states. Something about bouncing bad checks, faking deeds, stuff like that. First thing I did when I left the station was go to the bank and check my account."

"Let me guess," Sandy predicted. "I bet you didn't have a cent."

"Oh, I wish, but it was actually much worse than that. My account was over drawn and my credit line completely maxed out."

Tate took out his chaw and chucked it into the flame.

"And just like that, my entire froggin' fortune," Tate said as he snapped his fingers. "— *Up in flames*. Purty much every bit of it. Except for my capital investments, everything else was gone."

"Capital invesments? You mean the stores?"

"An empire of plywood shacks," Sandy muttered.

Tate shook his head. "Turned out we'd been squatting the whole time. Didn't have a deed, or a *real one* anyway, to a single site."

Sandy shook his head. "So he actually went through the effort of *counterfeit paperwork*. That seems harder than doing it right."

Kleal shook his head with a menacing smile. "That Manny he was a piece of work. Promise the sky, but couldn't deliver you dirt."

"Lookin' up at it now I guess, from six feet under. *Ain't that right, Greg*," Vuke drunkenly slurred.

Greg either very slightly shook his head no or didn't respond, all the while maintaining his cryptic Cheshire cat smile.

Tate answered for him. "Well I ain't seen him around these parts. He's either in jail or slipped town. I was mad as hell at first but then I just decided to let it be. The night I finally got closure was at the Green Frog when old Sonny said the drinks were on the house. He was the only one to console me when my Frog Legz dream finally, once and for good, drowned."

"And Gerald and Leroy, did you ever settle up?"

"Gerald, he married that girl he met that night. Trixie was her name. He was more than happy with that. I think they moved up state. I'll never forget the day he left. He'd kinda come full circle on the whole thing, had it all sized up. 'Sometimes with the financial stuff,' he said, 'you take it on the chin' to which I responded, 'Yeah, lucky in love, unlucky in poker, you can't count on winning every hand.' I'll never forget he gave me the strangest look and said how with Trixie he was lucky with both. She was a catch that Trixie. Darned if she didn't laugh at all Gerald's jokes. As for Leroy, he drew a harder bargain. Eventually we agreed he could have my frogging territory. I circled the places and we signed our names on the map at the Green Frog. Sonny even said he could have the map so I gave it to him straight off the wall. Leroy was hesitant at first until I sold him on Manny's view that froggin' was *'just like fashion:'* he just had to be patient and give it some time and it would be roaring right back even bigger and more profitable than before. Threw in some coolers to sweeten the deal. He wanted my secret sauce recipe, too, but I wouldn't budge. In the meanwhile, he got into the long hauling business, cross country stuff." Tate shook his head. "But you know how it is with most of the old boys. Mostly I sort of lost touch."

"How about Candy?" Vuke asked.

"Last I heard Candy moved to the Carolinas, a big house in the hills," Sandy replied. "— Never did marry you know."

"Any guy she ever dated *never could* handle how she got so many looks. You know, of all the bad things that went wrong for me, it was nice knowing Candy was still out there, unattached, that maybe I still had a chance."

"Ha! You and Candy? It was her and Manny that were the hot ticket," Vuke let slip out.

"Manny and Candy!?" Tate exclaimed. "That's news to me!"

"Welllll," Vuke backpedaled as Henry gave him a face. "Oh, no, that wasn't Candy ... that was ... Jenna-ba ... *um* ... Jenna Barnack ... *um* ... Barnacles ... Jenna Barnacles ... yeah, that's right."

Vuke seemed relieved when he finally got the name out.

"Yeah, okay, Jenna whoever," Tate approved. "I can buy that, but not Manny and Candy together – no way! I'm positive they would never do a thing like that. It would be in violation of our corporate trust, and full disclosure rules."

Kleal muttered something under his breath. "Oh yeah, him and Candy, it was *full disclosure alright.*" It wasn't loud enough for Tate to hear but everybody else got the gist.

"So 'bout Manny?" Sandy spoke up in attempt to connect all the dots. "What's his story? Did he just disappear?"

"Old Manny. Good ol' Manny," Kleal sinisterly sneered. "Let's just say that maybe he finally paid the price for messing with *One Too Many Charlies* over the years."

Vuke thought to add something in mid slurp only to have beer spray through his nose. *"Cough, ahem ... yeah ... cough ...*

we all know what happens when ... *ahem* ... you go messin' with ... *cough* ... One Too Many Charlies."

•••

"ONE TOO MANY CHARLIES?" a baritone voice rang out. "—Is not ONE enough?"

Rusty looked over to see a silhouette move toward the inner ring of the campfire to take center stage. It was Huddy! Rusty had previously assumed that he'd dozed off for the night; apparently not.

"AHHHHH, gentlemen, EXCUSE ME while I try to WAKE MYSELF UP," the retired sawyer sang as he slapped at his arms and cavernous chest. "YOUR STORIES, well, they were — and pardon me for sayin' again — PUTTING ME TO SLEEP ... until, HA! Did I hear my ears right: ONE TOO MANY CHARLIES??? As if there could ever be MORE THAN ONE!"

Huddy circled the flame as he spoke.

"If Charlie were here, OH THE STORIES *YOU'D HEAR*," Huddy thundered. "Those stories, HIS STORIES, chronicle this HARSH and UNFORGIVING land that, like a MESSIAH, he strode across. You'll find no better friend in Charlie, BUT DON'T CROSS 'IM!" Huddy warned.

The pupils of Huddy's eyes danced in a trance as the men followed along transfixed, eager to hear what he was going to say next as Rusty *tried* to follow along even though much of the story, at least to him, wasn't going to make a hundred percent sense.

"OH, THAT CHARLIE. Y'all think you KNOW what it means to live in this PLACE, DO YA? Well let me tell ya — YOU DON'T! NOT EVEN CLOSE! The AGE OF CHARLIE is a time you know NOTHING ABOUT. A swamp ain't A FIT PLACE TO LIVE for no man, not even ME! If it weren't for DROUGHT my FATHER would have never brought us here."

"If a drought is what you call it when it's men, *not Mother Nature*, draining the water off," Henry exhaled under his breath with some smoke.

Huddy nodded in agreement toward the thought. "HODGE COME HERE to take leave of DEMONS. Even the INDIANS were PUSHED HERE: a LAST REFUGE, a last stand. AND STAND THEY DID. PROUDLY. One foot in the SUN and one in the RAIN, one foot DARKNESS one foot in the LIGHT, one foot in the FLOOD and one in the DROUGHT, one in the PAIN one in the BLISS, one on the GROUND one in the GRAVE, one on the PLATFORM one on the TRAIN. If PROGRESS is what you want, don't expect it to happen on YOUR TERMS ... or to last VERY LONG. This place has defeated man TEN TIMES OVER before any man DEFEATED IT, and NO MAN TRULY BELONGS here 'CEPTIN' CHARLIE."

Rusty couldn't believe what he was hearing, and couldn't have been more thrilled. At long last the legend of Campfire Charlie was being revealed, or so he thought. Rusty listened in awe at Huddy's honest voice, humbly firm and sympathetically resolute: he spoke in a lyricism and authority that demanded respect. From the sounds of it, Charlie straddled the fence between the pivotal and poorly understood era when the swamp was still primal, untamed, and when the first of the big canals and levees were put in; a time when all things seemed possible – natural bounty like modern-day man has never seen and engineering endeavors that were as grandiose as they were poorly thought out, half-baked in conception and half-baked again in how they were built — a "build it or bust" mindset, *and bust it they did!* — splitting the swampy frontier open like a ripe melon and spilling out a big fat mess that somehow got sold as both proof of the progress and the crux of a problem that could only be shored up and fixed with more surveys, more blueprints and most of all money, machines and men digging and sawing and sweating seven days a week at double, triple quintuple the cost, and most of all, through it all — somehow, incredibly, the swamp holding strong.

"That is, until they brought in a thing called the WALKING DREDGE," a melancholy Huddy Johnson moaned. "It was the MONSTER OF THE MARSH, a machine the swamp COULD NOT DEFEAT. Foot by foot and mile by mile, that walking dredge HAMMERED her, BLASTED her, DUG out her GUTS and THRUST a STEEL DAGGER straight ACROSS HER THROAT to leave her liquid heart TO BLEED OUT."

Huddy had an absolutely defeated look on his face.

"THAT was the END of the AGE that Charlie KNEW...."

Sandy interrupted with no small amount of skepticism. "So this Campfire Charlie, did he, you, anybody write anything down? Because I'd really love to check any of your primary sources – *if you have them* – for any mention of such a legendary figure."

The orange orb of light pulsated.

A phalanx of bats twisted in the darkness above.

Huddy laughed: "FACTS? Oh, I see. You want ... COLD HARD PROOF. Well, what if I was to tell you THERE WAS a person, A WOMAN, who wrote it all down, most EVERY WORD. Everything that Charlie ever SAID he did. Transcribed BLACK on WHITE."

Sandy's ears perked up slightly, although his look could best be described as doubtful at best.

Huddy continued: "SHE was a COLORED woman, a pretty thing, someone the moment I met her I knew she was a FRIEND, like KIN. If you don't know who I'm talking about, ZELDA was her name. She arrived SOUTHBOUND by rail on the CITRUS EXPRESS. Don't know why or how but Charlie always had a way of SHOWING UP whenever that train whistle BLEW. And why Zelda even chose this place is ANYBODY'S GUESS. Of that woman's many admirable traits, she was PATIENT above all else."

"You aren't talking about Zelda Hayes?" Sandy chimed in with an earnest look. "I'm pretty familiar with everything she wrote. She travelled all over the state doing research on folklore. Interviews with lumbermen, hunters and other backwoods types, mostly Black folks. She was voluminous for sure, especially at the crossroads of where the Seminole and African cultures meet."

"UNCLE LINCOLN and me, we got to know her well," Huddy confirmed. "TO ME, all the old timers' JOKES and TALES were nothing but ENTERTAINMENT, something to PASS THE TIME. But ZELDA thought those STORIES were something MORE THAN THAT."

Sandy shook his head pretty adamantly. "It's a history that would be lost without her accounts, that's for sure," he agreed, "— But Campfire Charlie and Zelda? *I don't think there's a link.*"

"OH, THERE WAS, Dr. Sandy... and I'll NEVER FORGET; Saturday night at the JUKE, pretty much everybody cleared out, GONE HOME, and all the jugs gone DRY, so tired we were from a long week's work ... only to be STARTLED AWAKE by the sight outside; TWO SILOHUETTES around the flickering flame — Charlie HOLDING COURT and Zelda BY HIS SIDE, a FULL MOON shining down."

"Wait a minute," Vuke slurred turning to Kleal, "So Charlie ... he was a white fella, *right?*"

"As white as me," Henry exhaled.

Huddy belted out a laugh that reverberated through the woods, leaving Vuke (and Rusty for that matter) even more perplexed, not that Huddy slowed down to explain what had been discussed. Rusty looked at his father. The flickering shadow and light cast an appearance of war paint across his face, as if he was an Indian of the High Plains.

"She wrote on the southbound train COMING DOWN and she wrote on the northbound train GOING BACK. Zelda the INK and Charlie the PARCHMENT. Black lines EMBEDDED on white. When the MUSE finds her MORTALS there is no turning back. She came down a singular train TWO RAILS of the SAME TRACK. One rail rolling BACKWARD into the past. The other rolling FORWARD into the UNKNOWN, the still unseen."

The flame flickered.

The embers hissed.

Sandy was getting increasingly drawn in to the heretofore undiscovered historical thread. "The train connection intrigues me, Huddy. You don't think Charlie was a rail man, do ya? That would sort of make sense. Could've worked the steamboats, too?"

Huddy nodded knowingly. "The FULL SUM of what Charlie did, maybe only ZELDA KNOWS. Something about that woman she could see STRAIGHT INTO YOUR SOUL. Wherever she walked she ALWAYS BROUGHT PEACE. I think that's what drew Charlie to her. She gave those TUMULTUOUS times some sense of ORDER, a kindly ASSURANCE that the TRAIN OF TIME would NOT FORGET. As for your question, *GUIDE* is the WORD. EVERYBODY WHO CAME HERE sought Charlie for that. Hunters, speculators, the railroads, the lumber firms ... EVEN THE EMPORER HIMSELF."

"The Emporer? Really? Whoa! This is really making me think," Sandy guffawed with a look of genuine surprise across his face. "I can see Mr. Gilchrest needing Charlie. Perhaps he was even a little afraid of him as well. But where in Zelda's narrative is any of that?"

As Huddy circled the flame, a drop in his shoulders portended the personal and heart-wrenching turn in the story about to come next. "—And then came the winter Zelda DIDN'T SHOW UP; ONE hours, TWO hours, three DAYS, a WEEK late; HAT IN HAND, I'll never forget, Uncle Lincoln walking ACROSS THE PLATFORM to the GET THE NEWS firsthand from the STATION ATTENDANT himself; he was a NEW FELLA, young, and QUITE POLITE, his reply as SOUL-CRUSHING as it was MATTER OF FACT: *'Um, did you say ... the Citrus Express?'* he *asked as he shuffled through the paperwork on the desk. 'No sir, I don't see it on the schedule. Not today or tomorrow ... or, um, any day this week.'"*

Huddy stared stoically into the darkness.

"It was later THAT SPRING that Uncle Lincoln DIED. SIX BLASTS of the TRAIN WHISTLE — *I can STILL HEAR THEM now.*"

Rusty looked around at the other men in attempt to decipher what that meant.

"*Dead man goin' back on the train to Hopeland,*" whispered Tate. "*God rest poor Lincoln's soul.*"

The fire sizzled.

Sparks popped.

Huddy's body disappeared into the darkness of the dying light at the same time his mind and soul plummeted back into the past, his voice providing the only proof he was still there at all.

"THEN CAME THE DAY to lay Uncle Lincoln's body DOWN TO REST when — *Lo' and Behold* — *if I didn't hear that SEVENTH WHISTLE BLOW!* And so I TOOK OFF running by foot AS FAST AS I COULD — but not for the station, no I bypassed that — going straight through THE CYPRESS, a place we called 'The Hill', past the JUKE-JOINT and cattycorner to the MILL, underneath the shade of the GRAPEFRUIT GROVE and finally to the fresh dug-up dirt at the near bank of the BIG CANAL the WALKING DREDGE had recently gouged out where, across the water, up on the LEVEE, I watched THAT APPARITION APPEAR: *It was ZELDA'S TRAIN chugging around the bend!*"

A smile spread across Huddy's face. Though standing at the fires edge, he was lost to the present, away on that sunny afternoon long, long ago, his arm outstretched to the sight of the passing train.

"And SURE ENOUGH, there he was, UNCLE LINCOLN at the very same window where Zelda ALWAYS SAT, and her by his side WRITING EVERYTHING DOWN. But the moment he saw me," Huddy mouthed in a trance-like state, "— he jumped up and dashed forward, OR DO I MEAN REVERSE, leaping and striding SOUTHBOUND as the train CHUGGED NORTH, the contradictory motion OF MAN AND MACHINE causing my uncle to momentarily stay in *ONE SPOT* — hovering over the tracks — one car, then THE NEXT and the next until FINALLY he made his way to back railing of THE CABOOSE to WAVE GOODBYE one LAST TIME."

Huddy stared at the fire.

His story appeared to be done.

"Is that true, Mr. Huddy?" a bewildered Rusty asked.

Huddy inhaled deeply before answering the question. "That's the way IT WAS ... IF IT WASN'T, that's the way IT SHOULD HAVE BEEN."

Sandy had a question, too. "So, whatever happened to Zelda? I could be wrong, but all of her published work chronicled Polk County. No mention of around here."

Huddy squatted by the fire. He picked up a stick and stoked it. Sparks flew like hellish fireflies into the smoky air.

"MY GUESS," Huddy mumbled to himself, "—Is that she CONTINUED to write as much as anybody could DO ANYTHING that was as PRICELESS as it never PAID THE BILLS. Maybe they've never been found, but it's A LIE, ignorance, EVEN WORSE, to say they don't or NEVER DID exist."

Affirmation of Huddy's faith in his memory was counterbalanced by Sandy's growing incredulity with the sequence of events. "No, the station attendant *was right:* The mainline stopped going south from Perry once the major tracts were logged. And as for Zelda Hayes, she died penniless working as a maid in the Hill Country, Chattanooga if I recall right. Only a fraction of what she wrote ever saw the light of day. And Charlie? Probably the best proof we've got of him is *that photo*, you know the one, of him running the Walking Dredge ..."

"CHARLIE *RUNNING* THE WALKING DREDGE!?" an unconvinced Huddy bellowed out to contest the point. "No ONE MAN, *not even Charlie*, could run that dredge ALONE. That MONSTER of a MACHINE took a dozen men on the BEST of days, and EVEN THEN it was the other way around. It was THE MACHINE THAT RAN THE MEN — that is, when it wasn't BROKEN DOWN."

"That's just the thing," Sandy followed up. "Even on that photo the jury's still out, some say it was a guy named Theodore Watts. I guess what I'm saying is this: I've run across more evidence there might be a Sasquatch than I've seen proof that old Uncle Charlie exists. If he's anything, he's probably a composite character of many men and many events. Sure there's lots of stories, but let's face it. A lot of stories are probably made up."

"Well, for what it's worth." Vuke hesitated, "—I always heard it was Charlie in that photo running the dredge."

"Yes, yes — of course," Sandy acknowledged. "That's what everybody thinks, *but where is it written down?*"

"Thing about Charlie," Henry exhaled in Huddy's defense. "— It wasn't *what* he said, it was *how he said it*. Notes on paper, even if they survived, could never have recaptured that, maybe a fraction at best. And that photo? It's really anybody's guess."

Greg Kleal looked eager to finish the conversation up, but was also peeved about on point. "Did ya hear how they're raising funds to declare that *Hunk of Junk Dredge* a historic landmark — Can you believe that, a *landmark!?* — and put it on display in a state park."

Henry scratched the back of his ear and then took a drag from his tiparillo. "Ironic as hell, don't you think, that the one thing they want to declare a National Treasure is the very thing we, or they — *Charlie's generation* — used to tear up the swamp."

"Yeah," Kleal sneered, "—That Charlie, he got away with so bleeping much! We lionize him now, but if we tried to do *today* what Charlie did *back then* they'd put us in the Hoosegow and *lock* us up for life!"

The conversation was abruptly interrupted by a succession of three loud smacks — *Thwap! Thwap! Thwap!* — smashing down just beyond the view of the campfire's outer orb of light. A startled Dan Vukovich immediately stood up.

"Who goes there!? Step forward and show yourself," Dan demanded into the night.

...

The shadowing figure of an old decrepit man entered the orb.

"Charlie in the Hoosegow!?" the mysterious intruder mocked. *"— Did I hear ye gents right?"*

The old man didn't so much walk as he *shuffled* through the dirt. Behind him in each hand he clenched the stems of two giant palm fronds. One and then the other he jammed into the embers. The fire responded with a diabolical roar that instantly turned the inky night into the shining intensity of day, the illumination of which the new entrant used to give each man a hardened stare. *"Charlie in the Hoosegow!?"* he repeated with contempt as the ephemeral flash of light returned to night. *"— Ha!!!"*

Rusty couldn't believe his good fortune: If Huddy's stories of Campfire Charlie weren't enough, now he had the actual man, alive and in the flesh, standing before him to tell his tale himself. Perhaps overhearing the men's critical comments was what had made him so upset, thus leaving him no other choice than to step forward out from the dark and defend his good name. Nobody likes being talked about behind their back.

Despite the hero's somewhat malingered state, Rusty's overriding impulse was elation, a tingling sensation in his chest. "And thank God," Rusty thought: from the looks of it, the man didn't appear to have much time left on earth before he was gone for good. For a guy that had a reputation for *not aging,* Lord Almighty if it didn't look like it had finally all caught up with him all at once. Hunched over, weathered and a raspy wheeze of a voice, Charlie was a pitiful shadow of the youthful spirit and vigorous health so prominently on display in the old black and white photographs. But make no mistake, he was no shrinking violet either, no, not even close; he was more the type of man that even the Grim Reaper would delay meeting at all costs.

While it was a little disconcerting to see Charlie so old, to Rusty it also *"clicked"* and made logical sense. Of course, Charlie would *have to be* an old man by now. No one, not even a legend, could escape the ravages of time unscathed. To his credit, the old man seemed to acknowledge as much himself. In a sort of out of body experience, the geezer had the self-awareness to separate the well-chronicled feats of his storied youth from what had now become his decaying self by employing a manner of speech that produced an altogether peculiar effect: he outright and absolutely refused to refer to himself in his retelling of his memories using the first person — *"I"* — rather opting to use the third-person — "Charlie" — in its place. Whether the man did it on purpose or inadvertently it was hard to tell. Perhaps it was an overt act to protect the reputation of his legend from the ravages of his advancing age, or maybe it was a sign that his senility had caused a fragmentation in the continuum of his life.

"Lockin' up Old Charlie? Ha!" the geezer said as he beat his chest with a thud. "Don't you think for a second that Charlie wasn't *way too smart* for that. Don't 'spose any of you *fine gents* could guess what'd happen to you if you even dared?" Charlie raised his boney finger to the flame and extended his talon-like shadow of his crooked finger to each man, one by one, and called out each man by name: first Henry, then Huddy, Tate, Vukovich, Sandy and Kleal. It was especially striking to witness the broken-down old specimen of a man's tongue-lashing of Greg Kleal. Even if *he was* once a legend, it seemed fool hearty in the extreme. Greg Kleal was a dangerous man in broad daylight let alone around a remote campfire deep in the woods.

Defying his reputation, Greg didn't seem offended one bit, rather just curious. "Don't you mean *Jimmy Thistle? He* was the lawman ..." Greg pondered out loud and then added politely, "— Of course, I'm not trying to be rude." Greg turned to the others for confirmation. "Just want to get the record straight so we're all on the same page."

"*Ha! Thistle!* Now there's a worthless piece of ..." Charlie snarked. He kicked violently at a log, instantly atomizing the embers into a constellation of sparkles and hissing ash. "Thistle was worse than a turncoat, even lower than that. My only regret in life is that I didn't get a chance at him in my prime years — *oh, 'cause if I did!"* The old man left what he had in mind to the imagination of the others. Considering the crowd, it wasn't asking a lot.

Rusty could accept the man had aged. What bothered him was how bitter he'd become. The youthful man his father showed him in the old photos — which, granted, were blurry and scratched and just a snapshot in time at best — had always exuded an affable charm, a man without a worry in the world, a lightness of being and a youthful spirit with a perpetual skip in his step; or in other words, a man who was the polar opposite to the ragged and haggard figure circling the campfire. Despite his febrile state, the man looked unhinged and ready to explode. What in the world could have happened between then and now to so startlingly and sadly have altered the man's view of the world?

"But don't you boys worry about Jimmy Thistle," Charlie howled as he jabbed his clenched hands in the air at the invisible villain. He stood in front of the fire in a way that made him look like he was being consumed by the flame. "Because I'm here to tell ya Ol' Charlie, yep — *Good Ol' Charlie* — he had a way of dealing with bad actors! *Lawman!? Justice!?* You've all come to the wrong place if you're expecting any of that. *Good or bad?*

Out here there's only *bad and worse!* Everybody wants to remember Thistle like he was some 'do more good than harm' latter day saint. What a bunch of bunk! I'm here to tell ya firsthand, flesh and in the blood, that Sheriff Jimmy Thistle — *before, during and after the badge* — was the biggest scoundrel that this state has ever seen. Makes all of you and all your misdeeds, even your worst, look like a damn Sunday school church picnic in comparison. He didn't take no for an answer, not from beast *nor man.* Nothing got in the way of Jimmy Thistle getting what he wanted. What he couldn't get with his charm he'd get by hook or by crook or by brute force."

A shift in the wind blew the smoke Rusty's way. By the time it cleared, the evil-eyed Charlie was standing right in front of him staring at him menacingly in the face.

"How old are ya, boy!?" he exclaimed with an executioner's voice.

Rusty was embarrassed, horrified actually, to be noticed — let alone *singled out.* Beads of sweat popped out of his pores. He was stricken with the sudden indecision of fight or flight: should he lash out at the man or flee in the woods?

"I know how old ya are," Charlie answered for him before he could respond. "You're old enough to know better than to hang out with this vermin group in this God Forsaken Swamp. *Ain't nothin' here for ya! Thistle already took care of that!"*

The man circled the flame and pounded his chest, the force of which caused him to cough something phlegmy up into his mouth which he hacked at a little more and then spat out. "My advice to you is to run as far away ... *ahem hack cough* ... as you can ... run for the hills ... *ahem hack spit* ... and don't you ever come back!" The exertion seemed to tire the man, or possibly it was a soothing effect to finally expel the excess bile. Whatever the cause, the octogenarian (or however old he was) proceeded to speak with a less acidic, almost subdued voice. *"You know why I tell you that?"*

Rusty had no idea what to think or how to respond other than he was scared and dared not open his mouth.

"Because when I was your age I was sneaking on tip toe up on little baby birds and thwacking them dead with a stick, one nest then another and then on to the next!" The demented old man emphasized the point by picking up a knobby branch from the kindling pile and violently and awkwardly striking it to the ground until it broke into shards and there was nothing left to beat, just a stub in the agitated man's ghastly hands. "— Just like that!"

Rusty's fright instantly transformed into disgust. And for the first time ever he was actually mad at his father, too. All the stories he had to listen to about Charlie being a hero and then for it all to come to this? What was the point? More than a letdown it was a betrayal of the father-son bond, as if something sacred had been shattered, something holy befouled. Charlie wasn't a hero, no, not even close. He was the exact opposite: an imposter masquerading as a gentleman and who'd managed to escape detection his whole life, and even worse than that, here he was in his final years — obviously nearing his deathbed — and confessing it without a kernel of guilt or remorse but rather in pure spite, if not also with a bit of twisted delight. Internal anger flooded into Rusty's heart. He could think of no bigger or better wish than him being *bigger* and Campfire Charlie *younger* — not a frail man but still in his prime — so that the both of them could travel back in time and relive the apocryphal event, this time Rusty taking advantage of his knowledge and cutting the diabolical man off at the pass before he got to the rookery and protecting every last nest. That of course not being possible Rusty started to choke up. Having remained stoic to this point, emotions were now welling up.

"*Well ... you're ... a ... mah-mah-mah ... mean man ...*" he stammered back in a resolute but crackling voice.

In a surprising turn of events, Charlie adopted a grandfatherly tone. "Now don't go start cryin' on me, young fella," the geezer gently pleaded. "— I know you're Henry's boy, *Rusty's your name, right?*"

A chill ran down Rusty's spine to hear Charlie call him by name.

"And I do understand, *I truly do*, how you might feel. You must hate me for admitting such a dispicable act."

The repentant old man even tried to hand Rusty a kerchief. Rusty wasn't haven't any of it. He pushed his hand away.

"Now don't take me wrong, Rusty," Charlie implored. "— Please don't. From the bottom of my heart, whatever little bit of it is left in this here chest, I can assure you're most certainly wrong on *both* counts. First, I was not mean. No, *mercy killing* is the more proper term. And second, like I said before, I wasn't a man when I did it, not even close. I was barely your age," he added. "If you can believe it that a withered old man that looks like me was ever a boy?"

Rusty was more confused than ever. He glanced across the campfire at his father who raised the ember end of his tiparillo in the air and gestured with his hand, all body language his son understood to mean his line of inquiry was on good ground.

"Well well ... wha-wha-wha ... wha-why did you kill them, sir?"

"Thank you for asking?" Charlie answered in a perfunctory and quite even-keeled tone. "— I killed them because I couldn't stand the sound of them chirping for their mothers who would never return." The old man capped off his response by chirping as best he could in a baby bird's voice, *"Cheep cheep cheep."*

A moment of silence followed.

Just the campfire. Its crackle. The pulse of the embers below.

"Seventy-five years later that sound still wakes me up in the middle of the night. But trust me, what I was doing — and you're right, *it was* an unthinkable and ugly act — was my best choice on a long list of bad options. What else was I supposed to do? The mothers were dead. The chirping babies were doomed to die."

Charlie thrashed the stub of a branch he was still clenching in his fist as hard as he could into the night. Rusty listened as it rustled through the leaves and landed somewhere out of sight.

"I'll have you know I said a prayer as best I could before I snuffed the life out of each one." Charlie paused with a painful look in his eye as he tried to pull himself away from the moment to gather his thoughts.

"Wha-wha-wha happened to their muh-muh-mothers?" Rusty interrupted with a cracking voice.

"They got caught in the crossfire of Jimmy Thistle," Old Man Charlie morbidly laughed as he again kicked at the flame with his boot. An explosion of embers and hissing of gas dispersed into the night air. "Mercy killing is what I was doing — *Jimmy Thistle's dirty work."*

"He sha-sha-sha shot their mothers?" Rusty repeated, still in shock.

"He did," Charlie acknowledged solemnly. "— Right off of their nests. Almost made shooting fish from a bucket honorable sport."

"He shot the ba-ba-ba baby birds' mothers?" he repeated yet again, this time to himself. Rusty was abhorred. Outdoorsmen like his father abided by strict rules on the sizes and seasons to hunt and fish. With the deer hunt the rule was you never took a doe, and especially not in spring.

"More meat on a deer fly. Yeah, but he *ate* alright. Ate like a fat cat. Big fat sirloin steaks. He sold their plumes to the highest bidder and then went straight to the bank. As for me? After all that unpleasantness, I didn't even make a cent."

"But I could've lived with that," Charlie confessed. "— If it was just a *one-time* event. What's most disgusting of all is what happened next. Back comes old Thistle, this time the *toast of the swamp*, sporting a fancy hat and wearing a *shiny badge* — Mr. Big Shot Game Warden! — saying how all the new canals had attracted nuisance gators that were attacking women and children on boats and eating all the game fish, and how it was his job to 'civilize the swamp' and make it 'safe for swimming' and a bunch of other sales pitches like that. I can still see him smiling with his big white hat and his pointy badge."

As terrible the story was, at least it was starting to make more sense. Jimmy Thistle was a master at playing both sides of the fence. First as a bad man in a lawless land and then later donning the white hat to clean it all up.

Charlie continued. "So Thistle and his top man, Twitchy Thompson, were sent in to investigate a report of a little boy who lost his dog to a gator attack while fishing at Trails Bend. Next thing you know, in comes Thistle, him and his puurrty badge." The old man snapped his fingers. "And just like that he took fifty gators, and that was just on his first sweep. A week later Thistle returned and took fifty more, and over thirty a few days after that. Of course, by that point Thistle knew enough to keep his hands clean, and his alligator-skin boots shinier, all the while his gang of henchmen were neck deep in gator hides and blood and guts."

After so many decades Charlie still shook his head in disbelief

"But it wasn't the plumes and it wasn't the hides that earned Jimmy Thistle his reputation. The smoothest of smooth operators, he capped off the carnage by masterminding one last final and despicable act."

Rusty waved his hands in front of his face and covered his ears. He didn't want to hear it. He'd heard enough and couldn't bear anymore.

"Please don't say it! Please don't say!" Rusty kept repeating, *"— I've heard enough!"*

"He gave that boy a puppy."

The new revelation stopped the boy's impassioned plea dead in its tracks. Rusty went from being very upset to rather confused, even doubtful in fact. The new information just didn't make sense. Either that or he didn't hear Charlie right, to which he summoned the courage to ask the old man to repeat: "You said that ... Jimmy Thistle bought the boy ... *a puppy?*

"A puppy," the old man confirmed. "That's right."

Rusty got his confirmation, but he was still unsure. The only path to enlightenment seemed to be to hear the old man out.

"And it wasn't just *any puppy,*" Charlie proceeded to explain. "It was the most adorable little baby Laborador Retriever that little boy had ever laid his eyes on. And you know Thistle, he made a big show of it like only Thistle could do. Got the story *front page* in the newspaper like all scoundrels posin' as a hero do."

Charlie kicked at the fire again. This time he whiffed.

The old man looked up with a wild and faraway look in his eyes.

"And if you haven't guess by now about who that little boy was, I'll give you a hint. You're staring right at him. That little boy was *me.*"

Rusty was more confused than ever. Up until this point Charlie had been an ageless and affable man without a worry in the world, a man who was perpetually in his prime. Now, in the matter of a half hour, Rusty had learned that Charlie was nothing of the like, not one bit, but rather an old man severely rattled by the bad memories of his prepubescent youth.

"But you said that *you* had a way of dealing with *Jimmy Thistle,*" a more resolute Rusty spoke up.

Now it was Old Man Charlie's turn to be confused. The boy's inquiry had clearly caught him off guard, baffled him in fact, to the point that the octogenarian seemed to lack even an inkling of an idea of how to respond — then, in a flash, a look of total clarity washed across the old geezer's face; or maybe *bemusement* was the better word. Whatever the case, the continence of the old man had discernably changed: In place of his scowl, a paternal smile of reassurance spread across his face. And no longer bent over in a crooked hunch, he stood tall and straight like an upright plank of wood, a veritable pillar of humanity, and not a scourge at all.

"Not me!" the old man clarified. *"— I was talking about Charlie."*

"That's not Charlie. *It's Albert Lee Hodge,"* Sandy followed up to affirm. *"He's the owner of this camp."*

All the man broke into riotous laughter, and most of all Mr. Hodge.

"He thought ... ha ha ha ... that I WAS CHARLIE!!! REALLY!?" A mixture of air and fluid snortled through his nose. *"Oh, in all my days! That's a good one! That really is good!"*

•••

It took Rusty a moment to rejuggle the facts: Albert Lee Hodge — not Charlie — was the little boy in the story who long ago did the mercy killing of the baby birds and it was Albert Lee Hodge, the owner of The Lodge — not Charlie — who was the old man standing in front of him now.

Rusty turned to Mr. Huddy still confused about one point: hadn't he mentioned seeing Charlie in real life on multiple occasions? And his cryptic tale about Zelda; whatever happened to her? Just as Rusty was about to open his mouth to ask, Huddy responded in a cavernous trance as if he had been expecting the question in advance: "Charlie never STICKS AROUND," Huddy answered. "— By the time you realize it's him, HE'S GONE like a ghost."

Rusty did the quick math in his head. If Mr. Hodge was such an old man there's no way Charlie, or Jimmy Thistle for that matter, could still be alive; other than as a sighting from a spirit world, an over-imaginative mind playing tricks, or Zelda's long-ago lost notes.

Separate conversations had broken out by the time Rusty had finally started to figure it out, even if a lot of it still didn't make sense.

Mr. Hodge and Henry were discussing something in private, after which — without saying a word — Mr. Hodge left, presumably, Rusty could only guess, to go into The Lodge to retire for the night. Huddy and Sandy Parrish did what they could to get the campfire back in order as Tate grilled Vuke for more details on Manny Pantera.

•••

The men stood back as they watched the new wood ignite and spread the orb of light to reveal Greg Kleal with an unsatisfied look on his face, like he was restless and waiting – and now ready – to discuss something else. "Say Henry, you wouldn't happen to have any *scuttlebutt* for us about tomorrow night?"

Rusty's father seemed to carefully consider the request as he lit up a cigarillo with a smoldering stick he pulled from the flame. After getting it lit, he inhaled deeply, then exhaled, and said that he did, after which he stood up, took another puff, and walked off. A few moments later he returned with a bundle of papers tied together with red string. He carefully untied the bow and turned on a headlamp he'd strapped around his forehead and started to read.

The men listened intently as he went through each page one by one, paragraph by paragraph, sentence by sentence and word by word. At the end of each paragraph he'd say *"end of paragraph"* and if words were quoted or italicized or capitalized he'd also say that. The men listen respectfully, even intently, if at other times looking bored. Sandy rubbed his face and yawned only to suddenly wake up.

"HEY! *Back up for a moment, did I hear that right?*"

Henry backed up and re-read the last few sentences.

"What happened to the *Freshwater* before Preserve? *Did you skip over that?*"

"Yeah," Henry nodded. "I noticed that, too."

"I thought the deal was they were gonna *both* conserve the land *and fix the water, too.* Dropping the Freshwater sounds like backpedaling."

"Forget about the water!" Kleal barked, trying to shut everybody up. "What I wanna know is *What About Us!?*"

Rusty's father held his hand up Kemosabe-style to keep the peace. "—Just let me finish, okay, and then we can discuss."

The men grudgingly obliged although still, on several occasions, Henry had to pause as the men broke into a rebellious roar — *"Hey Henry, Whoa ... What the ... Can they do that?"* — all over words and seemingly little minor distinctions that Rusty couldn't predict.

At the end there was a moment of silence.

Rusty couldn't tell if the men were quiet because they thought Henry still had more to read or if they were in shock and unable to speak.

"That's the new *Creation Document*. And it'll be the new Law of the Swamp once all the signatories add their names."

Another moment of silence ensued.

"That's ridiculous Henry. The only law of the swamp is all up here," Greg Kleal said tapping at his head. He pointed to the other men. "It's all around the campfire. It's unwritten. It's understood. It's been passed down. One generation to the next. It's ours alone."

Henry nodded.

He did not disagree.

"Of course it is Greg. We know that. Ain't nobody disputing you there. The problem is the outsiders, they don't think like we do. They're gonna go by whatever words are in this *Creation Document* ...," he paused. "—Whatever gets signed into law."

Vuke rubbed at his chin in attempt to think it all through.

"But us who got a handshake deal, Henry, we get to stay, right? Canal diggers and developers. They're the ones getting kicked out."

Henry looked away from the campfire into the darkness. Except for the crackling of the wood and the chirping of the frogs, everything was quiet for several moments.

"Remember that time I floated you two bills to fix up that mess."

"Yeah, what about it. I paid up."

Rusty's father shook his head. "Of course you paid up. We had a handshake deal."

Dan's eyes lit up.

"Well darnitt Henry! That's exactly my point."

"Now how 'bout the time you fell behind on your mortgage because your boy got sick. Had to pay his medical bills instead. What happened then?"

Dan's face dimmed. "Don't get me started on that, Henry. They tried to take my house away."

"And who's *they?*"

Dan shook his head. "I don't know. All I got was letters in the mail. I never actually met anybody face to face."

Rusty's father nodded.

"I don't mean to put you on the spot because I know it all worked out. You're boys all grown up with a wife and kids and you kept your house."

"I can't thank you enough for that, *you know that Henry*. And all the other stuff, too. Life used to be a struggle. Now I got everything paid off in full. And money in the bank on top of that." Vuke corrected himself. "Not that I'd put any of it in the bank. *I'm not that dumb.*"

Henry continued talking like he didn't even hear as he tied back up the papers and picked the pile up. "My point is that once this thick wad of paper gets signed, you can kiss all the handshakes in the world goodbye. Hell, it won't even be the person that wrote it that enforces it, they'll be long dead and gone. Instead you're gonna have some guy in a suit holed up in a windowless office somewhere up in Washington D.C. reading through it verbatim, word for word, and then giving orders to his henchmen to do — or not do — whatever it says."

Henry plunked the papers in the dirt and looked into the fire. He waited awhile and then looked around to all the men.

"It was just too big, fellas. Way too big. *And way too fast.* What they had planned. First the airport. Then the freeways. Then the strip malls and subdivisions after that. The whole swamp was on a path to being blacktopped to oblivion, just like the coast." Henry took a deep draw on his cigarillo. "— We couldn't have saved it ourselves without the Government's help."

"It's a deal with the Devil and you know it, Henry," Kleal scoffed.

"Burt says he'll make sure we're in the plan."

"So Burt *wrote* that document then, is that what you're sayin', Henry?"

Henry stared blankly into the fire. "Burt got us a seat at the table. We're lucky to have any representation at all."

Greg's gave a big grin across his pumpkin-shaped face as his head moved back and forth in disbelief at what he was hearing. "We gotta get it in black and white, Henry," he said as he pounded his fist in his palm. "— And not just about swamp buggies being allowed, *I'm talking about us, our property rights!*"

"I respect everything you're saying Henry, but I gotta be honest — I agree with Greg," Vuke rose to Kleal's defense. "— There's no mention of us. That raises red flags."

"This turns us into squatters on federal lands!" Tate carped. "If Sid gets reduced from twenty down to three acres, that leaves my camp on government property!"

"Yeah," Dan barked. "— So we're just gonna sit and take it? It's bullshit!"

Henry looked at them soberly with an expression that said it all. It was outside their control.

"Well Dammit, Henry. We know it ain't gonna be the same," Sandy snarked back. "Just give it to the boys *straight and plain.*"

Greg didn't wait for Henry to respond. "This is a *complete disaster,* Henry," he said as he threw his stubby arms in the air. "— We might as well burn all our shit down and go home."

"Home?" whispered Tate. "—This is home ..."

Henry prodded the fire with a stick.

Embers rose into the air.

"I wish I had better news, but this is what I got."

"We'll find out the rest tomorrow," Sandy added.

Greg sneered. "Gonna take a *lot longer* than that before we figure out the rest. And by the time we do, it's gonna be *way too late.* Why don't ya toss those goddamn papers in the fire, Charlie. It's getting dark. I think we all need a little more light."

Chapter 9:
Patriotic Fervor Grips the Land

Apr 14, 1860
The steadfastness of my letters has paid off.
What a great honor it is to host Thursby in Cincinatti! Opportunities abound he will soon find out.

Jul 23
My faith in French is rewarded.
Thursby's acumen as an engineer and businessman has won us lucrative contracts. His speculation has tripled our money in the last month alone. We rival the biggest firms and dine among the town's best.

Aug 3
Thursby and my niece have fallen in love.
I jokingly caution that Thursby is quite the unfaithful rake to which they both laughed. Molly hadn't thought of Claire's opinion about marrying a Virginian. Yet Thursby's proposal was as much a surprise to my sister as it was to Molly, and quite predictably it did take Claire a few days to acquiesce. Thursby, if anything, is a good judge of the female temperament.

Sep 12
Business is booming.
French is a man much in demand. A non-stop stream of clients walks in and out through our door. This town *is his*, just as I said it would be.

Oct 23
National politics is the talk of the town.

Everywhere I go that is all I hear. Thursby is a true American, the best among us. But I can also sense he is conflicted about what a good Virginian should do. The upcoming election looms.

Nov 10
Lincoln is elected!
There is talk of open succession and that some states may leave. Thursby has always spoken highly for his love of Virginia, but given his business acclaim and his military decorations from Florida, I am confident he will serve in the Federal army should a rebellion break out. Surely his love for my niece and our prospering business will keep him from regressing to his home state.

Jan 20, 1861
Secession now seems imminent.
"It'll never come to that," French insists whenever the topic comes up. "— I know my Virginians, we're not like South Carolina. Cool heads will carry the day." Thursby repeatedly cuts me off short and steers me to brandy and cigars "—Enough of this wretched politics."

Apr 15
War breaks out.
The idle threats have taken a bloody turn with the standoff at Fort Sumter.

May 3
Bad news arrives!
Thursby has left for Virginia with no clear plans for return.

May 26
I find out today where I will be commissioned.
Why do men fight who were born to be brothers? Godspeed Thursby, wherever you are, until we meet again ...

Chapter 10:
Downtime at The Lodge

Second Day, 3pm

Rusty closed the book and shut his eyes. He opened his eyes and looked around the room. A sword. Two wood chairs. A vase on a table in between. A magnifying glass. A shelf with some books. A space in the row of books where he'd pulled the one he was reading out. And a black and white framed photograph up on the wall. On the other side of the glass a man in a military uniform looked out. He wore his uniform perfectly as soldiers do: a peaked hat impeccably placed, lieutenant's bars pinned to his lapels, and a Labrador Retriever faithfully sitting by his feet. Rusty had read about the Great War and heard stories from an uncle of Dwight's who had driven an artillery truck across France. Rusty often thought about how people in old black and white photos looked ghost-like, as if they lived in a reflection or shadow of the real world, in a time and place that had passed, that was devoid of color and was fading away. Although it was just a photo, the man seemed to be there with him in the room, silent and all-knowing and watching all the time.

When something began stirring under the work bench, Rusty realized he'd unwittingly roused a slumbering dog. The ancient creature hoisted itself up on its haunches and started sniffing Rusty's thigh. It had matted grayish blonde fur and seemed to be missing most of its teeth. Rusty wondered if the dog might not be the identical animal as the one at the feet of the soldier on the wall when better judgement prevailed: the canine in the frame had likely been dead for decades, as perhaps was the young man, too. Rusty didn't know. He scratched the old pooch behind the ears and brushed off some dander that had caked up behind a floppy earlobe. In doing so, he spotted an old shoebox on the floor near an ammo can. The lid featured a distinctive logo of a daper-looking mustachioed gent with a bow tie and the chain of a three-piece suit connecting either side of his vest: "*Walton Massey: Shoes for the Sharp-Dressed Man, Coconut Grove's Finest Shoe Merchant*" it read underneath. Seeing that the dog had knocked the lid askew, Rusty bent down and pulled the box up out of the corner and put it onto the table to give it a closer look.

Muffled voices were audible outside. It was Huddy and Tate, the latter pressing for more information on what the eating arrangements were going to be later that night and the former expressing his opinion that the Round Up was going to be bigger than previously planned causing the latter to loop back around with anxious concern there might not be enough food. The topic switched to orchids as Sandy approached.

"First thing happens when the feds tip their hand is the poachers are gonna come in and pick the place clean. Saw the same thing happen at Snake Bight back when I was a kid ..."

"*How's that bad for you??* Tate snickered. "— Less orchids in the swamp pro'bly means mo' business at your shop."

"Tate, this isn't about money, it's about the fate of the swamp. When all the lawlessness erupts and before the Feds move in, we're gonna be the ones holding down the fort. That's what the Round Up is all about."

"And not get paid for it, I suppose?" Tate sneered.

"LOREN TATE, after all these years, I would have thought BREAKING EVEN would be a MAJOR VICTORY for you," Huddy bellowed. Although the other voices were muffled, Huddy's voice reverberated through the exterior wall as if he was standing with Rusty in the room.

"Well, as long as you keep servin' me seconds, Huddy" Tate chortled back. "—You're home-cooked food is enough payment for me. And besides, I always said it t'aint what the swamp can do you for you, but what you can do fo' the swamp."

"JFK, not a bad quote," Sandy deferred. "—I couldn't have said it better myself."

"*Noooo, not JFK!?* I'm the one that gave that sayin' to him — not the other way around — back when he stopped in to do some stumping at my Frog Legz store."

251

"Oh, you're so full of it, Tate! He wouldn't go near your low-class plywood shacks," Sandy scoffed. "And Frog Legz, I can't remember: was that with an 'S' ... or a *Zee-ee-e?*"

"Sandy, I'm in a good mood, so don't even start."

Of course starting was never the question with Sandy – it was if and when he would stop, and just how far he would go. "So JFK was borrowing phrases from you, really? Or was he there to see Candy Martinelli like everybody else?"

"It was before your time Parrish. That's why you don't know. Used to be a day the swamp-rat vote mattered. Now, not so much. Demographics have changed."

Eventually the voices faded away, once again leaving Rusty inside alone with his book, the box, the dog and the soldier behind the glass.

Rusty lifted up the lid and blew off a layer of dust to find a hodgepodge of items packed within: a faded purple ribbon with a medallion at the end, a handful of other pendants of various colors and shapes, lieutenant bars, a brass chain with artillery shells dangling from every third link and a yellow envelope with a brass prong that that was flattened to secure it at its flap. Rusty thought about how Dwight's Uncle George had his military medals and other souvenirs prominently displayed in a glass case in the front room. Just from the few times Rusty had been there, the images on the photos and the other mementos were etched in his head. That was a big contrast to how the medals in The Lodge were shuffled away into the tattered cardboard box, although Rusty knew it wasn't a sign of disrespect. Saving them meant something, especially for so long. He studied each of the medals one by one. A few were tarnished and smudged to the point they were hard to read while others were perfectly preserved as if never touched. The lieutenant bars seemed to be the same or similar ones to what the man wore beneath the glass on the wall. He guessed that the brass chain was for holding a time piece across a three piece suit in the same style of Walton Massey on the lid of the box.

•••

Rusty looked at the soldier on the wall and the soldier on the wall looked back. It didn't take long for the two of them to reach an understanding that the items in the box were probably his. The yellowed envelope contained two photographs stuck together by a cockroach egg case which Rusty separated with a gentle tap. The first photo showed two soldiers posing at a dock. They looked like they were having the time of their lives. But wasn't that always the case when people posed for photos? If people only looked and acted that way all the time the world would be a happier place, or maybe the past was just a happier time, and the future that followed sad. The fella on the right was holding a cigarette in his hand with the crook of his arm wrapped around the other guy's neck. A large ship loomed behind. Rusty flipped the photo around. It read, "*Old Chums, New York, January 1917.*"

The second photo had a pinhole on its upper right corner where it had been tacked to a wall for display but long ago removed. It featured a man in denim overalls holding a fishing pole and wearing a straw hat in the style of Huck Finn in front of a bucolic lake. The envelope also contained a neatly pressed newspaper clipping, with brittle creases, that Rusty carefully unfolded. The words *"The Taneytown Beacon, May 11, 1918, Obituaries"* were neatly handwritten across the top. The clipping read as follows:

> *Services will be held at St. Mary's Catholic Church on Friday for our beloved son, Waldo Kenneth Wilcox, 22 years of age, who fell fighting for God and Country in France on April 25, 1917. He is survived by his loving parents Barton and Ophelia and his sisters Dorothy and Claire. They are joined in bereavement by Wally's fiancé, Tina Gaffney of Baltimore. Words cannot express our sorrow. We resign our beloved into the loving arms of Jesus.*

All the clues were finally adding up: the man in the framed photo was probably Waldo. To die *so young* seemed like a waste, but at the same time Rusty didn't so much see a life cut short as he did an "old soul" who had lived a long life, as if in being allowed to hang on the wall and look out the window (day in and day out for probably decades), it had somehow afforded him a *full life*. Still, Rusty felt bad for the young man's family. He guessed Taneytown was near Baltimore or somewhere close. He envisioned the poor man's family at the church, a flag draped over a casket, everyone in prayer and tears. He also thought about how those tears had long since dried and doubted if there was anyone still left to grieve. All in all, the soldier had a thankful look. Maybe Rusty being there, thinking about him, helped the man in the framed photo feel good.

Tucked behind the newspaper clipping, Rusty discovered a third photograph. It featured one of the two service men in the first photo, *"Old Chums" in New York, 1917,"* only in the new photo the same person didn't seem as happy and was notably alone, standing solo in front of an ornate arch in a rather picturesque city square. The man's face had aged somehow. At the same time, Rusty sensed that the picture of the arch was not taken too long after the "Old Chums" photo in New York. He turned the photo over to see if he could find out. Written across the back were the words *"Arc de Triumphe"* and some other cursive writing that was too faded to make out. Rusty studied the two pictures, first the one on the wall and then one in front of the arch, when suddenly the image of a familiar person in the background of the second jumped out. Rusty laughed at the coincidence but quickly brushed it off as just that, although the man did seem to be wearing Charlie's telltale hat and had a relaxed look like he was enjoying a cigarette, he doubted Campfire Charlie ever made it to France.

Rusty felt a nudge at his side.

The dog was nuzzling with his snout trying to get under his arm.

Jimmy Thistle might have been tough, but he couldn't have been all bad if he'd given a young Albert Lee Hodge such a nice dog, although the dog on the wall was probably the great great great (great) grandfather of the dog at Rusty's feet. Rusty gently draped his arm around the animal's frail backside and rubbed his belly as it rolled on its back.

"*Good boy,*" Rusty said as he patted him. "*Good boy. Good boy.*"

...

Same day, 8 am

"There he is!" a voice called. It was Sandy waving him over to the picnic table. Huddy greeted him with a plate of steaming hotcakes, corn hash and spam from the grill. "Get WHAT YOU CAN WHEN YOU CAN GET IT," Huddy advised, "— While Gator Tate is STILL ASLEEP."

"Sure am glad I got mine," Sandy quipped as he savored another sip of coffee. "—Food has a way of vanishing when Gator Tate is around. Still not convinced him eating all his product isn't what did his Frog Legz scheme in. Oh, and by the way, that's Frog Legz ... *with a Zeeee-ee.*"

"Where are Dan and Greg? Anybody seen them?"

"Those two, who knows? —Probably stayed up all night. Kleal's worked night shifts so long the only good shut eye he gets is in the afternoon."

"Maybe they went out with my father?" Rusty guessed.

Huddy and Sandy looked at each other blankly. Rusty interpreted that to mean a maybe, but probably not.

Tate barged in from the path to the outhouse with a distressed look. *"Now ... t'ain't that just great! I see how you boys play!"* the big man whined. "— Let ol' Tate sleep through a meal! What is the world comin' to? I bet'cha it's all gone, done all ate! And the mornin' after I treat ya'll to frog legs, special sauce'n'all."

"Actually Tate, it was Greg and Vuke that brought the frogs."

"That's splittin' hairs and you know it, Parrish!"

"And Huddy that grilled them up," Sandy continued.

"Don't you start with me Parrish, not this early!"

Huddy's arrival with a towering plate of steaming hotcakes immediately defused the escalating situation.

"I'm gonna be here a while, Rusty," Tate garbled as he went to work with his fork and knife. "Got a lot of catchin' up ... *munch munch* ... to do still with Huddy. Huddy, ain't that right?! Hate to see ... *munch munch gulp* ... you throwin' out any of that batter if you don't have to. You know pancake batter ... *munch munch* ... attracts bears."

"Well, not as much as DEER GUTS," Huddy chuckled. "— But I guess you're right, we should probably FINISH IT all up."

"Quite the civil service of ya, Tate," Sandy agreed. "Batter patrol is one of the most important jobs in camp."

"Yeah, well, you know me, Sandy ... *munch munch* ... I'm always happy to help."

Rusty stood up to excuse himself, in part to avoid watching Tate grotesquely devour his hot cakes — he chewed with his mouth open causing morsels to fall out and regularly used his thumb which he repeatedly licked as he ate — but mostly because he saw a good window to get back to the book he'd been enjoying in The Lodge.

"Don't go far, Rusty" Tate groveled into his food as Rusty started to leave. "I was hoping the two of us ... *munch munch gulp* ... could do that final sweep on the runway ... like we discussed ... *munch gulp*... tractor's ready to go ... *munch gulp slurp* ... Greg and me, we loaded up the wagon with some loose dirt ... *gulp munch* ... so we're all ready to go."

"Well, just come and get me when you're ready," Rusty requested. "—I'll be up in The Lodge."

"Hate to see anything happen to the Counselor ... *munch munch* ... on account of us missing a pothole," Tate garbled to Huddy as he loaded more cakes on his plate. "— He's a good man."

"And even more important than that," Sandy piped in with a Lukewarm vote of confidence, "—*He's the only man we've got.*"

•••

Same day, 10 am
"I'm inside," Rusty hollered toward the door. "—Come on in!"

"Well, maybe it's better ... *if you just come out.*"

"I'll be right there," Rusty said as he put down his book.

Tate was swishing his hand in the cracker barrel when Rusty emerged on the porch. "As a personal rule, I try to stay outside The Lodge. Especially now I know Albert Lee is on the grounds. *He ain't in there, is he? Um, I just ... wanna be sure.*"

"Does he really hate you that much. Just over spilt deer guts. And from so long back?"

"Oh, I don't know. Getting a man to clear his mind of a grudge, that can take a lifetime I guess. But why bog ourselves down on the past when it's such a purty day. Look at that cloud up there. Almost looks like a pile o' hotcakes with syrup pouring down on top, don't ya think? Boy, that Huddy he sure knows how to cook!"

"And what exactly is The Lodge anyhow?" Rusty asked. "Is it just the *main building*, or is it the *entire camp?*"

Tate was impressed. "Actually, that question's more comp'icated than you can guess, with historical and philosophical underpinnin's. Come on, we'll talk about it more as we walk."

Rusty was glad to have some free time to more leisurely poke around the grounds. What had seemed like such a foreign and slightly intimidating place one day back was already taking on a familiar feel, and one he was ready to explore. Apparently his father had the same idea. In place of where his buggy was parked was just a two track of matted down grass going off in the direction the man and machine had left. His father was a rare combination: an early riser who was also the last to go to bed — that is, assuming he ever slept at all. And where did his father go? Rusty imagined him a High Plains Indian canvasing a wide perimeter across the territory to get a better lay of the land. While respected by all for his strong moral code and authoritative demeanor, he operated less like a lawman than he did a free-ranging lone wolf, a man who didn't bother to give commands because he could do it all and usual better himself.

"Hard to believe they're all caught in a blizzard back home in Missouri, up north," Rusty broke in during a lull in Tate's story. "They could be digging out for weeks."

"Yep, but that don't mean we get a free pass from the weather down here," Tate opined as he eased onto the driver's seat of the tractor. Rusty stepped up and sat down on the small mound of dirt being hauled in the attached mini trailer in back. "— I'd take a blizzard over a hurricane any day, especially one with a hund'ert foot surge."

"Hundred feet! That's taller than these trees," Rusty said looking up. The patchy light felt alternately warm and cool on his face.

"Hold on!" Tate called back as he approached the strip. "Not much of a rise but it t'ain't take much to turn this apple cart over."

Rusty had a better idea. "Why don't I just hop off. It's just a foot or two. I think I can handle that." While such a miniscule change in height wouldn't seem to make much of a difference, it was a huge vertical distance in the swamp. In terms of vegetation, it was the equivalent of a thousand foot vertical difference on the continent, and maybe closer to five thousand feet out West. With respect to the airstrip it made all the difference. One foot above the natural slash pine grade meant it would rarely, if ever, flood.

"As you wish!" Tate concurred as he gave the tractor some gas. Once up on the strip they got to business. Spotting the holes was easy with the strip being mowed. Some of the depressions were caused by the growth of plant roots over time, others were from burrowing critters whose tunnels had collapsed, and others from falling trees.

"This here, though, ya see it," Tate pointed as he steered the tractor to the left. "That's what they call a solution hole. It's caused from a limerock cavern forming underneath."

"Like an underground river?" Rusty responded as he shoveled out some dirt from the wagon — four spade full in all — followed up by Tate riding over it with the tractor tire to pack it down and smooth it out. "Huddy done right to fatten me up with them cakes knowing I was gonna need extra ballast to *steamroll* the airstrip flat!" Tate patted his stomach to emphasize the point. "Yep, that's the type of hole that never gets fully fixed. Sort of like my stomach. There just ain't no filling it up, at least not for long."

•••

Same Day, 1 pm

By midmorning they'd done their job: they'd filled all the potholes from end to end of the grass-covered airstrip. Tate was celebrating the completion by rewarding himself with a fresh chaw when he spotted a fruit tree cattycorner ahead. *"Well I'll be! How could I forget!?"* The big man furtively looked from side to side as he thought over the situation. "Tell ya what, Rusty. It t'ain't my right to be taking them, but if *you* go grab a' one, I'm sure ol' Albert Lee won't mind one bit."

Rusty returned a few minutes later with a fruit the same color as its name only it wasn't round, it was shaped like a bell.

Tate's eyes bugged out. "That's a good'n! Go ahead and give it a peel."

The rind was so loose, Rusty didn't even need his pocket knife to get it started: it all unraveled in one piece. Although he was a little skeptical, too. "— This isn't a *sour orange*, is it? My father fooled me with that once with an orange at Deep Lake." Rusty laughed a little bit to himself thinking back to how he had to spit the whole thing out in disgust.

"Not sour, nor is it an orange. I done knew I'd fool ya on that. Actually what it's called is a Half-and-Half. Give me a sliver, would ya, and I'll explain."

"Half?"

"No, just a sliver. Never was one much for fruits in general ... *smunch* ... *smunch* ... Just like your father doesn't like apples, I'm not sure why ... *smunch* ... *smunch* ... but this one is ... *Wow ... mmmm deeee-EE-licious.* Okay, if you twist my arm about it, gimme the full half." Tate spit out the seeds as he talked. "Half-

258

breeds they call it ... *smunch* ... *spit* ... *spit* ... Often called the sweetest orange, but ..." Tate halted speaking as he tried to get the facts right in his head. "*Spit* ... *spit* ... *spit* ... it's actually, and you might wanna check with Sandy on this ... *spit spit* ... I think it's part banan'er ... *smunch smunch* ... and part peach. And it never done good on the market ... *spit* ... *spit* ... *spit* ... because is so darned filled with seeds ... *spit* ... *spit* ... *spit.*"

"So a banana and peach — that makes an orange?" Rusty responded doubtfully, not that he was going to argue the point.

"I think so," Tate hesitated. "Not a plant-ol-ogist like Sandy, but I know my fair share. See over yonder that elephant-ear lookin' plant," Tate pointed. "That's a banana tree. They probably hybridized it with a peach pit they smuggled in from across the Georgia line Up North."

"Smuggled?"

"Yes sir, it was snuck in across state lines."

"But it's only a peach pit?"

"Well, let me tell ya, Rusty. Lotta battlin' between Georgia and Florida back in the day. In the War of 1812. And if I'm not mistaken, Florida won. That's how we got the panhandle."

"Well, whatever it is. This *peach-orange* sure is good."

"Actually, now that I'm thinking about it, it's probably part pineapple and part apple that somehow combined from a *lightning strike*. Yep, Flawda might not get any blizzards, but her history is written in her storms, some of 'em named and others that you never o'heard of." Tate hoisted his sizeable frame back on the tractor. "Ya know, I'm proud o'ya. Proud o'ya like you was my own son. I just wanted to say that." Tate turned the key and steered the wheel back toward The Lodge. Rusty walked beside the tractor as Tate continued to talk.

"Yeah ... *brum brum brum* ... your father ... *brum brum brum* ... he's a good man."

"How about *your father*, Mister Tate? Was he the one... *brum brum* ... that showed you the ropes ... *brum brum* ... out here in the swamp?"

"My pa?" Tate responded with a look of surprise, taking a moment or two to respond as he continued to drive. "Well, I guess in some ways it was the ghost of my pa ... *brum brum brum* ... that lured me into the swamp ... *brum brum brum* ... on account of it being only knee deep ... *brum* ... *brum* ... it was his way of ensuring I didn't drown to death. At least that's the story I was told ... *brum* ... *brumm.* And to me it makes a lot of sense."

The big man wiped a fleck of dust from his eye and blew some snot out of his right nostril. "Damn hay fever!" he unconvincingly complained as he blew some more out of his left. "You see, my father died at sea when I was just three years old ... *brum brum brum* ... during the Hurricane o' ... *brum brum* ... So the story goes ... *brum* ... *brum* ... I actually don't got no memory of him myself. Can't really miss a person you never met."

"Gee, I'm sorry to hear that, Mister Tate ... *brum zumm brum* ... that's really sad," Rusty said as he simultaneously observed Greg Kleal and Dan Vukovich down by the gator pond horsing around.

"Well, I had a good ma ... *brum brum brum* ... and, you know, her sisters ... *brum brum brum* ... and my Uncle Arby ... he sort of picked up where my daddy left off."

Rusty spotted bad and good news up ahead. On a bad note, although not a surprise: Greg and Dan were up to their usual no good. Dan was climbing a tree on the bank with the end of the rope swing clenched in his teeth as Greg dangled a big fish above Gertie the Gator's snoot. Rusty was hoping to God it wasn't Elmer, but had a sneaking suspicion it was. The good news was that Rusty was blocking Gator Tate's view which, combined with the loud sound of the tractor, shielded Tate from the shenanigans going on. Rusty wearily eyed the unfolding scene not sure what, if anything, he could do. Dan let out a Tarzan yell as he launched the full heft of his lumbering frame into the air and the rope went taunt, followed by him flailing over the surface of the water like a carnival act gone wrong. At the high point of its upswing Dan let go and ker-plunked into the tea-colored pond. After doggy paddling to the limestone bank he cracked open a fresh patriotic-colored can and tossed a second one to Greg. The distraction allowed Elmer to flap free and escape causing Greg to curse and Rusty, a good hundred feet away, to pump his fist in the air in a euphoric cheer right in Tate's ear, "— Awesome!"

"*Awesome?*" Tate repeated with a perplexed glance. "— What's so awesome about Uncle Arby losin' all his savings at the dog track?"

"Well, um. What I meant was ..."

"No, no need to explain," Tate immediately dismissed. "He actually tripled his money before he lost it all, so I guess in a way you're partially right."

Vuke and Kleal finally caught Tate's attention by lighting off a round of blackjack fire crackers that loudly popped and kicked off a sulfurous cloud of smoke. Rusty had to grab the wheel to keep the tractor straight as Tate turned around with alarm to see what was going on.

"Oh, no worries, it's just Greg and Dan shooting off some fireworks," Rusty replied as a succession of roman candles flew through the sky.

"Welp, as long as their not messing around at the Bass Pond. After all the fishin' I did, I think Ol' Gert and Elmer deserve some rest. *Speakin' of rest*," Tate reminded himself, "There's a hammock strung up between two trees in the dome across the path from Tinker's camp. Thinkin' now might be a good *break in the action* for Ol' Tate to take a nap."

•••

Rusty found himself yawning, although not from being physically exhausted: he was bored. More and more it was looking like the Round Up was shaping up to be a *Round Down*, the type of party lots of invitations were sent out but not many people showed up — and understandably so. People have busy lives and full-time jobs. The Lodge was in the middle of nowhere. Holding it in town at the bowling alley would have been a lot more convenient for everyone, or if it was absolutely necessary to hold it in the swamp, they could have picked a place that was more accessible, by car, right along the Tamiami Trail. The Trail's End Motor Inn would have been a perfect spot. The Lodge did have a great aura about it, but what was the point if nobody was going to show?

"So you're gonna be at Tinkers, Mister Tate?" Rusty asked as he headed up the steps to the porch.

"Well, maybe not just yet," Tate said with an indecisive look as he was overtaken by the aroma of food floating over from Huddy's tarp. "—Little concerned that Huddy might need help. Don't want nothin' to be burnin'. And my stomach's grumbling. Ya hear that?"

"That wasn't thunder?"

"No, that way my stomach!" a suddenly revived Tate rejoiced. "I'm definitely gonna need a snack to tide me over to the next meal."

"Snack? I'm still stuffed from breakfast!"

"Well dernint, of course you are," Tate complained. "— That's because you were first in line and got *all the big cakes*. By the time I got there I had to scrounge for whatever crumbs were left." Tate turned back for a final word before he rounded the corner towards the cooking food. "You should take a break, too. Maybe hunker down with your book in The Lodge. And put a good word for me with Albert Lee if you get a chance!"

...

Same day, 4 pm
Rusty woke up to the sensation of a looming shadow blocking the light. He must have dozed off. The smell of thick aftershave filled the room.

"Who gave you permission to come in here!?" growled an angry voice at Rusty's back.

The box slipped out of his lap and fell flat on the floor with a thud. Fortunately, nothing fell out.

The dog bolted out from under Rusty's arm to join his owner by the side. Previously his friend, now the dog started to bark.

"I-I'm sorry...I-I-I was just ..."

Mister Hodge finished Rusty's sentence for him. "— Snooping around other people's property is what!"

I was just ... um ... taking a break ...

"A break!? Everybody else is out there breaking their backs trying to get everything prepared and you're in here taking a snooze?"

Chapter 11:
Grim-faced Lawyers Appear

Apr 22, 1865
A great weight has lifted from our shoulders.

The war has been disruptive, but maybe now that it has ended our Great Nation can start to heal. It has been almost three years since I've last heard from French.

Jun 7
Stopped by the old office.

I regret selling our business at such a steep discount at the outbreak of the war. But with French gone, what else was I to do? The lawyer who bought it insisted on French's name staying with the deal. However, without the man in the flesh to back up the work I doubt the benefit lasted long. But behold, all is not lost — it's a shot in the arm to see that Arnold's Tavern is still at the corner! Good to know some things don't change in Cincinnati. Dropped in to catch up and make a nostalgic toast, "— To old times and friends past, until we meet again."

Jul 20
I have been bestowed a huge honor!

"In recognition of my extraordinary service to the county in the Seminole War and War Between the States," I have been "cordially invited" to a ceremony in New Orleans — all expenses paid. I have suffered this terrible cough for many months, if not a year. I cannot recall last when I could breathe deeply without pain. Perhaps travels south will do my body well.

Sep 3
I depart from Cairo.

263

My symptoms improve as the climate warms. We have entered the cypress. I make acquaintance with a hunter of some acclaim. A woodpecker called the Ivorybill is his latest quest. Many of the groves where they once abounded proved barren, but this trip, his third, he believes to be his charm. Upon hearing my cough, as he was a dentist prior to his overseas investments paying off, he spoke highly of the rejuvenative powers of the warm mineral springs in Dolesom Heights, where he sent many of his patients, especially the severely depressed, and which I am of the inclination to pursue as a last resort should my latest batch of medicinal elixirs not provide a full cure by the fruition of this trip. The ship is scheduled to arrive in New Orleans tomorrow.

Sep 7
Festivities in New Orleans are entirely first class.

Last night at the opera was extraordinary. Tomorrow, I will be in attendance at the Ballroom Gala in the famous Grande Hotel. Many luminaries and debutantes will be present. I am very much looking forward to taking it all in.

Sep 8
I am immediately called away upon my arrival at the ball.

A young captain informs me that my presence is requested at General Butler's quarters on "a matter of grave international importance." My hopes for meeting the general are dashed when two grim-faced lawyers approach. The business concerns the recent high-jacking of a ship. No other details are given. I am to report to the Embassy Hall first thing tomorrow morning. In light of the news I am unable to enjoy the evening's festivities and retire to my quarters early.

Sep 9
After formalities, the lawyers quickly get to their point:

They request my service as an expert witness in a murder case. It seems a ship from Havana, Cuba — a blockade runner — was high-jacked at sea by a confederate officer named Captain Brown and a civilian accomplice, a Mr. Columbus Tate, the latter of whom pleads his innocence. They are very keen on using my knowledge of the Florida Frontier to shed light on the validity of Tate's many claims, or if he too should be charged alongside

Brown. Paperwork is signed and more details are discussed. Tomorrow I am cleared to see Tate.

Sep 10

My health takes an unexpected turn for the worse.

Just when I think I am past the worst of it my swamp fever returns. Symptoms include an uncomfortable buildup of phlegm in my throat accompanied by slights chills and shortness of breath. I will stop by the apothecary on my way to the jail, that is — assuming I possess enough strength to walk.

Chapter 12:
Circling the Wagons

Rusty dashed out the door to find himself unexpectedly in the middle of an intimidating scene. A ruddy face man with a bear-like build was throwing his arms up in the air and screaming at the top of his lungs —*"Yee-Ha! Ya-Ha!"* — as another man, presumably his friend, forearmed him in the chest as hard as he could. A sinister-looking bowie knife dangled from the second man's side and a skull and crossbones decal adorned the back of his vest. Across the way, an old swamp rat sporting a beard down to his belly and a pistol jammed underneath his belt barked instructions at two younger fellows who Rusty guessed were his sons. A third group of men threw hatchets at the trunk of a sable palm. The first missed the tree completely, the second hit at a lopsided angled and clumsily bounced to the ground while the third penetrated deeply into the bark. *"That put's me up two!"* the man cackled as he lifted a milk jug full of clear liquid to his face, gulped greedily and winced.

Rusty's preoccupation with the ruckus ahead caused him to lose track of two burly men barreling rapidly around the bend. Startled at first, he immediately relaxed. It was Dan Vukovich and Greg Kleal. Never had he been so relieved to see the two men.

"Are they all here for the Round up?" Rusty ran up to ask as he pointed back to the unruly mob.

"Yeah, looks like the carnival act's arrived," Kleal smiled.

"They're just a little rough around the edges, is all," Dan said in more polite terms.

"So they're okay?" Rusty tried to confirm.

"Absolutely great!" Greg said in an upbeat voice as he nudged Vuke at the sight of a buggy that resembled a military jeep rolling into to camp, "—*Well I'll be damned.*"

"Say, Rusty," Vuke followed up with a distracted voice. His eyes were glued to the buggy. "—Why don't you, um, go see if Huddy doesn't need some help."

"This thing's really got 'em crawling out of the woodwork, that's for sure," Dan nervously assessed. "If Emory's here you know Pepe can't be too far behind."

•••

Huddy had his operation in full motion by the time Rusty showed up at his tarp. "NO IDEA we'd have THIS MANY guests," he mumbled above the kettles and the upward radiation of heat. "— A FULL GUT of grub may be the ONLY THING that SETTLES 'em all DOWN."

"Is there anything I can do to help," Rusty asked.

"WELL, we're gonna need MORE WOOD from over at TINKER'S." Huddy pointed to the tractor. "There's a WAGON by the lean-to."

"The same one Gator and I used to haul dirt to the airstrip?" Rusty asked with all the confidence of an old hand.

Huddy nodded. "That's the ONE. Fill it up FLAT and that should BE ENOUGH."

"And that-a-way, right?" Rusty pointed at what looked like the entrance to the trail.

"Can't MISS IT," Huddy confirmed, "—It's the FIRST CAMP on the right. If you start seeing CYPRESS you've gone TOO FAR."

•••

Being on another mission put Rusty at ease. There really was nothing quite like physical work to relieve stress, not to mention it would give him another notch on his belt in terms of earning his keep at the The Lodge. Dwight called it sweat equity. Plus it might give him an inside track on getting seconds, that is – assuming there was going to be enough food to go around. All indications were that the Round Up was shaping up to be much bigger affair than originally planned. Not that he had any idea what the Round Up was supposed to be about.

Rusty glanced back at the gathering crowd as he disappeared into a hole in the palmetto thicket and then down the trail.   The tight inner circle from the previous night had officially given way to something a little less controlled, and still growing. There was no telling what it was going to look like by the time he got back.

Despite Huddy's assurances things got confusing pretty fast, to the point that Rusty started to second guess if he was on the right path. The trail quickly shrunk from a wide corridor to a narrow two track. Would the ride take a minute, or would it be closer to five or ten, or even longer? In retrospect it was a silly question not to ask Huddy before he left. The primary landmark was supposed to be the tall cypress trees on the other side of Tinker's, a place they called Boot Hill, it serving as the indicator he'd gone too far. Rusty did his best to stay alert. He doubted he'd see a sign with a big arrow pointing the way, but if he kept his eyes peeled he would probably be able to figure it out — and hopefully not get turned around: like climbing a tree, no matter how high he got, Rusty knew his success would only be measured upon returning to the ground.   Neil Armstrong's biggest step wasn't leaving his footprint on lunar dust but completing the voyage by safely splashing into the water back on Earth.   The mission wasn't to Tinker's, it was to Tinker's *and back*.

Many sizeable branches blocked the trail. Rusty wondered if there'd been a big storm that recently knocked them all down, or had it been such a long time since anybody used the trail? Not that the branches were all that big. In most cases it was as simple as idling the tractor and rolling them to the side. At one point he had to stop at a dangerously deep rut. After a little hemming and hawing, Rusty decided he could straddle the cavernous pit without getting stuck.   It wasn't long thereafter that Rusty suspected he'd overshot the camp; or had he taken the wrong path?

The sudden sound of men's voices offered a ray of hope. More than likely they were on their way to the Round Up and knew the country well.

Rusty cut off the engine.

"Hello," he called out.

Rusty was a bit bewildered.   The voices were no longer there.

"*Hello*," he asked again.

Still nothing. No sound. Just the silence of the woods and a lingering mechanical knock or two from under the tractor's hood. Rusty wondered if he'd inadvertently barged into a conversation he wasn't supposed to hear. Tate had mentioned the story about smugglers. Maybe there were bandits on the loose. What else could explain them being so loud and then suddenly going quiet like that? He looked overhead at the tops of the cypress gently swaying back and forth. He listened in the direction of The Lodge. Maybe the voices were coming from there, or up a parallel trail, or maybe it was coming from a creature like a fox: he'd never heard the sound himself but he'd heard stories how the animal could eerily mimic human voices when it howled at night. But that didn't make sense either. The voices coming from the cypress were as clear as day, and most of all friendly.

"Hello," Rusty repeated, this time a little louder. "Is anybody there?"

Not hearing a response, the boy tried to convince himself that it had all been in his imagination or that it was just the sound of the wind. What he did know was that he'd gone too far. Everything around him was mostly cypress. That meant he'd have to unhitch the wagon and do a three point turn. It was at the exact moment that he re-started the engine – *Errrrrnt rumble rumble rum rum* – that the mysterious voices resumed.

"This young bunch ... *brum rum brum* ... I tell ye. They want it all."

"Yep. They don't know when they're licked either ... *rum brumble rum* ... At least we had some sense not to get too big ... *rumble brum* ... for our britches. We knew when the gittin' was good ... *brum brum* ... and when to git out."

"And we kept it *in house*" chimed in a high-pitched Slim Pickins type voice, "— Not all the shenanigans on the coast."

The clarity of the voices was matched by the invisibility of their source. The only thing Rusty could detect no matter how hard he scanned was an uncluttered forest floor of shallowly-submerged knobby cypress knees and fluted trunks, and again — just like before: the moment he cut the engine the voices immediately stopped. At this point, Rusty didn't give it all too much thought. Maybe he'd caught the echo of a distant conversation that had carried through the woods from The Lodge the same way Huddy's voice had ricocheted through the old growth cypress on the buggy ride up. Rusty had heard stories of radio signals beaming back to earth after decades of bouncing around in outer space before magically appearing on

AM radios thousands of miles from the original transmission spot. Or maybe everything he heard was all in his head. Contradicting all those conclusions was the return of the dialog the moment he re-hitched the trailer and turned the engine back on.

"These fellas, well ... *rum brum rum* ... they ain't quite as close knit. Going in all sorts of directions ... *br-brum brumble rum* ... and a bunch of them bad."

"A man owned up ... *rum brumble brum* ... and owned up alone in them days. He knew you'd be seein' the same folks when you got back ... *rum brum-brumble rum* ... and they'd keep yer seat warm. Now they's like crabs in a barrel."

"Not to cast aspersions upon nobody," said the third. "— But the big feller ... *rum-brumble-brrrummmm* ... come out mighty fast."

"Coulda done some fast talkin', ya know."

"The thing is, considerin' the situation ... *brum brum brum* ... I don't believe the talk would be fast enough. He always did strike me as shaky ... *brum-brumble-rum-brum* ... I think he started talkin' about somethin', though ... that's fer certain."

"Gotta let 'em make their own mistakes. We had o'plenty in our day, too. "

"Better days, them were", said the first fellow. "Much better days..."

...

By the time Rusty rolled back into camp, the waiting game was over — the Round Up had officially begun. What a day ago had been an abandoned ghost town had become a boom town bursting with life. While some of the men definitely looked rougher and more dangerous than the crowd his father normally ran with, the equal presence of women, children and pets presented a paradoxical vibe: the growing crescendo of a revolution combined with the carefree backbeat of a family reunion.

Rusty's concern about three men in camouflage overalls concealed under the shadows of a spindly laurel oak (they were making hard glares toward the direction of an unsuspecting Dan Vukovich chatting to a contingent under the Robertson's tarp) was offset by the affectionate scene of a possum curled under the crook of its owner's arm being handfed some loose nuts by a girl and a boy. The comforting aroma of biscuits and scones intermingled with the smell of machine oil, mudded tires and diesel fumes.

Rusty was about to call out Dan's name to warn him of the impending ambush when, after giving the woman he was talking to a departing peck on the cheek, Vuke turned and noticed his would-be assassins by himself without any help. The scene had all the makings of a showdown in an old Western movie — a build-up followed by a stare down, and peppered with incendiary words — but in this case it ended with a round of ebullient salutations. Not enemies at all, they were simply friends that hadn't seen each other in a long time.

Rusty felt a little bit silly to be falling prey to such paranoid thoughts. It was a reminder that he was the new guy with a very limited, and probably often incorrect, understanding of "who was who" and what was going on. Having mistaken Mister Hodge as being Charlie the other night was the perfect example, and probably the final nail in the coffin that Charlie was long dead — or did he have that wrong, too? Maybe Charlie was still out there, somewhere, possibly even in the crowd, or soon to show up. Or, at least there was a big side of Rusty that still wanted to believe that might be true. Maybe Charlie wasn't any *one* single person but rather an architype who spanned through the ages, different men on many stages who played the same part. Maybe it wasn't all hearsay, innuendo and false leads. Maybe the man in the Stetson hat still had a hand in the game.

•••

A German Shepard rushed up and cowered at Rusty's feet.

Rusty reached down and gave the dog a pet only to have it retreat to the side a girl about his age following up behind.

"What's your name?" she immediately asked.

"Oh, I'm Rusty."

"I'm sorry, how rude me," she corrected herself. "I'm Lori. I should have said that first."

Rusty of course didn't think she was rude. She couldn't have been nicer. Or prettier either.

"Say, you aren't the kid staying *in* The Lodge?"

Rusty hadn't thought anybody noticed, let alone cared. "Yeah, why?"

"Oh, the other kids they told me to stay away from the mean old man, *even when he wasn't there.* He keeps "baby devils" on his porch."

"Oh that," Rusty said with confidence. "— It's just a cracker barrel. No big deal."

"How do you know? Is he your grand-dad?"

"No, he's, um, a family friend," Rusty answered, "—And this is his camp."

"Duh! Well of course it's his camp, dummy!" she said with a conceited laugh. "Everybody knows that."

"Oh Lo-ooor-iii !!!" an adult-female voice sang from a tent.

"That's my mom. I better go back. We're about to eat," the girl explained with a flirtatious smirk. "We're tenting up with the Roberstons. You should come on over if you get a chance."

Rusty was just about to thank her for the offer, and even thought about walking her over to the tent himself — after all, given the number of unsavory characters on scene, it was probably most prudent, especially for such a pretty girl, to not let anyone travel alone — when a skinny kid with a devilish smile snuck up on Lori from a shortcut in the trail. He had his finger pointed vertically over his lip as a sign for Rusty not to give him away.

"Guess who!?" the boy exclaimed as he covered Lori's eyes with both hands from behind.

Lori let out a gasp but wasn't fooled one bit. *"I know it's you, Chilton. Now let go!"*

The boy obliged, but not right away, and when he did he gave her a pinch.

"Chilton! You know I don't like that!"

"So who's your friend?" the adolescent boy asked as he sized Rusty up. "He looks like a new comer. Who's he with? And doesn't he know he's not supposed to be on Mr. Hodge's porch? I'm sure the old geezer doesn't appreciate that."

"Oh, yeah, this is Randy, uh, I mean Rudy."

"Rusty's my name."

"He's Mr. Hodge's grandson."

"Well that's a LIE Lori! I hope you know that. Mr. Hodge is a hermit. He ain't got no family. Only reason people are nice to him is they want his money when he dies."

Rusty was about to correct the story but didn't get a chance.

"Come on, Lori. Let's go eat," Chilton said as he pulled her down the trail and, as he did, taking time to give Rusty a leering glare. "— *We don't wanna miss grace.*"

Lori turned back at the last moment with a helplessly look just as she disappeared around the bend. There was a side of

Rusty that wished he'd intervened, but again, as the new guy, it was difficult for him to discern if they were good friends fooling around, or if there was something more sinister lurking underneath.

...

On a lark, Rusty worked himself to the edge of camp where he climbed up and stood on a beefy branch of a laurel oak and looked out from a bird's eye view: he wanted to pick out the one person in the crowd who best matched Charlie's description.

If Charlie was there he would stand out but also be playing it cool, hanging out in back, in the same way he did in the old blurry black and white photographs. His stately stature and Stetson hat always perfectly placed, he exuded the toughness of a cowboy with an urbane touch, an uncommon blend of both charisma and grace. The only problem was that no single photo ever showed a clear view of his face even if Rusty had a pretty good sense of what he would look like if he did see him, which was admittedly unlikely given the timeline of his life. The only man in camp that even remotely resembled that look in fact was his father. Rusty was struck by that. So many times Rusty had asked and the answer was always the same: *"Oh, you'll know Charlie when you see him! You'll know he's the one,"* or *"Well, he's the type of guy who ages well. Could be forty-five ... could be sixty eight ...."* That was contradicted by Huddy's insinuation that the Charlie *he saw* the night before, when they picked him up at his camp, might be more ghost than real life. Meanwhile Sandy seemed to express skepticism that the man ever existed at all, *"Talk of Charlie's exploits is mostly that, just talk."*

Sure enough, Rusty's gaze honed in on his father, and not because he was easy to see or somehow in the center of things. If anything his father had a knack for *not* drawing attention to himself. The moment you thought you knew where he was he'd vanish only to unpredictably appear when you were positive he wasn't around. His high cheekbones. His slanted eyes. His deeply tanned skin. Rusty shook his head trying to process everything in front of him. The Round Up, The Lodge, His Father's Life: none of it made any sense. Was it all real life, or an avoidance of everything it entailed? He gazed intently at his father, standing beside and speaking to Albert Lee Hodge. From that distance Rusty wondered what he would think of the man if he weren't his father. Would that give him any better

273

understanding, or a new perspective, on who he was? He wasn't sure. One thing he did know was that his father walked a path that would be impossible for him to follow, let alone even being able to find the tracks.

Whatever the case, the Round Up was quite a bit different to the times Rusty usually spent with his father in the woods. There was sometimes a friend or two, but nothing anything ever remotely as big as what the Round Up had produced. Being in the woods with his father was all about the simple things. Where life slowed down. Morning dew, breakfast cooking over open fires and cigarillo smoke, diesel, dust, fire and thunder — the image of his father standing in three feet of water, stretching a sun browned and strong arm across domes and strands, joking, smoking, bestowing arcane backwoods wisdom. His father was the swamp personified. Rusty knew nothing of his father but this. There was nothing aside from the wilderness and his father's sanctuary within it.

Albert Lee was listening with great earnestness to what Henry had to say. By all appearances it was something infinite and significant, most likely about the state of the Round Up, how it was going and who was going to show, the update of the present being tinged with a lament on what once was and, up ahead in the future, what might soon be. It was striking to see his father, a man of very few words, speaking at such great length and with such animation. It was a side of his father he rarely if ever saw, and only in glimpses and at a distance, if ever at all. And then, as if the man sensed his son's spying gaze, he cut the conversation off and disappeared.

Soon thereafter a low rumble gave way to the cataclysmic crunching of brush as an absolutely enormous swamp buggy burst onto the scene, *VRROOOMING, CRUNCHING* and then *LURCHING* to a show-stealing stop. The machine was hissing as if had suffered a wound from its war with the previously undersized trail, now widened, and was decorated on the side with big honking decal lettering that read — *MCNASTY*. Rusty had every expectation of the operator being as equally large and loathsome as his oversized ride when an enfeebled face sporting a tattered hat peered down over ledge of the chrome-plated beast. The gent whimpered plaintively and kicked in frustration at the goliath of rubber and shiny steel, jamming his toe as a result, and thus ending his impressive, if also obnoxious, entrance with the pitiful coda — *"Dear me, my poor achin' back*." A chuckle or two ensued as the crowd's normal decibel level quickly resumed.

Henry appeared out of nowhere in full stride by his son's side, motioning him to follow along. "Go ahead," his father pointed and patted him ahead. "— Introduce yourself. He'll be happy to see you. It's been a good couple years."

At this point Rusty had laid to rest any preconceived notions of who anybody was, let alone what to expect.

"*Rusty!? Is that you?*" the frail man marveled from the heavily chromed upper deck as he desperately searched for a way to dismount. After several aborted attempts, he finally found his way down a stainless-steel ladder. When his boots finally touched the pine-needle strewn earth, the man breathed a sigh of relief as might a sailor making port after a long and harrowing voyage across a treacherous straight. Rusty was surprised he was the taller of the two.

"*My my my, look how you've grown,*" the man doted with the easy intonations of an uncle you immediately trust, yet whom you lack the name to match the face because it's been so long since you last met, if you even recall him at all. "Don't s'pose you remember me?" he added.

Rusty just smiled. He didn't want to be impolite, but it couldn't be denied keeping track of all the faces and names was tough to do when he was only in the swamp at best a few weeks each year.

Nor did the man take offense. "I bet you'll never guess where your father and I met?"

All Rusty could think to guess was "somewhere in the swamp."

"Well ... it was sort of *swamp like*. But we called it *The Jungle* and it was near half a world away." The man laughed as he patted Rusty on the arm. "— Does that ring any bells with ya? Do you remember me now?"

He looked at his father and then at the man and then at the two as they bypassed formal introductions and firmly embraced. While the process of elimination seemed to increasingly be on his side, he'd been burned too many times to guess wrong again.

"Um, well, I know, um — you're *not* Campfire Charlie," Rusty quipped. It was the only name he thought he could completely rule out.

"Well I had a little Charlie in me back in the day" the frail man acknowledged. "But these days," he added pointing to his withered frame, "—Not so much."

"Quite a tricked-out buggy you have there," Henry offered with a wry smile. "— Pretty Impressive, Sid."

Sid! Of course! Rusty remembered now. The man was Sidney Gruman, better known as "Sick Sid," one his father's best buds from his Air Force days overseas. Rusty also knew him as the father of Allen and Shane, the two teenage boys they helped get their buggy unstuck from the mud on a previous trip a few years back.

"Henry, both you and I know their ain't no reason for a buggy to be this damn big. More for show than being practical. It breaks down more than it goes forward, and boy does it guzzle gas." Sidney wiped off his glasses and rolled his eyes. "And it t'aint mine, you know that Henry. I borrowed it from Shane. Darned ridiculous to be honest. Just look at this thing. I don't understand these young folks anymore."

"Well, it's an attention getter, that's for sure," Henry added as he inspected the chrome pipes.

"Yeah, the wrong kind of attention," Sid snarked. "Thing is, Shane has a ton of potential, but ever since what happened to Allen, it's just hard to give him any advice."

Henry nodded without passing judgement.

"Anyhow, enough of that," Sidney groused as he turned to Rusty with an uptick in his voice. "— Let me tell you some stories about your dad. Back in the day, your father was the best crop duster on this side of the pond. Still be doin' it too if they paid an honest wage."

Henry laughed. "Got out when the goin' was still good ..."

"Gotta hand it to you there, Henry," Sid said, then turning to Rusty. "You're father's always had a knack for that ..."

•••

Rusty heard an acoustic guitar and singing on the other side of the palmetto behind him.

Around the corner he spied the source. It was Lori! She was sitting around the campfire next to a man, possibly her father, who was singing Bobby Angel's mega crossover country hit, *Tonight you're Wrapped in my Mind.*

I ramble into town and throw some whiskey down. And look up at the women sitting pretty. They're up on the rail and I think about the jail. How it's better not to cheat and keep your nose clean. Outside the crescent moon smothers out a ragtime tune. And I look up at the stars that hold no promise. I turn back before long, neither there do I belong. And I go to my room and put head down on the pillow ...

As Lori's father sang the first line of the refrain alone — *"No I don't need to know where you are tonight"* — she leaned in to harmonize her fluttery tenor with his booming baritone to form an alternating, overlapping and hauntingly beautiful duet: *"Because tonight (because tonight), because tonight (because tonight), because tonight (because tonight),"* and then both together they sang, *"— Because tonight, you're wrapped in my mind.*

Rusty admired the way Lori's father handled the guitar. The finger picking looked complicated but he played it with ease. He was an old hand with the instrument; his singing around the campfire was as much a tradition as it was a treat.

It was down in San Anton' that I broke most every bone. And fever gripped my body like a vice grip. The nurse rubbed water on my chest and listen to me confess. As the day grew long and the night grew shivery. It was sometime before dawn when I woke and she was gone. She left everything she had except her prayer book. It made no sense at first but then I seen it matched my curse. That had run me down like a wildcat in the arrayo ...

Again Lori and her father alternated on the refrain, this time Lori's voice sounding even more stunning that the first time around.

Her dad: *BECAUSE TONIGHT*
Lori: *Because tonight*
Her dad: *BECAUSE TONIGHT*
Lori: *Because tonight*

Both together: *Because Tonight
You're Wrapped in My Mind.*

Rusty was mesmerized but the sum total of it all: the crackling of the fire and the light that it cast, the fancy fret work and finger picking of Lori's father on his rosewood guitar and, most of all, her. At that moment he was sure he'd never seen or ever would again such a pretty girl, both inside and out. He stood there in complete infatuation trying to soak it all in.

> *The trail out of town, I leave on it without a sound. And I got all my belongings in my saddlebag. First light hasn't broke and night covers me like a cloak. And your eyes shine in my mind like two emeralds. It's the only way I know. I learned it long ago. In a time and place that's disappeared forever. The things I didn't say I can hear them replay. It's what settles me soul and brings me no sorrow.*

As the final refrain drew to a close, father and daughter smiling and looking deeply into each other's eyes, and ending on a sublime syncopation of the words in the title of the song — *"And tonight, you're wrapped in my mind"*— the entire Robertson family and all the other onlookers broke out into a heart-felt applause. Lori had stolen the show with her incredible voice, and in the process also grabbed a piece of Rusty's heart. As pretty as she looked in the flicker of the campfire light – and to be sure, he would never again listen to the Bobby Angel classic without also hearing her voice in the refrain – Rusty's heart also sank when he saw Chilton step in with a polaroid camera to take a photo of the father and daughter campfire stars, winning him a firm handshake from the chord-plucking patriarch and a glowing compliment from the matriarch Mrs. Robinson whom he'd borrowed the camera from.

"Oh Chilton, you are so thoughtful. A fine boy indeed. Family to us."

Rusty couldn't be sure but her father seemed to approve.

As for Lori it was obvious. She tolerated Chilton but that was about it.

Rusty quickly vanished behind the palmetto when we saw Chilton turn his way.

Chapter 13:
Suffering the Consequences

Sep 12, 1865
Arrangements have been made.
The Embassy has agreed to cover the expense of my carriage ride as well as my requisite medicines at the apothecary.

Sep 13, 8 am
I am impressed by Tate's firm grip and beaming eyes.
He possesses the relaxed demeanor and sinewy strength of the Florida Frontier I remember well of its youth. He, too, bears a resemblance to someone I have known in the past, but whom at the moment I cannot place. One thing is for sure, he is a Floridian through and through. Onward with of the retelling of events. Below are my notes.

8:15 am
Tate reveals he was born in Pennsylvania.
His family migrated south to work on a mission along the southwest coast. After his father, a reverend, died he was adopted by his uncle on the east coast, a fisherman, whom he lived with until one day he didn't return after a mishap at the boatyard. He and his brother Abel have worked a variety of odd jobs ever since.

8:25 am
Tate proceeds to explain his ordeal as beginning south of Ft. Stafford where Abel and he were fishing for mullet in Gallivan's Bay.
When I inform Tate that I was the commanding officer of said fort for the duration of the recent Seminole War, he

abruptly interrupts: he means the town, not the military post. The fort, he clarifies, has long since burned down and is a chapter the town would soon like to forget. An effort is afoot to shorten the name to just *Stafford* to make it more business friendly and attractive for settlers, including trade with the Indians.

8:30 am
Tate and Abel are hailed down by a party of Confederate soldiers led by the broad-shouldered Captain Brown.

The captain quickly commandeers their boat as they approach. Brown pulls a tattered map from his breast pocket marked with the letter X, threatening them to find the spot, "— *Or Else!*" It doesn't take long for Brown to reveal his mean and diabolical nature, a man that nobody dare spite for fear of being singled out for cruel punishment, even death.

8:35 am
Many holes are dug on many islands.

Despite working day and night, progress is thwarted by the meager nature of their digging instruments, including a soup ladle and conch shells that continually break. Brown's paranoid behavior takes a severe turn for the worse when a federal patrol boat is spotted beyond the outer islands. Brown bans all campfires as a result, and strictly orders all lanterns to be covered by blankets at night. The men work in constant fear of Brown lashing out at the slightest provocation, most often for no reason at all.

8:40 am
After many days of digging in futility, the party teeters on the edge of madness.

Blackflies and mosquitoes ravage the men's bodies and minds. When the second in command, a Lt. McGuire, finally summons the courage to complain, Brown responds with brutal force. A mutiny ensues. McGuire manages to escape with half of the men in the Confederate boat, leaving the Tate brothers marooned with Brown and a few of his loyalists — the worst of the lot. Bickering arises on who should assume the lieutenant position now that McGuire is gone. After a tussle and some loud words an egg-shaped man named Peacock prevails. One man is shot. Discipline is clearly dissolving in the miserable heat.

8:50 am
Brown drops further into insanity as the pace of digging slows.

He orders the men to dig twice as fast to make up for the lost hands, "— *Or Else!*" The men are unable to dig below a hard white capstone repeatedly encountered at a depth of two feet. The men's hands are bloodied and swollen to a pulp. None say a word for fear of losing their rank. No one is sure of their status with the mercurial Brown or who to trust.

9 am
The men are greeted by a sudden, and quite fortuitous, turn of events.

Abel awakens from a strange and unrestful sleep with a clairvoyant thought regarding the map: after folding it along a diagonal crease and holding it into the morning sun in reverse, the map finally makes sense. All the telltale landmarks are easily found. Three feet underneath a limestone outcrop a box is removed. Brown threatens the men with his pistol to stay away, "— *or Else!*", as he transfers the contents of the box into a satchel which he secures with a kerchief and a double knot.

9:15 am
Any relief from recovering the mysterious cache is short-lived.

Brown's initial wave of euphoria quickly gives way to a catatonic stare. He orders his loyalists to join him individually on the other side of the beach, one by one, each time returning alone until it is just the three of them left: Tate, his brother, and the demonic Brown.

9:25 am
Brown demands they set course for Havana.

Abel's suggestion to delay their departure until dark is met with a severe tongue lashing and a pistol to the face. Tate's defense of his brother is equally struck down. Brown listens to no one, even if it is good advice. "— You WILL Set A Course For Havana ... *Or Else!!!*"

9:30 am
The voyage is quickly cut short.

A federal vessel enroute to Ft. Jefferson overtakes the ship no more than five miles off coast. Brown accuses the Tate Brothers of "tipping them off" and seizes control of the wheel in a seething rage. Shortly thereafter, tragedy strikes: a salvo of grapeshot from the federal vessel collapses the mast on Abel killing him instantly and capsizing the boat. Brown and Columbus are cast afloat.

9:50 am
Tate drifts alone at sea for many days.
At some point he discovers his feet touching bottom only to realize he is standing on the back of a large creature, possibly a whale. Land is nowhere in sight. In a desperate bid, he grabs hold of a giant turtle that leads him to a desolate stretch of sandy beach.

10:10 am
Tate rests under the shade of a palm tree for some time.
He slowly regains his strength by eating the heart of the coconut and drinking its milk. Abel is often on his mind. Tate's spirits are lifted when he sees the silhouette of his brother walking along the surf only to open his eyes to the sight of Captain Brown pointing a gun in his face.

10:15 am
Brown kicks at Tate to get up.
Tate's pleas for reason are met with violent threats: "You will lead me inland to Lt. McCabe and the Confederate Calvary," the deranged captain commands, "—Or Else!" He is covered in seaweed, missing an eye, and clenching tightly at his mysterious satchel, still wrapped with a kerchief and secured with a double knot.

11:00 am
Slogging inland proves grueling.
There is no dry land anywhere. Brown loses his boots in the mud and is bit on the leg by a snake. Tate is able to fashion a makeshift eye patch out of a sand dollar and three blades of braided chord grass which Brown initially wears but later hurls into the weeds.

11:05 am

Tate and Brown arrive at an abandoned Indian village.

Tate attempts to dry out his feet at a smoldering campfire. Brown scavenges for and finds a cache of food which he greedily hordes, refusing to let Tate partake. His gluttonous binge abruptly ends when Tate spots a group of Indians approaching by canoe. Brown commands that they flee through a deeply flooded grove of cypress to escape. Tate is ordered to go first, to fend off snakes, "—*Or Else!*"

11:10 am

Brown succumbs to violent retching during the retreat.

Tate's initial concern of Brown's expulsions exposing their position to the pursuing Indians gives way to a more dire threat: gators sliding off the banks from every direction and disappearing into the liquid murk. Tate is able to wade into the relative safety of shallower waters, but Brown remains stuck in a chin-deep pool as the gators approach.

12 noon

Tate watches helplessly as several giant alligators close in.

Although Brown fights valiantly, cursing and striking at the beasts as hard as he did his men, it doesn't take long to see he is overmatched. Brown lunges for Tate's outstretched hand in a last ditch effort to escape, but all for naught: the moment they clench palms a torrent of splashing erupts and Brown is pulled below (with the exception of the captain's detached arm which Tate continues to clasp by the hand). After ten minutes, an alligator emerges from the opposite bank dragging Brown's badly mangled body in its mouth.

12:02 am

Other gators move in to fight over Brown's carcass.

As the first gator shakes whatever life remains out of Brown, a second gator clamps down on the captain's outstretched legs — pulling lengthwise on his body like a medieval rack — at the same time a third gator chomps down on the prostrate man's chest causing blood to spurt out. Tate takes advantage of the internecine battle to bull rush the grisly scene with a hollowed-out log, causing the gators to scatter. Tate succeeds in pulling Brown's body behind the protective shield of an uprooted cypress tree trunk, but is unable to arrest the flow of blood due to his missing arm and puncture wounds to his chest.

12:10 am
Brown's wounds are severe but not mortal.

In addition to what I have already mentioned above, they include a missing eye, severely bloodied feet, a swollen tongue, several lacerations to the head, continual retching of a black bile and a bad case of the hiccups which renders him incapable of finishing a sentence.

12:20 am
Any vestige of hope for the captain is snuffed out by a sneak attack by yet another gator from behind.

Brown is again pulled under before Tate can react, although the captain does briefly resurface to warn Tate to stay away from his satchel, "—Or Else!" Tate helplessly watches as the turbulent water turns placidly still. The tranquility is only broken by the faintest of ripples as cypress needles fall on the water's surface from the shadowy tree canopy above. This time for sure Captain Brown is dead.

12:40 am
Tate pays his last respects.

It is only in doing so, as he proceeds to make a sign of the cross, that he comes to realize his hand is still being firmly gripped by the dead captain's detached arm. Tate's attempts to let go are met by a reflexive strengthening of the bodiless hand's grip, possibly a sign of rigor mortis setting in. Eventually he is able to pry free of the tightening squeeze by wedging the meaty arm into a crook of a tree and heaving himself back. Emancipation from the hand coincides with a new disturbance in the water. Tate watches in great astonishment as Brown emerges from the murky sludge as irritated as ever and cursing up a storm, belting out several pretty impressive "—Or Elses!", before reclaiming his satchel and dutifully collapsing in the muck.

Chapter 14:
Incoming Charlie Overhead!

Rusty was so engrossed in reading his book that the raucous sound of the crowd outside had all but faded away. Or had the entire gathering gone completely silent? The utter absence of noise disturbed Rusty to the point that he noted where he was reading and put the book down. It was almost as if nobody was there, as if the entire lead up to the Round Up had been a dream, as if it was just another normal trip: his father and him alone, by themselves, at a remote backcountry camp. Or maybe he'd slept through the entire event – maybe that was it. Or had he unknowingly dozed off? Nothing was more disorienting than waking up from a late afternoon nap, the kind that it takes a while to figure out what time it is and where you are at. He could have easily been asleep for days, possibly decades. Rusty rubbed at his chin to make sure he hadn't grown a long "Rip Van Winkle" beard, that he was still a kid. To his greatest relief his skin was still smooth. Rusty wasn't keen on becoming an adult, let alone an old man. He liked the age he was at and halfheartedly hoped he would never grow up.

That's when he heard a new sound from overhead.

Rusty opened the screen door and went to the end of the porch. Sure enough, the crowd was all there, a hundred percent intact, if also strangely frozen in place. To a person, each and every member of the Round Up had stopped what they were doing and were looking up with the eager-eyed anticipation of children waiting for – and for the first time *seeing* – Santa's sleigh overhead.

The airplane made a wide arc in the sky. Its red and green lights blinked against the twilight's orange hue. Rusty watched it circle once then twice and then fly away.

"Is it leaving?" he wondered aloud as he continued to stare.

285

Evidently some people in the crowd were thinking the same.

"No! Look! It's coming back!" an enthusiastic voice announced.

The outline of the Cessna and its blinking lights were clear against the setting sun. It was approaching and dropping in altitude, heading straight for the airstrip. Rusty squinted his eyes to try to make out its shape. At ground level he saw the apparition of two men with torches: It was Sandy and his father demarking the landing strip with light to help guide the plane in.

The engines of the plane filled the air. It was at tree top level coming in to land.

Everyone cheered when the wheels finally touched down, but for Rusty the feeling was more a sense of relief: his mowing and rehab work on the airstrip had been a success, or at least it had prevented a crash. The crowd began gathering at the edge of the grassy runway as the plane taxied back. The pilot came out first followed by a nervous looking man carrying a briefcase, but it was only after a third man appeared that everyone broke out into uncontained cheer. The much ballyhooed guest of honor had finally arrived, and with style points to match. He was donning a buckskin jacket and walked with a confident stride in brightly polished snakeskin boots. In each and every way he looked larger than life, exuding the air of a movie star or some other dignitary of the state, and for once and without a doubt Rusty knew it was definitely not Campfire Charlie — whoever the man was, he was *way too upscale* — except perhaps for one striking similarity in detail to the mythical legend: tilted ever so slightly on his head, he wore a Stetson hat.

Rusty's father met him halfway between the plane and the crowd. They briefly embraced and then walked to the side with Henry gesturing to the crowd to *stay put* as the two men walked alone towards The Lodge. Rusty instinctively headed inside as the two men approached. He tried to look busy reading as they entered through the screen door.

"Oh boy, this place doesn't change. Brings back memories, Henry! Easier times, easier times. How I miss them. Let me tell ya, Henry, you think *you* have problems, Tallahassee is a pain in my rear."

Henry worked the hand pump at the sink. "Here, ya go Burt, take a drink," he said as he handed him a tin cup. "These are the most pristine waters in the state. Here's to *keeping* them that way."

Rusty watched as Burt took a shiny metal flask from his jacket and splashed a little in both cups. "To the good old days, clean water and good whiskey," Burt toasted as they both downed their drinks.

"I wish it was pleasure, not business. Really do," Burt beseeched. He pointed to the deer mounted on the wall. "Say, that isn't the one that Tate spilled the guts ..."

Henry chuckled at the memory. "Yeah, we were all having a good laugh on that earlier."

Burt took the opportunity to pour a generous second helping of whiskey from his flask and gulped it down quickly. "Henry, this deal I got worked – *it's a complete ace*. Nothing to worry about, this is *air tight*. We didn't have many cards going in, but I'm a pro at bluffin', always was."

Henry interrupted. "Yeah, but what about that whole section on ..."

"Hennnnrryyyy," Burt gently cut him off with a sweeping gesture of his hand and an easy smile. The whiskey had finally kicked in. "How long have we been friends, Henry? How long?"

Henry shrugged without expression, "Sounds like you're talking past tense."

"Awww, Henry. Don't be like that. Look, I've got friends in Tallahassee. And D.C. Powerful friends. Barring them throwing me in jail which, *trust me*, isn't gonna happen. Not now that I'm in office. We're gonna work all the loose ends out, alright?" Burt gave Henry a politician's pat on the back and looked him in the eye. "It's gonna be fine. Getta hold of yourself."

"It just seems like, the longer this all drags on, the more and more we're getting kicked out of the loop."

Burt was no longer listening. Something caught his attention at eye level at the perimeter of the room. Rusty thought he was walking over to look at a framed photograph hanging from a nail, perhaps one that he himself was in (or a close friend), when instead he ended up at a piece of bare empty wall and just admired the planks. "Really amazing this Miami Slash Pine. They don't build 'em like this anymore, no sir. Ya know, the hard resin, that's what gives it its shine." He gave the wood a couple of hard taps. "And it's the same solidified sap that makes it naturally resistant to bugs." Burt sighed as he ran his finger down the grain of the wood. "Yeah, you wouldn't believe the cockroaches that I see coming out of the woodwork asking me for favors, *paybacks*, these days. If there's such a thing of having too many friends and not knowing who your friends are, that's where I'm at. I used to fear my enemies. Now I'm not sure which is which. And quite frankly ..." his voice trailed off, "— There's a lot of people I can't be seen with, I can't even call them back."

"Burt, that's one thing we all understand. I was just hoping things might be a little easier for some of us."

"Henry, nobody should take it personally." Burt decreed, still marveling nostalgically at the pine planks. "Sometimes I wish I'd built my own house with this stuff. The problem is ... *there isn't any left.*"

Turning his attention away from the bug-proof wall, Burt noticed Rusty for the first time. "Glad to see you're reading, sport. That's really great. Literacy happens to be one of my priorities for the Florida youth, part of my long-term vision for the economic future of the state."

"Well, um, I go to school in Missouri."

"Of course, of course. I know that. But lots of opportunities in the Sunshine State, if you ever decide to move." Burt turned to Henry. "This is your boy. Rusty, right?"

Rusty stood up as Burt approached to shake hands only to have it unfold into what could be better described as a sort of business transaction in which the avuncular statesman obviously excelled; more than a press of the flesh just to be polite, Burt delivered the sum of his gravitas in a deftly choreographed act — a multi-layered two handed clasp mixed together with a reassuring smile, poignant eye contact and an impeccable selection of words — to create a "moment in time" that sealed the deal: above all else and perhaps only exclusively so, if Burt Silver knew anything he knew how to *sell himself* — everything after that was icing on the cake. "I can see the resemblance," Burt commented as he held Rusty's shoulders with his hands. "Same cheekbones, same eyes."

"Yeah, we have fun," Henry agreed. "It's good to have him down."

Burt glanced at Rusty's book approvingly. "Colonel Stanley Powell. A great American. And in my opinion a book that every American should read."

Rusty's eyes lit up. "You've heard of him?"

"Have I heard of him! That's my Great Uncle Stan! On my mother's side. Second marriage and all that ..."

"So you met him? Didn't he live a hundred years ago?"

288

"Well, um, he was pretty old. I was just a little whippersnapper." Burt positioned his hand parallel to the floor just above the height of his knee. "— Only about ... yea big."

The conversion ended abruptly with the sound of footsteps up the stairs and knocking at the front door, to which Burt nervously shuffled back.

"Who's there!"

"Who do you think?" Sandy replied as he opened the door and gave the congressman an icy look. "Counselor, Henry" Sandy nodded. "I think it's about time the Congressman said his peace."

Burt looked out the window. "So, what's the vibe?" he said as he snuck another swig from his flask.

"They're chomping at the bit to hear what you have to say," Sandy answered. "I am, too."

"Well, let's get on with it!" Henry suggested as he held open the door. "After you, Burt."

Henry turned to Sandy. "You and I, let's go first to clear a path. Rusty, come on and put down that book. This'll be important for you to hear."

Rusty glided through the front door just as it was about to shut. The three men had already descended the steps and were walking down the path. Rusty had to jump off the edge of the porch to catch up.

Burt approached the crowd waving and shaking hands as he made his way into the circle that was forming around him. He was obviously well known and evidently popular among this crowd. He was greeted with back slaps and firm handshakes and warm wishes from all around: *"Evenin' Congressman"* ... *"Quite an honor"* ... *"Good to have ya back!"* ... *"Stick it to them boys in Tallahassee"*... *"Give 'em hell, Burt."* When somebody hailed him as *"The SILVER BULLET!"* it immediately clicked in Rusty's mind where he'd seen the man before: on the many giant billboards up and down the highway closer to the coast where he hawked his legal services for the common man. *"Been arrested or jailed unfairly? Call Burton Silver: The Silver Bullet. Criminal Law for the Innocent Man."* On those placards, Burt exuded power and charm: a man who knew the system, how it worked, and how to work it for anybody's favor. He was ready willing and able to be in your corner for the right price. Rusty was a bit overwhelmed, but also took it in stride. While it was an unexpected honor to be part of the legal legend's entourage, he also couldn't help feeling a little bit let down. Entry into Burt's hallowed inner circle had the contrary effect of diminishing the colossus he knew from the billboard to the level of just an ordinary man, even while at the same time it elevated Rusty's status in ways he couldn't fully comprehend. Whereas before he had been regarded as just another nobody in the crowd — virtually a ghost — the same eyes that had "looked right through him" earlier in the day now saw him in a whole new light; and in particularly, one set of eyes, *Lori's*, whom Rusty briefly exchanged glances with as he rushed by in the energized air of Burt Silver's wake. Rusty desperately wanted to stop and talk but the gauntlet was moving him, not the other way around, and the crowd was too dense — it was impossible to go back. Rusty tried to jump up and down to find her again but the moment had passed. He was only shoulder height compared to most of the men and The Silver Bullet's speech was about to begin.

"Before we get down to business I brought some refreshments," Burt informed the gathering with a generous voice. The aviator stepped forward and opened the lid to a giant cooler on cue. "Brought ya'll some whiskey from my recent trip to Scotland as a small token for your loyalty and support." The pilot dispersed the bottles in several directions with the assistant following up with small paper cups.

"Silver, I hope you know what you're doin'," Sandy stepped in to interrupt under his breath. "Half these boys were lit up before they got here. A lot of them aren't gonna like what you have to say to 'em."

"Lighten up a little, would ya, Parrish," Burt grimaced through his teeth as he continued to smile to the crowd. "Just a gentlemanly gesture ... and to soften 'em up."

Sandy dubiously obliged with a swig. "Gotta hand it to ya, I know my single malts and this is smooth."

Dan Vukovich sauntered his way to the front of the crowd.

"Hiya, counselor. Or should I say... *Congressman?*"

"Hello Dan," Burt responded flatly, purposely avoiding eye contact. "Sorry I couldn't help you with that little trouble you had. Surprised to see you here, frankly."

"Didn't need any help, Burt. *Not this time.*'" Dan faintly chuckled, "— they had nuthin'. Just wanted to ask me some questions about some trips I made down south."

Burt's assistant called over to Henry with a terrified look as a wild-eyed hatchet-man and his ragged companion wrestled over one of the bottles. "Gimme that, you Sumbitch. You already got one, that's mine!" The melee was over before it had barely begun thanks to an ancient man knocking one man to the ground and grabbing the other by the collar with a calloused hand. His other hand was holding a rifle. It was Albert Lee Hodge. "You are gonna behave, ya hear?" he growled in a low voice that everyone could easily hear. "If it were up to me, you two wouldn't have been invited. Now git under that oak tree and stay there! And God help you if you move from that spot! *Now Git!*" The old man walked away with the bottle and took a thirsty swig.

Sandy laughed under his breath. "Albert knows how to keep the peace. And it ain't from coddling. It's because men are terrified of him. Like him or not, they fall in line soon enough. Even the bad actors give him respect."

"Well, he did have a rifle, too."

Sandy laughed. "Not that old thing. It's a Civil War era musket. Only way you're gonna hurt anybody with that is walloping them with it in the head. And Albert wouldn't dare doing that. It's his grandfather's gun from Antietem."

"Still," Henry abruptly broke in. "— I'm sure Albert Lee wants us to get this Round Up over with as soon as we can so he can get back to being alone. I think we should get on with it."

A gun fired into the air from the back of the crowd. It was Albert Lee standing on top of Sid's oversized McNasty buggy with his smoking musket pointed into the air. Contrary to Sandy's claim, the gun did work. The crowd hushed to a murmur as they looked his way. Albert Lee pointed his bony finger across the crowd to Burt and barked out an order, *"Now Everybody, Listen up!"*

"All right, folks! And thank you very much, Mr. Hodge, for agreeing to host this event," Burt said with a broad gesture as he removed his hat and held it to his chest. "Everyone in this crowd — *and most of all myself* — are incredibly honored. Albert Lee represents the best of our citizens. A true hero of the Great War." Burt humbled his voice. "I still remember it like yesterday the day I met Albert Lee at my father's general store in Opa-locka," he digressed, "— selling hides, telling stories. That's the Florida that was. Salt of the Earth folks that built the place up from nothing. Thank you, Albert. You leave me, us, with big shoes to fill."

After a heartfelt moment of silence, Burt deftly segued his attention to the crowd. "Wow! How incredible it is to see all this interest from you folks. Henry, Sandy, Huddy, Loren ... and all your children ... the Robertsons ... it's really overwhelming to see you all here! You all deserve a round of applause!" When Burt started to clap, his assistant stepped forward and held up his clapping hands for everyone to do the same.   Many attentive faces looked on. The roughest looking men of the bunch were up on buggies. Several children were sitting on a giant laurel oak branch like a row of birds, among them included Chilton trying to show off and Lori next to him looking unimpressed.   The charismatic counselor slash businessman and now congressman had complete control of the crowd. All eyes were on him. His assistant was spooked by a barking dog as he handed a briefcase over to Burt.   The crowd of skiffers, swamp rats, hermits, and ne'er-do-wells leaned in eager to hear the news. Burt Silver, the famed Silver Bullet, the same big shot Miami lawyer who had fought for the rights of the Trail Indians and got them a sweet deal for gaming rights, the same Burt Silver who halted the confiscation of property by the federal government in Homestead, and also who fought to save homes from the Interstate by pushing the project farther into the Glades, who rubbed shoulders with scoundrels, smugglers and environmental crusaders of every ilk, had now taken up the crusade for the rights of hunters and the owners of camps and hunting lodges in the flooded woods. The big airport project had been halted. For three years Burt worked every D.C. and Tallahassee connection he had to keep the feds from grabbing all of the swamp. He got a deal. It was a good deal and hard fought. Above all, it was a deal the crowd he was about to address wasn't going to like one bit.

Burt took a document from the briefcase and held it up.

"You wanted a deal boys! And I got ya a deal! Boy oh boy oh boy, what a deal. Some people, some powerful people, they wanted to run *us* out of these woods. Well, in steps the Ol' Silver Bullet and I said, '*Well now, we'll just have to see about that!*'"

The crowd erupted in a cheer.

"The Silver Bullet!!! Get 'em Burt!"

Burt took a deep breath.

"But let me give it to ya straight. It was tough. They're some tough people. No, they aren't nice. So, let me give it to ya straight. The government is coming in. Period. We weren't gonna stop that. Everybody knows that, right?"

"THEY AIN'T HERE YET!!!" an angry voice barked as another man flailed in his attempt to jump from the buggy to a tree branch.

Burt pointed in the direction of the voice. "Not yet, but they're coming. And it's gonna be alright. It's gonna be okay. It's gonna be *fine*. I've secured guarantees. Guarantees that nothing we have now won't be taken away, ever. Never."

"SO WHAT'S THE DEAL?"

"GIVE IT TO US STRAIGHT!!!"

"Okay, here's the deal. The government proposes to manage the area including your properties. There's no getting around that. It will take a few years, but eventually this will be a federally managed property, with all that implies."

A collective moan roared from the crowd. One man shook his head in disgust, spat and abruptly walked away. Others cursed under their breath.

"However," said Burt, jabbing a finger in the air and waving it in a wide arc, "traditional practices such as hunting, the use of off-road vehicles, and airboats will be permitted *in perpetuity!*"

An audible grumble filled the air. The men were beginning to stew.

"What about it being a *'freshwater'* preserve?" a genteel-looking man asked as he stepped forward from the horde. His voice had a Jimmy Stewart authenticity, slightly stammering, polite but to the point. "I thought that was part of the deal?"

Burt nodded knowingly as if to imply the question hit on the very exact topic he was about to talk about next and, like all soothsaying statesmen, started with a personal anecdote he knew would resonate among his brethren and perhaps more importantly, buy him some time to refine his response.

"Adam's right," Burt frankly acknowledged with a solemn nod. "That's an excellent point. Good to see you, Adam, by the way. And how's the family?" Marge and your parents, Vincent and Jill, they really were, *always will be*, the best. Never forget the time I sat with y'all up at Cedar Key talking about all the issues so near and dear to our hearts. It was two days later at Sunday Mass that I made my decision to run, in a large part on what we discussed on that porch, and of course, guided by the Wisdom of God. My platform was simple as it was pure, just three things: Families first, stamp out special interests and, um

...." Burt faltered for a second as he gathered his thoughts, it being unclear if he forgot the final point or he suddenly realized his story had no connection to the question he'd just been asked. Soon enough Burt recovered his composure and picked up where he left off. "Freshwater and the environment, conserving our way of life," he proclaimed with a resurgent tone. "The first thing I did when I landed here tonight was go inside and get a drink of fresh *unpolluted* water. Henry and his son, Rusty ... where's Rusty? ... isn't that right?" Rusty was horrified to be brought to the attention of the crowd. He nodded slightly and smiled as the mob of unruly faces stared at him like a high-wattage spotlight, making it all but impossible to hide. The upshot was seeing Lori on the tree branch waving and cheering him on, "Go Rusty!" Chilton beside her was scowling.

"That's what this place is all about. Freshwater," Burt continued. "We're never gonna lose it. It's gonna be here for your kids and your grandkids and your grandkid's kids." Burt pointed around the crowd. "Now that I'm in Tallahassee, your lodges, your camps, your rights are at the top of my list. You've got my word on it and I guarantee it!"

The crowd went wild. "YOU GET 'EM BURT!!!"

"I told the folks in D.C. we don't need another Park. This is a Preserve. This is about preserving PEOPLE'S RIGHTS! If those folks in Washington think they're gonna come down here and run you folks off the land like they did the Parrish's out of Snake Bight and other families out of other places, *I GOT NEWS FOR 'EM: That ... will ... NEVER ... HAPPEN ... AGAIN!*"

The crowd went crazy. "YEEEAAAWW!"

In the thunderous applause, Rusty overheard Burt bending down to whisper something in his assistant's ear, "Go tell Carl to crank up the plane. *We're gonna wanna haul ass outta here as soon as I'm finished.*"

"But that doesn't mean there aren't going to be restrictions." Burt continued. "Those of you who own properties have the following option: You may take a $15,000 buyout, or be reduced to three acres with further restrictions on building. That's how the agreement stands now. But I'm going to mitigate that. I've slowed down the process. This is all ten, fifteen years out."

"This don't sound like good news to me!" a big fellow leaning against swamp buggy chimed in. "What about those of us who got camps on other folks' property? Most of us got handshake deals with the property owners. And that's most people here?"

Burt sighed. "Look, I've secured fifteen years to maneuver. Nothing's set in stone. We have the momentum here. Why would I be here talking to ya'll if I didn't think I could win? For now, this is the best deal we're gonna get. This is a victory. Heads up everybody. We won! Okay? This could be a lot worse. Trust me. *And I mean a lot worse.* I'm already working on securing squatter's rights. This is a battle we're gonna win. It's just gonna take time. But time is our ally."

"We don't need *time*, we need answers *now!*"

The energy in the crowd had changed. They were no longer with Burt or in agreement with his deal. Men began hurling curses at the government and arguing among themselves. Rusty overheard a balding and wiry man swear he'd "go down shooting" with anyone coming in to take over his camp.

Henry stepped in front of Burt and held out his hands, not as a speaker, but in the style of a Wild West Sheriff that was exerting order on an increasingly unruly crowd, or was he serving as the security detail for a guest of honor whose fraud had been exposed? Out of nowhere Greg Kleal appeared by Henry's side – his head on a swivel smiling from ear to ear – followed by Tate clearing a path from the left to secure the crowd at Henry's flank. Moments later Rusty spied Huddy staking his claim at a strategic spot on top of Henry's Buggy in back and could hear Sandy in the middle mixing his reasoning voice to help quell the rising tide of unrest.

"Is that everything, Burt?" Henry asked without turning back. "Is there anything else?"

"How 'bout I ask the Counselor a few more questions behind Tinkers," Greg maliciously sneered under his breath. "*—Might take a while.*"

"Actually, Henry, I just spoke to my assistant. And we're out of time. Love to stay, love to stay, but we're running late." Burt lifted his hat to the crowd as he and his aid retreated towards The Lodge and then around the path in the direction of the plane. "This is a fight we're gonna win!" Burt exclaimed to the deflated crowd. Burt hadn't delivered them a clear cut victory so much as he had confronted them with the grim reality that their time was running out and, if they were looking for a savior, the Silver Bullet probably wasn't their man.

Rusty watched Burt flash a V for victory sign to the dispersing crowd as he and his assistant pulled themselves up into the plane. A moment later they were picking up speed down the runway and lifting off up into the air. As quickly as he had arrived, Burt was back in the air and turning toward the gulf coast, first the sound of the engines going silent and then his lights disappearing behind the darkened silhouette of the ancient trees and into the night sky beyond.

Chapter 15:
Alligator Battle for the Ages

Sep 13, 1865, 2:01 pm

"Surely," I inquire to Tate in a sobering tone, "Brown's chances for survival at this point must be," I pause, "—*very slim?*"

Tate concedes that although the maniacal man was still "as irate as ever" — albeit also relegated to a much weakened state, gurgling up a bilious and bubbly foam through his mouth and nose and grimacing in intense pain any time he moved, "even an inch" — the captain never lost his grip of command, adamantly ordering Tate to deliver him out of the hell hole at once, "— *Or Else.*" After following several game trails that dead ended into even deeper and more dangerous snake-infested pools (resulting in a predictable cavalcade of curses and threats from Brown) Tate's dogged persistence pays off: they break out of the miserable thicket into an open prairie of sunshine as far as the eye can see — a sparsely-vegetated meadow that is only shallowly-flooded, just shin deep. Tate points the way to an island of high ground, covered with giant gumbo limbos and other hardwoods, about a half mile slog away.

2:10 pm

It seems I am having a reaction to my many medications.

Or is the problem I do not have enough? My Dr. Shiloh's is nearly depleted. I struggle mightily to keep my eyes open. Tate shakes me repeatedly and props me up in my chair, also assisting me in re-inking my pen which in a stupor I mistake as a medicinal elixir and drink half the vial before gagging and continuing with inscription of my notes.

2:20 pm

Tate and Brown arrive on the island to find company:

A flock of buzzards — "hundreds of 'em, even thousands" — are all hopping about. They quickly hone in on Brown. Tate swats at them with a stick as best he can, but it is no use. Every time he beats one away two more move in from the other side. Tate hurls Brown's stiffened arm into the flooded prairie as a last resort, to which the hungry birds converge; but their problems are far from over. The commotion has surely revealed their position to the pursuing Indians. Tate cannot see them directly, but he can hear their voices — it's only a matter of time.

2:30 pm

Brown's many wounds take their toll.

He falls into a semi-conscious state of calling out for a long-lost love, an "Evangeline" or an "Angelica" or "some other pretty lady's name like that." Tate has no other choice but to shush him up, threatening him with a really good "— *Or Else!*" Tate says it felt good to finally get back at the captain with his own line, an admonishment to which Brown does not seem to take any offense.

2:39 pm

After another coughing fit I again interrupt Tate.

"Why on Earth didn't you simply leave Brown? You were his captive, not his captor ... nor even a friend. His actions directly led to the death of your brother. You owe him nothing!" Tate responds affirmatively — nodding that I'd taken the words "right out of his mouth" and perfectly described "exactly what he was going to do" — when sheer exhaustion suddenly got the best of him and he collapsed right where he was on the spot, against the trunk of a Gumbo Limbo, and nodded off.

2:51 pm

Next thing Tate remembers is being startled awake by an unusual sound.

Expecting to hear Brown still moaning about his "Clarabelle or Lindalou or who have you," Tate is somewhat perplexed to find the captain in a comatose state, not even snoring a peep, "— which is saying a lot considering all the other nights he was really sawing away at the logs." Tate places his hand overtop the captain's mouth to feel for any traces of breathing. After a good minute or so, and to his greatest relief, he finally detects a faint puff from the captain's mouth. Tate describes himself as "incredibly thankful" to know at least Brown isn't dead.

3 pm
"Thankful!" I gasp. *"—For what? The captain dying would've been the best possible thing."*

Tate adamantly disagrees. He says that the last thing he needed was the responsibility of fussing around with the many burial arrangements Brown requested, a list that included "placing him in a proper casket of bald cypress, constructing a mausoleum made of 'the finest Italian marble' visible at a hun'ert feet, reading a whole list of passages from the Good Book, plucking diff'ernt flowers to represent each of his different lost loves and other such niceties as that; all of which was capped off with his most fearsome '—*Or Else!*' yet."

3:20 pm
I am aroused to the sound of Tate snapping his fingers and waving his hands in front of my face.

When I inform him that I was "only resting my eyes" he comments that my eyes were never closed. As everything is a bit of a blur, I ask Tate to remind me where we last left off. "Ah yes," he recalls, "—We were at the arrival of the strange glow."

3:22 pm
"Strange glow?" I query as I polish off whatever drops of Dr. Shiloh's are left. "Surely it must have been the moon, rising from the East, probably a full one, too?"

Tate confirms that's exactly what he thought, too, at least at first — but it doesn't take him long to see something much more ominous was unfolding. "Ya see, the glow wasn't rising out of the East at all," he explains, "—but rather approaching *at eye level* from the North, hovering over the water about yea high and being held up by the bony fingers of a long and craggily arm." Tate hurries back to inform Brown of the calamitous news: The Grim Reaper is moving in!

3:45 pm
After several good slaps to the face Brown finally wakes up.

The captain's mood quickly sours at the realization that it isn't "Abigail or Leandra or whoever else he was dreaming about" whispering in his ear, but rather Tate whom he pulls his knife on and threatens him with several *"—Or Elses."* Despite almost getting slashed, Tate is happy to see Brown is more or less back to his normal self.

3:50 pm
Tate describes Brown's reaction to the Grim Reaper's approach as nothing short of fearless.

"Bring'm On!" he barks among other taunts, including "I'll beat ya down with me missing arm," (which he orders Tate to find), "and with me other arm tied behind my back!" and "Won't be the first Grim Reaper I ever killed!" Tate feverishly attempts to talk sense to the dying man — encouraging him to repent from his sinful ways while he still had the chance so that he might be granted forgiveness and entrance into Eternal Life (even if on the inside Tate suspected he was looking at "a good couple centuries in purgatory at the least") — only to be sharply reproached by the captain and mule kicked in the chest.

4 pm
Seeing no other option, Tate climbs up the trunk of the biggest of the Gumbos to await his fate.

The view from the top of the branch is "better than a lighthouse," Tate claims, including the following spectacles: the moon above the size of "dinner plate held at arm's length," the flooded prairie below "bathed in the softest candlelight ever seen," and a breeze so fresh "it practically cleaned his teeth when he inhaled." Not that all was good with the world. The perch also gave a clear view of the Grim Reaper closing in from the North and the Indians paddling up from the South.

4:05 pm
Nonetheless, Tate is overtaken by an "extreme calm" in the face of death.

He fashions a cross from two twigs and prays as hard as he can for the good angels to rescue him before it's too late, and sure enough they do: It doesn't take Tate but a few seconds of praying before the angels respond "with the sweetest most gentlest *whistling*" he ever heard.

4:13 pm

"Whistling angels?" I interrupt in disbelief. "Playing the harp or bugle, okay, but whistling is a vulgar habit best confined to the gates of hell."

Tate chastises me sharply for cutting him off, to the point — at least for a moment or two — I wonder if I'm not looking at Brown, not Tate, and even find myself half bracing for a dreaded *"—Or Else!"* only to have him just as quickly regain his composure. Tate confides that he couldn't have found "a better place to die" up in that tree, although he also admits that Brown's constant cursing and retching were a distraction, "— but in all other ways," Tate says, "it was as close to God as he ever felt, even more than reading a verse from the Good Book in the front row at church."

4:16 pm

"But of course you didn't die," I remind him as I as I quietly, or rather — quite forcefully — clear my throat. Or could it be, I ask myself, that I'm talking to a ghost?

Tate assures me he is alive and in the flesh, all thanks to "the angels" that turned the Grim Reaper into a regular ol' man. Next thing he knows he looks over at the glow and just sees a "white feller pole-boating toward him in a thirty-foot skiff." Tate describes the man of tallish build, with a long nose, a real aristocratic-look, and most distinctive of all — *whistling,* and just where the angels left off, only better, "—not to disparage the angels of course." Tate further claims the whistling was so pleasant it drowned out Brown's cursing which is saying a lot.

4:19 pm

I am overcome with an overwhelming need to leave the room.

No more than three steps out the door, my gag reflex triggers a forceful expulsion of the contents from my guts. Tate rises to his feet and rushes to my assistance, and may have very well saved my life, reassuring me the entire time *"it's no big deal"* and that *"I'm nowhere near as bad off as was Captain Brown"* and other soothing things like that. In the meanwhile, given my current state of imposition, he offers to write in my journal himself.

4:30 pm

The following entry is written by me, Columbus Tate.

So's like I was sayin' about that white feller in the skiff. He and and the Injuns arrive on the Gumbo island at the same time, Honest Truth and Cross my Heart wouldn't lie in a hun'ert years. But Brown was ready for em. Right off the bat he hits em with a couple "—Or Elses!" that tops all the other ones by far, just really straight from the heart. Let me tell ya, there was something about that feller in the skiff Brown didn't like one bit, almost like they knew each other from a previous life. Called him "a deserter," not a "true Virginian," a traitor to "The Cause" and other such shameful things like that. Gotta hand it to the feller on the skiff, though. He took it right on the chin he did. Didn't lower himself to Brown's level one bit, nor did he seem scared which is saying something too. Next thing I know the white feller and the Injuns are waving me down from the tree, clearly showing that they come in peace. Update on Colonel Powell. He's back on his feet. Whatever the doctor give'm seems to have done the trick. Thank You and Yours Truly, Columbus Tate.

5:30 pm

Resuming with my notes, I request Tate to "back up a little" to catch me up.

When Tate starts telling me about him and Abel fishing for mullet in Gallivan's Bay I tell him that's back too far. Eventually he gets to a couple vivid descriptions of Captain Brown's "—Or Elses!" which we agree is a perfect place to pick up and we go from there, although Tate has to pause to allow me time to try to hack some phlegm loose, the entire time of which he assures me my affliction is probably nothing more than a seasonal allergy and that he's known other people, although *"not personally,"* who recovered from *"way worse"* by a special doctor hitting them real hard with a brick on the back. Upon further consideration, Tate corrects himself that it "might have been a *preacher*, using a *Bible*, to hit the man on the *head*."

5:45 pm

Next thing Tate remembers is waking to the gentle thrush of water and whistling in his ear.

Brown and Tate are being pushed up a tranquil, meandering stream, Brown on the skiff and Tate in the canoe. The water is clear to the bottom which is "white as pearls." Tate looks over to see the white man feeding a small hawk perched on his shoulder a morsel of food, after which the merlin-like creature spreads its wings and flies away. Eventually they enter a labyrinth of fizzing pools. Something about the water rejuvenates Tate immediately. Before too long Brown is alert and back to his old self, too, cursing up a storm and saying, '—*Or Else!*'"

6 pm
Whatever the medic gave me I am finally feeling its effects.

Jotting down notes as best as I can about what Tate says came next. After a day at the springs Brown is fully cured. They go back to the village. Not the same one, but bigger. Practically a city. There's a ceremony. And many busk fires. The Indians take a liking to Brown's cursing and start to end all their conversations with "—*Or Else!*" There is an extended courtship. Many of the women change their names to Evangeline and Clementine to try to win his heart. Brown marries one of the Evangeline's by mistake. While Brown is being occupied straightening the situation out Tate is able to slip out of camp using a map and a good dugout canoe given to him by the feller on the skiff. Tate is happy to finally be free of Brown and eventually makes it to a stretch of remote beach where he succeeds in hailing down a passing ship. The moment Tate is about to board Brown surprises them from behind a clump of sea oats and immediately overtakes the ship.

Sep 14
The Spanish Consulate is eager for a decision

The two grim-faced lawyers greet me at the door. I tell them the case is much more difficult than I originally thought. I ask for more pills to steady my nerves.

Sep 15
Carefully reviewing my notes.

Looking back I am struck by the breadth of what Mr. Tate has described. While I am intrigued by his account of the mineral spring — it obviously is a font of tremendous healing powers, and could possibly even cure my chronic cough (not to mention also provide me relief from my growing dependence on Dr. Shilohs Medicinal Elixir and Greenling's Natural Cure of Bartibuate Sulfide pills) — I cannot let personal matters interfere from the official capacity I was brought in to resolve.

303

Sep 16
I am no fool.

Tate would have me believe that he accomplished more in three months with the abhorrent Brown than Drake, Magellan, and Smith combined with a royal commission and a fleet of ships. Some of his story was believable – at least at first – but the longer he talked the less plausible it became, and in particular Brown's high-jacking of the Cuban ship. There is no way a man with only one arm could overtake a crew without any help. I don't care how many *"—Or Elses!"* he used. It just doesn't make any sense.

Sep 17
I have reached my final decision:

Tate is obviously guilty. His story is an outlandish fabrication. My recommendation will be for Tate to stand trial with Brown.

Sep 19
I am feeling better in every way.

The arrival of dry air has made for cooler nights, and much improved my sleep, giving me a skip in my step despite knowing I will be the bearer of bad news for Tate. As I approach the jail I am flabbergasted by the sound of a familiar and quite cheerful song. It is Tate whistling *The Risin' of the Moon!* When I commend him for performing the *"the second most"* rousing rendition of the song I have ever heard, he doesn't disagree: "No matter how much I whistle that song I will never rival the whistling of the white feller on the skiff." A bolt of electricity jolts me to my core. The feller on the skiff, but of course – How could I have missed it? *"His name,"* I beseech, *"—What was his name?"* Tate thinks about it for a second and then says he doesn't know, or can't remember. "Are you sure?" I interrogate him with grave intensity, "— He really had *no name?"* Tate nods in the affirmative: "Other than a funny phrase they called him in Muskogee, which literally translated to something like 'He Who Draws Crazy Lines in the Sand.'"

Sep 20
The two grim-faced lawyers are not pleased.

When they demand a copy of my notes, I deny their request and instead present them with the following note.

Dear R&R,

I am writing this letter to inform you that Columbus Tate possesses vital information to a confidential matter of national security interests that I am not privy to discuss. Effective immediately, under authority of the United States Government, I am authorizing that Columbus Tate be relinquished into my custody, thereafter which I will escort him back to Fort Stafford.

Sincerely,

CSP

Chapter 16:
Late Night Shady Dealings

Burt's fears of the crowd turning into a mob had been largely overblown. After a brief bought of collective disappointment, the vast majority of people were largely peaceful and mostly started to disperse, except for a few strident die-hards who gathered around.

That didn't stop a man in green fatigues and combat boots from trying to rally the retreating troops. "Let 'em come! I say we stand our ground!"

"Yeah, we'll slug it out with the feds," one of his cohorts agreed.

"Sure we might lose," another voice reasoned, "— but at least the government would know we won't go down easy."

"They couldn't run the Injuns off! Dammit," the ring leader fumed, "— they'll wish they'd never stirred us up! Let 'em come and try us!"

A more level headed man stepped forward to offer his two cents. It was Lori's father! "So, what do you think you're gonna do with guns, boys?" he said with a slow shake of his head. "That's foolish at best, dangerous at worst. Let's not spoil a good thing. Burt's our asset."

"*AssHOLE* is more like it!"

The guitar virtuoso raised his eyebrows at the bluntness of the talk. He couldn't entirely disagree, nor did he see the point. A flurry of new complaints rang out.

"Yeah, have you been reading the papers? He's in some real hot water on the whole Sea Oats Springs development scandal thing. Honestly, I don't follow it completely, but they're hot on his trail."

"And a lot of other things, too. It's all starting to pile up. I don't give him much time in Tallahassee."

"He's talking about buying *us* time? He's the one that's gonna be *'doin' time'* if ya ask me ... in Raiford!"

Lori's fathers stood his ground on his view. "Listen, we aren't gonna go back to the good ol' days. Those days are gone. But let's not look a gift horse in the mouth. We won. Let's pat ourselves on the back. We stopped them from turning this place into a giant subdivision. Boys, that's what would have been defeat, *not this*. For the first time in a long time, the woods won! That's pretty incredible considering what's happening along the coast. The only thing your griping and threats are gonna do is make things worse, a *lot worse*."

"Are you sayin' we should just roll over, Gene?" one of the angry men asked Lori's dad.

"All I'm saying is take a deep breath. We're on the right side of history here. Let's keep it that way."

"I still don't like it, Gene. I feel like we gave up too much."

"Change is hard," Lori's father conceded. "But I'd rather it be us doing the changing than the trees being bulldozed away. The trees are smiling. Can't you see that? We helped them win. I'll be proud of what we did until the day I die. Might be our ticket to heaven, too, you ever think of that?"

"Gene, I don't know."

"Trust me, sleep on it. Give it a chance."

•••

Gator Tate was speechless. For once it seemed he had nothing to say. Rusty remembered his father telling him that Tate had been in his camp in the Big Cypress for over fifty years, but didn't really own it. It was just a handshake deal with the foreman of the cattle company. Now he was going to lose his home. While Tate lived in Sweetwater, he spent most of his time in the Glades and the Big Cypress. Rusty saw anxiety in Tate's eyes, as if he had just been told he had a terminal disease. Uncertainty now clouded the only sure thing in his life.

Sandy Parrish stood silently as options were discussed. The Graveyard, his family camp, would remain safe from destruction, albeit reduced. He looked as if he wanted to comfort Gator Tate but knew better.

When Rusty spotted Albert Lee making a campfire in the previous night's pit he went over to give him a hand. It didn't take long for a flame to take hold on the wood. The old man seemed content with how thing worked out, or rather – if he was upset or happy he didn't show it. After a while he mumbled a bunch of things that Rusty couldn't understand about "honor" and "friendship" and "the way that things once were" partly to the flame, partly to himself and partly to others as they walked by. "Wish I could turn back the clock to when it wasn't so messed up ... maybe give the younger generation a chance." The old man broke off a piece of stick and threw it in the flames. He did that a few more times. Rusty closed his eyes to blink only they stayed closed. "– If Charlie were here he would've figured this thing out." Suddenly Rusty jolted awake. *Did he say Charlie?* The boy tried to focus his eyes on what he saw in front of him and straighten up. If he'd dozed off he didn't remember it. In the interim other men had gathered around the flame. There were many conversations. The moment he was following along with one, another one would break out and it would split in two. When Rusty heard Charlie's name mentioned for a second time he was more determined than ever to stay awake, but his eye lids were heavy. His mind was continually drifting off. The Round Up hadn't gone as hoped but Charlie could still save the day. He always came through at the last minute. If Rusty remembered anything from what his father had told him he remembered that. Campfire Charlie would be coming and Rusty was determined to stay awake.

•••

Rusty woke to the sound of raised voices and cursing unsure how long he had drifted off. His father was holding back an enraged Gator Tate. This time it was serious: Sandy and Tate were really at each other's throats, Sandy on one side of the fire and a snarling Tate on the other and a bunch of men picking sides. Despite the potential for violence and the rising energy among the men, Rusty couldn't resist the catatonic hypnosis of sleepiness slipping in; no amount of willpower was capable of keeping him up.

In a moment he was gone. It was just his father and him on a highway somewhere in a desert flying fast down a ribbon of asphalt. Or maybe it wasn't a desert because everywhere in every direction it was covered with trees. And mountains. Many mountains. The air smelled like juniper. A thick rich scent. The highway stretched for miles. They passed a sign that read

"Jackson Hole 35 miles." His father lit up a cigarillo and turned on the radio to the sound of a garbled mess of static and an agitated voice. Sensing someone was in the backseat he turned to look only to be deterred by an invisible force. Mumbling. Someone was mumbling. The mumbling was very strange. Rusty's father tuned the radio to another station that was crystal clear. The radio host was a man named Charlie who his father greatly admired because "he told it like it was." Finally the force field broke and Rusty looked back to see an infant baby wrapped in a brightly colored blanket with a repeating pattern of white, black, red and yellow stripes. When Rusty turned back to the wheel to see who was driving, his father was gone and Dwight was in his place. "Got the big contract for the new subdivision at Ruby Falls," his step fathered announced. "— This is the big break I've always dreamed of. Our own company, father and son." Dwight and he were in a parade of construction trucks and other heavy equipment riding under the canopy of a deeply shaded woods. Actually, they weren't in a truck but running through a forest filled with mushrooms as big as houses that were sprouting up everywhere he looked. As they crested a hill the rising sun was staring them in the face. He tried not to look into it but he couldn't hold back. He kept staring and staring straight into the sun until his eyes turned black and then there he was, back at The Lodge sitting in front of the campfire listlessly watching the incongruous scene of Sandy Parrish and Gator Tate smiling and laughing, and side by side, in the presence of a man in a Stetson hat who was stoking the campfire and chattering up a storm of words that was captivating all the men but Rusty couldn't make out, not even a word. Rusty tried to get up and listen more closely, to open his eyes. Every time he managed to open them they just as quickly closed. The last thing he remembered was his father trying to introduce him to the man but for naught. No matter how much Rusty tried he couldn't prevent himself from dozing off.

•••

The next thing Rusty remembered was waking up to the sound of a raccoon or something scurrying around on the roof of The Lodge. He wondered what time it was. He had to go to the bathroom, but the only bathroom was an outhouse down the trail. He slipped on his moccasin slippers and walked out the door. The ground was wet with dew. A song was softly playing on the radio from one of the nearby tarps.

> *My Maria, there were some blue and*
> *sorrowed times ...*

Just before the outhouse he spotted his father sitting with two other men around a dim campfire. They couldn't see him but he could see them. One was Dan Vukovich and the other was Greg Kleal. Greg was sitting in a folding chair whittling a stick with a big bowie knife. Dan was holding a can of beer in his hand standing up. His father was smoking a tiparillo. He looked vaguely displeased.

Dan produced a gym back and opened it up. "Starting capital, Henry. Thirty grand."

Henry glanced over at the bag. He looked impressed.

"I want you guys in on this. I can't do it myself. I'm telling you I got friends down south. They're gonna set us up. So are you in? I got this all worked out."

"We're way too smart for that shit, Vuke," Greg Kleal fumed as he peeled a strip of bark off the stick. "— Way too smart."

Greg's fat body was wedged into the lawn chair to the point it looked like he couldn't get up. His grin was from ear to ear. "We need to keep things in-house, Henry. Until this all blows over. We shouldn't be doing nothing. To be honest I'm pretty fuckin' nervous."

"Nothing to be nervous about. It's all worked out."

Henry took a drag on his cigarillo and looked Dan hard in the eyes. "Dan, you're solid, right? We really weren't expecting you, Dan. Not so soon. I have to admit it's a little —."

"Henry, hey! Henryyyyyy! What are you trying to say?" Dan said as he threw his hands up in frustration and turned the other way. Dan tried to compose himself for one final pitch. "They had nothing. We've all been pinched before. Look Henry, what about those two years I did in Atlanta. If there was ever a time I was gonna give something up, it would've been then. This is nothing. Think about it: that was two years before Burt even got me a deal. I'm tellin' ya I'm clean as hell. All buttoned up."

Rusty's father exhaled and stared back into the fire.

"What'd you give 'em, Dan?"

Dan refused to give in. "Godammitt, Henry! That's rich! That's really fuckin' brilliant! Henry I didn't give 'em anything.

Henry! Henry! Shit! So I sat down with Bill Tanner. Okay. No big deal. Henry how long we been doin' this? How long we been friends, Henry? C'mon. Fuck! Fuuuuck! Henry."

"You FUCKING WEASEL! I oughta end you right here, right now," Greg Kleal spat out as he stood up. He motioned at Dan with his bowie knife, making menacing circles slowly in the air. "Fuckin' rat-bastard is what you are! Talking to Tanner. Fuckin' Tanner. Who's Tanner talking to? Too many people talking. Somebody's gonna connect the dots."

Henry shook his head in frustration. "Sit down, Greg. That won't solve anything. We gotta figure out what we're gonna do next. I knew this was coming eventually. Greg, put your knife away. Okay. Just put it away. Tanner's the least of our worries."

Dan Vukovich took a beer from the cooler and angrily hurled it into the woods. "Henry, I swear. *Henry! You can't possibly believe that!* And now you have Greg thinking the same thing. *Fuck!*"

"Spare me the horseshit, Dan," Henry sighed. "We've always been honest with each other. The less said about it the better. I already know everything, Dan. I guess that's what bothers me. You shoulda just disappeared, Dan."

Startled by the sound of footsteps, Rusty retreated back to The Lodge.

•••

Albert Lee Hodge was sitting at the table when Rusty rushed in.

"Is everything okay, son?"

"I was just, um, had to use the bathroom."

Albert Lee nodded. "Don't suppose you were still awake when we had our special guest."

"You mean Mr. Silver?"

"No, after that — it was very late?"

"Not ... *Charlie?*"

"Oh yeah, Charlie," Albert Lee replied glibly. "No, I mean the panther. A big one."

"A panther!" Rusty gasped. "Is it still out there? I've never seen one."

"Well, I'd imagine it's long gone by now," Albert Lee guessed. "It was chasing a doe and her fawn. They ran right through camp."

"Can we at least go to where it was at?"

"What I suggest is you go on back and get some sleep. Ain't nothing good going on around here at 2 am. We'll look for the tracks in the morning when you get up, how's that?"

Chapter 17:
In Search of Lt. French

Sep 28, 1865

If Tate is thankful for my intervention I cannot tell.

I was able to see to it that he be awarded a $50 stipend as recompense for the loss of his boat and travel expenses. We depart by steamer for Stafford at noon.

Sep 29

Word on deck is that it's smooth seas ahead.

The trip should take us directly from New Orleans to Fort Brooke, and then from there another day, possibly two, to Stafford.

Sep 30

I am astounded by the size of the ship and its many new amenities and advances in design.

The ingenuity of the American spirit is a thing to behold, only matched by the quality of people on board. No longer a backwater frontier, the Florida peninsula is attracting civilization's very best. The women have enough plumage in their hats to put the highest-society of New York to shame. Many men wear fine tailored suits.

Oct 1

So good it is at last to be on the open water.

Land is no longer in sight and the warmer weather is again doing me well. Managing my cough with Dr. Shilohs and Greenling's for now.

Oct 2, 10 am

We arrive on deck to the sound of a salesman's pitch

"Ladies and Gentleman, Ladies and Gentlemen," a charming voice orates, "— I present you with a chance of a lifetime! An opportunity you will not want to turn down! Millions of acres of land ready for cultivation. Land that will magically appear from the swamp upon the dredging of the river and the digging of this canal. Friends, Peace brings with it Prosperity and a Destiny, GOD'S PLAN, to harness the potential of this Garden of Eden, the veritable sunny Italy of the Americas." As the man comes into view through a gap in the crowd, I can see he is wearing a fine vest and the more expensive type of straw hat. He is using a cane as a pointer to accentuate his remarks. Many of the onlookers are star struck by his mastery of legal and engineering terminology, as am I; still others seem amused and quickly move on. Approaching closer, I see his briefcase is opened into a diorama of pamphlets and legal contracts which reads Charles O. Nightingale across the front: C.P.O, Esquire, Chief Financial and Legal Officer of the Nightingale Drainage and Development Corporation. "I implore you. You Sir! And You Ma'am!" the businessman proclaims, "to join in our grand vision for the development of this Great Land!"

2 pm

This salubrious breeze reaches deep into my soul.

In my heart it reaffirms the reason I return. If there ever was a place to meet God and His Ministering Angels, I would not prefer the peaks of a lofty mountain or any of the high places of the Earth. It is the vast Gulf Waters lapping on south Florida's wilderness shores that would make Solomon silent with awe.

Oct 3

Tate has fallen prey to the huckster's pitch.

When I tersely remind him of his stipend's intended use, he recites through the promotional brochure's many claims of how Stafford is "preordained to surpass Venice in its architectural grandeur in just a few short years with a bustling port that will rival New Orleans in commerce once the Great Canal project is complete."

Oct 4, 8 pm

I meet with Captain Parker on Tate's behalf.

He graciously welcomes me into his cabin and carefully hears me out. He says he "understands completely" and, if need be, assures me he is ready to "see to it" that the matter is "properly resolved." As we walk along the upper deck, we are befriended by none other than Charles O. Nightingale himself. He apologizes profusely about the "coarseness" of his sales pitch and the misunderstanding with "that fine young man, Columbus Tate" whom he hails as "a future leader" and "our country's very best."

10 pm
During bourbon and cigars I become convinced the investment is legitimate.

In recompense for my backing, and as "a courtesy for my patriotic service to our great country," Mr. Nightingale offers to bring me on as a "silent partner" at a special discount rate – identical to the one made available to Captain Parker: fifty shares for the price of one. Perhaps sensing my hesitancy, he raises it to a hundred and I agree on the spot.

Oct 6, 3 pm
Our journey takes an unexpected turn.

High seas. Darkening skies. The captain redirects the ship south and orders everyone below deck.

11 pm
Sleep proves impossible, my sickness returns.

I pace as best I can to ward off nausea. As I look out at the gloom through my small porthole window I find my thoughts drifting back to my leisurely days with Thursby watching sunsets from the East Tower, listening to the gentle waves lapping on the shore, and discussing future plans. That was a time when all things seemed possible. Today I feel my better days have passed.

Oct 7
Waters have finally calmed.
I am having trouble getting out of bed. I will rest for now.

Oct 8
Finally feeling the strength to venture out on deck.

Damage is minimal, or perhaps the worst of it has already been cleaned up. The moment I turn the corner I again find myself in the throes of Nightingale's colorful pitch. He seizes the opportunity to introduce me as the "famous war hero" who is "all aboard" on the deal, even going so far as to imply the endeavor is backed by U.S. government bonds which I was specifically brought on to oversee. A horde of new investors clamor to the table in the patriot fervor that ensues. Not wanting to put my investment in jeopardy I stay silent on the point.

Oct 9, 9 am

My waiter hands me a sealed envelope at breakfast.

Having not the faintest of clues to what it could be about I quickly open it up to discover there is someone onboard who was made aware of my presence during Mr. Nightingale's speech, a man named Sam Hunter. To the best of my knowledge I cannot recollect ever having made the acquaintance of such a person. He claims to remember me well from my Florida days and requests my presence at the stern of the boat tonight at sunset.

6:11 pm

I watch the sun set but no one appears.

As I prepare to return to my quarters for the night, I am approached by a man whom I do not recognize by face but the moment he speaks I am struck by the familiarity of his voice. His selection of words is remarkable and quite unmistakable. It is the grandson of Shadows Inside on his mother's side with the Walks Alone Clan. He and his contingent are returning "on business" to Florida, "but do not plan to stay." I am somewhat embarrassed to hear him say that his grandfather spoke highly of me. When I mention my plans to return to the old fort with a refugee from the recent war, he nods his head but stays silent on the point.

Oct 10

Tate has been badly beaten and is nursing a bloody lip.

A bystander by the stairwell steps forward to explain the sequence of events: Tate had entered a high-stakes card game of Sixty-six the previous night, under the promise he was "well vested" and had plenty of cash. By all indications he was winning big for much of the night, "and should'a walked away a winner," only to "lose it all" in the wee hours of dawn and prove unable to pay. After "a good roughing up" by several of the other gamblers, and just when they were preparing to toss Tate over the rails into the gulf, Nightingale was able to intervene on his behalf by agreeing to forfeit the full sum of Tate's stipend to cover his gambling debts. It is unclear to me if Nightingale was not one of the gamblers himself.

Oct 11

Tate is determined to get his money back.

Mr. Nightingales is amenable to reinstating his shares in full, minus fees, if Tate can succeed in steering five new customers his way. Tate has accordingly immersed himself in a large dossier of papers entitled "*Nightingale's Ocksfurd School: Principles of Land Drainage and Real Estate.*" While his sales pitch lacks the touch of Nightingale, it could become passable with a little more work.

Oct 12

I awake from my slumbers gasping for air.

Shadows Inside is standing in front of me. Now he is gone. I walk up on the deck to clear my head, to try to remember what he said. Nobody is there and the water is still. There is barely a breeze. I sit down on a bench and face out into the void. Shortly thereafter, I fall asleep, or maybe I am just in deep thought. I think about digging the hole for Stafford and wonder if I may not yet do the same for French. At some point I lean over the rails to find myself looking at my quivering reflection on the water below. Shadow Inside's voice resonates in my head. He tells me there is a Bottomless Waters where the water always spins. It takes whatever is bad and buries it deep in the Ground. It is there my journey must begin. As long as the water is high, Shadows Inside says its weight keeps the Great Devil below and there is nothing to fear. But when the sheet of Water Life withers away the Great Devil becomes very upset. He climbs out of the earth though the Still Water and rules the Sky Land. It is a time of great hardship for our people. I open my eyes to the sight of Sam Hunter next to me on the other end of the bench. We sit in silence until eventually Sam stands up and leaves. I must say, every time I begin to understand the ways of these people they suddenly withdraw into unfathomable mystery.

Oct 13

Tate is doing better.

After a day or two of no luck, his utilization of such phrases as "no risk, a hun'ert percent guaranteed, and get your money back no questions asked" wins him over a handful of investors, including two missionary sisters from a convent in New Orleans, a widowed grandmother and a young man and his pregnant wife. In the wave of his relief, Tate also confesses that some of the testimony he provided to me at the jail "was a bit of a stretch," but *only* the part about what he and Abel were doing before they got pressed into service. They weren't fishing for mullet but rather running guns for the Confederates. Tate swears they only did it for the money and never believed in "The Cause." Everything else he swears up and down was true, including the part about Brown hijacking the ship with one arm and the mysterious satchel whose contents are still unknown. I am inclined to wonderment about anything Tate says.

Oct 14

I had no idea how far we blew off course.

We are arriving directly at Stafford as a result. Not an Italy at all, the river inlet is lined with a hodgepodge of dilapidated shacks. The sordid sight has caused an outcry among a contingent of the investors to get their money back. A rowboat appears to be missing and Nightingale is gone. Tate meanwhile finds himself cornered by one of the angry investors he lured in. Knowing full well that smart money has patience and my insider knowledge that the investment opportunity is legit, I intervene on both men's behalf, buying back the man's shares at full price, much to the appreciation of his pregnant wife.

Oct 15, 11 am

Sam Hunter catches me as I prepare to unboard the ship.

He says his grandfather is with us more now that he is gone, that the distance is long and the journey hard, that obstacles await for those who go south of the Big River, and that I should sing my death song when the time comes. Most of all, he wishes me well and is glad that we met.

4 pm

Tate needs a day to "tend to business" in Stafford before we continue upriver.

There are several women looking out from the second floor balcony of a prominent house, which I can only assume is not his own, although judging from the way he is greeted I am not sure what to think. *"Tell Evangeline that her precious Columbus is back!"* a woman in a low-cut blouse calls toward the stairs. I am greeted by yet another woman, similarly dressed, who is kind enough to fill me in on the comings and goings of the fledging town. After a drink to wet my throat and it altogether being an otherwise resplendent late afternoon, we agree to take a walk to the two nearby Indian mounds, which we discover by way of a path between a bush, its two hills perfectly round and alabaster white of the smoothest shell although proving difficult to climb, but eventually climb them we do, where at the top, after several failed attempts, as the shell is loose we repeatedly slip, this lovely woman – Angelica she reminds me is her name – giddily opens up to express her great interest in helping me find "my lovely little fort" and how it would be her "greatest honor" to walk with so handsome a colonel, hand in hand, through its doors, on the inside of which, I gesticulate in euphoric anticipation, there still may be some confiscated rum. It is only later from her second story window that the sobering reality sets in. What had been a sweeping view of the water from the East Tower is now completely obscured, nor can I any longer see the tree line of cypress toward the inland frontier. The location of the fort and the view it afforded seems lost to time.

Oct 17, 9 am
Tate and I meet at the dock.
I mock in disbelief at the river captain's preposterous claim of just a three-hour trip to the Great Falls. Upon informing him that during my tenure as the commanding officer of Ft. Stafford during the Third Seminole War, the same trip took the better part of four days by *canoe* which, as a much smaller vessel, did not require "warp arounds" — i.e. a complex navigational procedure using ropes tied around trees to maneuver through the many hairpin turns, the most notably being Devils Mouth — as surely his vessel will: the river captain's interest is piqued. He wonders out loud if I might then not know the veteran from the Seminole campaign who is currently being held at the prison in Ft. Harvie for murder.

9:20 am

As there were many troops in near three dozen forts, I explain to the captain I may know the name – but probably not the soldier or the man.

Whatever the case, the captain proceeds with a summary of what he knows of the situation. The prisoner, it seems, held claim to the crucial headwaters – called "The Bend" – renowned for its location at the source waters of the falls and its bounty of migrating fish that were easily caught, but also coveted by land speculators who have long hyped it as the linchpin for creating a navigable channel to the Big Lake and unlocking the bounty of the Danforth Tract. When it became exposed that the riverfront rights in question were procured under false pretense, in the guise of royal land grant, but actually no better than a navigational lease, and on a Confederate loan from a bank that had since collapsed, the man had no other choice but to "lash out" at the legal and engineering forces bearing down on him, first in the form of spraying buckshot at "prying surveyors" and later cutting cables to the dredge as it approached Devils Mouth, after which the he was apprehended on the spot, although his half-breed coconspirator successfully averted capture and fled away into the woods. The prisoner is interned at Fort Harvie for the nonce.

9:30 am

Although French was a friend of the savages, I doubt it could be him.

Thursby was a man of diplomacy first who never lost control of his stateliness. But on the chance that the prisoner might have information about my friend's whereabouts, either by way of his connections from the Seminole War or knowledge of comings and goings in the inland frontier, I suggest we stop at Ft. Harvie to put the matter to rest. At this point, any information about Thursby's fate is worth pursuing, for peace of my own mind and that my poor sister may move on confidently with her new life.

10:10 am

Tate and the captain enjoy a smoke as I proceed to the garrison.

The sergeant, a man by the name of Blatt, greets me a bit suspiciously at first but, upon recognizing my name from the

Seminole Wars, quickly warms up. Maybe ten years younger than myself, I am struck by the sergeant's resemblance to how I myself may very well have looked back in my Seminole days, not only with regard to the cut of his frame but also his mutton-chop beard, now popular among the officers but in my day relatively unseen. Blatt doubts I will be able to make sense of the prisoner's mad ramblings, a sentiment that is also reiterated by the guard as he leads me down the hall. I arrive at the cell to the sound of clanking irons, a terrible stench and shadowy darkness only broken by a shaft of light from the meager window above. A figure takes shape in the gloom, followed by a startling salutation, "— *Captain Powell ... is that you?*"

11 am
My heart fills with hope!
Could it be — French? My thoughts race as to how I might leverage my influence — or exploit any possible means (and in that regard surely Tate would help) — to free the man and deliver him away from the horridness his life has become, only to dismiss such treasonous thoughts by what I hear next. *"Pirates!"* the prisoner exclaims in anguish. *"They've come back ashore, Cap'n Powell. No, but this time it ain't just a ship. No, it's even more than a whole fleet. The pirates they are everywhere. They've overtaken the land! Ye can't tell 'em from regular people. They look like anybody else, Captain Powell."* I am saddened to see Simon in such a pitiful state but there really isn't much else I can do. When even a sane man takes a stand against progress, it's as futile as waves crashing against solid granite.

2 pm
It doesn't take long upstream of Ft. Harvie to see the reason why the trip to The Falls will be so short.
What had once been a roundabout journey through the endless series of meandering oxbows has been replaced by a newly-dug canal that cuts "straight as an arrow" up the river valley. It is an engineering spectacle to behold. The riverboat captain explains that the new canal was touted as the solution for opening up the economic potential of the inland frontier, an effort that "may yet" bear fruit – but in the short run has caused more harm than good by way of significant flooding

downstream. There is talk of building a levee to correct the worst spots.

3:20 pm
Why the boat captain is pulling to shore I am not sure.

Upon my inquiry he looks at me with a humorous grin. "But of course we have arrived at The Falls," he chuckles, "—*even if just in name only.*" It takes a moment, but slowly the new reality sinks in. I can see the jagged cut in the limestone and spoil piles of earth along each bank. What was previously sublime scenery, a cascade of overlapping pools over a staircase of ancient limestone steps has been completely blown through. In place of the gushing freshet of water is an eerie absence of sound. The water languishes, only moving slightly. We float past a baying calf stranded on a shoal just as we dock. The work was completed earlier in the year in an effort to open the "water-locked lands." The one group, led by a conglomerate of cattlemen and farmers and backed by the Buckingham Bonds Company, want to use the river as a big drain for drying out the waterlogged land at the river's source and along its banks. The other group, a shipping interest known as Meridian & Jones, has filed papers in federal court to make it navigable from coast to coast. The way they are going the man suspects it may require calling in the militia to settle the dispute, "assuming they don't all kill each other first."

Oct 19
We stock up on supplies at the frontier trading post.

Purchases include a thirty-foot skiff, navigation equipment, hard tack for three weeks, a lantern and oil, and a three pound bag of dried rice.

Oct 20
Our journey into the interior commences.

We pole upstream and then south. For some distance from the river the thicket is pretty well gone. Most of the large timber is cut. Ran into a cattleman by the name of Summerlin who assures us we are on the right path. He produces a map that I immediately recognize as French's work, although most of what is shown on the paper as riverside forest has since been logged. There lurks a fear in me that the days of this natural bounty are numbered. I do not see agriculture viable in this land any time soon.

Oct 27
My bearings put us at the Bottomless Waters.

Tate isn't so sure judging from the fact the shoreline doesn't reveal the telltale spinning of water Sam Hunter so vividly described. Or are we mistaken? After looking at the water for a great while we determine it is spinning, albeit only very slowly.

Oct 29
Rained the forepart of the day.
The Course of this day nearly South, wind from N. E.

Nov 4
We enjoy a feast around the campfire.

As is often the case around the primitive aura of the burning wood, we find ourselves being drawn back in time and talking about lives past. Tate's description of his many adventures on the Sarsaparilla as a boy gave way to my recollections of French, probably talking to myself as much as I was Tate. My admiration for the man runs deep, how he lived life on his own terms, his chivalrous demeanor, his willingness to see the best in mankind, his propensity to fight for truth, a larger good, a man whom money came easy but who was never consumed by it, a man, as are all men, who was dragged back by his past, but how everything that was good about him was about the future, his plans to travel West, his dreams of not riches but new frontiers and unspoiled lands. His adventures on the Hobart Plain had infused in him a great sense of what it meant to be free. There rises within me an urge to live out French's life, as if he didn't die, as if he had embraced his future instead of slipping back and succumbing to what he should have let be.

Nov 11
We have made much progress over the past week.

The country is unlike anything I have ever seen. Imagine a vast meadow flooded with freshwater in every direction as far as the eye can see. The water imperceptibly moves, not in separate stream channels but as one mass. Tate attributes the source of the water as overflow from the Big Lake.

Nov 20
A fine Day

Nov 28
Unable to light a fire, we make use of the last of our oil to charge the lamp. I cut the sawgrass and pile it high for two beds, something I'd seen the cowmen do.

Dec 2
We have reentered the cypress.
Tate says we are getting close. He attaches an eagle feather to an end of the stick using a trick he learned from an Indian guide named Early Joe. The going is slow. We find a waterlogged rifle in the wet marsh not far from a long strand of cypress that Tate identifies as Brown's. When I comment that I remember Brown having a pistol, he reassures me that Brown had both.

Dec 6
Tate seems increasingly unsure.
He's added an owl feather to the end of the stick and admits we may be lost. As we are now down to our final supplies, I have resolved with no small incertitude that, no matter what, that I will be heading out West upon our departure from this dismal swamp. Tate is of a mind to fetch Evangeline and make a new start Up North. Out of the blue he mentions that Angelica was quite smitten to have made my acquaintance, especially in light of my high social rank and influence.

Dec 7
Tate points to a clump of vegetation across the prairie about a half mile ahead.
Due to the shallowness of the water we abandon our skiff and go by foot. The stench grows as we near the island. Tate swears that it is the same place despite the lack of water and the vegetation being mostly dead. Tate points out the charred remnant of the Gumbo Limbo where he awaited the arrival of the man who we both agree may or may not have been French. Our arrival at the island causes the vultures to disperse, thus revealing the source of the stench: a bleached pile of gator bones, no less than three dozen skulls. It is a sure sign of poachers and that we must be nearing the coast.

Dec 8

Tate insists we are on the right path for the springs, but I am not sure.

What I do know is that my strength has returned. Several times I retrace my steps to retrieve my much fatigued friend who assures me each time "we are indeed very close." He is increasingly limpid of breath and disheveled of mind. I insist that he rest in the shade while I retrieve water from a scratch well I dig in a small grove of rocky pines.

Dec 9

A bright spot through the dense canopy fills our hearts with hope. We break into the opening to discover we've arrived at a desolate stretch of coast that I believe to be Gallivans Bay.

Dec 13

Tate and I fetch a ride in a passing boat.

It took us some waving down to convince them to stop. Apparently there is still talk of Brown being on the loose, but upon seeing we had four arms among us they welcome us aboard. Our rescuers are two brothers, negroes, buttonwood rickers, who travel up and down the mangrove coast, mostly selling their charcoal to the coastal communities that have sprung up along the forts. They are used to seeing Indians, but not many "white folks" in these parts. It is not until land is out of sight completely that reality sinks in and Tate expresses his heartfelt regret, but I will not let him mention a word of it. The mission was successful "on all fronts," I decree, not the least being my health. I inhale deeply, filling my lungs with the clean air. "Your cough is gone," Tate marvels. "And to think we didn't even find the spring!" Such is the sanctity provided by the special aqueous land through which we passed and may its spenditude forever remain."

Chapter 18:
The Legend of Col. Stanley Powell

Rusty stretched and yawned. The light from the window was shining in his eyes. It was also what woke him up. His feet almost but not quite touched the end of the cot. He felt simultaneously groggy and refreshed at the same time, a sure sign that he'd overslept. Rusty stood up and looked out the window. The view was reminiscent of the aftermath of a traveling circus or carnival that just left town: the grass was matted down and crisscrossed with spaghetti pattern of tire tracks, with the caveat that it wasn't abandoned in a completely derelict state as a result of the "code of the campfire" having also left its mark — there was no sign of trash anywhere; the attendees had one by one and all together picked up and packed out any and all lingering debris. The Round Up was over — that is, assuming it had ever begun? Rusty tried to think back to the sequence of events: the trip up to The Lodge, his chore of mowing the airstrip, his many hours of reading, the campfire stories, the tractor ride to Tinkers Camp, the arrival of Burt's plane and the many characters and conversations he had overheard. He wondered which parts of his recollection were real and which were a dream and how the sum of it all was irretrievably jumbled together in an alphabet soup in his head. Rusty also thought about Lori and how he probably missed his chance. Most of all, Rusty couldn't shake the bad feeling about Dan Vukovich and Dan Kleal. Something about that conversation wasn't right.

Mr. Hodge was sitting at the table drinking coffee when Rusty entered the main room. He motioned for Rusty to sit down. "Well, I always said, if you're not gonna be the first, you might as well be the last." The old man went to the counter and returned with a bowl of steaming mush and a spoon. "— Hope you don't mind, I took the liberty of cutting up some apple in it too."

Rusty was glad he did. By itself the oats were rather tasteless. The spoonfuls with a chunk of apple had a sweet taste and a nice crunch to match. Maybe apples weren't so bad after all.

"Feels good to get this place back to normal. Crowds, they just ain't for me. The more people, the more problems," Albert Lee quietly confessed to his cup of coffee. He took a sip. He put his mug down. "Especially now that times have changed. More and more with these younger folk I feel hopelessly out of touch. But I don't think it's me," he emphasized. "Most definitely it's them. They don't see what they're doing. They don't know what this place was." The old man laughed like he was telling an inside joke that only he understood. "You know, I don't even feel that old, I really don't. But when I look in the mirror there ain't no denying my time has passed. Guess I don't like mirrors the same way I don't like crowds. Don't like what I see in either anymore." The aging man picked up his cup and took another sip. He put his cup back down. "That's the thing I like about this place. No mirrors. No crowds. Just owls. Gators. The trees. They don't change. They look the same as they ever did." He turned to Rusty. "I see them with the same eyes I did when I was your age."

"Mister Hodge ... last night ... did everything go ... *alright?*"

"Oh, you mean with Burt Silver?" the old man snickered. "Yeah, everyone had their hopes up but I didn't expect a whole lot." Albert Lee took a deep breath to think how to say it politely without sounding rude. "Burt Silver," he said, finally settling on a response. "— I guess the best way I can put it is that he isn't the man his father was. I'll just leave it at that."

After a brief moment of silence Albert Lee proved incapable of taking his own advice. "*His father* ... now there was a *truly great man*," he elaborated. The old man seemed poised to point out a long list of how Burt didn't measure up — "The two of them actually quit talking the final year of his life," he began to remark — when Mr. Hodge saw the plaintive expression on the boy's face and immediately understood it wasn't the counselor he was inquiring about.

"Oh, you mean *your father*," he corrected himself, "— About that business last night?"

Albert Lee raised his cup of coffee to his lips and took the last sip and in doing so pushed his chair away from the table and stood up. He took Rusty's empty bowl with him and washed it clean under the hand-pumped stream.

"There's probably a lot of things about fathers that sons never really know."

"So nothing's wrong."

"Oh, there's a lot wrong," Albert Lee frowned as he returned to the table with a tumbler half filled with a pulpy orange fluid. "But, um, nothing a shot of fresh-squeezed sour orange won't make any worse. I diluted it down with some well water. It's about the closest thing to a universal tonic for what sooths human soul." Albert paused to think over what he just said. "— Not sure if it's the magnesium or the Vitamin C."

Outside the window, the place looked as abandoned as when they'd arrived. As far as Rusty could tell it was just Albert Lee and him. There were no other voices inside or out. Rusty wondered if maybe everyone hadn't departed without him in their preoccupation with getting home or in disappointment with whatever the Round Up was or wasn't able to solve. Or perhaps they left him there on purpose to inherit the responsibilities of the The Lodge when Albert Lee Hodge passed and moved on. While there was a side of Rusty that liked that idea — he would no longer have to go to school or carry the weight of the many real-world responsibilities increasingly being doled out to him by his stepfather Dwight — there was an even bigger side of him that knew he couldn't forsake or forget the many people and things that were waiting for him in Missouri up north. Not that Rusty was worried, at least not yet. His father had a habit of leaving him alone in camps on previous trips for hours on end. That was nothing new. If Rusty had learned anything from his father it was how to enjoy his free time. Seizing the opportunity Rusty retrieved the book from the nightstand by his cot and opened it up to where he left off.

...

About twenty minutes later Albert Lee cut him off.

"So, watcha readin'?"

The question took Rusty by surprise. After all, there weren't many other books on the shelf, maybe just a few dozen at most; nor did he even know why he picked the exact book he did. His selection was as arbitrary as it was lucky: he was enjoying the book very much. When Rusty lifted the front cover up for Albert Lee to see, the man took the contrary action of putting on his bifocals but walking the opposite way. "That's too far away, just tell me the name."

Rusty read the title verbatim.

"Outnumbered, Outgunned, and Alone:
A Compendium of Colonel Stanley Powell's
Journals, from the Seminole War to the
Stand at Boulder Ridge."

Albert Lee nodded all too knowingly. "Prefer a book with a happy endin' myself," he morbidly laughed.

Having completed his journey across the room, one careful step after the next, he gave a quick study of the other books on the shelf. "Well if you're gonna read that one I recommend you take a look at this one, too," Albert Lee suggested as he slid the book out. "— Not that I condone the message."

Rusty leaned across the table and lifted the tome up. It was heavy and longer horizontally than it was tall. The front cover featured two large dinosaurs. One stood erect, on two legs, roaring with all its might and the other was knee deep, all four legs, in the shallows of an expansive lake. Along its bottom where two names: Claymont Heard in bold large print and Mary B. Wise printed smaller underneath. At the top center was the title of the book:

An Illustrated Guide to Prehistoric
Animals of the Ancient Past.

Rusty turned to Mr. Hodge to ask him more about what he meant — more specifically, what was so important about the new book and why did he have such a dim view of the book he'd been engrossed in all weekend long — but before he could ask, the elderly man moved towards a shadow and seemed to fade into the pine-planked wall, the same one that Burt Silver had nostalgically tapped the night before; or was Rusty imagining things and did Albert Lee just exit through the door. Rusty was about to stand up to look around and see, and in retrospect wished that he had; it was the last time he would ever see Albert Lee Hodge again.

Not that Rusty gave it all that much thought at the time. For all he knew Albert Lee was stepping out for a moment and would just as soon return. In the meanwhile, Rusty opened the new book to the first of its many illustrated scenes — a double-page spread entitled "The Origin of Life" — but which quixotically featured the exact opposite of what any reasonable kid would expect from such a momentous event: instead of a Garden of Eden or similar bountiful grove was a Mars-like expanse of barren rock reminiscent of the apocalyptic outcome of a prolonged war, if not a descent into the bowels of Hell. The only thing missing was the Devil and his dingy dungeons of damned souls and gutted out tanks and artillery shells smoldering with fumes. In their place were fiery meteors hurling down from an angry sky, splashing and sizzling into a tepid tropical sea. On the upper right, an incongruous image of a magnifying glass amplified a tiny droplet of water to reveal a vast trove of biological squiggles, amoebas and other microscopic shapes. Below it was the provocative question: *"The Beginning of Life on Earth?"*

Rusty interpreted that to mean it was a mystery: that is, that they still didn't know; or was it implying that life began somewhere else, on another planet or solar system or galaxy other than on Earth first? It seemed funny for life just to start "out of nowhere" from such a barren scene. It was not so much a chicken or egg quandary as it was why either existed at all, although judging from the pages that followed the hypothetical question seemed to be somewhat of a moot point: the book wasn't so much concerned about the question of where or how life started as it was devoted to illustrating the many sizes and shapes that life took on as time progressed. One page after the next, simple single cell creatures morphed into bigger and more complicated forms of life, culminating in the Age of the Trilobites but also not stopping there: each creature on each new page had a number immediately to its side which corresponded to a table on the lower right. Next to number three read Hexapods and next to number seven read Nautiloid. The many creatures appeared to be as much animal as they were plant and without a doubt didn't have much of a brain, maybe just enough to eat and reproduce; the entirety of which was submerged in the water with not an inkling of an understanding or need for dry land.

Outside a buggy revved to a start.

Rusty briefly glanced up. Not recognizing any of the men on board, he quickly returned his attention to the book, this time flipping back to the front cover to see which person – the illustrator or the author – was listed first only to confirm his suspicion, and disappointment, that the order seemed reversed: the illustrator was *second* and the author *first* even though it was the drawings, not the words, that were by far the most captivating element of the book and, judging from the meticulous nature they were drawn, also required a lot more work. It made Rusty wish that Powell's journals had pictures, too; or would those images corrupt the vivid landscape the book had painted in his head?

Rusty thumbed forward to the epoch where he'd left off.

Early Sea Creatures was interesting for its lack of anything remotely resembling a modern-day fish with the exception of the jellyfish which, to Rusty's surprise was identified as a 'sea nettle' (a term he'd never heard) on the index on the lower right side next to the number six, the full list of which included a sea scorpion at number two, a crinoid at number eight, a school of ammonites at number five, a brachiopod and several more that Rusty could not pronounce and the rest of the numbers one through fifteen. Rusty was baffled on two fronts: how was Ms. Wise able to make such precise drawings using only their fossilized skeletons as a guide and how could such robust-looking animals have had such a head start on the rest of creation only to now, in modern times, become extinct. Common sense said that being first should have been an advantage for thriving, surviving and being the most abundant life form on Earth. Maybe being last was best. The first was a curse for being constantly replaced.

As he turned from one panel to the next the scenes became wilder and more full of life, and the life on them increasingly strange, wild ... and down-right dangerous.

Prehistoric Sea Monsters showed a montage of bizarrely shaped beasts, some with long necks and sharp teeth, and most with their mouths open like they were ready and ravenous to eat anything in sight – and presumably each other – all of them in a swirling standoff that was surely going to erupt into a bloody battle royal that massacred them all. Despite many of the creature's menacing glares, Rusty held out hope that bloodshed could be averted. Then again they had to eat something and it probably wasn't going to be plants. Rusty thought about what his father said the other night — or was it Lori's father, or possibly Burt? — about how "keeping the peace" takes more strength and work than going to war; perhaps they could all co-exist, although judging from their looks peace and happiness were two different things. A giant squid lurked behind a boulder at the entrance to its cave. That was fun to find. And behind that a large tortoise swam upwards toward the light. Was it fleeing? No, not at all. The animal was not in retreat but moving forward out of the depths and following a speck, which upon closer inspection was actually another tortoise in the distance leading the way – *out of the water* – to the surface of the Earth where he or she would be riding a wave through the surf and up on the sandy beach — and more specifically, the land where the dinosaurs roamed.

Unlike most of the previous panels that devoted just *one page* to an entire geologic epoch, the Age of Dinosaurs had a much more generous spread: one panel after the next was an assortment of star-studded and action-packed dinosaur scenes.

The first featured a family, or was it a herd, of long necked and lumbering brontosauruses at the wooded fringe that, around the corner, opened up to a large lake by way of a rocky stream which, on second thought, Rusty concluded might be a river given the gargantuan size of the animals at its banks. The background was consumed with a range of purple and parabolic-shaped mountains that gave way to a bevy of tropical trees that meandered from the foothills onto the open plain.

The notorious Tyranosaurus Rex was running in full gallop across the next page on what looked like a swamp buggy trail. Rusty was struck by how closely the painted scene resembled the Floridian swamp: a wet prairie covering the ground and egret-like pterodactyls gliding in the clouds above, but it was the ravishingly hungry T-Rex that took center stage. It had its head down and tail up as it chased after its soon-to-be vanquished prey that were stupidly fleeing as a group in a manner reminiscent of trying to outrun a speeding locomotive by running down the tracks instead of simply skirting off to the side. Despite the funny-looking horns on their heads and being painted a dull olive green, they had an altogether human and quite fatalistic expression in their eyes about what lay *ahead;* or more specifically in this case, what was rapidly approaching from *behind.* Instead of continuing to flee, one of the creatures decided to succumb to its fate and surrender to its pursuer face-on. On a good note, that gave the others a chance to safely get away, or at least see one more day — if not a full life — thus leaving him to wonder if there was such a thing as a Dinosaur Heaven in the sky. Rusty scanned to the page's lower right corner to identify the hapless creatures name: a Parasaurolophus next to a number three. He pressed the book down in the center crease to better see the T-Rex roaring in anticipation of ripping its undersized prey apart with its mammoth mouth and razor sharp teeth causing Rusty to conclude if there was a Dinosaur Hell the T-Rex would definitely take center seat.

The few panels that followed showed similarly gory scenes: a triceratops goring a stegosaurus, a spinosaurus and an ankelosaurus going head to head, and a school of velociraptors attacking a brachiosaurus's neck.

It was thus somewhat to Rusty's surprise that the last panel showed the Dinosaur Kingdom all at peace, or a détente at least, if not a final truce. Whatever the cause, there they all were — living in harmony on *one single* summary page around a common lake in the middle of what looked like a vast and soggy Serengeti Plain. In the background, several smoldering volcanos were spewing noxious fumes into a putrid purple-colored sky, the closest of which was spouting up fiery balls of viscous rock. Not that the dinosaurs noticed. They each looked as busy as they were bored, and completely unaware of the cataclysm that would soon make them extinct. A short paragraph at the bottom of the page explained.

> *Dinosaurs thrived for a much longer time than man has lived on earth. About 65 million years ago dinosaurs as shown on this page were plentiful. They perished suddenly and the reason is a mystery. The Tyrannosaurus Rex, once king of the earth, is now relegated as bones extracted from the dirt and reassembled by man.*

Rusty flipped ahead to a smallish family of bunny-eared mice scurrying down a wooded path. Two of them paused for a moment to eat a nut on a giant rock. The message was clear. With the dinosaurs dead, it was the *lowly mammals* that had inherited the earth. The human race was not made in the image of an Almighty God but the evolutionary progeny of a common pest, the lowly rat, and the accidental beneficiary of the dinosaur kingdom's freak demise, not the triumph of some celestial grand plan. Perhaps that explained the ambivalence Mr. Lodge's expressed about the book.

More and bigger mammals adorned the next page and still more after that, including giant sloth number ten and a saber toothed cat, seventeen, and another creature that looked bearlike with the exception it had the head of a horse and which Rusty didn't even bother to look at the name that connected with its number due to his eagerness to find out what was going to happen next and finally there it was on the next page: three prehistoric humans making camp around a small fire on an elevated rock ledge – a little boy and his mother tending the flame, and a man standing erect and looking down on a cornucopia of animals and plants that ran off from horizon to horizon in an unending expanse, as if ruling "above" (and not a part of) what he saw below; if also not in full control.

What caught Rusty's eyes most of all, however, wasn't any of the illustrations Ms. Wise had meticulously drawn or the simplistic text that Mr. Heard had effortlessly penned, but rather the juvenile scrawl of pencil lead handwritten at an angle on the top right corner of the page: just a simple drawing and two words.

How many times had Rusty picked up a children's books at the local library in Missouri to find it defiled by the "back and forth" spasm of random crayon scribblings, sometimes even foul words, thus ruining the reading experience for him and everyone else to come? It was something he hated every time he saw it. This rather minor handwritten addition, however, had the opposite effect. Instead of spoiling the literary integrity of the book, it provided a thought provoking and quite transcendent touch:

> *"Campfire"* and *"Charlie"* were the two handwritten words; the drawing – a diminutive *Stetson hat* drawn at an angle on the father caveman's head.

Rusty's jaw dropped. How many times had he closed the book on the Campfire Charlie case only to have another piece of evidence or information unexpectedly emerged from thin air to make him rethink it all? With Campfire Charlie that seemed to be the trend. No other page had graffiti of any sort. The book was practically in pristine condition except for that one page, those two words and that tiny hat. Rusty wondered when and who scrawled it, and why. Was it a joke, a clue, or did it have no meaning at all? The one thing that was *very clear* to Rusty was that he wasn't the only person with Campfire Charlie on his mind. While there was no way of telling when it happened — was it a week or decades old? — it *had to* have come after the publication date as shown on the title page a few pages in, September 2nd, 1945. Of Charlie's many mythical feats, his ability to be omnipresent but equally and always missing seemed to be his signature parlor trick; with one more magical act up his sleeve as Rusty was about to find out on the very next page.

At first glance it seemed nondescript enough, even quite bland. In the place of Ms. Wise's elaborate panoramas of the prehistoric past were just a few black and white photographs and the title — *"The Men Who Discovered the Bones"* — written across the top. On the left was a rather corpulent and long-whiskered archeologist named Charles Marsh posing with his ragtag field crew of men. On the right was a stand-alone portrait of dashing-looking fellow named Edward Dinker Cope. Mr. Heard described how the men were as famous for their pioneering work in the field of paleontology in the American West as they were for their gritty passion of trying to beat each other to the punch and trip each other up, often at the expense of not properly documenting their work. The morale of the story seemed to be that cooperation, not competition, was the golden rule of maximizing humankind's collective success; not that Rusty was all that interested in either rival. Instead, his attention was focused on what was spelled out on the caption below the photo on the left: three people to the right of the vainglorious Marsh stood none other than a humble, rather rumpled if also sturdily-built Colonel Stanley Powell.

Rusty quickly switched books to double check his improbable discovery, going to the Table of Contents first. Sure enough, there it was: Powell's journal entries on the "Dinosaur Bone Wars" was the very next chapter he was about to read.

I.   *Third Seminole War, 1857-58*
II.   *War Between the States, 1860-64*
III.   *Reconstruction, 1865*
IV.   *Return to Florida Frontier, 1866-1868*

V.   *Dinosaur Bone Expeditions, 1870-72*
VI.   *Standoff at Boulder Ridge, 1874-1875*

The odds seemed incredibly slim, or perhaps that was the reason Albert Lee Hodge had given him the book, so maybe not; but even so, what the childless patriarch couldn't have possible known (and whom Rusty would never see again) was the uncanny coincidence of Colonel Stanley Powell and Campfire Charlie sharing the *same sheet of paper*: one the back and the other the front, on opposing sides of the same exact spot. Rusty held the book open up in the light flipping that singular and special page back and forth to marvel at the perfect placement of the unsuspecting Siamese twins, Campfire Charlie on the odd side and Colonel Stanley Powell on the even. Eventually Rusty settled on placing the book on the table to study the fuzzy picture of Powell as much as he could. He studied it with the same intensity that he had previously done so many times before with the Campfire Charlie photos over the years. After a few good minutes of soaking in every detail, Rusty decided there was something about Powell's photograph that wasn't right — although it wasn't Powell's fault. The issue lay not in the man but the incongruity of the image — both his visage and his stance — with the one Rusty had already formed in his head from so many hours of binge reading the colonel's journal accounts during his downtime in The Lodge the past few days. The sensation was not unlike looking into a carnival mirror to find a reflection he didn't expect. The person he'd imagined Stanley Powell to be the whole time he was reading his journal was, if not himself, then definitely someone seeing the world through his eyes. Reading the journal had the magical effect of transporting Rusty back in time and resurrecting the long-deceased author back to life. He and Powell were somehow two and the same, an improbable bond across time and space, if not even a hint that time travel might actually exist. It was in that moment that Rusty also understood what was so desperately lacking from the Campfire Charlie accounts. Charlie and his stories were all passed down by mouth. Unlike Stanley Powell, Charlie hadn't written anything down. Sure, stories of his exploits sounded good around the campfire, but were any of them true? Where was the hard proof? The handwriting in the book was obviously that of a child's who, when he or she wrote it, probably also still believed in Santa Claus, too.

Rusty remembered the day just a few years back when he first figured out that Santa didn't exist. It was the year that he traveled to Florida to visit his father for the first time, and the very same winter in fact that the Legend of Campfire Charlie was born.

Not that Rusty was a man, no he was far from that, but figuring out Santa wasn't real was somehow empowering, a major step toward growing up — if also a little baffling: why did the premise even exist and what compelled parents to go to such great lengths to simultaneously nurture it and cover it up knowing it wasn't a matter of if but when one day the truth would be come out, and in doing so would lay bare the whole spectacle as a lie, them as liars, and even worse — saddling the children with a guilty feeling about growing up. Still, there was a side of Rusty that couldn't shake the idea that if you went back far enough in time you would find a real man inside a snowbound house on the eve of winter's darkest day, bearing gifts for children around a rosy glow of a flickering fireplace, that the man was most definitely not an invention of modern times but rather an expropriated and updated vestige of the ancient past. Yes, today he was everywhere and nowhere all at once but that should not be confused with meaning that he does not or never did exist.

Maybe Campfire Charlie was the same.

It wasn't a black and white question of whether to believe in Campfire Charlie or not, but the quandary of why his memory was so firmly entrenched and how far you had to trace back to find the singular person, the Original Adam, from whom the legend was born. The answer was as close as it was far away, if not impossibly out of reach, and that could only be found by recrossing the Rubicon if it was still there at all.

In the meanwhile, Rusty picked up his book and commenced reading at the chapter he last left off: Colonel Powell's Adventures in the Dinosaur Bone Wars.

Chapter 19:
Dinosaur Bone Wars

Jan 16, 1871
Chloride's meager accommodations make sleep difficult.
The folks here are hospitable enough, but still hard put by the bitter winter in which many perished. I can see the new row of crosses in the cemetery from my window as I write.

Jan 17
The Jack Morman innkeeper proves informative.
A frenzy of mineral speculation in the area has mostly tapered off. There have been a few claims, mainly of the "lesser metals," although there is still hope for finding gold. A trove of large bones "several times as long as a man is tall" has been unearthed by a cut in the river, "a curiosity more than anything else" if also stoking fears that the giant lizard of Hopolo legend is roaming about. Others seem to see it as proof of the valley being a burial ground or gateway into the bowels of Hell. As for the innkeeper, he is firmly of a mind that the bones are simply the remains of the drowned creatures that didn't make it on Noah's ark before the Great Flood. When he asks if I'm a God-fearing man I say that I am. The conversation ends on a bit of an ominous note about a sheriff named Dixon he describes as "the only law" in these parts. "You play by his rules, or you ...." He stops abruptly and makes a show of polishing the silver as a smallish chap approaches the bar to finish the thought. "Dixon's only rule is he ain't got none," he leers as he tosses a silver coin on the bar. The innkeeper pours him a drink. I'm left to wonder if the man wasn't spying on me the entire time.

Jan 18
Rawlings instructions were brief but direct.

I am to oversee the details of excavation and the "all important security." Due to the secretive nature of our work, the full plan will not become apparent until all the men arrive.

Jan 19
I leave under the cloak of darkness.

I loop around and other times ride ahead to cover my tracks and set false trails. This is lonely country indeed. I am looking forward to the company of fellow human beings.

Jan 22
I set up camp at the confluence of the Joola and the Santa Marie.

The sunken river bed provides both cover and a clear view from the lookout on the nearby butte. Ready access to water is also an advantage. Cold at night. I am chilled to the bone beneath my blanket. Fire gives little comfort in this inhospitable country.

Jan 23
Our success depends as much on not being detected as it does the technical feat at hand.

Rawlings was advised to pay off the authorities in advance, but refused as the university's budget is limited. Accordingly, Rawlings arranged for the other men to arrive in three groups from three different directions to throw off spies. Still spooked by the strange encounter at the inn, I find myself looking over my shoulder at every turn. I am alert to Dixon's spies, but another menace lurks. I now suspect the patron may have been one of the so called half-breeds: the descendants of a sect of breakaway Mormans that splintered off from Brigham Young before he found his Zion at the Great Salt Lake. Long assumed to have succumbed in a labyrinth of rock called "The Turnstiles," rumors persist that they "went native" with a reclusive local tribe that took them in. The Lopjckaae, as they are locally known, combine a strange blend of Christian rituals and pagan ways, including swirling impregnations of indigo ink under their skin, arrangements of cubical rocks visible for miles, ceremonial sacrifices of an antlered rodent, and their self-identification as a lost tribe of Israel, as prophesized by Manasseh (1 Kings 11:35).

Jan 29
Knoop and Horger arrive first across the Hobart Plain.

Mike Knoop knows the exact location of the site from his previous job as a scout for a gold mining outfit that went belly up. Even without being queried he mentions Red Dixon as a man we will want to avoid "at all costs." Knoop hasn't seen him shoot a man personally but he's heard many stories from other miners who have. While it's unclear whether his nickname is a reference to the unnerving crimson tint in the whites of his eyes or from his pleasure in seeing others bleed, his sadistic behavior is without dispute, including a fondness for ending his victim's misery with an odd sweep of his stovepipe hat before sending a bullet into their heads with the following words, "— Tell the Devil ol' Dixon sent ye."

Jan 30
Horger is a beer barrel of a man with huge hands and a great drooping mustache that covers his mouth.

I can follow the generalities of Knoop's dialog with Horger, as I am part Bavarian on my mother's side, but just barely — it is a crude medieval dialect that I have never before heard. He mentioned the word "Pavel" several times before I realize he is saying my name.

Feb 4
The canyon shakes violently from a mysterious source.

Knoop believes it to be thunder but I am not sure as there is no rain, nor has the sky darkened in any discernable way. The rumbling may be the result of blasting from behind a distant butte, possibly a crew of Marsh or Cope. The secret of our find may already be out.

Feb 5
"G'noof," as Horger calls him, leads us between two narrow cliffs.

The lantern slowly illuminates and reflects an almost frightening sight: a preposterously large jawbone protruding out of the sandstone wall, many — if not a hundred — times the size of the largest alligator skull I can recall ever seeing in the Florida Swamps; and from which I reflexively stumble back. The

340

minacious continence of the beast permeates through the rock as if at any moment it could break free from its tomb and quickly devour us all on the spot.

Feb 6
The necessary equipment is brought to the fore.
Shovels, picks and dynamite we already have in hand. The mules will be arriving with Benbow along the river trail and the wagons with Bowdrie across the Northern Slope. Getting the larger specimens out intact will be a challenge but Horger, as translated by "G'noof," says that he's "done similar work for Cope and has seen worse."

Feb 10
Minnows, Benbow and Dillon arrive in a frazzled state.
They claim to have been trailed by an unknown assailant for several days before they dropped into a fissure near Sagebrush, out of sight, and picked up the river trail by way of an ephemeral wash through Lopjckaae land. When I mention the strange rumbling Minnows nods in confirmation that he's heard similar sounds as well.

Feb 11
We gather at the campfire as darkness closes in.
The crackling sound and flickering heat conjures an easy comradery among the crew. Dillon is a shortish, muscular stump of a man, and quite brash, but I have gauged a keen intelligence in him. He learns quickly and has the makings of a leader. He hails from California near San Francisco from a family of whalemen. Charlie Minnows comes across as a kindly but feeble-minded braggart with no lack of things to say. Dillon immediately dissects his wild account of heroics concerning "saving General Sherman" during the Battle of Bentonville — including penetrating enemy lines in an air balloon and swinging from a chandelier to thwart an assassin's attack on Sherman — as nothing more than another of his fabricated tall tales. Minnows defers. Despite his propensity for grand lies and cold stupidity, Dillon vouches for Minnows as a solid worker. Matt Benbow is an Alabaman, quick-witted and gentle of speech, but hard to read. I regale a few stories from my years on the Florida frontier before I withdraw to my tent to plot tomorrow's pre-dawn security sweep.

Feb 14

I awake this morning to an unusual sight.

The river's edge has crept closer to our camp overnight. I am a bit perplexed by the situation given the uninterrupted run of hot days, with nary a cloud in the sky let alone a hint of rain. Upon further consideration of the facts, I have concluded it to be a geomorphological, not a meteorologic, event. The geology to the north where it abuts the pitted plateau of the Hobart is renowned for episodic disequilibrium events including boiling springs and venting steam from deeply fractured rocks. As for the encroachment of the water at the river's edge, I rest at ease: our camp is located on a slight bluff. We risk no chance of getting wet, nor does the dig site which is perched even higher up.

Feb 17

More stories spew from Minnows around the campfire tonight. As sometimes I do, I scribe the men's words directly as they speak.

Minnows: "Stuck it rich with silver in the Sierras, I did. Dun got me enough to be on easy street the rest o' my life, ten thousand worth."

Dillon: "Did ya then? 'Spose that's why you're stuck out here digging up bones from the dirt? Partner must've robbed ya blind."

Minnows: "No he didn't nuther. Now that's a lie! I'm the one that got the better half. All I had to do was give up my horse."

Dillon: "Not your Kentucky Stallion?"

Minnows: "That's right! And it was worth it, 'til I got to Crooked Cliff and my mule died drinking from a sulfur spring. I put as much as I could in my coat pockets but most I had to leave behind. Buried it at the base of a saguaro under a square-shaped rock. Didn't realize how many of them cactus there were until I returned. Must'a checked a good couple ten thousand before I finally gave up."

Dillon: "About sums up a prospector's life. Hard to gain, easy to lose."

Minnows: "Even if I found the stash, the silver market already collapsed. Fortunately I had enough in my pocket to get me a good barber to pull out my achin' tooth. So I made out alright."

Dillon: "I s'pose you used that money to buy that ranch you always talk about."

Minnows: "Ranch? I don't remember. — Oh yes! The ranch. Lemme tell you ..."

Dillon: "Here we go ..."

Feb 18

It doesn't take long to see Dillon has a nose for this work.

His discovery of an outline of a colossal arching spine and ribs embedded in the sandstone further up the rock face has altered our plans. It will take twenty wagons easy, maybe more, and twice the mules to clear out the debris. Minnows babbles on endlessly about a man named Cactus Jack he helped blow up beaver dams on the Magnesium Flats to win claim to prime riparian tracts through the Swampland Reclamation Act as Horger and "G'noof" — speaking in their medieval brogue — devise a plan for extracting the expanding trove of bones. Dillon advises that additional blasting will be required but considers full excavation not only possible, but a "necessary situation" given the rarity of the specimen and its pristine state. My view is on the contrary: the change stretches our resources too thin and exposes us to unnecessary security risk. What we were originally planning to do in one run will now take several return trips through treacherous land.

Feb 19

Despite Minnows reputation as a liar, I am repeatedly struck by the enticing threads of insight that unpredictably pepper his constant drivel of words, even if the chance of him ever repeating any of his stories the same way is about as likely as lightning striking in the same spot twice.

Minnows: "Indians ain't normal in these parts. Ya notice?"

Dillon: "Normal how?"

Minnows: "Ain't all Indian for one, half something else. They worship a creature that looks like the Devil. Antlers on its head and big ears and sech."

Dillon: "How come I ain't seen any?"

Minnows: "It's just a small thing is why. Only yea big. Still, by my calculations, we're on the exact opposite side of the earth that Baby Jesus was born."

Dillon: "Calculation? You can't even add nine plus ten."

Minnows: "That's a lie! It's twenty one. Truth is, it don't take a lick of math. Ya don't need any more than good Sunday schoolin' to know where the Devil lives."

Powell: "You mean Dixon?"

Minnows: "Devil ain't that bad!"

Feb 26

By the time we see the plume of dust it's too late.

I direct the men to hold down their weapons as the outline of two riders with wagons in tow approach. Dillon and Benbow provide cover as I greet the men at what Knoop calls "the gauntlet." They are two Texas bohunks, one Johann and Moses Kranarvik, who present me with a letter "signed by Rawlings" explaining the situation at hand: the brothers are to serve as our wagoneers in Bowdrie's place. They don't know for sure but word through the grapevine — according to the younger Kranarvik, Moses — is Bowdrie jumped ship to work for another dinosaur hunter, "a man named Marsh," for twice the pay.

Feb 27

My mood sours.

The Kranarvik brother's arrival in broad daylight across the open plain was a major security breach that Bowdrie would have known to avoid at all costs. Benbow's wavering reassurances that he saw "nothing unusual" from the lookout means little. I am now of a mind it is only a matter of time.

Feb 28

My mood lightens around the campfire.

Horger, as translated by "G'noof," is clearly impressed with the quality of the Kranarvik brother's wagon. The construction and all the connections are first rate, a "perfect blend of old country craftsmanship and new world ingenuity of design." Judging from the Kranarvik's stories about Big Buffalo Trail and Julip Trace, by every indication they are long-hauling experts beyond their years in knowledge of the trade. Minnows makes a futile attempt of measuring up to their exploits with a new series of outlandish stories about his "Yukon Territory Days," each of his antidotes proving more fanciful than the last. One of his more ridiculous stories culminates with a herd of hairy elephants using their whale-rib sized tusks to joust back a ferocious onslaught of triple headed hydras that could both fly and spit fire from a hundred feet, from which he took refuge in a cave and where he discovered an injured wolf that he named Mingan and slowly managed to nurture back to health after which, full strength, they joined up with a traveling circus where they entertained the adoring crowds with an assortment of carefully choreographed tricks, included jumping through flaming hoops and balancing "dishes and sech" on his nose, before the call of the wild proved too strong and he ran off with a she-wolf into the Boreal Woods. As we have grown accustomed, Dillon eventually cuts him off, calling him out on his bluff and to which Minnows makes no effort to contest. Despite Dillon's biting remarks, the two are on good terms, the best of friends. At a minimum, the banter serves as a much needed source of levity, especially in light of the drudgery of our work and the many dangers that lie ahead.

Mar 1

Horger is indeed an adept sculptor in performing the tedious work.

The great and terrible head of the ancient beast steadily emerges from its rocky lair, sockets that held monstrous eyes take shape as bone is separated from stone. Knoop operates as an in between to Dillon and Minnows on clearing as Benbow hauls away the debris with the mules. A large boulder at the end still needs to be removed, "probably with a series of small blasts," but Dillon assures me it's a minor detail given Johann and Moses's success at getting the wagons so close.

Mar 2

Minnows is at it again around the campfire.

Charlie Minnows: "Wuz a champe'en prizefighter back in ol' Kentucky. I whooped Blackhawk Davey and forced him into retirement!"

Dillon: "Blackhawk Davey? Ha! You couldn't whip your own grandmudder, Charlie, and that's a fact. You skedaddled from that skinny fella in Denver who called you out for spitting tobacca on his shoes."

Minnows: "That fella was a cold eyed killer. If'n I was armed I would have had to plug him. Self defense of course."

Dillon: "He's a school teacher, Charlie. He was already so full of whiskey that you coulda whooped him with a feather. But

345

as I remember you had to take leave and hurry out the back door."

Minnows: "Well, a fighter doesn't go looking fer trouble and I avoid violence, that is, when I can. Call it a code, if you will."

Dillon: "I know what I call it."

Mar 12

Just when we appear to be on the path of success, tempers flare.

The complexity of the dig requires the men to work multiple roles from which the the Kranarvik brothers bristle, preferring instead to bide their "spare time" panning for gold in a riffle just upstream of camp.   They are devoid of any sense of responsibility for helping with the larger cause.

Mar 14

Johann returns from the river with several small nuggets.

The biggest is the size of a pea. Knoop says it's pyrite "without a doubt," but no one else seems to know one way or the other for sure.

Mar 20

These men are hard workers each with their own style. For Horger it is his sonorous humming, Knoop the easy skip in his step, and of course there is nothing quite like Minnows' constant onslaught of stories to break the tedium of the excavation effort at hand.

Minnows: "These big ol' leviathans are still around. I seen one in New Mexico Territory. Ye can't let em see ye, no sir! Once one of them sniffs th' air and looks around like a big ol' heron, ye better get under a rock or in a crevice."

Dillon: "Aw Charlie, your usual nonsense is tall enough, but even you wouldn't have us believe that there's any of these things walking the earth! Charlie, I say, it's a shame you can't even write your own name, much less a book! You'd make half a fortune penning dime novels for rich and idle ladies in New York. Buddy, you'd be a celebrity in no time flat!"

Minnows: "Now lookee here, Dillon, I have been known to fib a bit, but as I sit in front of you — in front o' God'n the whole Holy Family — I seen one of them giants! I don't know if the desert sun was bakin' my brain or of if it was the roots I was chewin' for my toothache, but I seen it!"

Dillon: "Explain me this, you liar: why ain't you ever seen any of the like when I'm around? The only common thread in all your stories is there's never a witness to back up your dubious claims."

Minnows: Sure there were witnesses. Two Mexicans was with me. You met one of 'em couple years ago in Denver. Edgardo Sanchez."

Dillon: "So why didn't Edgardo pipe up about it?"

Minnows: "Cause you met him before he got eaten by the giant lizard. Wasn't much for speaking in English either. Not his strength."

Dillon: "Dammit Charlie! Now I know your full of shit!!!"

Mar 25

A strange melancholia has set in.

My attempts to ride it off during my security sweep prove unsuccessful. The bleakness of the landscape envelops my mind. I ride into multiple canyons toward the sound of a woman cackling, possibly a member of the Lopjckaae half-breeds, which ends in me being rewarded with what at first appears to be a rare sighting of the fabled antlered rodent. Closer inspection reveals it to be nothing more than the shadow cast from a craggily cottonwood stump, not the creature at all. Later, back at the crevasse watching the men work, I am bedeviled by a bandana flapping in the breeze tied to the handle-end of shovel standing upright in a pile of rock debris. The men amiably laugh as they go about their business but I detect something sinister in the rustling piece of cloth. As the other men are distracted helping Horger dislodge the jaw, I remove the bandana with a mind for burning it in the campfire later tonight only to have it fly away across the dusted plain. Each time I approach the demonic rag, it eludes my grasp until finally I succeed in catching up to it when it snags on a tumbleweed. Wishing no more of its torment I use a flat rock to dig a shallow hole and bury it on the spot.

Mar 28, 4 pm

A drifter unexpectedly shows up to camp at dusk.

What at first seems like the makings of a tense situation is quickly defused. For certain it has snapped us out of our funk, which I know suspect was a result of eating the strange toad-headed fish that Dillon found flopping about in the shallows and Benbow killed with a rock. The feeble old gent, a man by the name of Winston Hoots, is simply lost and quite incapable of doing any harm. His dusty vestments and voracious appetite speak to the failures of his mineral pursuits.

6 pm
As the man is half deaf, we speak freely in front of his face.

Dillon believes Hoots to be the fabled "lost miner" we've all heard stories about from the major gazettes back East, as judged by his skeletal looks. Benbow rightly points out that miners are not known for their plumpness "except the ones who strike it rich." Minnows, meanwhile, is happy as a jay to have a fresh face in the crowd to hone his vast repertoire of outlandish tales. Tonight he regales us with his many exploits in "Mountain Country" on the lee side of the Northern Slope where he assisted in a rescue up on Donner Pass and tracked the Sassafras River to its source at which point he met an Indian maiden that nursed him back to health with a clear broth of willow bark and chanterelle.

8 pm
Just when it appears the miner is on the verge of drifting off into a catatonic sleep, the feckless Minnows lets spill Kranarvik brother's recent discovery of gold.

The news jars Hoots awake with a feverish look, leading me to believe his hearing isn't so bad after all. Dillon quickly interrupts to clarify the meager find as nothing more than "fool's gold, pyrite," not the real thing, but the damage is done — the old miner is eager to see said specimens himself.

Mar 29, 10 am
Hoots identifies the nuggets to be gold "without a doubt."

Our efforts to dissuade him otherwise by leading him to the crevasse and showing him the true nature of our work proves more ruinous still. Horger's immense pride in showcasing his progress to date — *"Das Monster wird gerne Minenarbeiter essen,"* he beams — is met by a ghastly look by Hoots. We'd be better advised letting loose a hungry mountain lion from its cage, he says, than freeing the "Thunder Beast" of Hopolo legend from its grave. He highly encourages us to cover up the loose bones immediately and flee the area "before it's too late."

5 pm

Despite his dire warning, Hoots shows no urgency to leave camp.

At first I speculate it is because of our ready supply of food. He vulgarly devours every morsel with a crude smacking of his lips. But it doesn't take long to see his true intent is to pass on whatever knowledge he knows about the fabled beast before he moves on. Hoots proves himself to be a master story teller much to the men's delight, pulling us all in with his meandering account of the many unfathomable mysteries and remarkable twists in the storied history of the "Thunder Beast" and the destruction it has wrought. Despite our unblinking attentiveness, we understand all too well his fantastical account to be nothing more than a tall tale passed down from miner to miner each one claiming it as his own before telling the next. All the men seem to be in on the joke except for Minnows whose teeth chatter as loud as a rattlesnake ready to strike, a situation that only worsens after Benbow concocts a preposterous story of having spied the ancient dragon's giant tail sticking out from behind a butte from the vantage of the lookout some ten miles off while Knoop spins a yarn of Horger and him having to traverse across several of the monster's gargantuan paw prints and claw scrapes on the way in. So good is the storytelling that, by the end of the night, it seems we have created a monster out of nothingness that not a soul in the circle doesn't doubt lurks in our midst; and most of all the gullible Minnows who is scared half to death. Hoots ends with a stern warning should we encounter the beast, "— Stand as still as a rock. Not even a blink of yer eyes."

Mar 30

The Kranarviks are convinced Hoots is after their claim.

The brothers firmly believe that they possess a small fortune rather than a worthless bag of metallic rocks. One sleeps while the other keeps watch with a twitchy finger on the trigger of his shotgun — a recipe for any number of things to go wrong. Meanwhile, Minnows has taken to collecting logs for building a raft that he thinks he can float down the Joola should the "Thunder Beast" attack. When I inform him of the presence of treacherous rapids downstream from our camp, Minnows vividly recounts his experience of thrice floating over Niagara Falls in a barrel and doubts anything on the Joola is near as bad.

Apr 1, 7 am

Just when we thought he would never leave, Hoots is nowhere to be found.

For Benbow this reaffirms his suspicion of the miner being the fabled ghost, but for the Kranarvik brothers the explanation is much simpler: the man is a thief. Half their gold is missing as is one of their better saddle bags. When Knoop corrects them that it's "fool's gold," a scuffle breaks out. I have Dillon and Benbow separate the belligerents. I will withhold wages if any other incidents of this kind occur. I inform the men that it will be reported to Rawlings as a violation of the contract. I am dismayed by the lack of order of the civilian mindset. We would be much further along under the discipline of a military command.

9 am

Hoots trail goes dead on the other side of the butte.

Johann and I scan across the vast wasteland of geodic mounds and tufts of tree-high grass in hopes of a sign but eventually give up. On our return trip we discover a fresh line of tracks headed toward "the gauntlet." Convinced it to be Hoots and despite my strict orders to hold down, Johann races ahead in a rage.

10 am

Around the bend at the boulder my suspicions are met.

Johann has been ambushed by two sentries keeping guard. Below, in the distance, is still grimmer news. Our entire camp has been overtaken by a gang of outlaws. Scurrying up the face of the butte it doesn't take long to spot the ringleader: a well-dressed and rather striking man who wears a stovepipe hat — obviously Dixon without a doubt. I can't be sure but I also spot what appears to be Hoots by the riffle behind a clump of tamarind panning for gold, although it may be someone else.

11 am

I circle around to the other side but again have no luck.

A third sentry blocks the way, effectively boxing me out. Dixon's voice reverberates off the canyon walls as he drags the elder Kranarvik through the shallows of the river by a rope tied around his bootless foot. A few of his henchmen watch from the bank, including a man in a derby hat and another man about half his height. After he is done with Johann he rides up to the river bank to see who's next.

Knoop: "It's pyrite I tell ya. Fool's gold."

Dixon strikes him in the face: "I'll be the judge of who's a fool and who's not."

Horger: "Gegrillt Französisch, werde ihn nach Hause bringen."

Dixon looks annoyed: "Tell him to quite it with that barbarous gibberish. Goo-goo ga-ga, it sounds like *baby talk*."

Knoop: "*It's German. He says we're digging up bones.*"

Dixon: "Trespassing's the word. Only thing your digging is your own graves."

2 pm

The weather takes an unexpected and rapid turn for the worse.

A strange flash is followed by a cataclysmic crackling as if the sky has split in half. Rocks fall from above as I scoot to the protection of the lookout, although maybe not soon enough. The instant I make it to the ledge I am struck on the head and everything goes black.

—:—

I awake at the lookout in immense pain, confused and soaking wet.

Everything is a blur. Rain pounds down into the canyon like a Hopolo drum. Rivulets and miniature waterfalls rush across the rock. Flashes of white are followed by obsidian black and then a thunderous roar. I grasp at whatever I can for dear life. Another flash reveals the sound's source: Not the sky at all – It's the "Thunder Beast!"

—:—

OH, THE HORROR!

Alive and covered in flesh! With carnivorous eyes and razor-sharp teeth! Its giant tail thrashes to and fro with violent force, alternately whipping giant waves of water against the canyon walls and backing up the river flow like a dam. When it stretches its neck to let loose another thunderous roar, its tail uplifts from the riverbed and unleashes a powerful wall of water downstream. I scream at the top of my lungs to warn my crew,

351

although the louder I scream the more my head hurts to the point I am feeling dizzy and may ...

—:—

I am sitting with Dixon on a peculiar slab of rock.

It doesn't take long to see we are *on top* of the butte. Just the two of us. Around a campfire. The sky is the strangest shade of purple I have ever seen. When he makes a sweeping gesture with his hat I understand that it is my time to die. I stare down the barrel of his Colt pistol and listen as the hammer pulls back. It clicks in place. Dixon presses his finger against the trigger. The hammer releases. There is an explosion and the bullet is propelled out of the shaft. Then another and one more, a fourth and then a fifth. Each bullet sinks into flesh and gushes out blood. A red flood.

—:—

If I am hit I cannot feel it.

Why is it I feel so calm and it is Dixon who has such a terrified look? I watch as his gaze lifts up, and up ... AND UP. When I see the shadow of the Giant Lizard slide across the sandstone crown of the butte the reason is revealed. Remembering what Hoots said, I stay in place like a statue as Dixon, in a panic, fires his final bullet, the sixth, into the beast and, unable to reload, hurls the pistol as a distraction in the opposite distraction that he flees toward "the shoot" – the only way down from the butte – but his ruse proves short lived: the menacing creature cuts him off at the pass before he can descend. I dare not move, not even a blink, as the fearsome creature plays "cat and mouse" with Dixon, eventually swallowing him whole and belching out his stovepipe hat.

—:—

Despite Dixon's demise I am not out of the woods yet.

A scorpion's sting causes a sharp pain at my leg. I swallow my yelp, but I must have twitched. Within seconds the "Thunder Beast" is within inches of my face, sniffing the air with its massive nostrils. Unflinching I stare into the lunar white orb of its eye.

—:—

I awaken to the sight of the full moon and cloudless sky.

352

My cautious hope that everything was a dream is punctured by a deafening vibration and the sight of churning floodwaters below. What had been a placid ribbon of water, barely a current at all, has been transformed into a rip-roaring torrent and an escalating series of waves. I rush to the water's edge to recover who and what I can.

April 2, 10 am
The new reality sets in.
Given the loss of most of our supplies in the flood, we decide to clear out at dawn. We have one wagon which is enough to haul out the jaw. The rest we will cover up for Rawlings to retrieve at a later date. The men are all very obedient. They speak nothing of my stovepipe hat.

12 noon
Horger greets us at the crevasse in a panic.
He is ashen as if he's seen a ghost and is mumbling in his crude dialect words that only G'noof can understand — *"Das munster wurde vom Felsen losgelassen und steuert auf das lagerfeuer zu. Sag dem ranger, bevor es zu spät ist!"* It is not until I enter the narrow cavern that I see why for myself.

12:9
The bones are gone, every one of them: the jaw, the teeth, the skull — even the collosal spine and ribs that were still entombed in the rock.

All our work has been for naught.

•••

End note: Historians have long debated the authenticity of these last passages, or whether it and other aggrandizements found in the full body of Powell's work were the result of a life-long struggle with alcoholism. Sir James T. Nesmith's posthumous exaltation of Powell, relatively unknown at the time of his death, helped recast American expansionism in a softer pastoral light at a time when rapid expansion of the railroads threatened to dismantle the hegemony of its animal husbandry roots; and as a result largely delayed serious scholarship of the passages in question through the decades leading up to the Great War — with the exception of speculation, spread by word of mouth among itinerant cattlemen passing through the Dakota Territory, and specifically Belfush, that inadvertent poisoning by a common tonic ingested to withstand the heat was probably to blame. Anthropologists, including Zhōu and Sturdevent, pursued several lines of evidence — culminating in extensive interviews with a diaspora of Lopjckaae descendants now living on the Lower Sassafras Delta and chemical analysis of a tar-like residue scraped from clay pots in perched canyon caves of the Upper Joola Ravine — to conclude that a concoction of three parts ocotillo pulp, two parts ground antler of the Hopolo Hair (now extinct) mixed with water from a local alkaloid spring, if drank after eating peyote, would indeed cause loss of consciousness for multiple days. More recently, contrapuntal revisionism — and, in particular, as espoused in the "knife-and-jelly" peace-time economic theory championed by Thorstein Juglar in his seminal work, "The Sustainability Principle of Boom and Bust" — has been used to suggest that Rawlings may have doctored the final account in attempt to exonerate himself from any liability claims at the behest of his alma mater, Dawes Acton Academy, now defunct. Nesmith's work, meanwhile, has largely been discredited based upon revelations of his regular habit of accepting financial payments to burnish the reputation of his subjects, most famously including defamed Spanish-American War hero and presidential hopeful Millard M. Dupree.

Chapter 20:
Sick Sid's Campfire Coda

At the campfire on the third and final night the mood was decidedly more relaxed. It was everyone from the first night except Dan Vukovich and Greg Kleal, plus the welcome addition of Sick Sidney who was holding court.

"It's gonna be developers on one side gonna pave it all over," Sid growled as he opened a can of sausages, "and the damned gov'ment on the other side runnin' folks off tellin' 'em what they can and can't do. But I cain't bitch too loud I 'spose. I done caught the tail end o' what was good, that's the truth. Last of the generation that lived free and easy."

Henry took a long thoughtful drag on his cigarillo. "Things kinda grew up on us, Sid." The firelight accentuated his father's high cheek-bones and strong jaw. He didn't look up from the campfire, but sat almost motionless save the gently flicking off a bit of ash onto the dirt.

"Well it ain't helping my cancer none, I'll tell ya that," Sidney snarled. "— Probably what provoked it in the first place."

Sandy chuckled at the complaint. "Hell Sidney, you've been cryin' about being sick for near twenty years. And I probably ain't the first to say you look better now than you did back then."

"Yeah, what about it?" Sidney scowled. "If I hadn't lost that extra weight it would have killed me for sure."

"But you look like you put on weight, Sid," Sandy politely pointed out.

"Would you quit distractin' the man, Parrish," Tate interrupted as he spit tobacco juice into a knifed out can. "Cain't you see he's on a roll."

Sidney stabbed at a sausage with his knife. "You remember when the Green Frog was in the middle of nowhere? Now

355

dammit if I don't hear folks talk about it like it's the edge of town."

"Attracting a bunch of bad actors, too."

"Used to be little hamlets that spotted the coast now more and more it's solid concrete right up to the Everbushes. I'm damn near tuckered by all the stop lights by the time I finally get to the woods. My rheumatoid arthritis doesn't help either. Recently I can feel it in my thumb."

"Damn airport mess ruined it for us," Sick Sidney continued. "We had a good thing going until the damn Port Authority come in and blew the whole damn wad."

"Yeah, Sid's right on that one," Tate spat back. "We had another couple decades at least if they didn't get all greedy and try to take too much at once."

"Couple decades!? Might wanna take a look in the mirror, Gator. Cause you me, the both of us, we don't got but a few good years left, pro'bly less."

"Speak for yourself, Sid. I plan to live fo'ever!" Tate proclaimed as he reloaded more chaw into his cheek. "Long as I got me my tobacca, don't see me ever slowin' down. This stuff is like instant vitamins and age repellant all wrapped into one."

"MAYBE the JETPORT was a blessing in DISGUISE," Huddy spoke up. "Probably what it took to protect the swamp FROM US."

Sidney was insulted. "What'ya mean *protect the swamp from us?* Hell, we tread light on the land. It's the water managers, sugar cane farmers and developers that messed it all up. Not us!"

Henry finally spoke up.

"Truth is you could even trace it back farther than that. Maybe if Cuba never had its revolution, the farms south of the Lake would have never turned into cane. And maybe if they never brought in air conditioning after the Second World War, maybe northern folks would have never wanted to move down. But once both of those happened, the government didn't have no choice but to put in all the canals and levees and pump stations. Then once that happened the farms and coastal development increased double, triple fold. Probably's gonna be ten times that in the next twenty years."

Tate spat out his entire new chaw of tobacco into his hand and hurled it into the flame. "Gosh Darnitt Henry, when you explain it like that you make it sound like we were doomed from the start."

Sick Sidney shook his head in disgust. "Yeah, it didn't take long after that for them to figure it was all *our fault.* Maybe somebody oughta remind them damn enviros we were the ones that made 'em save this place."

"Swamp would be all gone if it weren't for us. Now they're telling us they don't want us to burn. Meanwhile the water managers drain out half the water through the canals, and then act all surprised — *and call it a natural drought* — when all the gator holes go dry. Too many canals and they dug 'em all way too deep." Sick Sidney spat on the ground. "Manage the water! Ha!"

"Stealing the water is more like it. Just like they want to steal our land."

"Instead they're running us off like we're criminals."

Rusty's father stood up from his crouched position. He was getting tired of talking and wanted to leave.

"You know they couldn't catch Al Capone on drug smuggling so they tripped him up on tax evasion."

Sick Sidney looked at him confused.

"So what's your point?"

Rusty's father shrugged.

"I'm guessing with us it's gonna be the other way around."

Chapter 21:
Standoff at Boulder Ridge

Sep 4, 1868

Were it not for my own service against the secessionists, I could not remark upon a more bold, more cunning, or more noble foe than the Indians of the Northern Plains. He is magnificent to behold in battle and accepts his own death with no hesitation or fuss. I hope only to match his aspirations in this regard as I expect to be dispatched upon my discovery. My intention is that they speak highly of my prowess around their fire.

Sep 8

Camped in the pass, they prevent my escape. I have only the barren expanse of the plain, an assured demise lies in the decision to risk the flatland by day. If I quit my position on the ridge, I will be found out, if I remain they will track me here easily enough.

Sep 15

Howling from the plains, I howl as well. Larkins, Krausse, McHale and the rest ... Under protest I took the column to the ridge. I should have howled my life out at them, damned them to perdition for this fool's errand. That I breathe the breath of life is no consolation, for I no longer treasure my sad mortality. Howl! Howl to God in Heaven! There was no time! That brave column cut to ribbons on the plain. They saw it through with alacrity and God willing shall I.

Sep 16

Lit many small fires to confuse my pursuers, that it might seem I am more than one. Ten fires at the bottom of the ridge might ward off the savages for a short spell, but my ruse will be made manifest to them in time.

The Ranger, Continued

THE RANGER
Continued

The Ranger, Continued

The ranger poked a lava-red log with his stick.

He studied the way the fire crackled and flickered, the way it cast its light and threw off its heat. Everything was now perfect. The amphitheater in front of him was full of attentive faces, a packed house, and overhead above was the night sky – a dark void filled with pinpricks of twinkling galactic dust. Most of all, he knew what he needed to say. Finally and once and for all he was ready to address the crowd. But *still* somehow something wasn't right: either an element was missing or an unwelcome intrusion (or intruder) remained, or possibly both; accordingly, the ranger scanned the scene to try to figure it out.

The mustachioed man with the bag of marshmallows, half eaten, was slightly snoring, true, but not enough to be bothersome, no, he was just a harmless vagrant, possibly a veteran, a little down on his luck but otherwise alright (and quite easy to rule out) when an instant later the ranger saw it point blank, problem solved: it was the dull blue glow and telltale slouch of a person in the audience (this case a teenager) gazing deeply into his cellular device; that was the problem for sure and without a doubt. *"How amazing,"* the ranger thought – *"actually sad"* – that even in a place as remote as the Fifty Mile Bend campground the long tentacles of civilization were still reaching in, polluting the campfire with radio waves from the cellular tower over ten miles away. The magic of the campfire couldn't come alive until *all* the interferences of modern man were snuffed out. And it wasn't just the teenager, no, the ranger couldn't blame it all on him, as others were toting phones hidden in their purses or pockets, out of sight, which were similarly attracting radio waves from all directions North, East West and South, thus polluting the purity of the campfire's primitive pulse. The ranger knew that the campfire – *his* campfire, *any* campfire – couldn't become a campfire in the true mystical sense until the chaos and distractions of modern-day civilization were completely blocked out. Summoning the magic of the campfire requires playing by its ancient rules.

The ranger thought to himself how the digital mobile device had become the younger generation's new "freedom machine" in much the same way the bike was for him when he was a kid, his mechanical means for aiding his escape from the cramped up space of his mother's apartment to get outdoors to explore the greater universe on the other side of the door, whether it be touring through the surrounding neighborhoods at breakneck speed, or going to a precise destination like meeting with his friend Steve to shoot hoops at the basketball court, or lighting out on his own into the leafy sanctuary he liked to think of as "his woods" to discover new paths and breathe in its fresh air. The same sensation he got on his bike was taken one step further when he bought his first truck which he drove windows rolled down through the center of town and across every backroad to the farthest outskirts, sometimes even crossing the county line to the point that he no longer even needed the paper gazetteer he kept behind his seat to know where he was even if, at the same time, he liked getting lost so he could guess which turns he needed to make to get back on familiar terra firma black asphalt, then and only then confirming his route by pulling off on the shoulder and reaching back for his map.

The ranger's thoughts raced back to the present situation at hand, how he had to press – *and hold* – the ON button to turn his cell phone off for the reason the phone didn't have a stand-alone OFF button by itself, and how that was somehow symptomatic of the device's most insidious effect: they were hard wired to stay ON all the time just as we modern humans were increasingly programmed to never be without a binary-code processor twenty four hours a day and seven days a week. First came the desktop computer – more novelty than necessity, a glorified typewriting machine – just taking over a corner of a desk or a separate roll-out cart. That wasn't bad. At least you could escape it by utilizing the rest of the desk to talk on the phone or put pencil to paper to sketch out a thought, and at the end of the day walk out of the room to call it a night unless – as time passed – you got *upgraded* to a laptop which more and more became the norm, it being sold as a way to escape the dull drudgery of office life when in reality it was a Trojan Horse for doubling the stress by tricking you into believing you could and should be working all the time without rest. But it wasn't until the internet that humanity finally crossed the line. Not just *on*, the computer was *connected* all the time. Rooms that were once sanctuaries turned into personal convenience stores open to business and the outside world every hour, day and night. And just when we thought the invasion of computers couldn't become more ubiquitous and insidiously ingrained into our daily life, the cell phones and laptop computer morphed into a singular pocket-sized device called the smart phone to become the new pacemaker that was running everyone's lives, keeping people constantly on the go wherever they went, even while they sat, and always within arm's reach on the barrow next to the beds where they slept and dreamt. The ranger saw the smart phone as a dangerous disruption to the natural course of events, it both exponentially multiplying and paradoxically reversing the liberties of the *mechanical* freedom machines — his bike and his truck — that, instead of being limited to a simple and singular Point A to Point B route, the new digital device transcended space and time to virtually zap you to Points C through Z in a couple quick spasm-jabs of your thumbs all the while you hunched over in the sedentary cocoon of one spot. Smart phones were the ultimate socializing and anti-social machine all at once. The ranger thought how many times he'd been in places where people had inappropriately forgotten to turn off their ringers, how it had once been taboo but was pretty much accepted behavior now, common place in fact. What was previously rude was now widely regarded as an unalienable right. The ranger wondered in fear where it was all going and more importantly, what it was irretrievably doing to us. Everyone was plugged into a computer all the time, from cradle to grave; were we people or computers, their masters or their slaves? Of all the addictive and debilitating substances discovered by man — sugar, caffeine, tobacco and even the more elicit ones on the list — it was that little electronic gadget, the silly smart phone and its sundry Pavlovian chirps, that people most craved ... to the point of it becoming physiologically part of humanity's flesh and blood: an external organ of sorts, a life support, as essential if not more so than the rhythmic ticking of our four-chambered hearts.

With that in mind the ranger had a request.

"Any of you who have a phone on, if it's okay, I'd like you to shut them off."

For a moment the crowd collectively paused without a response.

"Do you mean turn off *the ringer*," a woman asked. "— Because I've already done that."

The ranger shook his head. "No, turned off completely would be best. In order for this campfire program to really come alive I need everyone to be unplugged."

"Well, I guess my battery *is* getting low."

"Is that okay everyone?" the ranger double checked as he scanned from right to left.

"What if there's a panther attack?"

The slumbering mustachioed man semi woke up from his catatonic state. *"Did somebody say something about my kitty cat?"* he groggily muttered. Just as quickly he jostled to the side and slipped back into a low-decibel snore.

"Trust me," the ranger reassured everyone with a friendly wave of his hands. "It'll just be for a little while. We're all gonna be fine."

The teenager raised his hand. "So, are you going to turn off your phone, too?"

The ranger patted his pockets to show they were empty. "Actually, as luck would have it, my phone and I sort of *parted ways* earlier today."

"Inside an alligator's mouth I bet!" a voice called out.

"No, nothing that exciting. Actually, I locked it in my truck."

The ranger paused for a moment as he watched everyone jostle and fiddle to retrieve their phones and turn them off; one by one as they did he could feel the electronic interference incrementally lessen and the strength of the campfire starting to amp up — the flame burning purer and less impeded — until finally it was burning at full force, a hundred percent free; the long tentacles of civilization had retracted back to the coast. The magic of the campfire was now palpable. He could feel it and now so could they. "Can you feel that everybody?" the ranger decreed. "We're finally free of modern-day distractions. The fire — *not our phones* — is what's connecting us now." The ranger grabbed a dried palmetto frond from the ground and hovered it over the embers to emphasize the point. The fire roared with delight as it consumed the pleated leaf. Tiny embers like magic dust floated up into the night. The ranger stretched out his hand to feel the warmth. *Can you feel that?"* the ranger asked.

Finally the ranger could begin.

He positioned his feet to address the crowd.

"So, what was it about this flame, if you go back in history, that drew the ancients to the campfire?" he inquired into the crowd. "You know: back in caveman times after we got done throwing bones at each other?"

The audience laughed. The ranger continued.

"I don't care who you are or where you're from. All our ancestors gathered around a campfire. *Why?*"

The ranger let the question sink in. He had one hand stretch out to the audience in front of him and his other reaching back toward the campfire. Directly above him, millions of light years into the void, far away into the deep mystery of space, the shape of Orion shined above, mirroring his exact same pose, with the light of Betelgeuse on its Western shoulder forming its brightest spot, a celestial campfire of sorts in its own corner of the universe.

The ranger asked his question again. *"What brought the ancients to the campfire? Does anybody know?"*

"To cook," a voice called out

The ranger nodded his head approvingly.

"To stay warm," another voice followed.

"Good. Yes," the ranger concurred. "Anybody else?"

"For safety."

"To dance!"

"Light to see each other face to face"

The ranger nodded his head. They were getting warm, but they weren't quite there, not yet. He reached his hands toward the dancing flame. "Yes, it was all those things that brought them to the campfire. And yes, around the campfire they did everything you said, but ..." the ranger paused to emphasize the broader point, "— it was in gathering around the campfire that they learned something even bigger, something even more fundamental than that."

The ranger turned around to once again feel the heat of the flame. He studied the pulsing of its cobalt-colored ember core and the continuous crackle of the sacrificial logs, its one-of-a-kind smell and the warmth radiating on his hands and across his face. The fire transported him deep back into time and space at the same time it anchored him down in the time and moment where he stood. It filled him with peace at the same time it gave him strength. It filled his heart with a sense of place within himself and also the rest of humanity, too.

"The campfire," the ranger explained, "is where our ancestors first learned to relax and, here's the important part — *To Communicate.* It was that communication around the campfire that fueled the ancient's inexorable advance to modern times." The silhouetted ranger stepped forward to finish his thought. "The campfire is what turned them into who we are today. If you think about it, in a way, the cell phone is sort of like our modern-day perpetual campfire machine, a tiny glow that we can take with us in the palms of our hands. I know it sounds crazy, but maybe there's a primordial reason we like our cell phones so much?" The ranger chuckled to himself as the kernel of truth behind the semi-preposterous thought soaked in.

"So then, today, a campfire: *what's the point?* Why do we return to the campfire in modern times?" The ranger held his hand to his ear as if he was holding an imaginary phone and then brought both hands in front of his chest and pretended to thumb-type on the screen of his imaginary device. "*Why bother* with a campfire to communicate when, with the smart phone, we've invented the ultimate communication device?"

Embers throbbed.

And the flame danced.

The wood crackled.

A log shifted and collapsed.

Smoke and sparkles of ash raced up into the night.

The ranger took three more steps away from the light into the crowd. "Really, if you look at it logically, modern humans have *outgrown* the campfire; it's as archaic as it should be obsolete. But for some reason *still ... today ... here ... we return.* Can anybody in the audience tell me why?"

"—S'mores!" somebody spurted out as a joke to a couple laughs.

The mustachioed man instinctively cradled his bag of marshmallows to a safer spot in his arms, but otherwise did not wake up.

"True, everyone loves marshmallows around the campfire," the ranger acknowledged. Sometimes a little too much, right?" He turned back to check on his slumbering friend. "*— But why else?*"

"— To stay warm."

"True," the ranger nodded.

"What else."

"— To get back to our roots."

368

"Bingo! That's it! You're exactly right," the ranger pointed in the audience with a satisfied look. He was pleased to see the answer came from the teenager in the second row. "We return to the campfire *to simplify*. To decompress. The campfire is where our ancestors first learned to communicate to take them forward in time and down the path to eventually becoming us. Today, the campfire is our portal for — not going forward — but *going back* in time to help us connect with our true nature, our deepest roots."

A gentle wisp of wind blew in from the trees.

The embers brightened.

Fireflies of ash rose into the night.

The ranger took a deep breath.

"Today, here, at the campfire — a*t this campfire* — is where we rekindle the ancient storytelling and traditions of myths and legends that can only properly be conveyed verbally. The stories that you won't find in books. The stories that were before books. The stories that can never properly be put in books. The stories that span back to the beginning of time."

The fire splashed a flickering light off the ranger's face and hands. The night swallowed the rest of his body out of sight.

"So, a show of hands: how many here have ever heard of Campfire Charlie?"

The ranger nodded with approval.

"Ah yes, I see a few of you have."

The Ranger, Continued

The Centennial Campfire

The Ranger, Continued

About the Authors

Robert V. Sobczak
and Rudi Heinrich are co-authors
of the Centennial Campfire Trilogy

Books include:

The Legend of Campfire Charlie

Last Stand at Boulder Ridge

Final book (yet to be named)

Robert V. Sobczak is a hydrologist with the National Park Service and author of the *Go Hydrology!* webpage, an online journal that celebrates and illuminates the water cycle, wetlands and waterways of the Big Cypress Swamp and Everglades ecosystems. Bob also likes water in other places, too. Bob got his start in water at the stretch of Deer Creek (a tributary of the Susquehanna River) that runs through Rocks State Park and which Bob likes to think of as "The Yellowstone of the Mid Atlantic Piedmont Plateau region of the United States." In his free time, Bob enjoys spending time with his family.

Rudi Heinrich is an interpretive park ranger at Big Cypress National Preserve and an active member of the United States Navy Reserve. In his free time, Rudi likes to delve deeply into any historical topic (just ask him) – whether it be a conversation with a good friend, a willing stranger (soon to be a newfound friend) or by reading a book. Oh yes, and above all else, Rudi reads lots (and lots and lots) of books and, judging from his conversations, remembers every word. Rudi is a native of Florida and an ardent student of its history, too.

About the Authors

WARNING: Handling of this record may cause severe lacerations and toxic inhalation of gas. HANDLE WITH EXTREME CAUTION and under parental supervision.

Mama Cherub

Clogging New Age

Blues

Folk/Rock

Live at Boulder Ridge

Bobby Angel

Greatest Hits 5

The Legend of Campfire Charlie Trilogy

Part Two

About the Authors

www.ingramcontent.com/pod-product-compliance
Lightning Source LLC
Chambersburg PA
CBHW020510260626
47156CB00006B/1952